INTEGRITY BASED POLICING

Policing the Streets
OF LAS VEGAS

DAN BARRY

outskirts
press

Integrity Based Policing
Policing the Streets of Las Vegas
All Rights Reserved.
Copyright © 2019 Dan Barry
v1.0

This is a work of fiction. Names, characters, businesses, places, events, locales, and incidents are either the products of the author's imagination or used in a fictitious manner. Any resemblance to actual persons, living or dead, or actual events is purely coincidental.

The opinions expressed in this manuscript are solely the opinions of the author and do not represent the opinions or thoughts of the publisher. The author has represented and warranted full ownership and/or legal right to publish all the materials in this book.

This book may not be reproduced, transmitted, or stored in whole or in part by any means, including graphic, electronic, or mechanical without the express written consent of the publisher except in the case of brief quotations embodied in critical articles and reviews.

Outskirts Press, Inc.
http://www.outskirtspress.com

ISBN: 978-1-9772-0074-7

Cover Photo © 2019 www.gettyimages.com. All rights reserved - used with permission.

Outskirts Press and the "OP" logo are trademarks belonging to Outskirts Press, Inc.

PRINTED IN THE UNITED STATES OF AMERICA

I remember when I first saw that beautiful blond waiting in line to get her meal card at Buffalo State College. Little did I know that 40 years later we would be blessed with four beautiful children and nine grandchildren! Forty years ago, as I fumbled to introduce myself to her, I never imagined she would even give me a second look. Thank God, she did, and the rest, including this book, I owe to her support.

CONTENTS

Foreword i
Introduction vii

1. Tube Socks 1
2. Bumper's Code 15
3. Don't Sweat the Small Stuff 36
4. High School Daze 51
5. Three's a Crowd 68
6. The Killer Bees 84
7. The Friendly Skies 100
8. Kids in Action 111
9. Anna Banana 128
10. Crossing Over the Rubicon 143
11. Doing Too Good of a Job 156
12. Yabba Dabba Doo! 166
13. No Good Deed Goes Unpunished 176
14. Payback 192
15. The Magic of Trust 213
16. "Ready, Fire, Aim" 225
17. Old Yella 238
18. Wedding Bells 249
19. Neighborhood Pride 261
20. A Matter of Trust 272

FOREWORD

With all the criticism aimed at American policing, a simple question must be asked, "Why would anybody want to become a police officer?" It's certainly true that this generation of police officers needs to be made of Teflon to deal with all the negativity they encounter on a regular basis. Officers also must be able to make split-second decisions that will be judged by others who have the luxury of time and safety to contemplate their actions. Everything officers do may be recorded and their tactics second-guessed by so-called experts who have never worn a badge nor carried a gun. I thank God that, despite this sad reality, many high-quality men and women are still eager to become law enforcement officers.

It's important to remember this is not the first time in our nation's history our police officers have encountered a trust crisis. From the outset of American policing, major embarrassments have damaged public approval. During Prohibition, with the growth of organized crime, policing was very corrupt and garnered little public trust. Fast-forward to the 1960s and police blunders were displayed on a new technology--television. Brutal tactics exhibited by officers during their responses to protests of the Civil Rights Movement, Vietnam War, and Democratic National Convention made police officers look like the Keystone Cops. In the 1990s, the Rodney King arrest and subsequent riots created quite a significant problem for law enforcement. Two other major scandals of the 1990s which harmed the reputation of law enforcement nationwide were the Mollen and the Rampart Commissions.

The major takeaway from law enforcement's past trust crises is restoring public trust is essential. This is by no means easy and requires solid leadership to achieve. True reformers have never sought to use the "rotten apple defense." Instead, they have investigated to look for the systemic and organizational missteps that needed to be remedied. This required men and women of high integrity to stand up and make positive changes. In dealing with our present situation, we all must learn from the past. The reality is that while technologies and names will change, the fundamentals remain constant. The virtues of courage, good loyalty, and empathy need to be foundational for reform-minded leaders.

My main goal in writing "Integrity Based Policing" was twofold: to identify the critical role law enforcement plays in our democracy, and to highlight the importance of morally sound decision-making. Situations and circumstances are constantly in flux. However, our moral compass needs to remain balanced. By focusing upon the virtues of courage, good loyalty, and empathy, we can improve leadership and organizational soundness. I also believe the best way to learn is by studying real life situations. This book contains lessons from the many peaks and valleys of my career, and I'm confident you will find my experiences both interesting and informative.

Sound leadership is something American law enforcement is in dire need of. During my thirty years of experience, serving at various ranks and assignments, I have witnessed policing at its best... and worse. I have seen powerful leadership in action and the positive influence it has on our communities. Unfortunately, I have also witnessed the converse, where weak administrators and toxic organizational cultures have been the norm.

As you read this book, it will become obvious that my Catholic faith plays an important role in my decision-making process. Being Christ-centered allowed me to remain focused in handling both ethical and legal challenges. All of these experiences demonstrate the importance of the three virtues of courage, good loyalty, and empathy.

In today's world, American policing must be at the forefront to maximize positive change in American neighborhoods. Over the past several years, our police officers have been under constant attack by certain elements of society. These groups have sought to drive a wedge between police and low income neighborhoods. These activists have attempted to denigrate police officers at every opportunity. The reality is that our police need to engage now more than ever to regain the public's trust. Community Oriented Policing is the tool that must be used to increase trust. The reality is that the police are the solution, not the problem.

In considering police/community relationships, many factors must be weighed. While it's easy to look at recent blogs, websites and YouTube videos, and blame individual events, the underlying causation factors require research and effort to identify. Evaluating the organizational culture, assessing community engagement, and offering recommendations for improvement, takes time. The Ferguson incident is an example of the dangers of jumping to conclusions before knowing all the facts. The day following the first night of rioting in Ferguson, the public outcry was all about the tanks and rifles used by the responding officers.

The term "police militarization" became the buzz-word on a majority of blogs, news outlets and cable stations. As a result of this, many people blamed the poor police/community relationship on military equipment used by police. While this may be one of the symptoms of a strained relationship, it is not the causation, or even a major issue. Other factors such as training, crime prevention, lack of diversity, lack of youth activities, and insufficient police outreach programs, must be reviewed. The use of overly aggressive tactics may be the result of many factors. Officers who lack confidence, weak internal investigation processes, training deficiencies or lack of community engagement, constitute just a few of the potential underlying reasons for excessive force. Without first identifying the main reason for this lack of trust, lasting reform will be difficult to achieve.

The reality is that today's police face different challenges than those encountered by prior generations. With all the technology, recording devices, and the lack of community trust, our modern police officers can't afford to make errors. In my rookie days, you were expected to make mistakes. The reality was that the academy taught new officers what the policy manual said, but working the streets taught new officers how to be real cops. In 21st century policing, officers might not ever get a chance to improve if they make a mistake that is videotaped.

Courage is the first essential virtue for a successful career in law enforcement. Courage is most often thought of in the limited frame of physical courage. It's obvious that law enforcement requires a high level of physical courage to be successful. Imagine a situation in which an officer refused to handle an incident because the officer was a coward. While physical courage is a necessary virtue for all officers to possess, courage in decision-making is also critical. As a leader, it's vital to make decisions based on what is the "right thing" as opposed to the "most convenient." This type of courage in decision-making is essential for true leaders. The ability to make decisions and act--to do the right thing--is a requisite for being a leader. Leaders who show courage by standing up for what is right as opposed to placating their superiors, are the ones who must be emulated.

In Chapter Six, "The Killer Bees," I describe an event that took place a few months after I was promoted to sergeant. I had discovered that two of my senior officers included false information in an affidavit and arrest report. They justified lying by alleging they were trying to get notorious gangsters convicted. When I spoke with my lieutenant about it, he told me to let it go. I knew that by proceeding to discipline the officers and dismiss the criminal case, I was upsetting my chain of command and the officers, but I made the decision to just do what was right. If we are not truthful in policing, we are no better than the criminals we put in handcuffs.

'Good' loyalty is the second virtue that is critical for leaders in law enforcement. This virtue is challenging but we need to remember that misguided loyalty can be disastrous. Motivation for many gang members, corrupt politicians and cases of the "code of silence," can all be attributed to misguided loyalty. In cases of misguided loyalty, it is focused on the wrong target. Misguided loyalty in policing causes officers to place their loyalty to other officers over their loyalty to the community they serve.

The "code of silence" is the term used to explain police being reluctant to give information that could get another officer in trouble. In most of the major corruption scandals, the "code of silence" played an important role by allowing misconduct to go undetected. Many of the officers who lied to cover up for other officers, attributed their untruthfulness to their loyalty for other officers. While being loyal to other officers is a positive thing, superior loyalty must be given to the community. Good loyalty dictates that officers remember they are sworn to serve the community, and loyalty to the community can never be subordinate to their loyalty to other officers.

In Chapter Eleven, I share an example of a cover-up that demonstrates the danger of misguided loyalty. In this situation, leadership of the sexual assault detail refused to investigate one of their officer's (the suspect) perverted conduct with a juvenile victim. My Catholic values guided me through this difficult investigation. The lessons I learned from this investigation validated the importance of practicing good loyalty. The fact that numerous officers had covered up this disgusting conduct, shows how dangerous misguided loyalty can be.

The third virtue that is essential for law enforcement leaders is empathy. This virtue also runs deep. The fact is that we need to show empathy to everyone with whom we come into contact. Because a person is in handcuffs or mentally ill, does not make them any less human. Always treat others as unique gifts from God, not as inanimate objects. Remember always to treat them as if they were your brother or sister.

In Chapter Two, *Bumper's Code,* I recounted my near termination experience after a high-speed chase. To this day, I can still remember the emptiness I felt in my stomach as I sat alone in internal affairs after being threatened with criminal charges. Fortunately, I can also recall my relief when Lieutenant Chuck Martin walked into the room and put his arm around me. Lieutenant Martin ensured that these overly aggressive interrogators changed their demeanor. He allowed me to calm down and acted as my mentor. We are in dire need of the sort of empathic leadership that Lieutenant Martin displayed that afternoon.

In the same chapter, I recollected the time another officer let a wanted suspect drive away and told him to meet us an hour later because the suspect had his two little girls in his car. Using this type of empathic discretion is certainly not consistent with written policy. In fact, it violates the letter of the policy, yet handcuffing a father in front of his children is something that should only be done in the most extreme situations. The challenge with utilizing good discretion is that it's difficult to translate into a written policy. Good discretion is a product of both the head and the heart. Empathy is essential to building community trust, especially in low-income neighborhoods.

I hope you keep these three virtues in mind as you read *Integrity Based Policing*. More importantly, I pray we all rise to meet the great challenge our vocation faces as we head into the future. By focusing on courage, good loyalty and empathy, we can improve community trust and better serve our communities.

INTRODUCTION

When I first told my wife, Allison, I was going to write this book, she asked me a difficult question. "What are you trying to accomplish by writing this book?"

I responded, "I want to help police officers and reform American policing." I soon realized that although my experiences centered on police work, the lessons learned are also relevant for other professions. The reality is that this book is not loaded with technical police jargon. My goal was to put pen to paper and create a manuscript which everyone could enjoy and from which everyone could learn. The importance of trust in policing cannot be overstated. I am confident that many other professions are also suffering from a lack of trust. Trust is vital for our future.

I was blessed to have been a part of one of the greatest police departments in the world, the Las Vegas Metropolitan Police Department. I have been fortunate to work alongside some of the greatest men and women in the world. Some of the names used have been changed because the purpose of *Integrity Based Policing* is to improve the future and not embarrass or offend anyone.

Creating this book was an enjoyable adventure with many peaks and valleys. The only constant was the importance of prayer. It seemed that as I was working on each chapter, great things happened that were answers to prayers. As an example, in Chapter One, I wanted to explain the reason most police officers are attracted to policing. I certainly did not want to bore people in the beginning of my book by quoting surveys or citing academic journals. As I stared blankly at my computer screen praying to God for guidance, my cell phone rang. It was my buddy, Chris Hoye, whom I had not spoken to in months. He was calling to set up a lunch for the next week. I immediately remembered the class Chris taught back in 1996 and I knew how to start my book.

Even in Chapter Twenty, our last chapter, I hit a brick wall. I could not think of a way to give readers a tool to take with them to increase ethical soundness, both individually and organizationally. I kept thinking that the best way to accomplish this was to discover an acronym that people could remember. As I read over the draft and recalled our biggest challenges, the importance of trust kept resurfacing. It seemed that, as I sought God's guidance, he gave me direction.

Public servants are required to serve in the best interest of all people living in their community. Service, guided by the highest ethical standards, must be the driving force behind police leaders' decisions. Ensuring that our actions are consistent with courage, good loyalty, and empathy, will greatly improve relationships with the communities we serve. Virtues, like truthfulness, respect, understanding, stability, and transparency, should never be held hostage to political expediency, media releases or wealthy campaign contributors. By focusing efforts toward these virtues, we will increase TRUST in our communities.

I hope you enjoy reading Integrity Based Policing as we strive to make our world a better place!

1

TUBE SOCKS

I was sitting in one of those gray metal chairs and gazing at my Pulsar wristwatch, praying for this boring class to end. It was only 10:30 a.m., and my stomach was already growling for lunch. The room was packed with more than fifty people, but it only had seats for thirty. My thoughts were racing through the many tasks I needed to complete before leaving for Quantico, Virginia the next morning, to attend the Federal Bureau of Investigation National Academy (FBINA). I was confident that this class was just another waste of time that I was forced to sit through.

I had been a lieutenant with the Las Vegas Metropolitan Police Department (LVMPD) for five years, and had been a member of the LVMPD for a total of sixteen years. More elementary level training seemed unnecessary. In my mind, what made this class even more distasteful was the fact it was mandatory, thus eliminating any possibility that it would be of value. The purpose of this class was to inform all metro brass about the inclusion of sexual orientation as a protected class. Not only was being a homosexual no longer a crime, but we now had to afford them special treatment.

As I looked around the room, I could see from the amount of fidgeting and chattering going on, many of my colleagues felt the same way. Most were adamantly opposed to this policy change, and recalled only a few years prior when homosexual acts were considered crimes against nature – meaning that they were felony crimes in Nevada. I was sitting between Dwight Allen, a 34-year veteran lieutenant, and my captain, Billy Elders, who had been on the job about one year longer than I. We all felt sorry for the poor, young instructor who was trying to justify this unpopular policy change to such a surly group. The instructor was a young sergeant named Chris Hoye. Chris sensed that his message was not resonating well with his audience.

Being a top-notch instructor, Chris realized he needed to do something drastic to keep his students from falling asleep. He paced back and forth in front of the classroom like a caged lion, then took a deep breath and walked back up to the podium. The expression on Chris' face reminded me of many great hitters in baseball, who, when down 0-2 in the count would step outside the batter's box to collect their thoughts. I knew Chris was not thinking about fastballs or breaking balls; he was attempting to regain the advantage and win back our attention in that crowded classroom.

He looked out over the entire class while taking a final deep breath, and asked a straightforward question. "What was the main reason we all became cops in the first place?" He walked around the crowded room, seeking answers and received the typical canned responses. Most said they wanted "To keep our community safe" or "Join an honorable profession and serve others." Chris then shouted in a deep and commanding voice – "That's bullshit! The real reason is that we all HATE BULLIES!" You could have heard a pin drop in that room, which only seconds ago, had been filled with chatter.

That was an "aha" moment! I immediately thought back to why I decided to become a part of our great vocation. Looking around the room, I noticed that the majority of the other veteran officers had similar contemplative expressions on their faces. The silence in the classroom was deafening as Chris stood at his podium with renewed confidence. Chris had just made an insightful proclamation, and it struck a chord with everyone in that classroom. The room was completely quiet, as all of us were digesting this information. The remainder of the class went by with renewed audience interest. I am certainly not saying that everyone agreed with this policy change, but we viewed this shift in policy from a different perspective. In fact, dealing effectively with bullies of all types is, without a doubt, the most important function of law enforcement.

It especially resonated with me.

I found myself thinking back to my elementary school days, when I was sent to the principal's office because I had gotten into another fight. I recalled Principal Edward Judd screaming at me.

"I'm going to kick you out of school if you don't quit getting involved in other people's business!"

I rarely got into a fight because someone started it with me. Normally, I stepped into a situation because a bully was picking on somebody else.

After class, I went to lunch with about ten other veteran sergeants and lieutenants, and all of us had similar responses to Sergeant Chris' declaration.

The next day I left to attend the FBINA in Quantico, Virginia. I was fortunate to be driving the 3,000 miles alone, which gave me time to contemplate Sergeant Chris's pronouncement. After the four-day drive, I was convinced, more than ever, that Sergeant Chris was entirely right. While attending the FBINA, I was with law enforcement officers from all over the world. Although I never conducted an official survey, I am confident all good officers hold a common disdain for bullies.

While most people think of bullies as people who use their physical size or strength to intimidate other people, the truth is that most bullies are spineless weaklings. There are two types of bullies: street thugs and those who hide behind their position to injure others for their own gain. The street thugs are easier to deal with than the other, sleazier types often found in positions of power.

My values, especially my disdain for bullies, are rooted in my family background.

I was the youngest child of an Irish Catholic family. We were originally from Jersey City, New Jersey. My parents instilled in me the importance of faith and always standing up for what was right.

Dad came to the United States from Scotland when he was a small child and quit high school to help support his family. My mom also never graduated high school because of severe poverty. Both of my parents grew up in the Hell's Kitchen area of Manhattan. Dad's work ethic was unlike any I have ever seen. He would leave for work at 4:00 a.m. and most nights not return home until 7:30 or 8:00 p.m. He drove a truck for a dry-cleaning company. In 1967, my parents achieved the "American Dream" when they purchased their first house, a converted bungalow, in East Rockaway, New York.

Mother had the most important job in the world: she was a fulltime mom. She made sure that we were physically cared for and the house was clean. Most importantly, she always ensured her children served God and helped other people. My parents instilled in my brother, my sister and me the importance of having unwavering love of God and America. She emphasized the need to do what was right and protect our neighbors.

I was never a good student and was sent to the principal's office often for getting into trouble. I am sure that I had Attention Deficit Hyper Disorder (ADHD), but in the 1960s we did not have that label. They just referred to me as a "little butt-head." They got my attention the old-fashioned way with wooden paddles, yard sticks, and the palms of some teachers' hands. It worked.

My brother, Pat, is four years older than I am, and neither of us ever took school very seriously. We liked boxing, and we both thought of school as something to do before we went to the gym. In the seventh grade, I got into a fight which was broken up by two Nassau County police officers. After that fight, the officers encouraged me to join the Police Boys Club (PBC) boxing team. Pat and I went down to the PBC gym the very next day, and we both discovered that the sport was our passion. Pat and I boxed throughout high school. I fought my last bout when I was seventeen years old. Pat boxed professionally for many years, and has run Barry's Boxing in Las Vegas for several decades.

By the time, I was a senior in high school, the combination of a few good left-hooks and some common sense made me realize I

was never going to be the "Middleweight Champion
so I shifted my career aspiration to law enforceme
jor hurdle. Most police departments on the East Co
cruits to have at least an associate's degree.

With my high school, cumulative average hanging below a "C," getting accepted to any college would be tough. Because the Vietnam War had ended, military opportunities were limited, so I had no desire to join the military. My high school counselor told me to "...forget about going to college and get a job driving a truck." Thank God for Nassau Community College, where, if I took some prerequisite classes and passed, I could attend on a probationary basis.

I graduated from high school in 1975 and worked full-time at a local Friendly Ice Cream Restaurant while attending Nassau Community College. I majored in criminal justice and started to take my education seriously. As a result, I breezed through my classes and received my associate degree in criminal justice in 1977. My grade point average had improved to a 3.0, and I decided to continue for my bachelor's degree at The State University College of New York at Buffalo for two main reasons – it had a great criminal justice program, and the girls outnumbered the guys 8:1.

On my first day at Buffalo State I met my soulmate, Allison.

By the time I graduated in 1979, the entire East Coast was going through a hiring freeze for all police departments.

Meanwhile, my brother, Pat, was still pursuing his boxing career. Pat came to Las Vegas for a fight and fell in love with the town. Shoulder surgery ended his boxing career, so Pat decided to hang up the gloves and pin on the badge of the Las Vegas Metropolitan Police Department. Because Pat was already on the LVMPD, it was a no-brainer that the LVMPD was the department that I wanted to join.

After college, I saved up $2,000 and took a Greyhound bus to Las Vegas. I paid $49 for the smelliest, most disgusting, and uncomfortable three days of my life. I spent the trip thinking about what a big mistake I was making. I knew that the odds of passing the testing, the Academy, and the field training were slim. Allison was still back in college and I needed to make sure my career was stable before we could get married. I spent most of the trip trying to sleep and dreaming about the magic of Vegas. I envisioned all of the things I was going to accomplish with my career. I wanted to make a positive impact on others, just like those Nassau County officers who introduced me to the Police Boys Club had had on me.

My dad was always an example of what it means to be a man of God. His deep faith always carried him through tough times, both as a child and as an adult. His father had the "curse of the Irish," causing my dad to quit school and go to work at an early age to help support his family. His family never believed in taking assistance from the federal government. He was deaf in his left ear and had limited hearing in his right ear, the result of an illness as a toddler. My dad said that as a child, he was teased and picked on because of his lack of hearing. This explains why he was quick to intervene when he saw others being picked on. My sister, Debbie, described him best. She said that he had the heart of a lion, and most important, he was always concerned about the welfare of others.

My best memories of Dad were of the days when he took me with him to his job. Dad was not a big man. He stood 5'8" and weighed about 170 pounds. As a young kid he would go down to the bars and fight bigger guys for money to give to his mother. He never bragged to us about having to do that but you knew by looking into his eyes that he was a man who would never back down. He used that skill as an adult to handle bullies. It made a lifelong impression on me.

One morning, while I was waiting inside his truck, my Dad went inside the locker room of Eastern Airlines to put uniforms into the lockers. A guy walked up to the truck and started screaming and cursing about missing a set of uniforms. As Dad walked back to the truck, the idiot continued to carry on. My Dad looked at him and told him to watch his mouth. The man was a good 100 pounds heavier than my Dad and at least half a foot taller. He did not take Dad's advice.

Tube Socks

He made the serious mistake of grabbing Dad's arm. I saw Dad roll his right shoulder and fire a right-hand that caught him square in the mouth. He dropped this big turkey like a bad habit. As blood streamed from the bully's mouth, my dad casually walked up to me and said, "I'm sorry, but he was being disrespectful."

The officers arrived and the big guy apologized. The cops did not take any reports or make any arrest because, back then, they were allowed to settle things by using common sense. My dad and the other guy shook hands, and we went on our way to our next stop.

Another time, Dad and I finished our route early and had time to stop by a diner on Sunrise Highway. Having "one on one" time with Dad was always special, but it meant even more when I was at work with him. I had just ordered a tuna fish on rye and Dad and I were discussing the Mets playing the Cubs that night at Shea Stadium. I remember hearing a loud commotion and seeing a man in the next booth screaming at our waitress. She was African American. He was white. The man was calling her a "fuckin' idiot" and an assortment of racial slurs. Dad jumped up and stepped in between the loud mouth bully and our waitress. He told the big mouth to shut up. The bully looked at Dad, and immediately lost his alpha dog demeanor. He turned around, threw some money on the table and silently left the diner. The waitress gazed at my Dad with a look of amazement and gratitude. She was not expecting a white man to jump to her defense, especially against another white guy.

Dad made sure the waitress was okay and other customers in the diner congratulated him and said they were glad the jerk had left. When things settled down, and we were finally able to enjoy our lunch, I asked Dad why nobody else jumped up. He smiled.

"That's what is wrong with this world," he said. "Nobody wants to get involved unless they are the ones being picked on."

That same night, Tom Seaver pitched a one hitter against the Chicago Cubs and the Miracle Mets were beginning to make their move into first place. Dad was always the type of man who walked his talk. I never had to look far for a role model because Dad was always close by. That year was 1969, and the Miracle Mets were only my second greatest memory of that summer.

Dad was always there for Pat and me during our boxing days. He made sure that we were up at 4:30 a.m. to do roadwork, and we never missed a workout. He ensured that when we rose above the talent level of the Police Boys Club, that we were trained under the best trainer in New York City, Gil Clancy. My dad was a street fighter so he allowed us to be trained by the experts, but he always watched who we were dealing with.

In the late 1960s and early '70s, organized crime figures would always hang out at the Telstar Athletic Club to watch fighters work out. Pat and I were the only two Irish kids in the gym and those mob guys were always talking to us. One day, an older Italian man, whom we knew from the gym, gave Pat and me two brand new gym bags filled with new bag gloves and jump ropes. He told us he liked us and felt bad we had such shoddy, old equipment. We both said thanks and were happy for the new gear. That night, our dad saw us walk in with the new bags and asked us where we had gotten them from.

"One of the older men at the gym gave us the gear."

Dad made us give them back to him the next day. It turns out this older man knew Pat was turning pro and wanted to get a piece of him. We returned the equipment.

"You're lucky your old man is watching out for you two," the man told us.

Dad supported my decision to become a police officer. His words of advice to me were simple.

"Always treat people with respect, unless they don't deserve it."

As I sat on the bus heading west, I knew that I was leaving behind two of the greatest people in my life – Mom and Dad. Although they may not have attained high school diplomas or college degrees, together they had more common sense than anyone I've ever met.

When the bus arrived in Las Vegas, behind the Union Plaza Hotel, my brother was there to greet me. I stayed with Pat and his wife, Dawn, for several weeks until I landed a job and found an apartment. I was fortunate to get a job as an apprentice bartender at Don the Beachcomber inside the Sahara Hotel. My first apartment was in Meadows Village, just across the street. My pay and the tips covered all of my expenses. Life moved quickly. During my first two months in town, I had already taken and passed the LVMPD test and was making a comfortable living. In 1979, Vegas had a personality that was magic for a young man. Everyone was kind and generous. It was as if we were all a big family.

My coworkers at the Sahara were supportive of my plans to join the force. They thought that law enforcement was a much better career than working in the casino business. Even Don Rickles agreed. One night while working at the service bar at the Congo Showroom at the Sahara, Rickles was getting ready to go on stage. He looked at me and waved me over. Thinking he wanted a glass of water or soda before he went on stage, I ran over to him.

"What's a young kid like you doing working in a place like this?" he asked me.

I proudly told him, "Mr. Rickles, this is only for a few more weeks, until I start the police academy." He smiled.

"That's good news to hear, kid."

The most common advice I received from my fellow coworkers was that Vegas is the greatest place in the world, but the further you can keep away from the Strip when you're off work, the better. After living here for the past thirty-eight years, I still know that is great advice.

I was notified that I would be in the February Academy of 1980.

Allison and I hated being 3,000 miles away from each other. It was a challenge. She was still in her junior year at Buffalo State, and it was important for her to graduate before we were married. We relied on writing letters and our weekly phone calls. This was long before the e-mail, cell phones, and Facebook days. I know that during my academy training, there were many weeks when Allison did not know if I would still have a job the next week, and neither did I.

On February 20, 1980, I began my career with the Las Vegas Metropolitan Police Department. The first morning was our orientation explaining what our Academy would demand and that many of us would not make it to graduation. Sergeant Paul Conner walked up to the podium and told us that he knew over half of us would not graduate. He then told us that the LVMPD Academy had the toughest standards in the nation and after looking at all of us, he could not believe that the standards had dropped so low. He and his staff of Teach, Aide, and Counsel (TAC) officers would ensure that only the best would make it out of the Academy and earn the right to wear a Metro badge. After a couple of hours of being told about the challenges that lay before us, the three TAC officers came running into the room and screamed at us to put on our running gear. We were going for a little run. We ran about five miles through the city streets. Since I was one of the youngest and in the best shape out of our class of sixty recruits, I finished shoulder to shoulder with the TAC officers. Bad move! Lesson one: Always be in the middle of the pack.

The majority of my class had been in the military, but I had never even been a Boy Scout, making inspections a major hurdle. So, the TAC officers decided to make an example of me and another New York transplant, Johnny Russo. During our first inspection, I was asked to give the definition of a crime.

"Sir, a crime is an act or omission forbidden by law with criminal intent, punishable upon conviction by death, imprisonment, fine, or other penal discipline, sir," I shouted. My TAC officer paused.

"What in the fuck does 'witt' mean?" he said, needling me.

"Sir, W-I-T-H, sir."

This was my introduction to the gig – a demerit, each of which takes a quarter of a point off my final score. Forty of them and I would be out. So here, during my first inspection, the TAC officer told me to take a gig for my stupid accent and give him fifty push-ups. He went on to Johnny, asked him for the same definition, and got the same exact result.

Again, the TAC officer asked him "What in the fuck does 'witt' mean?" As I was getting up from my pushups, I could not help but start to chuckle at Johnny's encounter. When the TAC officer saw

Tube Socks

me fighting back a smile, he left Johnny and pounced on me like a hungry dog on a steak bone.

"What in the fuck are you laughing at?' he screamed. "Your stupid accent is contagious and you got Russo all screwed up!"

He gave me another five gigs and fifty more pushups because of my demented sense of humor and being a bad influence on Johnny.

For the first couple of weeks of the academy, I was setting all kinds of wrong records for the number of gigs and pushups. I had more than thirty gigs, and we were not even one third of the way through. Making matters worse, I had just flunked our first practical problem. It looked like I would be buying another Greyhound bus ticket, this time heading back to New York.

The other guys in my class tried to help me get squared away at inspections. One of them suggested I get a really short haircut, to show the TAC officers I had the right attitude. I drove to the closest barber shop and told the barber to give me a buzz cut. In 1980, buzz cuts were not fashionable, and the barber asked me "Are you sure?" In about five minutes my hair was on the floor and I knew I looked like a complete idiot. Driving home, I was glad Allison was 3,000 miles away and could not see me. I thought at least the TAC officers would be impressed.

Sadly, the opposite was true. Part of our inspection required us to wear the uniform hat. Because my hair was now buzzed off, my head piece was too big and no longer fit. I could hardly see as the hat kept sliding over my eyes. A TAC officer screamed at me.

"Barry! What in the fuck happened to your head?"

"Sir, I got a haircut, sir."

The TAC officer gave me two gigs for having a cold head. He ordered me to take my hat off and show the entire class what a fucked-up head looked like. As I stood in front of my class and modeled my new hair style, Sergeant Conner screamed out, "He looks like one of those Hari Krishnas you see at the airport, giving out beads."

My academy nickname was born: "Hari Kari Barry."

Getting two gigs for having a cold head made me realize that I

Integrity Based Policing

wasn't going to get fired over gigs. I began to relax and suddenly, something clicked. I got a 95 on our next practical problem and survived two more inspections without a gig.

All of us in the academy feared Friday mornings. Academy staff would fire people on Fridays, right before lunch break. The procedure went like this:

Cut-out black paper hands would be posted on a two-way window in front of the classroom. The number of black hands denoted the number of recruits being fired that week. At about 11:45 a.m., the three TAC officers would march single file into the classroom, walk through the aisles and tap the recruit on his shoulder and tell him to get all his books and follow them into the sergeant's office. As the TAC officers were walking out of the classroom with the soon-to-be-terminated recruit, they would take down one of the black hands. They did this for each of the soon-to-be-terminated recruits individually, so this ritual often took over an hour. This agonizing process continued until all the black hands were removed. The only positive thing was that when they had finished with their terminations, we could take our lunch break and know we were still employed, at least for another week.

One Friday morning, I noticed three black hands affixed to the "mirror of death." Unlike the prior Fridays, I was not nervous because I knew that I had improved during the past several weeks. My remaining classmates and I were confident that I was safe this week. At 11:45 a.m. TAC officers marched in, headed right to a recruit in the back row and escorted him away. I was thinking, okay, "one down, two to go." When the TAC officers came in for the second person, I was convinced they were going to extract another recruit in the back row.

Nobody could even look at the TAC officers while they were conducting their sadistic ritual. We all had to stare straight ahead and pretend to be paying attention to the instructor. I could hear their footsteps on the tile floor and knew they were getting uncomfortably close. I was getting nervous because I knew they were marching down the row where I was seated. I almost couldn't hold my pen up because my hand was perspiring -- I knew they were only a few feet away. Then, I felt a tap on my right shoulder and heard the words that all of us were afraid to hear.

"Pick up your books and follow us to Sergeant Conner's office."
I did.

My mind was racing. Why were they going to fire me? By the time we reached his office, I was confident that, despite my recent improvements, I would be taking a bus ride back to the Big Apple, and my career with the LVMPD was over.

As I walked into his office on shaky legs, Sergeant Conner had a big smile on his face and looked like a giant ogre sitting behind his desk. He pointed to the empty chair and told me to sit down.

"Officer Barry, I guess you're wondering why I called you in here," he began. I nervously nodded my head in the affirmative, and he could tell by the look on my face, I thought I was toast.

"We normally call people in here to fire them," he continued slowly, hesitating as if to prolong my agony. As I sat there, I could tell that they all were enjoying watching me squirm in my chair. After about thirty seconds of complete silence, which seemed like an hour, Sergeant Conner continued, "but in this situation, I personally want to tell you that you have really turned things around in the right direction. Keep up the good work!"

My sense of relief was huge -- like a prisoner on death row being told that the governor had commuted his sentence, and instead he was going on a Hawaiian vacation with Jennifer Lopez! I could not believe that I was not getting fired and remember feeling the tension exiting my body.

I breathed a huge sigh of relief and without thinking about it sat back and put my foot over my knee. My joy was replaced by panic as I remembered that I wore white tube socks because I forgot to take my black regulation socks with me that morning. Immediately, Sergeant Conner showed his sniper eyes, stood up, and got in my face.

"You are a cluster fuck! You can't even accept a compliment without fuckin' it up!" Sergeant Conner and the three TAC Officers opened a major case of verbal whip ass on me for the next ten minutes.

Sergeant Conner told me that I was his new number one target, and he was going to enjoy firing me. I wound up getting another five gigs, and had to write a 5,000-word report concerning the importance of maintaining a professional appearance by adhering to our uniform standards.

The worst part of my punishment for this fashion faux pas was that, for the remainder of our academy, I was put in an embarrassing spot. I was ordered to wear white tube socks instead of the standard black socks for the remainder of the training. During all breaks, including lunch, I had to stand guard beside the empty podium in front of our classroom. To make me look even more foolish, I needed to pull my tube socks over my pant legs, while holding my PR24 baton parallel to the floor with my arms fully extended.

As I walked back into the class that day, I could sense all the other recruits were surprised. The TAC officers continued their ritual and fired the two other recruits. During lunch, all of the other recruits heard of my adventure and thought about changing my nickname to "Lazarus" instead of "Hari Kari Barry." Unfortunately, they decided to keep the latter.

For the remaining two months, I managed to somehow make it through to graduation. Our academy had *esprit de corps,* and we all pushed hard for each other. The older guys got me squared away with the military maneuvers and I worked with them on the physical training. Thanks to the help of others, and a ton of rosaries being said, I made it through to graduation. I may have ranked dead last in my academy class, but I did make it through!

2

BUMPER'S CODE

The sun was beating down on all of us, as we marched in the parking lot of Zelhah Shrine Temple in preparation for our academy graduation. We were told to be at this location two hours early as we needed to perform marching drills for people attending. I was fortunate to be in the back row, so I pretty much just had to follow the guy in front of me. After we completed our final inspection, we began marching into the hall. We'd made it.

I had worked hard to reach this day. I could not wait until the ceremony was over. I kept thinking how blessed I was to have made it through. I received so many gigs during the past eleven weeks that I lost count (I do know it was well over the forty maximum). I realized that while Sergeant Conner and the other TAC officers pretended to be our mortal enemies, they honestly did care about us. All of the recruits feared the entire academy staff, yet we respected them as men of honor and knew they wanted us – and the LVMPD – to succeed.

Academy staff did use grades as a benchmark, but they also looked for other important virtues like tenacity, courage, and integrity to decide who was worthy of wearing the LVMPD badge. Suddenly as the ceremony began, it hit me. This only ended the academy phase. The next day I would begin the field training program. My mind was racing about the challenges facing me and how blessed I was to become a member of our great department.

We had all been warned about the field training program being more difficult than the Academy. Back in the early '80s, it did not require much to fire a recruit. We heard horror stories about recruits getting fired over a mistake they made in the field and being told to walk back to the station and turn their gear in. As the speakers droned on, I tried to relax and I thanked God for letting me get this far. I was also glad that my hair had grown back, so my headpiece was no longer sliding over my eyes.

As I was getting ready to march onto the stage and have my badge pinned on, I spotted my mom on the other side of the stage. She had taken the red eye flight and arrived in Vegas only a couple of hours before the ceremony. When I spotted her in the audience the reality hit me: my new home was here in Las Vegas, not East Rockaway living with my mom and dad. This special day meant much more because my mom was there to share it with me.

Badges were presented in alphabetical order, not by class rank, so it didn't matter that I was last in the class. I was a part of the first row to receive our certificates and have our badges pinned on.

Academy graduation was probably the single largest accomplishment of my young life and having my mom present during the ceremony meant the world to me. Mom pinned the badge on my chest and gave me a kiss on the check with that look that mothers give to show their maternal approval. Another realization sank in as the ceremony was drawing to an end. I gazed over at my classmates, and realized this would be the last time we would all be together. The next day, we would be in field training and scattered throughout the valley.

We received our new assignments after the ceremony. I had been transferred to West Substation swing shift reporting to Sergeant Mike Bunker. I learned that I was the only recruit assigned to that squad. Everyone else in my class was going in groups of two or three to different squads.

Mom, Pat, Dawn, and I celebrated after my graduation by having a barbecue and enjoyed the weather at a local park. Because I knew my Mom was only in town for the day, I wanted to spend as much time with her as possible. Despite having a fun day, I did keep thinking about the uncertainty that lay ahead, starting the next day, in the field training program. Mom's flight back to New York was the red eye, so I dropped her off at McCarran Airport at 9:00 p.m., and I stopped by the west substation to get a locker.

I could feel the clerical staff was giving me the once over.

I told them who I was, and they laughed, and told me that I looked about fourteen. As I was leaving the station, I bumped into Sergeant Bunker. Bunker was a massive man, standing about six feet five inches and weighing over 300 pounds. He smiled at me and introduced himself. He confirmed that I was the only rookie assigned to his squad and said my field training officer (FTO) would be Bobby Jones.

In 1980, it was common practice for many new officers to be treated like slaves by their FTOs. Many of my academy classmates needed to be at their station at least forty-five minutes early to get their cars gassed up, washed, and the air conditioner set just right, before their FTOs would ever sit next to them in a black and white. Bobby Jones certainly wasn't a typical FTO. He treated me like his partner from day one. He told me on our first day in the car that we were partners and his job was to make me better than he was. I never had to refer to him as "Sir" but I always did. Of all his virtues, not having an inflated ego was at the top, the major reason he was a great partner and mentor.

Bobby Jones was an eight-year veteran who was respected as a "cop's cop." He worked his butt off putting bad guys in jail, but he also knew we were, most importantly, public servants. He was committed to Community Oriented Policing (COP) long before it was even introduced as a philosophy in the law enforcement community. Our area was the West Side of Las Vegas. The West Side was once the segregated portion of Las Vegas. African Americans still made up more than 90% of the population. At that time, it was the place that Metro brass didn't care about. Bobby Jones did, though, and so did most of the other officers who worked this great part of town.

Integrity Based Policing

"Do you know why they put you over here with me?" Bobby asked me as we settled into our car on our first shift together. I took a guess.

"Because it's the most dangerous area and they wanted me to improve in the area of officer safety."

Bobby laughed.

"They want to get rid of you and figure you won't be able to handle yourself."

The reality was that Las Vegas had been known as the "Mississippi of the West," and many white officers were afraid to work in this part of town. Bobby told me that, here, cops were required to work with the good citizens and forget about the color of their skin. I was fortunate that the color of somebody's skin had never been an issue for me.

Bobby told me that he would watch out to ensure I didn't do anything stupid. We worked together as if we had been partners for twenty years. One of the major factors that shaped my development as a police officer was a cassette tape Bobby always had playing in our patrol car. The tape was Deputy Chief Bob Vernon of the LAPD speaking of the need for police officers to be "Christ-centered" in order to be successful police officers. I was pleased to learn that my partner also shared the Christian faith and believed that our role as officers was an extension of that faith.

Our first call was a domestic disturbance in a government housing project. A grandmother reported that she caught her grandson smoking PCP and confronted him. Her grandson punched her in the face and took off running. When we got to her apartment, I saw an older African American lady crying. She confirmed that it was her 16-year-old grandson who had punched her in the face. She was raising him because both of his parents had died from drug overdoses. I knew she experienced physical pain resulting from being punched, but her real agony was the fear that her grandson was heading down the same deadly path. Bobby asked me to go back to the car and retrieve a report for misdemeanor battery. "This punk needed to go to juvenile home for hitting his grandmother," he said.

Bumper's Code

The typical Metro response in the early '80s would have been to not take any action and leave grandma to fend for herself. I was glad that we were going to do something to make sure this kid would be held accountable. As I was outside getting the crime report from my briefcase in the trunk of our police car, I spotted a kid matching the description of our suspect. I called him over, but he took off like a rocket. I remember thinking, "Should I chase him or go back inside and notify my partner first?"

I had too much testosterone and too little brain power. The chase was on. That day we did not have a portable radio, so Bobby, who was inside the victim's apartment, didn't have a clue where I was for about twenty minutes. I chased the suspect through Doolittle and the Weaver Projects, and finally ended up catching him behind the Nucleus Plaza. The fight didn't last long as he was more tired than as I was. After patting him down and slapping the cuffs on him, it was just a matter of walking him back to his grandma's apartment.

I knocked on the door, expecting Bobby to greet me like the prodigal son, but instead he rightfully jumped me. "Why didn't you let me know you were chasing him?"

I apologized and said I should have advised him before getting into a foot pursuit. After taking the crime report and making sure our victim understood her next steps, I escorted our prisoner to our patrol car to transport him to Clark County Juvenile Home.

Making your first arrest is an important event in a cop's life. I would guess that while many retired officers could not remember what they had for breakfast, they definitely would be able to give you all the details surrounding their first arrest.

After taking a few deep breaths, I keyed the microphone.

"Control, 3David12, we'll be 492 en route to CC JH one time."

Wow! I knew all the other units were wondering, "Wasn't that suspect gone prior to their arrival?" I knew that the other guys on my squad were going to be asking me about my first arrest and foot pursuit. During the short drive, Bobby had forgiven me and said that I did a good job catching our suspect.

The policy at juvenile is that before bringing any suspect into the facility, officers need to make sure their weapons are placed into a gun locker. I reached down for mine. It was not in my holster.

I did the required paperwork quickly, and then I made my confession to Bobby.

"My gun is missing. I must have lost it during the foot pursuit."

Here's an example of what made Bobby such a great leader. Without burning me on the radio, he called for a K9 unit to meet us over at H Street and Doolittle. He did not mention the gun. Sure enough, K9 Officer Theron Howard and his Rottweiler, Sterling, found it on the muddy outfield of Doolittle Center. In field training, if you lose your duty weapon, you're out. Bobby's discretion in keeping my disappearing gun between us saved my career.

Soon, Bobby and I were working like a well-oiled machine. I was even assigned to work undercover because of my youthful appearance. We targeted drug dealers at a local Dairy Queen and at the west end of Sahara.

One night, I was working in plain clothes and Bobby was watching me with his binoculars when a situation took place that showed me police work can often be hilarious. The west end of Sahara was nothing but desert and at night it was pitch black. The only light on Sahara was from the headlights of the vehicles parked on the side of the dirt road. Every weekend night from about 9:00 p.m. until 2:00 a.m., kids would hang out to smoke marijuana and pop Quaaludes. My job was to work the crowd and buy dope, and signal to my surveillance officers after a transaction took place. Surveillance officers would then request patrol units to roll in and make the arrest. My surveillance officers were positioned in the desert area and used binoculars to keep their eyes on me.

My job was simple. I normally had kids selling to me without even having to approach them. On this evening, I had already made numerous buys and was getting ready to wrap things up, when I heard a blood-curdling scream coming from the pitch-black desert. Was it a girl being raped? Beaten? I couldn't believe my eyes as I saw a young girl with her pants down around her ankles hobbling into the light with Bobby chasing after her.

As I got close to the girl with her jeans pulled down, I heard Bobby yelling, "I told you I was the police. Why didn't you just move to another spot?" It turned out, the girl had gone into the desert to relieve herself and was in the process of going when she spotted Bobby lying prone out a few feet away. She understandably panicked and headed back into the light. Making this incident even more comical was the sight of Bobby with piss spots all over his shirt. After she pulled up her pants, we decided to call it a night.

After a couple of weeks of field training, I was ready to be out on my own. I was nervous, but extremely confident that I was ready to go solo beat. I would miss having Bobby as a partner, but I could not wait to get out on my own.

On my last shift in field training, Lieutenant Chuck Martin tossed Bobby and me the keys and told us to stay out of trouble.

"It's his last day in training -- don't fuck it up!" Martin warned.

We laughed and headed out to the parking lot. The shift was unusually quiet, and it looked as if we would be able to follow the lieutenant's advice until I spotted two white kids jumping into a Trans Am in front of the Wild Goose Bar at Lake Mead and D Streets. The only reason white people came over to the West Side was to buy dope. I told Bobby I was going to stop them. As I called it out over the radio and hit the red lights, the Trans Am kicked it and the chase was on.

We rocked and rolled for forty-five minutes at speeds in excess of 100 miles per hour and blew red lights as if they weren't even there. The helicopter was not up that night to help, so we had to keep the car in sight. Other units joined us as we headed up Kyle Canyon Road. My heart was racing and I could barely see fifteen feet beyond my hood as we traveled in excess of fifty miles per hour on the dirt roads. The car kicked up dust so thick that it was entering the passenger compartment of our vehicle. It made us both cough. I couldn't even see the suspect vehicle, when I suddenly heard a large BANG!

The dust settled quickly and we saw the suspect vehicle had hit a cactus. It was totaled. I ran to the passenger side of the car.

One of the suspects had just kicked another officer between his legs and sent him to the dirt. So, I unleashed two power strokes with my baton to his calves, took the passenger to the ground and handcuffed him. The suspect's head was bloodied, and he was still resisting even as I put on the cuffs. I heard a voice screaming.

"Look what you did to his head!"

I kept my focus on the suspect, and shouted back.

"Help or shut up!" I looked up, saw that the person who yelled was wearing sergeant chevrons, and it was not Sergeant Bunker.

Both suspects were taken into custody, and we called for medical help to treat the injuries from the accident. The sergeant who had yelled at me was screaming at Bobby Jones. Finally, Bobby and I jumped in our car to follow the ambulance to the hospital to complete all the reports. It turns out that the car they were driving was stolen and they had been carrying several ounces of liquid PCP.

Driving to the hospital, Bobby asked me why I screamed at the sergeant.

"I didn't know who he was," I explained. "And besides, I never hit the suspect in his head. All the injuries were from the crash."

"He's pissed at you for yelling at him." Bobby said. "Just make sure you apologize to him."

When we arrived at the hospital, that sergeant and most of internal affairs were already waiting for us. The internal affairs sergeant told me that other officers would handle the booking process for us. The IA sergeant and I drove to the IAB office in his unmarked vehicle. It was the loneliest drive I ever had to endure.

The sergeant escorted me to a small interview room in IAB where two other investigators were already seated and waiting to interrogate me. All three of them screamed at me about what a worthless piece of New York shit I was and that the poor boy I had beaten was in bad shape. They told me I needed to resign immediately or they would have the district attorney prosecute me for battery with a deadly weapon and battery with substantial bodily harm.

My mind was racing and I knew that, at the very worst, this

Bumper's Code

punk might have needed a few stitches. But he was awake and sitting up in the ambulance. And I was positive that all my strikes were to his legs and his head injuries were all from the wreck. I sat there and feared that everything I had gone through was now going up in smoke. I was still on probation, I could be fired at will, and there was nothing I could do to defend myself. For a fleeting moment, I considered resigning to avoid any chance of getting trumped up criminal charges filed against me.

Then I realized they were just attempting to bully me into quitting. I sat there, quietly saying some prayers to Saint Jude. I had worked too hard to get to this point, to allow some bullies intimidate me, even if they were wearing badges. I decided not to say anything until I could talk with somebody I trusted.

I told them that I wasn't going to resign.

"We'll put your skinny white ass in Ely State Prison," one of them yelled. "Do you know what happens to young white cops up there?"

I held my ground while they yelled for another half hour. Then I heard a knock on the door. One of the IAB investigators opened the door, and the atmosphere changed immediately. It was Chuck Martin, my lieutenant.

"What's going on?" the lieutenant asked.

The IAB sergeant changed his demeanor and told Lieutenant Martin they were just doing a preliminary interview.

"You are going to start over, and I will be sitting next to Dan," he said, and sat down next to me.

When I first saw Lieutenant Martin, it was as if my guardian angel had just flown into the room. He patted me on the back and asked if I was okay. I told him I was happy to see him. Lieutenant Martin simply told me to tell them exactly what happened. The tone of the interview became calm. After about ten minutes, Lieutenant Martin and I left. During the interview, these once overly-antagonistic interrogators suddenly had morphed into professionals seeking to glean information.

It turns out that the suspect had several stitches and had been

Integrity Based Policing

released from the hospital before we even arrived at IAB. His head injuries were from the crash and happened inside the car. Lieutenant Martin advised me that the suspect was the son of some casino executive, which explained why most of IAB rolled out. Making matters worse was that the sergeant I had yelled at was a "blue flamer" who wanted to take over the Academy. Lieutenant Martin thought the sergeant was attempting to portray me as the poster child of bad training to illustrate why our Academy was all screwed up and needed him to fix things.

After that interview, I was sent home on administrative leave. Being on administrative leave is like walking the Green Mile – I was likely going to get fired. Before I left, Lieutenant Martin reassured me.

"Don't worry," he said. "I have your back."

I became more confident after hearing those four powerful words.

I met my brother, Pat, at the coffee shop inside the Ambassador on East Fremont. It was the first time that night I could contemplate what had taken place during this incident. Pat was assigned to the graveyard and had just left his squad's start-of-shift briefing when we met. He was told I had already been fired, and they were contemplating criminal charges. When I told him my side, he was relieved, but he still needled me like a brother.

"That's a relief. I would hate visiting you in Ely Prison. It's cold up there." A good laugh is medicine for the soul.

I didn't sleep more than a couple of winks that night. The headline in the morning paper made matters worse: "Metro Officer Beats Local Youth." I was thinking about joining the Marine Corps when the phone rang.

"Hello, is Dan Barry there?"

I answered, saying it was me.

The caller introduced himself as Don Dennison, the undersheriff. At this point, I felt as I had a few months ago sitting in Sergeant Conner's office wearing my white tube socks.

"Dan, it seems like you got into a cluster last night and I'm calling to find out what the hell happened," he said. He had been called by Chuck Martin, who told him I was a good kid with potential. Undersheriff Dennison advised me that because of all the media attention and who the suspect was, there would be a full investigation. He assured me he would personally review the case before any discipline was meted out. He asked me for the details. After listening to me, he gave me his word that unless I was lying to him, I would not be kicking rocks. However, I'd probably get forty hours of extra duty. Before he hung up, he jokingly gave me the good news.

"Your administrative leave is over. Get your lazy ass back to work today."

I was in my seat at the briefing and thought for sure that I would not be doing a solo beat for at least several weeks, if ever, due to the prior night's incident. Sergeant Bunker read off the lineup. I was to work 3E12, as a one-man unit. He laughed and told everyone in the room that he had been ordered by Undersheriff Dennison to graduate me from field training. That entire night was a blast. It was the first time I knew for sure that I had made the right decision to become a police officer.

After two weeks passed, I learned that I would be given forty hours of extra duty. This meant that instead of working four ten-hour shifts each week, for a four-week period I would be working five ten-hour shifts, with the same pay. I know this entire episode taught me a great deal. The type of leadership that was displayed by Officer Jones, Lieutenant Martin and Undersheriff Dennison, is "servanthhood leadership," something we are in dire need of in today's society.

Can you imagine a person of rank calling a probationary officer and being so candid in today's world? In all likelihood, the ranking officer who reached out would be severely disciplined. While it is true that over the past thirty years, law enforcement has made major strides in technology and tactical preparedness, we have regressed in the manner in which we treat the public – and our own people.

The most important event that happened during this period of time was my marriage to Allison. We had originally planned on

Integrity Based Policing

getting married back in Schenectady after I had completed probation. However, we missed each other too much to wait. On a beautiful Saturday morning, we entered the Sacrament of Holy Matrimony at Saint Bridget's Roman Catholic Church in downtown Las Vegas and tied the knot.

I loved being on my swing shift squad, however I was elated to learn that I was being transferred to a graveyard squad at the west substation. All police officers know that even if you're riding alone, you're still considered a rookie when you are on a training squad. The hours for grave were 10:00 p.m. to 8:00 a.m. and I was off on Tuesday, Wednesday, and Thursday. This was great for Allison and me since we had only one car. Another advantage was that I had days off in the middle of the week, which meant we did not have to wait in long lines to see a movie.

My first shift on graveyard was an experience that I'll never forget because that is where I met Bumper.

This squad was composed of eight officers and a sergeant. Sergeant Jim was newly promoted, although he had been a cop for over twenty years. He was extremely friendly. The other officers had a mixture of seniority. While some senior officers were attracted to graveyard because it was when the brass were sound asleep, few stayed on this shift for the right reasons. Officer Ron Morgan – Bumper – was one of those men.

Bumper stayed on that squad because he truly loved the people living on the West Side. He also knew that many of the new officers were sent there after field training. Bumper enjoyed teaching young guys the right way, not just the bullshit that was written in the policy manual. To Bumper, being a good cop was more than just being smarter and tougher than the bad guys. A good cop also needed to have compassion for the good people.

Sergeant Jim welcomed me to the squad and told me that he wanted me to work with Bumper. Bumper was built like an NFL linebacker and knew the West Side like the back of his hand. He was an eight-year veteran of Metro, who had served in Vietnam as a member of the Marine Corps. After Bumper and I got into the vehicle, he told me that he was going to show me how to work the streets. I was ecstatic to have the honor of working with him.

Bumper told me that the difference between working swing shift and graveyard was that all the hard-core assholes were out during graveyard. He advised me that as long as I treat people with the respect they show me, I would be fine. He explained that what makes the difference between an average cop and a good one is his relationship with citizens. After thirty years, I can tell you, Bumper was 100% accurate. The last thing he advised me before we parked in front of the New Town Tavern was that he would do the driving until he had confidence in me as his partner.

Bumper put the car into park, and he said he needed to go inside the New Town to use the head. He told me to get out and start talking with the folks hanging around. I did. I introduced myself to several of the men outside drinking cans of Colt 45. They were all friendly, and as I was about to go inside the bar, I heard a voice directed at me.

"Get back in your car, you little faggot."

I looked and saw a black man staggering toward me.

"Are you talking to me?"

"You heard what I said, bitch."

I told him, "Get in front of my patrol car." I was going to pat him down, but he continued to show off for the crowd.

"I would kick your punk white ass if you weren't wearing that badge."

I patted him down and responded, "I don't need a badge to whip your ass."

He threatened me, "Take it off and see what happens."

I walked back to the car and took my badge off and put it under the seat. My mind was racing, knowing that I already had one sustained complaint in my file for "use of force" and probably would get fired if I received a second one while still on probation. This idiot really made the decision for me.

I knew that if I didn't stand up to him, my reputation as a cop would be destroyed. I could also tell from looking at how unsteady he was on his feet, it wouldn't take more than a few seconds.

As I stepped back toward him, he threw a wild right that brushed the top of my head. I just started punching and hit him with about five solid shots. He went down like a pile of dog shit. He looked up and told me to stop hitting him. I slapped my cuffs on him and put him in the back seat of our patrol car. The people standing outside were laughing and clapping after our brief encounter.

Bumper was smiling as he came back to the black and white.

"They tested you early," he observed. "Normally it takes a couple of weeks before somebody calls you out."

It turned out this mental midget had just been released from prison and liked to challenge young white cops. On our trip to jail, the arrestee kept saying, "Man, you're quicker than white lightning." Bumper just smiled and nodded at me, showing his approval. I much preferred the nickname "White Lightning" to "Hari Kari Barry."

The rest of the shift consisted of Bumper taking me around to meet several people and handling a few calls for service. Bumper counseled me that developing trust required treating everyone else as you would want them to treat your brother or sister. For the rest of the night, we just got to know each other and made a few stops. The best part was that at the end of the night, Bumper showed his confidence in me.

"Tomorrow night, you're driving."

Because the majority of the suspects in the valley lived over on the West Side, it was not uncommon for us to spend our entire shift doing follow-ups for the detective bureau. As Bumper told me, the reality was not that the detectives were too busy. It was that they did not have the trust of the African American citizens who lived over there. Bumper had so many informants that we could not pass an intersection without one of them waving us down. It seemed as if every night we received information from one of Bumper's friends about a violent felon hiding on the West Side.

One night in briefing, we learned about a suspect who was wanted on numerous narcotic warrants. We were aware of this guy. It was not long before we spotted this suspect driving his green

Cadillac down H Street. When we pulled him over, we saw he had his two daughters in the back seat. Policy stated that when a suspect has felony warrants, he is taken into custody immediately and the car is towed. Bumper stepped in.

"I'll handle this."

I saw Bumper talk with the suspect for a few seconds, then the suspect got back into his Cadillac and drove off. I asked him why he let the suspect go. With a toothpick dangling out of his mouth Bumper sarcastically retorted, "How would you like to be searched, handcuffed and arrested in front of your kids?" Bumper then told me that the suspect was going to meet us in front of Nucleus Plaza in an hour. As Bumper predicted, in an hour the suspect was standing there waiting for us to take him to jail.

While we took the suspect to jail, he gave us great information on where two suspects from a shooting were hiding out. When we got to jail, the suspect was crying and thanking us for not jacking him up in front of his little girls. After we finished booking him, we followed up on his information and arrested both of the suspects from the shooting. Bumper's way was not always consistent with our policy manual. It was better.

In one crime spree, a group of African American kids had been robbing tourists on the Strip. The local media was all over this and the detective bureau was not passing information on to patrol. Bumper told me in the car one night that he'd gotten a call that morning from Detective Murray, a man he trusted, asking for our help tracking the knuckleheads down. Bumper drove over to the People's Choice Lounge. We went inside and just talked with some folks to see what they knew. We had been inside the People's Choice for about two hours, when an older black lady walked up to Bumper.

"Those white detectives in their cowboy boots told me they were going to kill those boys, but I trust you," she confided.

Within a couple of hours, Bumper and I had rounded up a group of three juvenile suspects and two adults. We also recovered all the evidence (guns and victims' identifications) hidden at different apartments. After we finished the paperwork, the detectives called us to verify that the series was solved. That day, the department held a press conference to announce how Metro robbery detectives cracked this major case. Not one word of credit was given to Officer Ron "Bumper" Morgan. It was at that time that Bumper taught me the most important eighteen words for any cop to always remember. Bumper's Code stated: "We do this job for the good people of our community, not to please the clowns at headquarters."

After a few weeks, Sergeant Jim told me that he wanted me to work with another partner who had just transferred over because he wanted Bumper to break in a new officer. Besides, my new partner and I were both New Yorkers and Sergeant Jim joked we were the "only two guys who could understand each other."

In the '80s, we did not have computerized suspect databases like we do today. It was all done with handwritten index cards. We had files in the station, but all good cops kept their own shoe box filled with these cards in the back seat of their patrol cars. We also had to carry a pocketful of dimes – for the pay phones. It was often comical to watch an officer stay at a pay phone while another officer would run back and forth from the command post to relay information.

However, in the '80s we had more community trust. During this period, cops were assigned to a beat and stayed there for a lengthy amount of time. Police officers knew the community's residents and the community knew – and trusted – them. It was at least five years before officers even considered moving to a specialized unit.

In today's world, it is not uncommon to see officers work different beats on a regular basis. Officers are encouraged to transfer out of patrol as fast as possible. It might take only eighteen months to become a detective, or join the K9, SWAT or traffic teams.

The most exciting news was at home. Allison and I were expecting a baby. In the tough economy of the early '80s, this meant we would have to move from our adult mobile home community. We had decided that Allison would be a stay-at-home mom, which meant that I needed to get a second job. Allison and I found an apartment that allowed children, which cost slightly more than what we had been paying for our mobile home. I also landed a part-time job in the warehouse of Montgomery Ward.

My new job was loading and unloading tractor trailers and stocking the warehouse. I also had to retrieve all the large items customers purchased and load them into their vehicles. I only earned minimum wage, but I often got tips when I helped customers. The hours were tough. Since I finished at Metro at 8:00 a.m. and had to be at the warehouse from 10:00 a.m. to 4:00 p.m., I didn't sleep much. The only saving grace was that I worked both jobs only two days a week, and worked three of my days off from Metro. But it was not the lack of sleep that got me – it was the heat. During the summer months, the temperature in Las Vegas is normally well above 100 degrees, and inside the metal trailers it was like an oven.

All of the extra work was well worth it when Rosie was born on Saint Paddy's Day.

Working with my new partner was great because he and I were good friends, and we were both passionate about working the West Side. A benefit of working graveyard back in the '80s was that many nights, especially during the cold months, it was quiet after 2:00 a.m. which served as a major perk. Because all of the guys on my squad were working two jobs, we would get a few winks while our partners covered. I had no problem getting some shuteye during the dead times. My partner was usually the one who stayed awake.

One night, I could see my partner was exhausted. During the briefing, we were advised of a group of thugs from San Diego who had pulled multiple robberies and had shot at police. We received information they were driving an older model gray Cadillac with partial California plates of "CGT." It was believed they might be on the West Side because one of the suspects had relatives living over there. I was confident.

"We're going to catch those assholes tonight," I told Bumper and his partner.

"If you two get them, I'll buy you a steak dinner at the Horseshoe," Bumper replied.

I shouted back, "You're on!"

It was so slow that night that we were able to check all the possible locations several times, and we were confident these suspects were not on the West Side. At 3:00 a.m., my partner told me he needed some shut eye and I told him to go ahead. I parked in the desert area, and after about a half hour, he was out like a light. I realized that the reason he did not like to sleep in the car was that he snored so loud. But I was bored, so I decided to recheck some of the locations to see if we might get lucky.

This night was so dead that even the bars were empty and only a few cars were on the road. But I saw a speeding car about two blocks ahead of us. I got closer to the vehicle and the car appeared to be speeding up. I realized that this might be the Cadillac. My partner was snoring so loud that I could barely hear the radio. Worse yet, the radio was on his side. We were heading on to I-15 from Washington. I could tell it was a gray Cadillac and it had California plates beginning with "GCT." I was driving at about 90 miles an hour. He needed to wake up.

"Wake up!" I yelled repeatedly. The louder I screamed, the louder he snored. I started punching him in the arm. He finally came to.

He snapped, "What the fuck do you want?" I told him we were chasing that wanted vehicle, and he needed to get on the radio and tell dispatch. He dozed back off. He thought I was messing with him and kept trying to go back to sleep. Finally, I pried the radio mike from his hand and told dispatch "we are in pursuit of that 415A vehicle."

That did it. He woke up.

The pursuit was going for a few minutes when the suspects rapidly and unexpectedly pulled over. This made me think that they were doing a "panther stop." The panther stop is where suspects pull over all of a sudden and open fire on the pursuing officers. I started planning tactics for our modified felony stop and made sure to exit the unit quickly in case they began shooting at us.

I stopped in perfect position and hit the gear lever. As I sprang the driver door and jumped out of the cruiser, I pointed my gun at the suspects and started to yell commands. Unfortunately, something not included in my tactical plan caught my eye.

Bumper's Code

Our car was rolling backward.

It turns out that I had hit the gear lever into reverse instead of park. I moved away from the car to avoid being struck by the open door, and I tried to keep my focus on our suspects. My drowsy partner had one foot inside the car, and the other bouncing on the asphalt while trying to retrieve the shotgun from the floorboard. Then, I heard a "thump."

Our unit had rolled into our backup unit, Sergeant Jim's car. I stayed focused, though. We got all five suspects into custody.

We recovered several thousand dollars in stolen cash and four firearms. After we finished securing the prisoners and retrieving the evidence, Sergeant Jim showed me the damage done to his cruiser's front bumper. I asked him if we needed to fill out a report. He began laughing.

"Just book those assholes and get something to eat." We did, and met Bumper and his partner for a well-deserved steak dinner.

Once during a lunch break, I learned the importance of never leaving my baton in the car. In those days, officers working graveyard developed close relationships with all the businesses open 24 hours. One of my favorite spots was a Mexican restaurant named El Jardin's. At about 3:00 a.m. during a midweek shift, Officer Brian Skala and I decided to eat lunch early at El Jardin's. This night was extremely quiet, and it looked like the restaurant was empty. We came in, sat down and were greeted by our waitress. As she handed us our menus, she told us that the night was dead, except for a bachelor's party that was taking place in the back room. In the background, we could hear music and people laughing.

We ordered our food and the waitress came over to our table and asked if we could help her. She said that a guest attending the party was getting rowdy, and she wanted him to quiet down and wanted us to advise him to settle down. We did. The man was very polite and kept apologizing to us, saying he did not normally drink. Brian and I went back to our table and finished our meal. As we were leaving, this same guest started screaming at me.

"You fucking piece of shit. I ought to kick your ass!"

Integrity Based Policing

We walked back into the party – still packed and going strong – and confronted the drunk, who was sitting in a booth. He was at least 6-feet 5 and was built like a refrigerator. This once-happy crowd had turned into an ugly mob and wanted to see a fight. Brian had the portable radio, but the noise inside the bar was so loud that making a transmission was impossible. He ran outside to call for backup units. The suspect came after me like a linebacker going after a quarterback. I sidestepped his attack and fired a right hand that caught him on the side of his head. Because my baton was in the car, my alternative was either my fists or my gun. This certainly wasn't a deadly force situation, so it was hand-to-hand combat.

The drunk had size. I had speed and sobriety. When he charged at me again, I was able to side-step and push him into a booth, and pin him face down on the bench. I stayed on top of him and kept him neutralized. It was so crowded that Brian couldn't even get back inside. I had to keep control until the cavalry arrived. The last thing I wanted was to incite the crowd, and have his buddies jump in. I made it a point to keep screaming, "Quit resisting, stop fighting!" If I kept punching him, I think the crowd would have jumped in and the outcome would have been ugly. The sound of police sirens was like beautiful music to my ears. My only goal was to stay on top of him. He was strong. However, he was too drunk to fight.

The crowd parted like the Red Sea, as "Stearling" (Officer Howard's 140-pound Rottweiler) entered the room. His paws clicked his arrival on the Spanish tile. Knowing that dogs do not discriminate when engaging on a target, I rolled off the suspect as Stearling snacked on the suspect's ass. Within a few minutes, the suspect and about ten other rowdy drunks were on their way to jail. The suspect needed a hospital stop first after being Stearling's chew toy. It took three sets of cuffs to get that suspect ready for his trip to the Gray Bar Hotel.

After several months of working two jobs, I realized that burning the candle at both ends was starting to create problems. One day, when I was taking a refrigerator off a trailer, the hand dolly slipped and the fridge landed on my big toe. It immediately swelled up and I could barely stand on it. Since I was only part-time, I was not eligible for workman's compensation. So, I just wrapped it up and finished my shift. That night, I was hobbling around and my partner told me to keep off it. He would handle things.

But no such luck. Our first call ended up with a foot pursuit involving a juvenile who had just stolen a lady's purse. It didn't take long for the suspect to lose me. I made a promise to myself that I would never work again unless I was 100%.

The next morning, Allison and I learned that our second child was on the way. As much as I loved working the West Side with men like Bumper and the rest of my team, I knew that it was time to transfer to an area command closer to home.

I spoke with Bumper about my decision to leave the West Side. He agreed it was the best thing for my growing family. We both knew that I would be back. In less than two weeks, I was notified that I could transfer to the South Substation to another graveyard shift squad. While I was happy to get exposed to a different style of policing, I could not wait to return to the West Side.

I had the privilege to learn from men like Bob Jones, Chuck Martin, and Ron Morgan (Bumper). All of these great men understood the importance of being a public servant. They all shared the knowledge that police can only be effective when they are trusted within the community. I thank God for allowing me the opportunity to learn from these great men. Throughout my thirty-year career, I often deliberated about Bumper's Code in serving our community. "We do this job for the good people of our community, not to please the clowns at headquarters."

3

DON'T SWEAT THE SMALL STUFF

After rumors began to circulate that I was transferring from the west substation, it was non-stop bantering until the day I left. In the early '80s, the officers working out west had a reputation for being hard-charging cops who did an excellent job. Since the west substation was the most dangerous and had the highest amount of violent crime, officers assigned there made many more arrests and handled the majority of the gun calls in our valley.

The south substation was nicknamed the 'country club' for patrol officers, whereas out West we took pride in being known as "ghetto cops." South substation's biggest priorities included officers maintaining a spit shine appearance and avoiding citizen complaints. Uniform appearance was not as important out west because many shifts included getting uniforms dirty. Being involved in fights, crawling through windows or into attics and stepping knee-deep into mud puddles are just a few of activities resulting in uniform maladies that were easily forgivable out west, but would drive sergeants crazy out south.

The easiest way to determine whether an officer was assigned out west or to the south substation was to look at their tie. Out west, as soon as an officer left briefing, the top button was opened and the tie clip would go through the open button hole. During the entire shift out west, the top button was open and the tie was not

Don't Sweat the Small Stuff

clipped. Most west officers would clip up their ties only when they were a few feet away from the station door as they were walking in to secure. Officers assigned to the "country club," i.e. the south substation, would never unclip their ties during a shift. The culture out south was that maintaining uniform standards was serious business, which included keeping their ties clipped. The culture out west was slack on wearisome procedures and more focused on arresting criminals.

This seemingly trivial difference in uniform standards led to a comical episode that served as an important leadership lesson. We had a new sergeant transfer out west from south who was on a one-man crusade to ensure that all of his officers became as paranoid about always having their ties clipped as the officers from his prior station. This sergeant threatened all of us at briefing that if he saw anybody with his tie unclipped, he would write them up. Our saving grace was that he hardly ever left the office and had little chance to see anybody outside the station. Bumper, being the informal leader, realized that he needed to intervene and decided that this young sergeant needed to be taught a lesson on "don't sweat the small stuff."

One night, before briefing, Bumper told everyone that he was going to conduct training for our new sergeant, and needed some help. Bumper asked me to get the extra set of keys to the sergeant's vehicle. All vehicles had two sets of keys hanging inside the key room. This sergeant always took out the same unit, so I needed to take one set of keys before we began our shift. As we left to work the streets, nobody except Bumper had a clue what this training would include.

All of us were like little kids on Christmas Eve, wondering what Bumper had in store for our new sergeant, and how he was going to respond. Fortunately for us, this night was extremely slow, which afforded Bumper the time to handle all the necessary logistics. At about 2:00 a.m., Bumper and his partner were shining their flashlights inside the dumpster, located behind the New Town Tavern. I was sitting on the other side of "F" Street watching this and wondering what they were doing?

Integrity Based Policing

Suddenly, I saw Bumper remove an object from the dumpster and place it into the trunk of his unit. I didn't have a clue what it was. However everyone was getting anxious about what was going to happen.

At about 5:30 am, this sergeant checked out for lunch at the 4 Kegs, which was across the street from the station. Bumper then cryptically advised the entire squad to meet him in the lot of the west substation. All of us were curious about what Bumper had masterminded.

The reason police speak over the radio utilizing the 400 code is to ensure communication is cryptic, concise and accurate. Our squad also had its own way of communicating that only members of our team understood. During briefing, Bumper had advised us that when he said over the radio that he was going, "483 at the Union Plaza," all of us were to meet in the parking lot of the west substation because the training was about to commence.

After parking my unit and switching to stealth mode, I handed over the spare set of keys to the sergeant's vehicle to Bumper's partner. I then saw Bumper open the trunk and remove a pig's head, which he had retrieved from the dumpster. It turned out that on that night, the New Town Tavern held a pig roast, and this was the item Bumper had retrieved from the dumpster. With the skills of a beautician, Bumper stuck a large cigar in its mouth, a New York Yankee baseball cap on its head and clipped a tie on its neck. Bumper and his partner then trotted across the street -- Bumper carrying the pigs' head and his partner hauling several phone books. When they got near the parked sergeant's car, they went into action. Bumper used the spare keys to gain entry. He placed the five phone books on the driver's seat and then, with the dexterity of a brain surgeon, gently placed the pigs' head on top of the phone books. With the pig wearing its Yankee cap, cigar in his mouth, and LVMPD tie, it almost looked alive sitting behind the steering wheel. They closed and relocked the door. Bumper and his partner then sprinted back to our location and we just waited until the sergeant finished his lunch.

All of us were in a state of hyper-anticipation and watched with

Don't Sweat the Small Stuff

binoculars as this unfolded. It was still dark when the sergeant exited the restaurant. He was totally oblivious to the fact that his entire squad was watching him from across the street. When he opened the car door, he jumped like a scared school girl and actually ran behind cover. We then saw something that frightened all of us: he grabbed his portable radio and began to transmit.

All of us knew that this thing was taking a felony ugly turn. We all used the darkness of the hour to scamper as far from the location as possible. Fortunately, there was an exit on the opposite side of the station, so our sergeant never saw the exodus of police cars. The sergeant screamed on the radio, "Control, my unit has been burglarized and a dead pig's head was placed in the driver seat."

He then requested the watch commander, homicide and criminalistics respond and process the scene. At this point, all of us kept quiet and responded back to our patrol beats. The watch commander was a salty old lieutenant who knew immediately this was a prank that was being blown way out of proportion. He canceled all the other units and told our sergeant to take a chill pill and quit messing with us about wearing those stupid ties. Nobody said another word about that prank and the sergeant did learn not to sweat the small stuff. The lieutenant told Bumper the next week that he owed him lunch for conducting that much-needed training.

Clearing out my locker from the west substation was not a pleasant task. I was leaving behind many friends and abandoning the neighborhood that I had grown to love. The one positive thing about transferring out to the south substation was that it encompassed the Strip, with superior eating spots and superior eye candy, as compared with the low-income neighborhood I had been working. Still, I was leaving behind all the good people who lived over on the West Side and I would not be as engaged with the citizens on my new beat. I gave all my field interview cards to my academy buddy, Johnny Russo. I emptied my locker, shook hands, and jumped into my 1976 Chevy Chevette to drive across town to my new substation.

As I pulled into the parking lot of my new substation, I

immediately sensed a major difference between the atmosphere that encompassed it and my previous home. Out west, I was accustomed to the ladies behind the counter being friendly with smiles on their faces. At my new substation out south, it seemed that everyone hated their jobs. They had expressions of disgust on their faces. Out south, it seemed even the smallest tasks required a number of administrative steps to complete. The morale at my new station was not going to be as high and the trust that permeated the West Substation was replaced by a sense of formality.

After putting my uniforms and gear into my new locker, I spent a few minutes walking around my new home. Even the briefing room was polished and every report was tucked away neatly into file cabinets. Several signs posted on the walls caught my attention: "No eating or drinking allowed outside of the break room," and "All items left out will be discarded." These guys seemed much more uptight.

The biggest difference was the attitude of the officers working on my new squad. Out west, we were focused on putting bad guys in jail and developing trust within the community. Here, we had a much greater transient population and the people we served appeared to be faceless. It seemed that kissing the casino bosses' butts, keeping tourists happy, and staying out of trouble were the overriding themes.

Even the way briefings were conducted was the polar opposite of west substation. Out west, it was all about arresting criminals and locating wanted fugitives. Here, the level of formality made productive communication almost impossible. The sergeants would sit at the table in front of the briefing room and do all of the talking. The only verbal utterances made by the officers would be to notify their sergeant of the car number they were going to drive. Other than details about a few major crimes that took place during the last few hours, crime was not even discussed. It seemed the most important topic was ensuring all units coordinated about where they were eating, so we did not abuse any "comp joints" (restaurants that give police free or highly discounted food).

Don't Sweat the Small Stuff

My new squad was made up of a mixture of seniority levels, and we had a sergeant who seldom left his office except to eat lunch or check out new prostitutes on the Strip. On my first shift, the sergeant told me just to listen to the senior guys and not piss anybody off, and things would work out fine. My new sergeant was a likable guy, but did not have the passion to be a true leader.

In fact, most of the guys on my squad were good people, but they were not concerned about finding felony suspects or fighting crime. I first realized this when I asked some of my new squad mates about the "hot spots" in our area, and nobody had a clue. It seemed that this new squad lacked any true mission and spent most of the shift responding to calls and stopping a couple of whores. The presence of thousands of tourists on the Strip meant that we did not get to know the citizens we were serving, so we primarily just responded to calls for service.

The only mission seemed to be "stay out of trouble and make sure to remain within your assigned sector/beat."

The most obvious crime issue was prostitution. In the 1980s, hookers were so thick on Las Vegas Boulevard that tourists actually had to walk out into the travel lanes to avoid being harassed by them. Many officers spent their entire shifts taking them to jail by the bus load. Despite our best efforts, we were not even scratching the surface, and this was a major source of frustration for all of us.

I found myself getting discouraged because I envisioned my role as making our streets safer and helping people, not playing taxi driver for prostitutes. I spent my time working the alleyways that were the havens for drug sales. I missed working with informants and tracking down bad guys. There is something about the rush you get when you track down a felon with a gun that dramatically outweighs the sensation you get when you arrest a working girl sitting handcuffed in a security office.

During one of my first few nights, I spotted a suspicious car parked in the desert near a pizza restaurant. I quickly realized it was just a whore giving a guy a blow job in the front seat. I pulled them both out of the car and interviewed them and discovered that the

Integrity Based Policing

male was the restaurant owner. My backup officer, Bobby Bennet, was also new to my squad and searched the interior of the car. He found a vial of cocaine on the rear floorboard, so I decided to book the male subject for possession of controlled substance.

The very next day Bobby and I were banished from the Strip. It turned out that the pizza joint always had been friendly to Metro and arresting the owner harmed this relationship. This pizza place would give us all free meals if we agreed to allow them to conduct business as they wanted. Bobby and I refused to apologize for taking the owner to jail. We were told we were not team players. This resulted in us being assigned the area just east of the Strip. That suited us just fine because the new area was packed with felons. Getting backup was sometimes a problem, but we coped.

After a few months, I transferred to a different graveyard squad that was composed of new officers. It was refreshing to get back to a squad where everyone was focused on police work. This squad actually worried about putting bad guys in jail. The difference in morale between these two squads was linked to leadership at the sergeant level. My previous sergeant was solely concerned with not pissing anyone off and making it to his retirement date. My new sergeant actually was a cop's cop who cared about helping people. It was the example the sergeant set and the type of leadership he provided that created a healthy policing environment, not the building.

It did not take long before the formality dissipated. Because I was one of the senior guys on the squad, I took it upon myself to transfer some of the old west substation traditions to my new squad. One of these traditions was pulling pranks.

We had a new officer transfer to our squad who was former military. He always had immaculate uniforms, and he was so concerned about his boots being shiny that he would shine them during the shift. During one briefing, I poured my entire can of Diet Coke into his pants back pocket. How he did not feel it, I will never know. He worked the entire shift and did not realize he had a long brown stain running down the back of his pant leg. This stain made it look as if he shit in his pants. I pointed it out to him at the end of the shift and the entire squad cracked up. He never sat in front of me at briefing again.

He did get me back. The next week, I was walking to the front of briefing room to check my mailbox. I felt as if I was walking on ice and kept sliding on the tile floor. Everyone in the room was cracking up and I decided to look at the bottom of my shoes to see why they were so slippery. They had been spray painted with fluorescent orange paint. I had to get a razor blade and scrape all of it off my shoes before I left briefing. It took over an hour.

My buddy, the Diet Coke victim, had watched me open my locker and learned my combination just to paint my shoes as payback.

In 1983, Sheriff Alexander was elected to office. His major campaign promise had been that he would "clean up the town by getting all the whores off the Strip within 120 days." To do this, everyone in our department stepped up to the plate. We were provided a jail bus during all shifts and prostitutes were arrested and detained instead of being immediately released. Within thirty days, Sheriff Alexander had kept his campaign promise. This accomplishment was achieved collectively through the effort of every man and woman at Metro and resulted in a sense of pride that benefitted us all. It is amazing how powerful clarity of mission can be in fixing problems.

Life was moving quickly on the home front, too.

After Caitlyn was born, Allison and I realized that we needed to buy our first home. During the early '80s, interest rates were sky high, and young cops were not making enough to qualify. Despite the fact that I had been working two jobs for more than a year, it still was not enough. Fortunately, a friend suggested that I talk to the manager of the Lucky Store where she worked. I met the manager, who told me the starting pay was more than twice what I was making at Montgomery Ward. The major advantage was that, in my new job, I would be inside an air-conditioned store instead of in the "hot box" that I was used to at Montgomery Wards. I hated leaving my graveyard buddies, but my priorities were clear. Transferring to dayshift at Metro would allow me to work more hours at Lucky so Allison and I could put money away to buy our first house.

Lucky was no picnic. My first thought was, "This job sucks!" Working in a supermarket requires you to know the location of everything, and there is no down time. Customers have no patience for a new person learning how to operate a cash register and some people are downright rude. But all the store employees made great teachers and did all they could to show me the ropes. Everyone got me trained on the register and knowledgeable enough to keep the job for several years. I met many great people, too. Policing tends to isolate you from others, but working at Lucky let me interact and socialize with hardworking people who had never worn a badge.

My new dayshift squad also provided a great learning environment. This squad consisted of a collection of great cops who wanted to teach me as much as possible. This team was made up of veterans who honored their roles as public servants and knew the importance of teaching the younger generation of police officers. My sergeant was a man named John Thorton. Sergeant Thorton was a Vietnam combat veteran who understood the true role of policing in our society. He believed in regular inspections and was always out in the field with his men. Despite the fact that we were assigned to the Strip, we did not kiss anybody's ass. I learned throughout my career, top quality policing is about being fair and objective without demonstrating partiality.

Sergeant Thorton had a reputation for attracting only the best officers to his squad. Despite having days off in the middle of the week, weekly inspections, pressure to produce and no tolerance for lay downs, our squad was known for high quality of work. Officers like Bobby Hitt, Jimmy Ayers, and O.C. Pigford reminded me of Bumper and Bobby Jones. Like Bobby and Bumper, they never worried about pleasing the brass – only serving the people who lived in their area. We were such a close-knit team that nobody even cared about individual credit. It was all about serving the community.

Sergeant Thorton knew all of our strengths and weaknesses and made sure that we all looked out for one another. Bobby Hitt

Don't Sweat the Small Stuff

was an outstanding communicator and could get a confession from a suspect better than anyone I'd ever met. Jimmy Ayers was a traffic expert and always set up the perimeters because he really knew all the streets and alleys.

O.C. Pigford was a 33-year veteran who knew how to work informants. Officer Pigford arrested the two suspects from the Truman Capote classic, "In Cold Blood." He told me that having to go to Kansas and witness the hangings of those two was the worst thing he ever had to do in his life.

At this point in my career, I did not have any strengths, except for my desire to learn as much as I could from these great men.

The most dangerous part of policing is not the raging gun battles. It is moving the vehicles from point A to point B. Traffic accidents have always been the number one killer of police officers. I was lucky to learn this lesson the easy way. One morning, I heard a "444" over my portable radio. The code "444" is the call that no officer ever wants to hear. It means that another officer is in dire need of help. The location was several miles away, but I still thought I could get there quickly. I jumped in my car, activated "code 3" and I was off. As I was clearing an intersection, I saw another black and white stopped at the red light. Then I heard "code 4" and for other units to disregard. So, I did. But I heard Sergeant Thorton's voice over the radio calling me to meet him at the station and I had a really good idea who was in that stopped black and white.

I walked into his office and I could tell I was going to get blasted.

"Were you the unit that rolled code through Tropicana and Paradise?" Sergeant Thorton asked. I told him I was. He told me that I had no reason to be rolling code and driving like an asshole, because I was miles away and traffic was congested. He told me that, for the next two weeks, I would partner up with other units until I showed him and my squad members I was mature enough to operate a black and white. I shook his hand and gladly worked as a partner to the other officers on my team.

This type of training is valuable and taught me an important lesson. While some would say that informal discipline leaves the supervisor open for liability, I know it is a powerful tool for any leader. Having the other officers involved benefitted me and the entire squad. Sergeant Thorton did what he thought was best for the department. A formal disciplinary action might not have had the long term positive impact on me. This worked.

The only other new officer on my squad was Tim. He had graduated from the academy in the class before mine and was a year older than I was. It seemed like all the senior officers on the squad were spending most of their time mentoring the two of us. One day, Tim told me over lunch that his wife, Georgie, was from Schenectady, New York. I told him that Allison was also from Schenectady. Small world. It turned out that Georgie's parents and Allison's parents were good friends back in Schenectady during the 1960s.

One Saturday morning, I was patrolling down an alley way in the area of Reno and Maryland Parkway when I spotted a car that was parked with its engine running. The car was a newer model Cadillac and had paper plates. I thought that it must be stolen, so I parked a short distance away to watch. I called out the event on the radio, and had backup units rolling. In about two minutes, I heard a loud scream and saw three Latino males jump into the car. I immediately tried to get behind them to pull them over, but the chase was on. We had no helicopter. It would be up to the ground units to take these suspects into custody. Lucky for me, three of my backup units pinned the vehicle in before it had a path of escape. All of the suspects were taken into custody without incident.

After we were "code 4" on the stop, I had another unit check out the apartment they exited. The officer in the other unit found that two men were inside the apartment bleeding from stab wounds. The Cadillac had just been stolen and the suspects were cocaine dealers. We obtained warrants for several locations and recovered many ounces of powder cocaine. When I finished all the reports and was walking out of the station, the swing shift lieutenant, Walt Myers, patted me on the back.

"Great work, Dan!"

I replied, "Lieutenant, this was an entire squad effort. I was just lucky to be a part of it."

Allison's brother, Steven, had just moved to San Francisco, and invited us to visit. We decided to take a well-deserved vacation. Because Rosie and Caitlyn were babies, we figured it would be a great time to spend a few days with him. I bought plane tickets and asked Tim if he could give us a ride to McCarran International Airport and pick us up when we got back. Tim agreed and drove us to the airport in our car (with the baby car seats). Since we returned on a day off, Tim would be able to pick us up using my car.

We had a great one-week vacation in the City by the Bay. We flew back to Vegas and went to baggage claim, expecting that Tim would be there to pick us up. We were at baggage claim when I heard, "Dan Barry, please call the information desk." The call brought bad news.

Tim had been in a car accident the day before and could not drive us home. I took a cab home and drove back to the airport to pick Allison and the girls up. Then, I called Tim to see how he was doing. The day before, Tim had been working and was dispatched to a robbery alarm at the First National Bank at Desert Inn and Maryland Parkway. Tim decided to bust the intersection at Joe W. Brown and Desert Inn. Bad idea! When Tim was in the center of the intersection, he was T-boned by a mini-van who had the green light. Tim told me that when he saw the mini-van it was too late to avoid the crash, and he thought he was dead.

Both the black and white and the mini-van were totaled and all parties were injured. Thank God, none of the injuries were critical; however, Tim had some eye damage from the flying glass. Talking to some of the officers who had seen the damage from the wreck, it is a miracle the injuries were not much worse. It was great to hear Tim's voice and know he was not seriously injured.

Tim said that his wife was in Schenectady visiting her parents when he got into the accident. He was home alone and had bandages covering both his eyes. I told Tim to sit tight – that I would bring him to our apartment to spend the night with us. When I picked Tim up, I could not believe that anybody left him alone in his condition. Both of his eyes were covered with about 2" thick of gauze and he was completely blind. I escorted Tim to my car and drove him to our apartment where I knew he would be safe until he could see again.

Tim began his stay at our house with art therapy – from Rosie and Caitlyn, who drew with magic marker on his bandages. I told Tim he could sleep on our roll out couch. Allison made a great meatloaf, and we all had dinner and watched a little TV – well, we watched. Tim listened. Once Tim and the children were all set, we called it a night. We set the alarm for 6:00 a.m. and Allison and I went to bed. At 3:00 a.m., I heard Tim's voice.

"Danny, I have to go to the bathroom."

I jumped up and ran out to my good buddy, who already was sitting up on our roll out couch.

I walked arm in arm with him to our bathroom. After Tim undid himself and ensured he was over the target, he just stood there.

"Are you fucking with me?" he asked.

"Tim, this is my house. Why would I be having you piss anywhere but in the toilet?"

Of course. So, Tim did what he had to do and went back to bed.

I was still juggling two jobs but my part-time job at Lucky was good. The boss was a great man and was happy to have me as part of his team. Primarily, I worked from 6:00 p.m. until 10:00 p.m. Most of the money from my part-time job was being put away to save for a down payment on our first house, but we still had a long way to go. The interest rates were still crazy high so Allison and I thought it would take years. Our apartment was getting too tight.

Fortunately, God had a different plan.

Even my job at Lucky was becoming more fun, since I now knew all the "ins and the outs." I was soon promoted to oversee both receiving and stocking. This meant that I was the one who needed to replenish all of the items on the shelves and in the dairy section. This was great as long as I was not tied up at a checkout register. When it was busy, I was always called up to the front to help with customer check out.

Because my boss at Lucky thought I was doing a great job and could trust me, I was able to recommend other people for employment at the store. My friend, Tim, asked if I could help land his wife a job at my store. His wife, Milo, had worked in a grocery store in the past and was looking for a job since their kids were going to school. Within two weeks, my manager, Robin, hired her, and she was working at the same store as I. Milo was a superstar and was promoted to supervise the liquor section.

The worst part of working in any grocery store is listening to that stupid public address system. For the entire shift, all I heard was that thing going off and having to respond when it pertained to my area. I also knew that the only phone line into our store was in the liquor section. The majority of calls were from outside lines checking to see if somebody could call home for a message. I decided to do the same thing to Lucky as I had done at the south substation--lighten things up with a few pranks.

On a crazy busy night, I called from the pay phone outside the store entrance into our liquor section and put on my best Chinese accent. Poor Milo answered the phone.

"Hello, Lucky, can I help you?"

I said, "Yes, my name is Mr. Lingus; I need to talk with my wife, Connie." I heard Milo get on the intercom and announce "Connie Lingus, please come to liquor." The customers in the store broke out in laughter and our manager immediately knew that I was Mr. Lingus.

O.C. Pigford was a part-time realtor, and asked me one day to follow him to a new housing development in the area of Nellis and Charleston. These homes were still under construction but were being marketed toward young couples. I still thought we could not qualify. But O.C. sat down with Allison and me and showed us that we were very close. I was disappointed, but knew in time it would happen.

That same day, I was contacted by Lieutenant Walt Myers about applying to test for Field Training Officer (FTO). I had been an officer for only two years and I didn't feel qualified to become an FTO. Becoming an FTO was exciting because it meant an 8 percent salary increase, thus allowing us to qualify for a new home. I spoke to Allison and we prayed about this decision. The next day I spoke with my entire squad about this transfer, and they all encouraged me to make the move. Lieutenant Myers gave me advice.

"Dan, the most important thing for an FTO is to have passion and to want to teach others what others have taught you." I was confident that becoming an FTO was the right thing to do. Within two weeks, I was an FTO and we were making plans to move into our first house.

That night I called Dad to tell him we were buying our own house. Dad told me he was extremely proud of me and said to keep God and my family as my top priority. This seemed obvious to me, but I had seen many people who failed to follow this advice and as a result their lives were destroyed. My Dad was thankful that his son did not have to work 80 hours a week, reminiscent of what he did to accomplish the American Dream. At the age of 24, I was the father of two cute little girls, husband to a beautiful wife, employed in a job that I loved, and a new home owner.

God is great!

4

HIGH SCHOOL DAZE

In 1984, I was a happy young man. Allison and I had just purchased our first house, thanks to my part-time job and the additional pay for being a Field Training Officer (FTO). We had two beautiful little girls, Rosie, and Caitlyn, and I was a member of the greatest police department in the United States, the Las Vegas Metropolitan Police Department. I had earned a reputation for being a "cops' cop" who, despite possessing a thick Brooklyn accent, was respected in this cowboy culture of the Wild West.

Being a city boy saved me from getting involved in a caper in which many of my squad mates were unluckily involved. One rainy night, a cow was hit by a truck on Sunset Road and Eastern Avenue. Several units responded for traffic control along with our sergeant, Billy Elders. The cow was covered in caked-on mud and had no visible brand, so the Animal Control Officer told Sergeant Elders the meat would probably go to waste.

That night at debriefing, Sergeant Elders, and the other guys on my squad concocted a plan to butcher the cow, thereby salvaging the meat. They planned to have a barbecue for our squad that weekend courtesy of this jaywalking cow. I told them I was not interested and went home instead of participating in this adventure. As I left the station, my buddies on the squad taunted me.

"You're not invited to our barbecue!"

The next day, I knew something had gone terribly astray with their butchering brainstorm. At briefing, I learned that my entire squad was under investigation for attempted grand larceny. It turned out that the brand inspector did locate a brand, under the layers of caked on mud. The owner was extremely upset that anyone – especially a group of cops – had attempted to claim his property. It took several weeks to complete this rustling investigation, but eventually everyone was cleared of wrongdoing. However, Sergeant Elders did receive the "Bum Steer Award" from our captain for his poor decision. The local media made a big joke about this caper and said, "Metro officers made a very bad MOOve."

Of course, I had a fun time busting their chops about getting beefed over some beef.

Being a police officer was so much fun that I could not imagine doing anything else for a living. Everything about the job was enjoyable, especially the brotherhood all of us shared. We saw ourselves as a group of warriors whose job it was to protect the good people from the animals who sought to make victims of them.

In the 1980s, police officers were not handcuffed by body cameras, the crusading media, special interest groups or their own administration like they are today. If officers had pure intentions, did not break the law or behave unethically, they did not have to worry about getting into trouble. We worked to make good citizens feel safe with little concern about pissing off bad guys, their attorneys, media outlets, or the American Civil Liberties Union. Taking a vacation was certainly not seen as a bad thing, but the reality was that in those days guys could not wait to get back to work. After a two-week vacation to New York with Allison and the girls, I remember being excited about returning to my squad the next day. Officers were so tight back then that a serious feeling of guilt would kick in if a brother officer was injured while somebody was taking vacation.

Driving home with Allison and the girls from McCarran Airport following our two-week trip, I remember feeling a mixture of being sorry that our journey was over and yet being super excited about getting back to work. The vacation was fun, but I was already mentally "back in the saddle" wondering if we had ever caught those burglars killing us in a neighborhood off Boulder Highway.

"Do you want to get pizza tonight?" Allison asked me.

"I don't care, whatever you want," I said absently.

She immediately snapped back "You're on vacation until tomorrow, can you keep your focus on us until then?"

I felt guilty for daydreaming about getting back to my squad. After I 'got my mind right' we did have a fun evening together.

The next morning, I got up and ran five miles, shined my shoes and watched the clock as it neared 3:00 p.m. At 1:45 p.m. I was already inside the South Substation getting myself primed for my first shift back to work. I wanted to talk to fellow officers to discover what was happening. I wanted to check my wooden mail box in front of the briefing room where I would find a hard copy of all of my correspondences. My mailbox was labeled in red to indicate that as a field training officer, I was a first-line supervisor.

Swing shift was a tough shift for the guys with older children, but because Rosie and Caitlyn were babies, it fit me perfectly. Swing shift also had nonstop calls for service and all the dirt bags were out and about, trolling our streets. Our main job was to stop all the thugs and twist them to get to the bigger thugs. That was, and still is, the best way to reduce crime in any neighborhood. The officers assigned to day shift needed to wait until late in the afternoon, and the guys on grave had only until 4:00 a.m., but us lucky ones on swing had non-stop criminals out and about. There were shifts when, if you did not arrest at least four felons, you were either wearing a blindfold or you had not left the parking lot.

As I approached my mailbox, I noticed that it was jam-packed with paperwork. The majority of items were administrative notices, subpoenas, training notices, and miscellaneous junk mail. One item did catch my attention. It was a phone message to call Deputy Chief Waugh about an opening in Narcotics. I immediately thought that these guys were extremely lame. Playing practical jokes was a major part of our police culture and after a two-week vacation, get ready because you're going to get screwed with. At this point in my career, I daydreamed about working up in narcotics, and this desire was well-known to all my fellow officers at south substation. This message was designed to have me call the chief and ask him about being transferred to narcotics. I knew that if I called, the chief would laugh and tell me, "Dan, I don't know anything about it." I crumbled it up and tossed it in the nearest trash can, thinking, "These guys are pretty dumb if they expect me to fall for that obvious of a prank."

That first week back from vacation went smoothly. In fact, nobody even pulled any sort of prank. However, the next week I was called by Lieutenant Walt Myers to come to his office. Lieutenant Myers was always the type of leader who didn't intimidate his people, so being dispatched to his office did not make my blood pressure shoot up.

"Did you call Deputy Chief Waugh about going to narcotics?" he asked. I told him that I hadn't because I thought it was a prank and didn't fall for it.

Holding back a laugh, the lieutenant said, "Dan, it's not a joke. I suggest you call him before five p.m."

This was a difficult call to make without sounding like a complete knucklehead. As I ran to the closest phone, I realized it was too late to do anything about that.

"Hello Chief, this is Dan Barry. I got a message you called."

"I called you two weeks ago and you're just returning the call?" I repentantly explained that I had been on vacation and thought his message could be a prank. He laughed and went on to explain that Sheriff Alexander wanted to put undercover police in local high schools to buy drugs and reduce violence. He told me they were looking for experienced officers who looked young enough to fit the role. He wanted me to consider taking this transfer.

I accepted.

I asked how I needed to prepare. He told me to call the commander of narcotics the next day, and he would set me up with the training. Chief Waugh also told me that this operation was extremely confidential and not to tell anyone about it. I was assigned to vice/narcotics section and could not go near a police substation until the operation was over. Chief Waugh said that the other two officers selected for this operation were Chris Van Cleff and Sam Hillard. These were the only two people I could speak with about this operation until after it was finished. The official justification for my transfer from patrol was that I was TDY (temporary duty) to the sheriff's office.

My next task was to tell my boss at Lucky that my hours would need to change, but that I could work the night shift. He understood the short notice and told me not to worry. He was happy because I could close the store for him. Then I had to tell Allison. She was nervous, but happy for this chance for me to expand my career. But how would we keep this secret? Most of our friends were police officers. I told her that we'd take things as they came and put the matter in God's hands.

The next morning, the narcotic's commander told me to report to the vice/narcotics office and to come dressed like a high school kid. Chris and Sam were already sitting in the hallway when I arrived. We waited together for the commander to greet us.

The commander was a gigantic man with a voice like an old grizzly bear. He yelled for us to come in and meet the squad that would be responsible for babysitting us. He said that we were a pain in his ass because narcotics should be out there buying big dope, not little nickel bags of weed from high school punks. He warned us about relationships with teenage girls.

"The first one of you caught fucking a high school girl will get it chopped off by me!" he barked in an intimidating tone. After these inspirational words, the three of us met with Lieutenant Mike, Sergeant Mark, and the rest of our new team.

Sergeant Mark had been in narcotics more than twenty years and knew more about working dope cases than anyone I ever met. Here was the plan: nobody except the principal would know our true identity. We would each be in one of the three high schools with the biggest drug problems. Chris, Sam, and I would each enroll under the pretense that we had moved here from other states.

Integrity Based Policing

Each of us would have a primary detective playing the role of an uncle.

We had three days to train. We were to be enrolled and taking classes by the next week. The method used to select which of the three schools we were assigned to was simple. Because Rancho was the most violent and had the racial problems, the guy with a flat nose and the Brooklyn accent would make the best fit. That would be me. Sam was a preppy boy type, so he would be one of the upper-class kids at Chaparral High School. That left Clark High School for Chris.

The three-day training plan turned out to be an exaggeration. It was more like a four-hour block. The majority of our time was spent on administrative tasks needed for us to be enrolled in school by the following Monday. We spent a full day at the Department of Motor Vehicles getting our undercover driver's licenses. We spent another morning waiting in line at Nevada Power to get some bogus power bills so we could register for classes. Then we went down to pick out the cars that we would use during this operation.

I selected a dark brown 1979 Firebird with heavily tinted windows. The car had a few dings, but it was definitely the coolest car on the lot. I was given the first selection of vehicles because I had drawn the short straw on selecting schools. It was during this time that my undercover uncle, Jimmy, and I were able to get our cover story laid out. Jimmy was also from back East, so it was believable that we were both New York transplants. I came to Las Vegas because I had been in and out of juvenile detention and was getting into trouble in New York. My mother wanted me to get away from my bad crowd and move in with my Uncle Jimmy. I was a first semester senior, and this was my last chance to graduate from high school.

I selected Danny McGuire as my undercover name. The first name is best if it is your own name. The reason for this is that when somebody calls out "Danny" you naturally turn and address them. The last name was selected because I fought a kid named Danny McGuire several times in the amateurs, and they were all wars that stuck out in my mind. Also, I wanted an Irish surname, so it seemed like a good choice.

The game plan was that, for the first week or two, I was just to get used to my classes and not worry about buying dope. I would register for all the basic classes and certainly not any of the academically challenging ones. This is because high school dopers aren't geniuses, and I wanted to be seen as a burnout with a thick wallet. I was given $200 in cash and needed to fill out an impress sheet to document all my expenses. Our marching orders were simple: 1) if a deal is set to go down after school off campus, call for a surveillance team; 2) never work on female suspects; 3) do not allow the kids to pinch your narcotics; 4) after work was done at school, get back to the vice/narcotics office to complete an activity sheet; and 5) always remember you are a police officer and after it is over, your actions will all be scrutinized by the media and defense attorneys.

My first day at Rancho I was so nervous. I thought everybody I met knew I was a police officer. I walked into the main office to register for all the bonehead classes on my list: Basic English, study skills, U.S. Government, and science. The best part was that I was finished before first lunch so that I could work on suspects during both lunch periods. My school day started at 8:10 a.m., so I could even meet people before school.

On day one, I arrived at my first class, which was already in progress. The teacher, an older blond lady, told me to introduce myself to the class. I blurted out that my name was "Dan Barry." After realizing I said my actual name, I blurted out "McGuire." I was so upset that I made this blunder during my first class it caused me to question if I were prepared to be in this role. Looking back, I do not even think anyone noticed my slip-up, but at the time it was a major deal to me. The teacher then told me to have a seat, and she would talk with me later about getting caught up.

I was certain that everybody in the class was suspicious of me, so I just pulled out my notebook and tried to look interested. For the rest of the day, I kept my head down and tried to fit in. After school, I drove back to the Vice Narcotics office and was relieved to learn that Chris and Sam had similar experiences at their schools. All three of us were wondering what we had gotten ourselves into.

Allison wondered, too. She and I discussed my first day and watched TV. Ironically, "Miami Vice" was on, a show about a couple of young dope cops who had the glamorous job of buying cocaine. They made the job of undercover cops seem exciting. It was Hollywood, and Allison and I laughed.

"Believe me," I told her, "it won't be that easy."

At least the second day was much more exciting. I parked my Firebird in the student parking-lot and several kids walked over and started to hassle me about having such a cool car. They made the mistake of threatening to kick my ass. I remembered that I was told to "just act like a punk kid would." So, I told them, "Let's go!"

I threw down my books and began to run after the punks, and they took off running like a pack of scared mice. Just then, I felt somebody grab me by my shoulder. It was a school police officer who screamed at me. After a few minutes, he escorted me to the dean's office. This incident resulted in a detention and I was told to have my uncle sign a letter about my behavior. I did not realize it at the time, but this was the best thing that could have happened to me. It gave me instant "street credentials" with the dopers. I headed over to serve my detention after school.

The detention room looked like a "who's who" in burnouts. During the forty-five minutes, I had at least three different conversations about scoring cocaine and weed. I also lined up a deal for the next day to purchase a nickel bag of weed. After detention, I headed out to my car and looked forward to getting back to the vice narcotics office to tell everyone about the day's progress. As I turned the ignition, I realized that my battery was dead. Since, my car was one of the few left in the student lot, I needed to walk a couple of blocks to the 7-Eleven and arrange for a jump.

As I walked up to the pay phone, I noticed some burnouts hanging around the side of the building that looked as if they were curious about who I was. I thought that they were probably sizing me up – contemplating whether or not to mess with me. I felt extremely vulnerable because I did not have a gun, and knew if they were legit bad guys they would be packing. I kept telling myself, "Just act like a teenage punk."

One of the crew asked me, "Do you live around here?" I told him that I was new to Rancho and my battery was dead and I needed a jump. He offered to give me a jump, and we just started shooting the breeze. After my car was running, he asked me if I was looking to score some weed. I told him that because I was new in town, I did not have any connections. He offered to sell me a dime bag if I was willing to trip to get it.

My mind was racing about whether I should go through with the deal or just set something up for later. I was all alone and could not get back up. I thought these clowns might rob me after seeing my cash. Reality sank in. I was supposed to be a high school doper, not a tactically sound cop. So, I said yes, and if it was good, I would buy even more from him in the weeks to come.

The suspect's name was Bobby. He jumped into my car and told some of his pals to hop in the back seat. I told them I was not taking any passengers because I didn't know him or his buddies. Bobby said, "Okay, it'll be just you and me." He directed me a few blocks to the alleyway of a housing project complex. He told me to park, and he would get the weed after I gave him the money. I told him I was not going to give him shit until I had the weed in my hand.

After about thirty seconds of his trying to haggle with me about giving him the cash, he agreed and told me to wait a few. Bobby jumped out of my car and disappeared into the complex. I sat there waiting for him. My mind was racing as I thought about the possibility of him returning with a gun and robbing me. I decided that I would keep my engine running and doors locked until Bobby returned. As I sat there, I looked around and saw numerous gangsters in the alley and I was the only white guy. I remember listening to Glen Frye's "Smugglers Blues" on my radio and just trying to look like I fit in.

Part of playing a high school kid meant not wearing a wristwatch, or a wedding ring, however, I knew that Bobby had been gone for at least a half hour. I also noticed that some of the gang members were starting to give me increased attention. As I was getting ready to drive off, I saw Bobby running up to the passenger door. He jumped in and told me "Let's get out of here."

I put the car into gear and drove onto Maryland Parkway. I asked Bobby if he had gotten my package, and he said, "Definitely, and its high-quality shit." After we got a short distance away, I parked the car and handed Bobby the money and took the weed. Bobby told me he was worried because a few weeks ago, a buddy of his was shot in that same alley while he was scoring some weed. I drove Bobby back to the 7-Eleven. I got his phone number and I told him I was glad we met. Before he left my car, he said he wanted to pinch the package. I told him, "No, you already pinched it before you came back to my car."

Bobby wasn't a student, so his identity couldn't be found by simply looking at school records. Back at the 7Eleven, I asked Bobby if the car he used to jump mine was his. He proudly said "damn straight" pointing to his 1982 Impala, and started telling me what a great deal he got on this car. I looked at his plate and made a mental note, jotting this information down after I drove out of eye-shot. This information allowed me to identify him and submit a criminal complaint. When I got back to the office, I ran the registration and attained the identity of Bobby. It turns out he was a 24-year-old and was registered for robbery.

I can still remember how great it was to be impounding the first package of dope I purchased. From that day forward, I didn't need to go looking for dopers. They were looking for me. A white kid with cash was like a magnet at Rancho. The best part of the operation was that the majority of cases were not from students. They were off-campus adults who lived in the neighborhood. The students knew where these addresses were and would take me to the doors and make the introductions.

One time, I drove with my contact to an address on the West Side. We got out and went inside the apartment while one of my surveillance units parked in front on the lawn. The crook was getting ready to hand over the dope, when he spotted the truck with a bearded white guy sitting behind the wheel. He began screaming at me "You're a fuckin' narc!" I told him that he was the narc and I would not deal with him again. As he came at me, I knocked him to the floor and ran out of the apartment. Later, I learned that the surveillance unit had written down the wrong address. Two weeks later, I returned to the same apartment without any surveillance units and purchased rock cocaine.

Greed is stronger than common sense.

In a few weeks at Rancho, my reputation had spread. I had several good students actually upset with me because they thought I was a nice guy who was getting in with the wrong crowd. I was invited to numerous Christian Bible Studies and other positive functions by kids who wanted me to get on the right track. Obviously, the teachers thought I was trouble and couldn't wait to get me out of their classrooms.

On one occasion, in the middle of U.S. Government class, a campus police officer (named Calvin) marched into the room. He walked right up to me and told me to follow him. Once outside the class, he searched me. I was clean. He told me that I was an asshole, and he was going to make me his "little punk ass project" and see to it I ended up in jail. I remember thinking, that is exactly what a school police officer should be doing. If I really were a dope-dealing kid, I would have been scared straight – or at least off campus.

Time went quickly during this operation, and it turned out that Rancho was by far the best school to be assigned. Near the end of the operation, Sergeant Mark told me that I needed to wrap up my buys and get the warrants together for our bust out – the day we would serve all the warrants and make all the arrests. In this case, I was no longer concerned about making new cases, and I had time to have some fun with certain teachers.

My entire time at Rancho, I played the role of a complete burnout who did not do homework or participate in discussions. In my government class, the teacher was a young lady who was extremely liberal. On one of my last days, we were discussing the

Watergate years, and she was giving a negative, one-sided portrayal of President Nixon and, in fact, all Republicans. When I raised my hand, she almost passed out. She probably just thought I wanted to use the restroom again. I spoke for about the next five minutes on how I did not appreciate her preaching her leftwing ideology as if it were gospel. I also told her that while President Nixon left office in shame, she had no right to paint all Republicans with the same brush. Her face turned red.

"That's an interesting position," she said. "However, it's wrong."

In another class, I was the only student who had not turned in a term paper. Without the "paper," I would not pass the class and could not graduate. The teacher had already given me several extensions and finally she said, "That's it. You are not going to graduate!"

I told her that she was acting like everyone else in my life by turning her back on me. I covered my face and pretended to be hiding tears. She wound up giving me a big hug and another extension.

The day before the bust out, Sergeant Mark told me that because I had the most cases, he wanted me to select the name of this operation. I asked Allison to help me think of a name. She thought for about five seconds and came up with "Hi School Daze."

Perfect.

The bust out was on a cold Wednesday morning. All of the local media outlets were present. Every student suspect was taken out of class, arrested on campus, and put on the prisoner transport bus. All of the adult suspects were arrested at home or at work. "Hi School Daze" had a major impact on drugs in our high schools for years to come. The majority of the citizens of Clark County were extremely pleased with "Hi School Daze" and wanted to see an ongoing effort to reduce drugs and violence in our schools. I am sure that we also had a small group of bleeding hearts who believed we had trampled the rights of the dope dealers. After that, Allison and I decided that we would have our kids attend Catholic schools, even if it meant me working two jobs for the next twenty years!

The next week, I returned to my squad and the work I loved

best. There is nothing like the feeling you get from jockeying a black and white around town and putting dangerous criminals in jail. I know "Hi School Daze" was productive and I am proud to have been a part of the operation. However, I did not enjoy working undercover as much as being in uniform. The daily euphoria I got from operating a black and white, and not knowing what was going to happen next, always made patrol my favorite. In patrol, you could be dispatched to a hot call or to stop a dangerous fugitive at any moment. While working in narcotics, the majority of my time was spent waiting and trying to keep a step ahead of the bad guys. Patrol can be compared to a boxing match, where narcotics is more like fishing. They are both positive activities. It is just a matter of which one floats your boat.

Because Chris and I were on the same patrol squad, the other guys were constantly messing with us. After one arrest, both Chris and I were late getting back to secure. As we walked into the station, all the guys were waiting by the door and demanded to see a note from our mothers on why we were late. On another day, I was handed an envelope during briefing with a dollar bill inside. I made the mistake of inquiring aloud where it came from. Lieutenant Whitney said in front of the entire briefing room, "It's your lunch money the bully took from you last week!"

Probably the funniest thing occurred when the guys were asking Chris why he did not get as many suspects as I did. Chris responded without missing a beat "Dan had more suspects, but my grade point average was much higher."

Once, Steve, one of my academy buddies, was busting on me about looking so young. After about thirty seconds, I told him "Don't worry, Steve. Next semester, they are going to use you as an undercover principal." The entire room cracked up and Steve quit messing with me – at least for the next few seconds.

Allison was relieved that I was back in patrol. I was finally able to clean up and take the family out in public again without worrying about bumping into a suspect that I was working. The rumors about me going through some type of premature mid-life crisis were gone, too. We actually could go to church again and talk with people after Mass. With all the positive media, Allison and I saw firsthand that citizens really do appreciate good police work. It was great reading and seeing positive stories, instead of the almost daily onslaught of negative articles. The best part of ending "Hi School Daze" was finding out on the last day of the operation, that Allison was pregnant with our son, Patrick.

Word spread like wildfire throughout the department of my work during this operation and commanders from covert operations were calling me asking me to transfer. My standard response was that I wanted to stay in patrol for a few years before I made a decision about transferring anywhere. I did, however, agree to work undercover to assist as long as I remained assigned to my squad in patrol.

During one briefing, Lieutenant Whitney called Chris and me into his office. He said that vice wanted both of us to work with them the next night. They had received numerous complaints about gay men soliciting prostitution at adult book stores throughout the Valley. Because most of the vice detectives were known at these establishments, they wanted to use Chris and me as undercover operatives. While both Chris and I weren't excited to act as "gay boy bait," we both agreed to work with our vice squad the next night. We were told that this was only a one night operation.

The vice lieutenant met up with Chris and me at a Denny's restaurant and explained that many of the adult bookstores in town were complaining about gay prostitutes using their businesses to get clients. These bookstores all had locations for private movie booths. These were tiny wooden booths (cubicles) with a curtain and a small screen that played pornographic movies. Patrons would deposit quarters in these machines and view porn. While the businesses (supposedly) believed that the patrons were pleasuring themselves, in reality male prostitutes were entering the booths with clients. Also, the majority of these booths had circular holes cut into the adjoining booth. This was to allow the "John" to insert his penis while the prostitute in the other booth performed anonymous oral sex.

The vice lieutenant said that because Chris and I both looked young, we would not have any problem getting suspects. He told us to meet up with his team the next night at 9:00 p.m. behind the Flamingo and Paradise Adult Bookstore. Chris and I were uneasy. The idea of playing a gay prostitute was not going to be fun; however, I knew it was only for one night. I wasn't going to tell Allison all the details. This was one of those assignments that needed to be done. After it was over, I planned to take ten hot showers.

The next night, after meeting Chris at the South Substation, we drove into the parking lot of the Paradise Adult Bookstore. Chris and I joked about not wanting anyone to assume we were a couple. We drove around the block several times to make sure we were there at exactly 9:00 p.m. I pulled into a parking space. Chris and I walked around the back of the business.

This would not be a typical night.

The lieutenant and the entire vice squad were standing between two parked tractor trailers. After a few minutes of joking around, the lieutenant started the briefing. He told us that playing gay whores would make this the most disgusting night of our lives. We knew that we needed to be careful not to entrap the suspects. They would have to bring up the sex act and money first, before we could arrest them. Exposing themselves was sufficient for the charge of "indecent exposure." We drank two beers, got a handful of quarters, and steeled ourselves to walk inside the lobby. It would take about an hour or so before we would be approached by anybody, we were told.

The place stank of sweat and urine.

I thought "how does a gay whore act?" In a mere thirty seconds, I was approached by a tall man in his late forties wearing a lime green leisure suit. He smiled at me in a manner that made me sick to my stomach. I had to keep my cool and stay in my role and just smiled back. He asked me if I wanted to date him and share a movie.

He stepped into an oversized booth and motioned with his hand to step inside with him. As I stepped inside, he immediately

Integrity Based Policing

closed the curtain and put some quarters into the machine to play some gay porn. I just stood there waiting for him to ask me for a blow job. He began smiling at me as he pulled his pants down and began stroking his penis. He began moving closer to me. I pulled out my badge.

"You're under arrest." His stupid smile turned into a panicked expression as he clumsily struggled to pull up his pants. I stepped out of the booth and grabbed his arm and walked outside into the parking lot.

A group of surveillance detectives walked him to the jail bus that was parked out back. The lieutenant and several vice detectives patted me on the back and said, "Great job. Damn, that was quick." I completed a short declaration of arrest on Bob Samuels and went back inside the business. Nabbing suspects was like catching fish in a barrel. After about ten more arrests, we headed to different adult bookstores. We made more than fifty arrests that night. It was a major success for the vice section. The lieutenant and the rest of the vice team were ecstatic because this was the first time in many years they had done anything proactive to address this crime.

Because all the arrests came so easily and we exceeded our goals, we all went to a local watering hole after we'd finished. All of the vice guys were calling Chris and me "fag magnets" and buying us more beer than we could drink. As we sat at the table, Chris made the mistake of leaving to call his wife, Joyce, from a pay phone outside. I took his absence as a chance to pay him back for the pranks he had pulled on me. While he was away, I told the vice detectives that Chris was really gay and that he appreciated all of them being so nice to him. When Chris returned, you could have heard a pin drop.

There were ten minutes of awkward silence. Finally, the sergeant told Chris that they appreciated him working with them, despite his lifestyle.

Chris said, "What in the fuck are you talking about?" The whole table busted up and Chris promised me that payback would be a bitch! We all headed home and I remember taking several good hot showers before I would even look at the girls or touch Allison.

When we got back to work the next week, it was non-stop ball-busting. All the guys were calling us "fag bait" and "Siegfried and Roy." That next Friday, we were having a squad party over at Sergeant Billy Elder's house to welcome Chris and me back to our squad. When Friday night came, Allison said she did not want to go because she was having morning sickness. Instead, we took the girls for a ride down the Strip and got some ice cream.

As we returned home, I saw that somebody had dumped piles of trash all over my front lawn. Our small lawn was covered with at least four-foot high piles of garbage. It was trash night, and somebody had picked up all the garbage cans on our street and dumped the contents on our lawn. Being a trained investigator, I knew it was Chris and the other guys on my squad. After Allison settled down, I went over and joined my team at the party. The next morning, after gathering all the empty trash cans on my street, I shoveled all the trash back into the cans, and laughed to myself. That was pretty funny, even though Allison didn't think so.

Pay back was a bitch.

5

THREE'S A CROWD

It was a busy night at Lucky. Every checkout line was ten to fifteen people deep. Because my primary responsibility was restocking the dairy case, every minute I spent working the register, the later I needed to work getting everything replenished. Although our store closed at 10:00 p.m., I knew I would be working until midnight. Making matters worse was a recent commercial on television that Lucky had aired, "Three's a Crowd." This stated that whenever three or more customers were in line at a checkout, another register would open. Unfortunately, this meant the entire evening I was working the cash register instead of keeping the dairy section stocked up.

I was in the middle of a very large order when I heard over the intercom that I needed to call my wife. Normally, this would not be a big deal, but with Allison in her first trimester, and Rosie and Caitlyn being babies, I was concerned about what was important enough for Allison to call me at Lucky. Allison knew that, unlike my police job, I could not just break away immediately and return her call. After I finished the large order, I told my other customers I was shutting down for a break. Obviously, they were upset, but it was something I needed to do. I ran outside to the pay phone and called home.

Allison answered and told me that all the news stations were reporting how Metro arrested some big shot during a vice operation targeting gay men a few weeks ago. I told her we arrested more than fifty suspects, and it was not a surprise that a complaint would be filed. In the 1980s, the Nevada Revised Statute included crimes against nature, and the ACLU and other groups had been working to change these laws. I told her not to worry about it because I had not heard anything about it yet, so I was not concerned. She told me before she hung up that the only name they had mentioned was Bob Samuels. Samuels, it turns out, was the state director for the motion picture industry. At that point, I knew we had nothing to worry about because his arrest was by far the most solid arrest of the night. I went back to my register and was happy that Allison and my girls were okay.

I got home that night just in time to catch the tail end of the late news, and watched Mr. Samuels' interview. The same face that I saw in that bookstore was on television complaining about getting manhandled by some undercover vice detective. He alleged that I had pushed him into the booth and arrested him for no reason. Samuels claimed he was at that location to explore it for an upcoming episode of "Remington Steel." He went on to say that he is a happily married man and was totally innocent of all charges. He said he was definitely not a homosexual and wanted to vindicate his name.

Before the segment ended, the governor was interviewed and he said what a great man Mr. Samuels was and how important he was for the economy of Clark County. The governor also added they were close friends, and he was sure that he was totally innocent. The last part of the segment was spent saying that Mr. Samuels had taken two polygraphs and passed them both. Back in the '80s, a polygraph test was considered to be a definitive test in measuring the truth. I went to bed feeling as if I was in the middle of a "Twilight Zone" episode and thinking, the truth would surface so it didn't pay to worry.

The next morning, I received a call from the vice lieutenant. He was calling to make sure he had all the facts straight. I described the entire incident in detail to him, and he confirmed that this was

Integrity Based Policing

exactly what was in the arrest package. He told me that Mr. Samuels was extremely close to both the district attorney and the governor, and he was getting pressure to drop charges. He wanted me to understand that when politics get involved, the last thing that matters is the truth. Sheriff John Alexander was a great man who stood behind his people when they were honest and doing the right thing. In a situation like this, the relationship between the governor, district attorney, and sheriff, certainly weighed heavier than the truth.

I said a few prayers and was glad I knew I had not done anything wrong and was confident they just wanted this entire case to disappear. After I got off the phone, I watched the afternoon news. This case was again the lead story. Allison and I were encouraged to learn that one news station had shot a hole in Samuels's alibi by contacting the producers of Remington Steel and being advised that he was not there to scout an episode for their show. We were thinking, "Thank God. They want to report the truth, and the truth will come out."

That afternoon when I got to the south substation, all the guys were telling me not to worry and that the truth was going to come out. My sergeant (Billy Elders), Sergeant Dave Groover and Lieutenant Randy Whitney, called me into their office before I even dressed out. Lieutenant Whitney led off by telling me to buckle up, and get ready for a wild ride. He had witnessed situations like this before in his career, and they were going to make me out to be a liar who arrested poor Mr. Samuels for no reason. He said that because I had the truth on my side, they would not go for my jugular as long as I did not push it. He predicted that they would just dump his case quietly.

His counsel to me was to lay low, that this thing would be forgotten in a few weeks. I told Lieutenant Whitney that I was not going to say anything that would embarrass the department. However, I could not let them dump this case and proceed on all the other prosecutions. He smiled and told me to hit the street and not to worry about it. This had grown out of his control. He did tell me that he knew I was telling the truth, and he would fight like hell to ensure nothing bad happened to me.

Three's a Crowd

As I hit the streets that night, I felt as I had when, years before, another great lieutenant had told me he had my back. This gave me an inner peace and I knew "This too shall pass." Although Chuck Martin and Randy Whitney never rose above the rank of lieutenant, they had a major positive influence upon all of us fortunate enough to have worked under them. True leadership should not be measured by how high a rank a person ascends. Success must be evaluated by the level of desire a person has to help others.

The Las Vegas Sun was an important source of information back in the 1980s. Back then, we did not have the Internet as the worldwide communication network, and the Sun was the best source in town to keep the public informed on the news of the day. Ted Knight, a powerful local columnist, was without a doubt, the rock star of local media. He was in constant battles with organized crime figures, corrupt politicians, and other shady folks that the people wanted to learn more about. A factor that added to his influence was that in the '80s, the media had credibility. What was said in the printed media or reported on television had a higher degree of credibility than today's media.

That Friday morning while drinking my coffee, I looked at Ted Knight's column and got sick to my stomach. His column said "If Metro can illegally arrest a prominent man like Bob Samuels, just think about what they can do to you." The article stated that poor Mr. Samuels was innocently down at the bookstore working to improve the economy of Clark County by scouting an episode of Remington Steel. While inside this location, he was shoved into a booth by a bearded 6'4" vice detective and told he was being arrested for being a faggot. The point of the article was to say that the LVMPD, especially the vice section, was a group of thugs who ran around arresting innocent people.

The article went on to say how Mr. Samuels was a happily married man and had done so much good for Clark County. Knight said that the reckless vice squad was violating everyone's civil rights, and that poor Mr. Samuels was just in "the wrong place at the right time." The proof, he believed, was in Samuels passing two

Integrity Based Policing

polygraphs -- one by his own polygraph examiner and the second by the district attorney's polygraph expert. While nowhere did it mention my name, I took this as a smack in the face to me as well as all the LVMPD.

When I arrived at work that afternoon, it was obvious that I was livid. Sergeant Elders told me the situation was creating too much heat for him and he didn't want anything to do with it. Thank God, Lieutenant Whitney and Sergeant Dave did not play the Pontius Pilot card like my sergeant did. Lieutenant Whitney and Sergeant Dave called me into their office to discuss the situation. Dave said that he knew Ted Knight, and he was obviously fed a pack of lies by Samuels' people. Both he and Lieutenant Whitney asked me if I wanted to speak with Mr. Knight about setting the facts straight. I told them absolutely. Dave told me that he would try to call Ted Knight and arrange a meeting.

Lieutenant Whitney assured me he would be with me every step of the way. I left the office feeling very good and looking forward to getting the chance to set the record straight with Mr. Knight. After I changed into uniform and was sitting in the pre-shift briefing, I received a message to call Deputy Chief Corbett. I remember sitting in the briefing, thinking that the chief probably just wanted to tell me he was in complete support of me and not to worry, the truth would come out.

After the briefing, I went into the dictation room and called Deputy Chief Corbett. He had always thought highly of me because of my work history and the job I did during "Hi School Daze." When I called Chief Corbett's office, he answered on the first ring and said, "Hello Dan. Did you read Ted Knight this morning?" I told him I had and was upset and planned to speak with Ted Knight about setting the record straight. The deputy chief turned his friendly tone into a stern voice. "This is a direct order. Don't talk with him or anyone else, and let this damn thing die!"

Deputy Chief Corbett went on to tell me that I had a long career ahead of me and my job could be in jeopardy if I did not let this thing die. He also told me that they were dropping all charges against Mr. Samuels. I told him that I wanted to have internal affairs do a thorough investigation on what took place that night. If I was lying, I told him I should be terminated. He told me that there would be no internal affairs investigation and that I just needed to let it die. After this conversation, I was even more resolute than ever to meet with Mr. Knight, despite what the chief had ordered me to do.

I remember thinking as I hung up the phone: at times like this, a person learns who his or her supporters really are. Dave Groover and Lieutenant Whitney possessed the courage and were definitely worthy of their leadership roles. It is easy to avoid conflict when truth is merely a buzz word, only of importance when convenient, like right answers given just to pass a promotional examination. Being a true leader requires courage to continually fight for the truth and do what is right, not just seek the path of least resistance to avoid conflict.

At about 9:30 p.m. I was called by Sergeant Groover over the radio. He asked me to meet him at the Carrows on Flamingo and Maryland Parkway. I drove directly there, parked my unit and went inside. I saw Dave and Randy sitting at a booth in the back of the restaurant. After I joined them, Dave said "Ted will be here in about five minutes." When Ted came in, I stood up and shook his hand. Due to the fact that I was clean shaven, and stood about 5'10" and weighed 160 pounds, he said, "You certainly don't look like that gigantic monster they described to me."

After I explained the facts, Mr. Knight said he would love to print a complete retraction. He said that the only thing he needed was for me to pass a polygraph test from an independent polygraph examiner. I told him anytime, anyplace and, anywhere. I was ready to take the test. Mr. Knight shook my hand and said that he would be contacting me within a couple of days to confirm the details.

After Ted left, Dave, Randy, and I sat around discussing our strategy. Both of them warned me that those tests are not always accurate, depending on who's giving the test and what they want to prove. I just remember saying, "Finally, the truth is going to come

Integrity Based Policing

out!" I could not wait for the test and to read the retraction in the newspaper. I was confident that, after the facts were out in the open, Allison and I would be able to get a good night's sleep.

The next day, Dave and Randy called me into their office and asked, "Are you busy tomorrow morning?" I said tomorrow morning would be great with me -- the sooner, the better. We were to meet the polygraph expert and Mr. Knight at 8:00 a.m. at the Channel 8 Studio. Lieutenant Whitney told me to make sure I got off shift early, and got a good night's sleep for the test. That night flew by as I anticipated the next morning. I was anxious, but extremely confident.

I woke up at 6:00 a.m. and shoveled down a bowl of cereal before I said goodbye to Allison and the girls. After driving to the Channel 8 Studio and parking my car at the back of the building, I walked inside to meet up with Dave and Randy. We sat there in the lobby of the studio until about 9:15 a.m. when Mr. Knight and his expert walked in. The polygraph expert was a lanky man and appeared to be in his late 50s. At about 10:00 a.m., the expert and I went into an interview room, and he asked me a series of questions designed to get my emotions fired up.

He started off by saying he thought that all ex-boxers were punch-drunken idiots and should never be police officers because they were too violent. I just listened to him, and knew he was attempting to get me angry. In reality, he was doing a very good job. He asked about the complaint involving the pursuit when I was in the field training program. He told me he knew I should have been fired for almost killing that poor juvenile. After several more accusations, he began to question my credibility.

This process lasted about thirty minutes, and he said he was going to get the machine fired up. I sat alone in the interview room until the expert returned and said that he could not give the test at that location. He made several phone calls, and finally said that we would take the test at Main Station. We all left the studio and drove to Main Station. The time was about 12:00 p.m.

As I arrived at Main Station, my stomach was talking. I could not wait to get the thing done. At about 1:30 p.m., I was finally hooked up to the machine. As he was asking me the control questions, like my name, date of birth and occupation, he told me my responses were inconclusive. The questions about Mr. Samuels's arrest were also inconclusive. When it was over, the expert said, "You were not even sure what your name is. You certainly were not truthful in your answers about the arrest."

I responded back to him, "You and your machine are fucked up. I know what the truth is!"

After the test, both Dave and Randy said they were sorry about letting me fall for that trick. They told me to take the night off, but I said I wanted to work the streets. That was my Friday night, so I had three days off after that to chill out. It is difficult to express how it feels when you know what the truth is, and yet all the evidence points in the opposite direction. Making matters even worse was that I knew I had violated a direct order from Deputy Chief Corbett which could result my termination.

I really was not worried about getting fired, however. In fact, I knew they would not push it. The fact that the truth was on my side gave me confidence, and there was nothing they could do to change that. As I was driving to the south substation to get ready for work, I saw a homeless man with one leg panhandling at Eastern and Charleston. Reality kicked in and I realized I had much to be thankful for.

I prayed and asked God why I was being put through this. I came to the realization that this would make me a better leader because I had lived through a situation in which only my true friends were with me. Many of the vice detectives were blaming me for not letting this thing die. Only people who valued the truth understood why this was so important. I just asked God to give me a sign that I was still on His path.

On Monday, two days after the test, at about 9:00 a.m., I was driving down Maryland Parkway after leaving court. As I pulled into a Winchell's Donut Shop, I noticed a sign across the street that caught my attention: Western Security Consultants - Polygraph

Examinations. I decided that I would go in and talk with the examiner about my situation. Luckily, when I walked in, the office was empty except for a receptionist. When I met the polygraph expert, Ron, he said, "It's about time you came in."

I went over the entire incident, including the polygraph I had taken two days before. He explained to me that several parts of my test did not pass the smell test. The test was scheduled for 9:00 a.m. and wasn't given until the afternoon, the fact that I hadn't eaten, and the switch in locations were some of the reasons why this examination was problematic. We then sat and I explained all the facets of the incident, and he agreed to test me the next morning. He told me to be sure I got a good night's sleep and ate a good breakfast.

That night, I had the first good night's sleep since the debacle began. Meeting Ron, I could sense he was after the same thing that I was after: the truth. That night, both Allison and I thanked God that I had met Ron, and we were confident that the next morning would put an end to this nightmare. I got up at 6:00 a.m. and had two eggs and some bacon. I drove down to Ron's office and we conducted the test at 10:00 a.m. and were done by 11:00 a.m. The result was that I was being truthful. After the test, I said about ten Hail Mary's and met Allison and the girls for ice cream. I called Dave and Randy and they were happy for me. Randy said, "Dan, we never doubted you, but I'm glad you fought the good fight." Dave was also happy for me, and told me to start having fun again.

After a couple of months, I began getting subpoenas for some of the other cases from that night. I called the district attorney's office and told them, I would not be appearing unless they refiled charges on Mr. Samuels. They told me that I needed to appear, or they would go after me for contempt of court. I told them that I would not be testifying on any of the other cases, and they could call IAB if they wanted to. I never went to court for any of the subpoenas, and they never went after me for contempt of court, or contacted IAB.

This entire incident resulted in a major shift on how I viewed myself and the role that I filled in our criminal justice system. Being in my mid-twenties, I was beginning to understand my role as a police officer was not the idealistic one that I had envisioned as a kid growing up. Other people with their own agendas would define the level of service provided to our community throughout my career. When a young man or woman first becomes an officer, they have visions of being warriors, constantly battling for the public good. Most new officers view the truth as their ultimate goal, and believe the agency is equally committed. Unfortunately, officers soon realize it is public perception, not the truth, which is their organization's ultimate goal. Individuals who stand up for the truth, despite the repercussions to their careers, are often labeled as malcontents and not team players. In reality, standing up for the truth is the thing that matters most.

After this experience, I began to see my policing career in a different light. Instead of making decisions based upon evidence, I started to consider the impact of my decisions on my family. During this entire episode, I was only concerned about the effect this would have on me and my career. It was not until after it was over that I looked at the impact it had on Allison and the girls. This entire episode happened while Allison was pregnant with Patrick, and caring for our two little girls. Allison was the one sitting at home reading the negative articles and watching the TV reporters insinuating her husband was a liar.

During this time, I was so self-centered that I did not share all the facts with Allison. I saw my home as the one place where I did not want to let the negativity enter, so I did not discuss it. When it was over, I promised myself (and Allison) that it would not happen again. In life, nothing is as important as the relationship you have with God and your family. They are constantly with you and will be there for you. Many so-called friends shifted their loyalty like sand at the beach on a windy day. All these people cared about was the perception others had of them if it became known that they supported me.

This episode was put into perspective when our son, Patrick, was born on Labor Day in 1985. Here I was, sitting in my Jacuzzi enjoying a cold one and realizing all the negativity that happened during this ordeal could not compare with the joy of having Allison, the girls, and our brand-new son. Only a few weeks prior, I had been acting as if I had all the problems in the world on my shoulders. I learned, that at all times, it is imperative to count your blessings before hosting a pity party.

I remember hearing a quote from Joseph Wambaugh: "When a young man first becomes a cop, he learns that there are two types of people: cops and assholes. After a few years on the job, he learns there are actually three different types: cops, assholes and cops that are assholes." Prior to this caper, I never understood what this quotation meant. I learned a valuable lesson through this experience: always fight for the truth and do not assume others are on the "up and up."

All things in life happen for a reason. While at the time I could not conceive of any possible good coming from this episode, I realized later that it prepared me to be a leader. I cannot count all the times throughout my career in which I reflected on the lessons I gained from this experience. Men like Randy Whitney, Dave Groover, and Chuck Martin have always served as a point of reference for me - even long after these great men retired. Without a solid ethical framework, police organizations can never earn, nor maintain, the public's trust. Even though I was unaware of it at the time, several important tenets of leadership came out of this experience that have served me throughout my career:

- Always seek the truth. When the truth is on your side, you have nothing to fear.
- Keep your spouse in the loop. While you may think that you are protecting your spouse, you are in reality, increasing the stress by not sharing the details. Remember: when "the fat lady sings" your spouse will be the only one standing with you -- if you allow it.
- Never be a fair-weather friend. If you won't stand with me

in battle, have a seat.
- Seek the counsel of leaders with honor. Having Dave and Randy by my side made this journey bearable. This might require looking outside your chain of command.
- God is in control. Pray often and ask for his guidance. Remember all you have to be grateful for and count your blessings.
- Do not act like Pontius Pilate and call yourself a leader. As Pilate did, you cannot wash your hands and absolve yourself. When a true leader sees an injustice, he or she has an ethical responsibility to take action. Only cowards use excuses like "it's not my problem," "this is causing me too much heat," "I'll let somebody else take action," or, "I can't for political expediency."

After the Samuels incident, Allison and I gave much thought to our future goals relative to my career. Until this point, we had planned on me transferring to a position in covert operations. That would have allowed me to use my undercover skills and still have time to be with Allison and the kids. My part-time job at Lucky was solid and I could keep it while working other assignments at Metro. Those goals shifted after this incident and I realized that the best way to have a positive impact on Metro and meet the needs of my young family was to prepare myself to make sergeant.

Prior to this event, I thought that I needed at least five more years of experience as a police officer, but after witnessing the lack of backbone in some people currently wearing sergeant chevrons, I knew I was ready. For the next eighteen months, I committed myself to focusing more on my growing family and less on my departmental reputation. I also recommitted myself to Bumper's Code: "We do this job for the good people in our community, not to please the clowns at headquarters."

The Civil Service rules for the sergeant's test mandated that a letter be sent to all the qualified candidates at least 90 days before the written examination. Most important, the letter was

Integrity Based Policing

to give a list of reference material to be included on the examination. The letter also was to include the number of candidates to be chosen to proceed to the second phase of the process, which is the oral interview. Based upon the results of the average of the written and oral scores, a list of the names of the sergeants to be promoted was compiled for a 12-month period.

The list of reference material was so extensive that no candidate could be expected to read all the books prior to the examination. After looking at the letter, I realized that I had about ten different textbooks to buy and read, along with a series of reference materials to comprehend. Many people had taken the test numerous times and never passed the written exam, and after seeing all the resources, I understood why. I knew that success during the testing process needed to be a balance of preparedness and good fortune. Since good fortune was out of my control, the only thing I could do to increase my chances of success was preparation.

I decided to transfer to the graveyard shift at the department at that time. This allowed me to study several hours a day, and still work swing shift at Lucky. For six months preceding the sergeant's test, I committed to studying at least two hours a day. During this time, our youngest daughter, Elizabeth, was born. Somehow, Allison managed to deal with most of the daily distractions and handle all four kids.

As the written test date approached, I was confident that my preparation was going to pay off. The amount of mental and physical preparation that goes into getting ready for a promotional examination is similar to getting ready for a big fight. The night before the test, Allison and I had pizza with the kids and gave thanks to God for allowing me to be fully prepared. The test was the next morning at 7:00 a.m. and I slept like a baby the night before because I knew I was ready.

I got up and went for a five-mile run, almost feeling guilty that I was so confident. Having breakfast with Allison and the kids that morning, I was more relaxed than I had been in months. I left my house that morning and drove right to Cashman Field to take the written test.

Three's a Crowd

As I walked into the reception area, I noticed it was packed with more than 200 fellow officers getting ready to take the test. The sad reality is that we all knew that the final standing would only promote ten or twelve candidates. I remember thinking as I stood in line that this phase would reduce the candidate list to only twenty-four candidates. The reality is that, out of the 200 taking the test, only 100 of them had even cracked a book. Out of the 100 who did study, less than half had ever completed college. The most encouraging reality was that only one, me, had prepared as I did for this examination.

As we walked into the large room, we were all handed a candidate number. This number would be our official identification throughout the process. When I looked at my number, I could not believe that my number was fifteen. That had always been my number, and I took this as another indicator that it was going to be a great experience!

After being told to open the package and proceed with the test, I could not believe how well prepared I was. I finished the test and still had time to review it several times. When I picked up my material to proceed to the scoring table, I was smiling and could not understand why all the other candidates were complaining about how difficult and confusing the test was.

As I handed my scantron answer sheet over to the civilian grader and waited for him to run it through the scanning machine. I looked up at the sign containing all the top scores with the candidate identification numbers. Within a couple of seconds, the sign switched to showing a high score of 92 with the id# of 15. The second highest score was 86. As I left Cashman Field everyone was patting me on the back and saying, "Great job!" I got in my car and drove home. On the way home, I was anticipating a celebration with my family. I prayed all the way home and began planning for the next phase of the process -- the oral board.

The oral board was scheduled for thirty days after the written examination. This process included having three police administrators from out of state conduct an interview with all the candidates

Integrity Based Policing

and rank them. While finishing first on the written gave me bragging rights, in reality it was the oral board that could move a candidate from #1 to #25. Only the top ten finishers had a realistic chance of making the rank of sergeant. Unfortunately, the oral board was extremely subjective, and the questions could range from specific things about situations in Clark County to global issues, like the impact of a weak economy.

I selected several close friends to help prepare me for the oral board. We would meet, and they would ask me questions that could come up and critique my responses. This process proved to be valuable as it gave me confidence. I rehearsed all segments of the oral board process: the introduction, reason I am the best choice, biggest problem facing our department, my career goals, closing, and questions about challenges. We met at least three times each week before the interview, and just as with the first phase, I knew I was ready when the date came.

Another important part of preparing for the oral board required just turning on the cassette recorder and practicing verbal responses. Possessing my thick Brooklyn accent made it imperative to practice enunciating, and slow down my responses so the graders could easily understand. Another important process included getting up at 3:00 a.m. and sitting at my kitchen table, while everyone was asleep, and practicing my responses. I also would have large stuffed animals sitting in chairs across from me to ensure I was maintaining eye contact. This was an important part of my preparation, but I knew I looked like a complete idiot.

A few days before the oral board, I had been practicing for about two hours and thought the kids and Allison were still fast asleep. I was in the middle of explaining to a large Tigger, the importance of monitoring officer complaints when Caitlyn, who was four, toddled up, and asked me why I was talking to her stuffed animals. I told her I was practicing for a very important test. She responded in her sleepy voice, "Daddy, you can practice with me." She climbed up on a chair and put Tigger on her lap and listened intently until she dozed off. I guess she was not impressed with my answers!

Three's a Crowd

The interview was scheduled to begin at 9:00 a.m. and was supposed to last forty-five minutes. Walking into the room, I knew that this was going to be a great day. I made immediate eye contact with all three of the graders, and we immediately hit it off. At about 10:00 a.m., a member of the personnel staff knocked on the door, and said that the other candidates were waiting. Before I left that room, I knew I had done very well.

Within a half hour, I was notified that I had received 100% on the oral board. This ensured my final standing as number one. I went home after the oral board and took the family out to Valley of Fire for a picnic. At that time, I knew I would be wearing chevrons within the next month. That Sunday, we went to church and said a special prayer thanking God for allowing the Bob Samuels incident.

On Christmas Eve in 1987, I received a phone call from Sheriff John Alexander telling me that I was being promoted to sergeant on January 2nd, 1988. I was then called by Deputy Chief Myers and informed that I was taking over a graveyard squad in the west area command. I remember thinking back to the words of encouragement that Bumper had given me several years prior - that I would return to the "West Side."

6

THE KILLER BEES

As I walked into the west substation, I was ecstatic to be back home. It was not so much the old building with the musky smell or the ugly canary yellow walls that had not seen a fresh coat of paint in decades, as it was the area of town we were serving. Coming back as a new sergeant meant that I was going to have a direct impact on the people living on the West Side. I could not have been happier because I had my own team to ensure that this community received the high level of service they deserved. I stuffed my uniforms into my locker with my shiny new sergeant chevrons, and thought about the adventures ahead and the experiences that had brought me back to this great building.

My first night taught me an important lesson about my new responsibilities as a sergeant. I learned this lesson from my mentor and former sergeant, John Thorton. That first night, he was the only lieutenant working.

My normal lieutenant was on a two-week vacation. I came to learn that he was a thirty-year veteran who had never worked on the streets for an extended period at any time during his career. He had spent most of those years in the detective bureau, and he did not have a clue what street policing was about. His biggest concern was ensuring that the captain never had to call him about a complaint. His personal mission was to see that all abandoned vehicles

The Killer Bees

in our command were towed in a timely manner. This would keep the captain off his back.

Fortunately, on my first night as sergeant, it was Lieutenant Thorton and me.

My squad had a mixture of talent and, sadly, it did not have a positive reputation. I had two senior guys who had been on the squad for more than ten years. The other officers were at various levels of seniority, anywhere from one to three years. This meant that, of my dozen officers, only two were permanent. The others saw this assignment as a stepping stone. The problem was that my two senior guys, unlike Bumper, remained there because they hated both the brass and the people who lived on the West Side. These two officers had worked in the same unit for many years and were the informal leaders because of their seniority. They were not highly respected.

So, there I was, excited and nervous in front of this squad during my first briefing, but I still had to appear confident. I was not confident, because I had seen so many others fall flat on their faces in their transition to the role of sergeant. I knew I would be leaning heavily on the lessons learned from working for some solid leaders while trying to avoid the mistakes of the clowns who never should have been sergeants. My goal was to be the hardest working sergeant on Metro - and also the most popular, and the most innovative by making things better.

That is where my first lesson came in. Being popular cannot be a benchmark in determining leadership.

I read a few items out of the log book and turned on the briefing phone line when the plaza desk called in. On my first night, I did not change anything on the line-up card and gave the typical pep talk.

"Stay safe and stop all the assholes you see!"

With that, I headed out the door and assumed command of NW13. My new responsibilities had not mentally sunk in yet, and I could not wait to get into action. I thought being a sergeant was just being one of the guys on the squad except now I wore stripes. I was in for a cold dose of reality before my first shift was over.

Although Lieutenant Thorton was working, the reality was that I was on my own. Our jurisdiction had 8,000 square miles and I knew that the watch commander would be too busy elsewhere to keep tabs on me. My first call was to a family dispute. I responded with several units. As we were getting ready to take the suspect to jail, one of my officers was clearing a rifle when it discharged. The gun was a .22 caliber and the round went harmlessly into the dark desert sky. I knew that this was an accidental discharge, and we needed to call out internal affairs and the watch commander. My desire to be popular kicked in, and I made a serious mistake. I thought, "Why make a big deal out of nothing?" Nobody was injured and nothing was hit. We would simply move on to our next call. We all cleared without taking additional action.

An hour before we secured, Lieutenant Thorton asked me to meet him at Carrows for a cup of coffee. When I got there, he was waiting in a booth.

"How was your first night wearing stripes?"

I smiled and told him, "It was great!"

"Are you sure?" he prodded.

My Irish Catholic sense of guilt kicked in and I immediately told him about the .22 caliber incident. He already knew. He said he had heard about it from an officer on the call. In the end, we wound up calling criminalistics to process the scene and internal affairs to investigate.

Lieutenant Thorton rightfully chewed my butt.

That is when I learned the difference between being a leader and just a person wearing stripes. I still don't know who told Lieutenant Thorton about my lapse in judgment. We completed all of the reports for the accidental discharge and Lieutenant Thorton told me not to worry. He also told me, "Remember, everyone is watching."

The next few weeks went by fast. I loved being a sergeant. The other two parts of my vow had come true -- our squad had become the hardest working and most innovative in the valley. Bumper had moved on and was assigned to a different area command,

The Killer Bees

and yet I knew all that he taught me was benefiting the citizens we served.

One night, my squad was focusing on a specific gang that had been involved in numerous shootings all over the valley. These shootings all stemmed from rock cocaine sales with which this gang was involved. This night had been incredibly slow and I was considering shifting our resources toward a traffic problem. I drove to J Street and Bartlett for one last look at our main target's house before making my final decision.

As I was parked about two blocks away in my black and white, I heard a shotgun blast and saw several African American males fleeing from the residence. I immediately hit the front door with my spot light and pronged out about five suspects with my shotgun. After I called the situation out over the radio, my entire squad showed up. Subsequent to the situation being stabilized, we located a Blood gang member who was shot in the leg. This had been a Donna Street Crip (aka DSC) party, and he was not among those invited. We also found eight ounces of rock cocaine in a dresser drawer in a bedroom. We hooked up all the DSC gangsters and even got the probable cause to charge the shooter. We arrested twelve of the most notorious DSC gangsters as a result of this incident.

The next week, I decided to write commendation letters for all my officers for their outstanding teamwork. To my dismay, I became sick to my stomach when I went to records and read the content of the arrests reports.

My two senior officers had written a report that was completely fabricated.

They said that they were contacted by a confidential informant who told them that this cocaine was hidden in the exact location where we found it. In fact, we all knew that the search was weak, but at least we got the crap off the streets, and we could twist the other suspects.

I called my lieutenant and told him what had happened. He told me to quit trying to save the world, and those senior officers did

Integrity Based Policing

a great job. He told me that if we played by the rules, we would never send any of those assholes to prison. I called both officers into my office, and they admitted "twisting the facts" so we could get a successful prosecution. They told me that was the way things were done on the west side, and I just needed to follow along.

I would not just follow along.

I set them straight, and told them that things were going to be different with me as their sergeant. They both sat back and said "Okay." I suspended both of them for forty hours and had the criminal case dismissed. If we lie like our suspects, we are not serving or protecting the good citizens. Deputy Chief Myers agreed that I had done the right thing.

The morale on my squad shifted after those suspensions. The only surprise was that it was for the better. All of the newer officers on the squad took notice that lying and other acts of misconduct would not be tolerated.

Both of those senior officers soon transferred out. This squad, once known for being reckless, was getting a reputation for being solid and the officers, high producers. Instead of a steady flow of officers transferring out, we had a list of officers requesting to transfer to NW13. Many other officers and sergeants told me that they were glad someone finally confronted the misconduct. The entire squad improved simply because I insisted on truthfulness.

After I had been assigned to that squad for six months, I received a phone call from Lieutenant Gene Smith, who was heading a new team designed to combat the influx of gang members we were getting from Southern California. He wanted me to come to work for him because he knew me and liked my work. The sergeant I was replacing had been disciplined and needed to leave immediately, so I needed to give him an answer by that afternoon. After I realized this assignment was dealing with gang members, the majority of whom lived on the west side, I did not need to think about it. I accepted this assignment.

Lieutenant Smith and Deputy Chief Myers gave me a simple goal: put 100 certified gang members in prison in one year. I appreciate

The Killer Bees

having clear objectives, so this was perfect. We could do anything from uniform sweeps, reverse stings and covert narcotics, to using confidential informants -- anything that was legal and ethical.

The best part was that complaints would be reviewed by Lieutenant Smith. This let us take the gloves off and not worry about pencil pushers taking needless complaints. Lieutenant Smith was the man who did more to run the mob out of Las Vegas than any other person, so I knew dealing with these gang punks would be a walk in the park for him. We kept an accurate chart of our progress and knew exactly where we were in relationship to our goal.

My team had six great officers who all loved coming to work as much as I did. Every shift was an adventure, and we were kicking in at least two doors each night. We never used SWAT to conduct our entries. We all had the experience and enjoyed making the gang members sweat. It did not take long to get the word "on the streets" that Las Vegas did not tolerate gang activity. Even judges knew about our detail and its success rate. We could even sign out certain inmates to do control buys, which was a move off-limits to other sections. We were that good.

On one occasion, we had an inmate who was going to do a controlled buy for us. He was in jail on a contempt of court charge. I personally called the judge and asked him if he would let us use the inmate to make the buy. This suspect must have gotten the judge extremely upset. I was told that if he was not in court the following Monday, it was my ass. The target address was one we had been trying to get into for several months and was packed with Donna Street Crips (DSC). We checked out the informant and did a solid recon on the targeted address. When we sent him to the apartment, we watched all of the doors and windows.

After two minutes, we saw three guys jump out the rear window, and they were off. We chased the suspects and caught two of them. Sadly, our informant was the one who got away. We spent the entire weekend going door-to-door looking for this guy. Then, we got a call early Monday morning that he wanted to turn himself in. We had put so much heat on the DSC that they were going to kill

Integrity Based Policing

him if he did not. He was standing in front of the judge when court was in session on Monday, as promised.

Every night we were finding guns, dope, and dangerous felons. We often used a tactic known as "reverse stings." Since gangs are in the business of narcotic sales, we would take over their operations for a night and arrest all the gangsters and customers. Here's how it went down. We would start by saturating a gang turf and arrest all the gangsters. We would secure the area to ensure no other gang members had come in from outside until the operation was over. Undercover officers would take the place of the gang members, and we would open the location back up for business. The gangster "posers" had cocaine that had already been pre-packaged. We would make the sale. Then a team of uniformed officers would move in and make the arrest. We would make sometimes more than 100 arrests. Then the media made it known that the LVMPD was in control of all the streets and alleys in Clark County. These stings had many vocal critics, such as the ACLU and defense lawyers, so it took a leader like Gene Smith to commit to continuing these operations.

These operations made gangs paranoid and demonstrated that they had no real power.

These operations also put buyers on notice that the gang member selling you your rock cocaine might be an undercover officer. The nickname that was given to my team was "The Killer Bees." This was because we were all over the valley and our raid jackets were bright yellow.

Another one of my favorite operations utilized cabs to trick gangsters.

During these operations, we purchased rock cocaine from taxi cabs. This served a dual purpose: suspects never expected it was an undercover tactic, and it also helped reduce cab robberies in the most violent areas of town. One caper that I will never forget occurred when we used a Yellow Taxi Cab. I had one of my guys, George, play the role of the cabbie and I was the passenger/buyer in the back seat. The plan was to drive to these areas and make some

The Killer Bees

buys, and then have the suspects arrested after George and I drove away.

One night after we had already made about six buys and were getting ready to secure, we were flagged down at Lake Mead and Balzar. I rolled down the window and an African American male stuck his head in and asked if I was looking to score. I opened the door, and he jumped in the back seat. I said I wanted a $20, and he reached into his back pocket and pulled out a small blue steel revolver. The second I saw the gun, I grabbed it and held his hand down toward the floorboard. After the gun fell, I pushed him out of the cab and took him into custody. The suspect was an older crack head, so it was not much of a fight.

Being the leader of the "Killer Bees" was the most enjoyable assignment of my career. We put in many long hours without putting in for overtime. We hardly ever took lunch breaks. We ran 100 miles an hour, but we loved being there. People would ask us, "Why are you working so hard?" Knowing that the community appreciated us and we had our bosses' full support made the challenges we faced easy to overcome.

Material things were not a priority for us. We were a brand-new unit. Having a nice office and quality equipment was not our reality. We worked behind the plaza desk in city hall, and had only four broken-down desks and a couple of chairs. Normally, we briefed at different substations, or all crammed into the lieutenant's office to conduct our meetings. We were always playing jokes on each other, but because quarters were tight, nobody had time to stay upset for long.

One night after we had completed a search warrant, our entire team was packed into our small room impounding guns and dope. Everybody was stressed because it was our Friday. We had another warrant to serve that night and we all wanted to go home. Some of the team wanted to wait until the next week, but I wanted to get it done this night. One of my hardest working officers was complaining about always working late. When he asked me for some Wite-out to correct a report he was typing, I decided to try to lighten the

Integrity Based Policing

mood. I unscrewed the top of a Wite-out bottle and tossed it to him.

This was an old prank that we all had been victim of at one time or another. When he caught the bottle, the top came off and the whiteout covered him. The entire team roared with laughter. He got up from his desk and ran to the restroom.

"He ran away like a twelve-year-old girl!" someone commented.

After about ten minutes, he had not returned. I went into the men's room to check on him. He was lying on the bathroom floor, holding his eye and yelling "I can't see!"

I turned around and I saw that my entire team was behind me and they all looked as terrified as I felt. One of my team members, a former nurse, looked frantic.

"Call for an ambulance!" she screamed. "The Wite-out must have gotten into his eye."

I asked her how dangerous this could be for his vision. She did not miss a beat.

"Hopefully, he'll only lose vision in one eye."

For the next few seconds, I held his arm and thought, "I ruined my friend's career and he might lose his sight." Unexpectedly, I noticed his lips start to quiver. Was he trying to keep from laughing? He was! And so was the rest of the squad. I knew it. Those SOBs got a great one over on me! He jumped up, and we hugged each other.

"We've been working on that one for the past month," he said.

We all headed back to our room and finished our reports. We did not serve that other warrant. We went out for a few beers instead. Maybe it was more than a few, and I definitely paid the bar tab.

That event taught me that although it is important to have fun and pull pranks, you always need to make certain nobody gets hurt – either physically or emotionally. We had fun together that time, but I have seen people get fired, demoted, and seriously disciplined for pranks gone awry. I have witnessed many people get in serious trouble by attempting to be funny. So, I am grateful to my gang team who taught me the importance of maintaining discipline early in my career.

The Killer Bees

As with many successful details, the gang detail was doing such a good job that the top brass shifted our focus. With gang violence low, they decided that we should become a pool of readily accessible officers which could be utilized for other problems. We were called on to enforce a new curfew ordinance on the Strip. This ordinance required unsupervised juveniles younger than eighteen to be off Las Vegas Boulevard after 10:00 p.m. on school nights and midnight on weekends. This was a brand-new ordinance, so they wanted to make sure we had a heavy presence on the Strip for the first few weeks. The gang detail was assigned so that the department would not have to pay overtime. This was a uniform assignment, so all covert operations were put on hold.

When our focus moved away from the gangs, violence escalated. We were ordered to return to our anti-gang mission. For the next month, we were back to firing on all cylinders and the gang violence began to decline again.

One Friday night, a group of juveniles got into a fight in front of the McDonald's on the Strip. When we came to work the next night, Lieutenant Smith told us to put on our uniforms and head to the Strip. One of my men, Mike Surick, tried to be funny.

"Does anybody have a coin we can flip to decide what the fuck our mission is?" he shouted.

Lieutenant Smith took off after Mike intending to kick his ass. Mike was in his early 20s and was agile in his jeans and sneakers. Poor Gene was in his 50s, and a three pack a day smoker wearing cowboy boots. Mike got away.

I would come to value Mike's quick moves.

One afternoon, an intelligence sergeant called me. He said that a kid who lived in the extreme west end of Charleston Boulevard was selling weed out of his house. The kid was seventeen, and intelligence was working up a case on his father for some real estate scam. I was asked if we could try to call this kid cold and arrange to buy a small amount of weed. After the buy, we planned to arrest the kid and get some valuable information for the intelligence

Integrity Based Policing

investigation. I took the number and figured we could get this done, grab a bite to eat and execute the warrant later.

I called my team back to the office, and did a preliminary check on the kid and the address. The kid had no criminal history and no firearms were registered at that address. I had Mike call the number to see if he could set up a dime bag buy. When Mike called the kid, he was told to come by the house in about thirty minutes. Our team had been putting the most dangerous criminals in prison for the past year. We were not too worried about this little white teenager. We decided we would do a buy and rip, which means we would do the buy and arrest him on probable cause.

We drove to the targeted house and Mike walked up to the door, stepped inside for about two minutes and walked back to his undercover vehicle. Within thirty seconds, he said on the radio "in pocket, let's meet at Pizza Hut." We drove to Pizza Hut and ate lunch as a squad. It was decided that after lunch we would go back and arrest the juvenile. We would have a uniformed officer with us, so they could not question our identity.

We finished lunch and called for the uniformed officer to meet us in the parking lot. I had everyone on my team expose their hang badges and had the officer in uniform to ensure we were easily identifiable as the police. We would knock on the sliding glass door attached to a converted garage, which served as the front door. Mike would knock on the door. Once he was in, I would follow, along with the uniform officer. The other officers would not enter unless we requested them. It was about 5:00 p.m. mid-July, and the brightness of the sun made visibility into the darkened room extremely difficult.

I stood behind Mike as he knocked on the door. Mike is 6'5". His body blocked my view into the house. I heard Mike say, "Police officer. You're under arrest." As Mike stepped in, he once again demonstrated his agility by immediately jumping to his left. I stepped into the doorway. The room was pitch-black but I could see a .45 caliber hand gun just two feet from my chest. I grabbed for the kid with my one hand while I reached for my duty weapon with the other. I pulled the kid in front of me and could see the suspect with the .45 looking confused. He was looking for a clear shot. He moved the barrel off of me because his son was in the line of fire. He was looking for Mike who had taken concealment behind a chair. As I began to raise my gun to fire, I saw what appeared to be two slow-flying projectiles leave Mike's gun and hit him in his chest. I saw the gun drop and his arm collapse. I didn't fire a round. I did not hear a thing. Then, reality snapped back in. I saw the suspect with two bullet holes in his chest and the .45 on the carpet. I heard people in the room screaming.

At times like these, the human mind often goes into a state of hyper vigilance. A second or two can seem like an hour. Seeing Mike's rounds moving, I thought I could have reached out and caught them in mid-air. In reality this entire encounter was over in about two seconds, but in my mind, it seemed like several minutes.

We immediately notified dispatch of the officer-involved shooting and requested medical assistance. One of my officers, the former nurse, checked for a pulse, but could not find one. He was dead. My team had kicked in hundreds of doors and dealt with armed gunmen on a nightly basis and never fired a round until this incident. It seemed surreal that this caper, which seemed so non-threatening, would be our first deadly encounter.

It took a few minutes to get the scene stabilized and I knew that Mike and I would have to give a statement to homicide. When the media showed up, I had another sergeant assume command of the scene, and I took Mike for a ride to my house to clear both our minds. The shooting took place less than five blocks from my house. Mike and I pulled into the driveway and Allison and the kids just thought we were stopping by to say hi. I told Allison what had just taken place. She made us some iced tea, and we just relaxed for about fifteen minutes.

Then we returned to the scene and walked homicide through every step of the incident. We also went to the homicide office and gave an interview. The coroner's inquest would be in about a month and until it was over, Mike and I were on administrative leave. This was a month of dissecting every moment and every decision made during this event. During this time, we needed to see the department psychologist, attend the coroner's inquest and then to go back to full duty.

Everything we did was legal and within policy, but I believe that I did not do enough to ensure a safe operation. I was overly confident that this incident was minimal risk. After all, it was only a little white kid selling weed! I could have done many things to avoid this deadly encounter. We could have just submitted for a warrant or arrested him outside the house — these are just two of the alternatives that may have made things turn out differently. However, once we committed to making the entry, everything we did was necessary.

The day after the shooting, I went to see Father Thomas Holland. I had been friends with Father Tom for many years. He was the priest at Saint Bridget's Roman Catholic Church, which was my first church in Las Vegas. He even baptized two of our children, and I would always go to him for guidance. I told him what had happened, and he counseled me that God puts all of us into situations to make us stronger. He told me that the one at fault was the person who decided to point his gun at us. We just acted in self-defense. We said a few prayers, had a few beers, and talked. I left his apartment knowing that our actions were not only right in the eyes of the law, but most importantly, right in the eyes of God.

I took Allison with me to see the psychologist because she and I are a team and I wanted her to get her feelings out. When we went into his office, he asked me if things slowed down and if I heard the rounds being fired. I was happy when he told me that my reaction was normal. Up until then, I thought that this was abnormal. He explained to me about hyper vigilance, and while it took less than two seconds from entry to shots being fired, it seemed to me to last several minutes.

"What was going through your mind when you saw the gun pointed at your chest?" he asked me. I told him that I thought I was

The Killer Bees

going to die and was upset with myself for not wearing a vest. I was also upset that we had not done a will.

"Okay, Dan," he said, "God gave you a break on this one. Now go and fix those things!" Both Allison and I gave him a big hug as we left his office. Our best friends, Johnny and Donna, were watching the kids, so we decided to go out on a date.

The next day Mike Peters, an attorney friend, called me to see how I was doing. I told him that Allison and I needed to get our wills written. The next day, we met Mike at his office to do just that. I tried to pay for it, but Mike refused to take any money. Since then, I have always worn a bulletproof vest while on duty. This situation showed me that it is the simple ones that can blow up in your face. Tactical planning is a critical step and can never be taken for granted.

While I had been a sergeant for only eighteen months, I had already been given the chance to learn many important leadership lessons from my experience. I also know that, while many items can be gleaned from academic sources on leadership, the most impactful ones are those attained through life experiences. Throughout my career, I have often reflected upon these lessons and realized that while many things change, these tenets remain solid:

- A leader cannot seek to please everyone. On my first night as a sergeant, I made a decision that, rather than follow policy and notify IAB of the accidental discharge, I'd choose to pretend it never happened. The embarrassment I experienced after Lieutenant Thorton confronted me taught me the importance of making proper notifications.
- The truth must always be paramount when serving others. If we decide to falsify information in an effort to make a stronger case, we are no better than the suspect in handcuffs. If we accept untruthfulness we are violating our oath of office.
- Maintaining a high level of trust is vital. After disciplining the officers who lied in their reports, I expected to see a decrease in morale and productivity. The opposite was my

reality. Officers were happy that complete honesty was my expectation, and productivity and morale skyrocketed.
- Mission clarity is an important element in achievement of goals. Both Sheriff Alexander's election promise to clear the Strip of prostitutes within his first 90 days and my mission to send 100 gang members to prison within one year, demonstrate the importance of having a clear mission. This clarity made achievement easier. Mission clarity encourages everyone on the team to be a part of the solution.
- While leaders need to make sure that the work environment is a positive one, never allow any acts that could injure others (physically or emotionally) to take place. I can still recall the pain I experienced when I thought that my officer's vision might be in jeopardy as a result of my Wite-out prank.
- A true leader, like Lieutenant Smith, never worries about receiving the credit. The reality was that when the TEAM wins, we all win. As Gene often said "I'm having too much fun putting bad guys in jail to worry about getting my name in the paper."
- Leaders need to ensure that honest and constant feedback to improve the entire team, both upward and downward, is the norm.
- Leaders can never become complacent. During the shooting incident, I did not perceive the danger and I put myself and my entire team in jeopardy.

The coroner's inquest is supposed to be non-adversarial, but during this inquest the team was the suspect. My team and I arrived at the justice court and were put into an empty courtroom until we were called to the witness stand. As expected, the inquest lasted only a few hours and the jury deliberated less than forty-five minutes. We were called into the courtroom, and the verdict was read.

"Justifiable homicide."

When I was on the stand, I was asked, "Why didn't you fire?"

The Killer Bees

I said, "The threat was gone after Officer Mike Surick fired his two rounds and I saw the gun drop." Mike Surick, my agile officer, had saved my life that day by firing those two rounds.

After the inquest, the team went out to dinner. We could not wait to get back to work.

During that year, we put more than 120 gang members in prison. Unfortunately, Lieutenant Smith announced his plan to retire. We lost our sense of direction. In reality, combating gang violence took a back seat to appeasing self-appointed representatives of minority groups. Instead of keeping our valley safe, our goal became to not get into trouble. Criminals benefit when the police have to work while wearing kid gloves. Criminals fear hard-core policing, and that is the only way to curtail gang activity. When the community accepted a certain level of gang violence as being normal, our community peace was gone.

The secrets of our successes under Lieutenant Smith were total honesty, unwavering loyalty to the community, the team, and no desire to take credit. Mistakes were used as platforms to improve, not causes for punishment. We always put the good citizens first. Lieutenant Smith was as old school as a cop could get. He never pulled his punches, and when he had a problem with somebody, they were the first to hear about it. Many people were afraid to work with him, but good officers relished the opportunity. He would always respect a person willing to look him in the eye and give him an honest answer. Gene said he was retiring to go into another business, but I knew that he was getting sick of our department operating more like a Fortune 500 company than public servants.

7

THE FRIENDLY SKIES

I couldn't wait to get back to doing what I loved most: putting bad guys in jail. I learned many things as a result of that fatal encounter. First, I had made a serious mistake by not adequately planning our tactics. I was confident this was just a zero caper and did not take time to ensure a safe entry and arrest. Next, I never should have made entry without doing a thorough risk assessment on our target. Numerous firearms were located inside the residence and I never even considered the danger that was waiting for us. I later learned that even though the decedent had no criminal priors, he had been diagnosed with terminal cancer. At the inquest, some family members said he may have had a death wish after this diagnosis.

Going back to work after the inquest was a big relief. With a major drop in gang violence and Lieutenant Smith already having announced his retirement, things at work were in transition. Instead of the focus being on gangs, the focus became a "shotgun approach," as opposed to a surgical one, which had made us successful. The gang unit had become a group of handy men fixing problems throughout the valley. Despite, all the bullshit we were going through, we knew that Lieutenant Smith was fighting for us. At Gene's retirement, I got drunk and knew that policing was changing fast and not in a positive direction.

The week of Gene's retirement, I received a call from Lieutenant

The Friendly Skies

Bobby Hitt. Bobby and I had been friends from the time we were squad mates on Sergeant Thorton's team. I always had a great deal of respect for him, and I knew it would be great to work with him again. He asked me if I would consider coming to narcotics. With Gene retiring and the mission in gangs being so jumbled, I said "Definitely!" Also, this assignment meant an 8% pay increase.

Things were going smoothly on the home front, too. Rosie and Caitlyn were in elementary school at Saint Francis De Sales. Patrick and Elizabeth had not yet started school, but were growing like weeds. Allison was also doing well, but with me still working two jobs, our time together was limited. The additional 8% for detective pay meant I was finally able to resign from my part-time job at Lucky. We had just moved into a larger house, and we were in good financial shape. Even with Allison being a stay-at-home mom and paying for the children to go to Catholic School, thanks to the additional pay, I could finally quit my second job.

When I told Robin, the manager of Lucky that I was leaving, I remembered how he had hired me six years prior and had always accommodated my unpredictable work schedule. He shook my hand and told me that he valued all the work I had done. I told him how much I appreciated everything he had done for me and my family.

Working at Lucky helped financially, but more importantly it broadened my view of the world.

Police officers normally tend to associate solely with other police officers. As such, they tend to think of people who are not in law enforcement as weird. At Lucky, many of my coworkers struggling to pay their bills had become victims of crime. They were good people who were afraid to walk the streets in their own neighborhoods, and they would tell me how much safer they felt when they saw a police car. Occasionally, a coworker who received a citation for rolling through a stop sign would tell me that paying this citation meant that they could not sign their daughter up for soccer, I would feel bad. I'm certainly not saying police officers shouldn't write tickets, but discretion is a valuable tool. Good officers are people, not robots.

The best part of going to narcotics was that most of my old gang detail was already there. In the late '80s and early '90s, candidates did not test for certain positions in Metro. Narcotics was one of those assignments. When there was an opening, the team leaders would look for the people best qualified to fill the position based on work ethic and experience. Although, many people protested that it was just the "good old boy system," in reality, it was not. The system ensured that the most talented people with proven skill had their chance to make things better. In narcotics, the potential for liability is great and proven leaders need to fill these vacancies.

Putting the wrong people in charge can have disastrous results. This can be compared to encouraging an amateur prize fighter to climb in the ring with a top ten contender and hoping he does not get a bloody nose. In reality, the system of having candidates go through a formal civilian-controlled testing process diminishes law enforcement quality.

Let me explain why the selection process is so important. Labor relation specialists will argue that the current system guarantees that these positions are filled by a fair and objective process. However, this point of view does not fairly weigh the candidates' work history and performance. Performance is extremely subjective and difficult to measure. The only factor objectively weighed is documentation of disciplinary action in an employee's file. Officers normally will have pristine personnel files if they are not proactive. The underlying message to officers who want to become members of a specialized assignment is if they do the minimal and stay out of trouble, they stand the best chance of getting the job.

Besides, the practice is not organizationally sound. The bureau commander must be the person who is ultimately responsible for the performance of his or her bureau. Because the bureau commander is only a figurehead in the current process, that person's role in the selection process is trivialized. This would be like holding the general manager of the New York Mets responsible for the Mets not making the World Series if all the decisions on personnel

The Friendly Skies

were dictated by the owners of the Cleveland Indians. It just does not make sense.

Fortunately, the other sergeants in narcotics were willing to mentor me. They were top notch and I learned from all of them. Narcotics had a high trust level, so other sergeants never worried about who was going to take credit. The atmosphere in narcotics was almost identical to that in the gang unit. High morale and everyone operating at a fast pace were the commonalities that made this transfer seamless. My new lieutenant, Bobby, was a mountain of a man. He was six-foot-five and weighed 250 pounds. He was a power lifter, and he could make a suspect melt when he stared him down. Lieutenant Bobby Hitt was a great boss and more importantly, a man of integrity.

Walking into the vice/narcotics office made me feel as if I were back in the gang unit. Several of my former officers were on my new squad. Bobby welcomed me aboard and told me that he had some good news. Ray, a detective who had worked on my gang unit, had been handpicked to join a federal task force. The only problem was that he needed to pack his stuff and be on an airplane for Los Angeles by 7:00 p.m.

I knew that Ray would be delighted. When I announced to everyone that Ray was going to join this task force, Ray smiled and said that he was excited for the chance to work on major cases with federal agencies. Ray's joyfulness was replaced by a look of panic when I told him to head home and pack a bag for his flight. He told me he couldn't do it. I thought he was joking until he told me that he had a fear of flying and could not even set foot on an airplane. I thought Ray and I needed to step away from the office and discuss this over coffee.

Ray and I drove a short distance to the closest Winchell's donut shop. Over steaming hot java, I explained to Ray that the transfer was finalized and his ticket was at the airport. Ray's face was beet red and he was shaking like a leaf. He kept repeating how these panic attacks were nothing to take lightly. I told him that his transfer would be rescinded if he refused to fly to LA. I explained how flying is much safer than driving.

But I am no Doctor Phil. Nothing worked.

Then Ray had an idea. What about driving? It was only about 10:00 a.m. and the five-hour drive would get him there in plenty of time. I replied, "Great idea. Let me talk to the lieutenant and get his approval."

When I got back to the office, I immediately went in to tell Bobby that Ray was going to drive to LA, instead of fly. I explained that Ray had a fear of flying and I tried to convince Bobby that we actually would be saving money on airfare. Bobby screamed at me.

"Fuck him, that fat piece of shit!" he yelled. "What do you mean he's afraid to get on a plane?"

"It's no big thing," I told him. "I'll cancel the flight and he still has plenty of time."

Bobby slammed his massive fist on his wooden desk and screamed, "Get that coward piece of shit in here!"

I went back out and told Ray that the lieutenant wanted to see him. Ray went in and sat in a seat in the corner of the office, as far away from the lieutenant as he could get. Bobby continued his tantrum.

"You fat piece of shit, either you get your fat ass on that plane or I'm going to fire you for being a coward!"

Ray sank his face in his hands and did not say a thing. I jumped to Ray's defense.

"This is bullshit," I shot back. "I know Ray's got balls, and because he has a phobia about flying is no reason to fuck with him!"

Bobby turned on me.

"Maybe you need to leave narcotics with him."

"That's probably a good idea." As I started to leave the lieutenant's office, Bobby and Ray cracked up. Bobby got up and gave me a big hug.

"You passed the test." Bobby wanted to see if I would stand up for Ray. I did. He said he knew he made the right choice selecting me.

After I realized that I had been "punked," I cracked up and told Bobby payback was going to be a bitch. Bobby then told me to pick

The Friendly Skies

a good spot for lunch. He would buy.

During our lunch, Bobby was able to provide a roadmap of his expectations for the entire bureau and specifically, my role. Bobby told me he was having me take over the administrative squad and that he wanted me to take it to a higher level. The sergeant I was replacing was a superstar, but was not as engaged with his detectives as Bobby wanted. After that I knew exactly what my mission was and I was glad that to have made the move.

This new job was going to be a challenge. My squad was responsible for a wide range of narcotics issues. It was a great spot because I wanted to improve my administrative skills. Frankly, I didn't have a clue what was ahead. But I had great detectives working with me who knew their stuff. I also knew that having a boss like Bobby meant I could always go to him when I had a question. This organizational culture gave me the confidence that I was up to the challenges.

My detectives were all experienced veterans. They knew that, in addition to rock cocaine, crystal methamphetamines and heroin were growing problems in our community. We were also starting to see the growth of prescription drug abuse impacting our neighborhoods. Another responsibility of my team was to be in charge of all the wire taps and pen registers concerning our department.

Law enforcement technology was still in its infancy in the early '90s. Text messaging and e-mail had not yet arrived, so most communication was written in hard copy. The biggest negative of being the administrative sergeant was that I served as the captain's gofer. Our captain was a very smart man who had a spit shine appearance. One day he told me to get his car washed because he was going to an important meeting with the FBI in a couple of hours. My team and I were in the middle of presenting a class on telephonic search warrants at an off-sight location. I reluctantly told him I would take care of it. I left the class and drove back to our office to tend to my captain's vehicle.

I drove my captain's car to the carwash and realized that I still had time to stop by a local Winchell's and grab a cup of coffee before heading back. Unfortunately, when I got back in my vehicle after my coffee break, the car would not start. I tried again and again. After several unsuccessful attempts, I diagnosed that the battery was dead and called for a tow truck. Worse still, it was getting late, so my captain had to use one of the pool vehicles to drive to his important meeting. I knew that he was going to be really furious with me.

As I was waiting for the tow, I noticed a small plastic sign over the gear shift lever.

"Place foot on brake before turning the ignition key."

I fired up the car and drove back to the office as fast as I could. Too late. The captain had already left for his meeting in the spare van. I knew that we had not even driven this van for several months, and it was filthy. Also, the air conditioner was out. This wouldn't normally be a big thing, but it would be for my captain. I knew I was in for an ass chewing when he came back.

I was right. When the captain returned, he went nuts.

"That van was a fuckin' pig pen. I had to move piles of shit to even sit in it. Cigarette ashes were all over and it was like a fuckin' oven!" he ranted.

I glanced at him. He was dripping with beads of sweat and his face was contorted, reflecting the displeasure spewing from his mouth. I apologized and said I would get it washed and serviced in the morning. He wanted to know what the problem with his car was. I told him I figured out the problem, and it was clean and waiting for him in his parking space. Obviously, he was not pleased with my response and repeated the inquiry, but only much louder. I repentantly said,

"You need to make sure you put your foot on the brake before turning the ignition." He looked even more flabbergasted.

Clearly disgusted, the captain spun around and began walking to his office. Then I noticed the gum dangling from his ass. My entire squad, who had been witnessing the captain's implosion, cracked up.

"What the fuck is so funny?" he barked. I told him we were laughing because of some joke we heard earlier in the day. Lucky

The Friendly Skies

for me, he did not ask me to repeat it. Sometimes, you cannot afford to be too honest.

My new assignment allowed me to learn about narcotics and the importance of working with others, both inside and outside law enforcement. My detectives were all experts in their own specific disciplines. We were responsible for electronic surveillance, covert technologies, prescription medication, case filings, department title IIIs, pen registers, liaison with all other law enforcement agencies, and department-wide narcotics training. All of my detectives had at least three years of experience in their present positions before I even walked in the door. Gary, my predecessor, had led that squad for five years. He was retiring after thirty years at Metro, and had a reputation for being one of the best sergeants ever to wear an LVMPD badge. I knew I had some big shoes to fill.

I realized that as a leader, I could not always know everything. Gary advised me to communicate with my people and make sure they had the resources they needed. Bobby Hitt told me," Make sure to trust your people and things will go fine." I knew that I could not be exactly like the sergeant I was replacing, but I believed that my differences could benefit my team.

I always enjoyed getting into the mix of things, so I knew that I could best learn the job by getting my hands dirty. My detectives responded to this and were excited that I was working with them and asking them questions. Soon, the workload leveled off, and we had more time to be proactive. Despite our wide variety of responsibilities, we developed a "unity of mission" and became a solid team.

During one team meeting, three of my senior detectives complained how they'd always wanted to make sergeant, but with the heavy workload they never could prepare for the test. So, we made a decision to work together and form a study team. For the two months preceding the sergeant examination, we met together for several hours, three times each week to discuss the material. It worked. All three of these detectives finished in the top ten and were promoted to sergeant within the next six months.

Integrity Based Policing

I had been a sergeant for only two years, but the thought of making lieutenant intrigued me. I knew that it would mean more administrative work and less time out in the street. The increase in pay was a big factor, but my biggest incentive was to have a larger impact on our department. The reality hit me that I was still learning my new job and to begin studying for lieutenant would be too much work. When the announcement went out, I did not even buy the required books.

Bobby Hitt asked me how my studying was coming. I told him that I was not going to take the test this time because I was still learning my job in narcotics.

"That's a dumb excuse for not getting promoted!" he said. He told me that the only way to make a positive change in the community was to have a larger impact. As a sergeant, you can improve things for your squad of six to ten officers, but as a lieutenant you'd command an entire shift or detail of thirty to sixty men and women. He told me that I was ready and would make a great lieutenant. So, I bought the books and began to prepare for the exam, which was two months away.

Bobby was constantly there to help me. Our kids were no longer babies, so studying at home was much easier. Just like taking the sergeant's examination, I was confident when the day of the examination arrived. The major difference was that the number of candidates was much smaller. While only four sergeants were assigned to narcotics, I discovered that four of the top five spots on the written examination were all assigned to narcotics. This demonstrated to me how a healthy work environment and having a leader like Bobby Hitt makes people perform at a higher level.

I worked with the other narcotic sergeants in preparing for the oral board. We met early in the morning and on weekends to make sure that we all finished in the top five. Usually, only five people a year were promoted to the rank of lieutenant. Unlike the oral board for sergeant, they did not tell you your score until all candidates had finished and the scores were finalized. This meant that I took my oral on Monday, but did not find out my score until Friday.

The Friendly Skies

That Friday, I learned that I had finished number four. I also learned that the other three sergeants in Narcotics were also in the top four – in spots one, two, and three. They joked that even though I was going to make lieutenant, I still finished dead last in my section. Part of being a leader is developing your subordinates to become leaders. The success of the narcotics section speaks volumes about the leadership of Bobby Hitt.

I remained in narcotics until I was promoted. During the narcotics Christmas party in December 1990, Undersheriff Eric Styles called to tell me that I was being promoted to lieutenant. While I was happy to get the call, I knew that leaving narcotics was not going to be easy. I told Allison and the kids that God had again blessed us.

I had the honor to work under great leaders, all of whom taught me these three major themes: always strive for the public good, focus on the truth, and build trust.

Amazingly three of my officers and all four sergeants from narcotics were being promoted during the same year. While narcotics accounted for fewer than two percent of the candidates, it accounted for the majority of the top candidates. This is evidence of the benefit of working in a healthy environment. There was something special about the organizational culture in narcotics. I came to the realization that it was the powerful leadership of Bobby Hitt that accounted for our success.

I often reflect on some of the lessons Bobby taught me. The reality was that he was a sincere and confident leader who never seemed to be overly stressed out. His confidence was contagious. I recall that Bobby always made it a point to:

- Find time to talk one-on-one with your people. Doing this makes two-way communication effortless, and it never has to be a facade.
- Ensure that your subordinates treat others with the same respect with which they wish to be treated. While the encounter with my detective about his fear of flying seemed

like a major problem at the time, I learned a valuable lesson from this experience.
- Feel confident that you have the support of your superiors and subordinates to achieve success. While all of my detectives were experts in their areas, I never worried they would use their knowledge to subvert the team's success. Remember success is a TEAM project.

8

KIDS IN ACTION

When the reality of being promoted to lieutenant finally sank in, both feelings of eagerness and anxiety overcame me. Although I looked forward to leading an entire shift of men and women, the reality was that my days of having fun tracking down criminals were over. Lieutenants spend the majority of their time managing people and resources. My days of focusing on putting bad guys away were now history. Most of my time would be spent crunching numbers along with other administrative tasks. As a lieutenant, my job was to make certain all my officers could do their jobs by ensuring a healthy work environment, leading by example, providing clarity of mission, and attaining the resources needed to accomplish our goal.

My mind was racing, perhaps similarly to those parents realizing their child is becoming independent. All moms and dads can remember seeing their child walk into kindergarten. Although they are happy to see their child set off on the academic journey, most are fighting back tears. The reality hits home that their baby's first words and steps were now married to the past. Despite other exciting milestones waiting for them in the future, they feel a sense of emptiness. Their pain stems from the certainty that their baby's first words and steps are gone forever, now to be relegated to memories.

After getting off the phone with the undersheriff and learning

Integrity Based Policing

I was being promoted the next week, I told Bobby Hitt the good news. He made the announcement to everyone at the Christmas party. He then told me to get home and celebrate with my family. Since Allison was busy Christmas shopping and the kids were in school, we celebrated that night at dinner. I spent the rest of that afternoon going to supply to get new uniforms and my lieutenant bars. I stopped by the northeast area command and spoke with my new boss, Captain Mike Jones.

I had known Mike throughout my career, and I was ecstatic to have the opportunity to finally be working directly with him. I first met Mike back in my Academy days. When he walked into our classroom, everybody snapped to attention, and he did something that I will never forget. Mike said he was not better than any one of us and told us to sit back down and relax. He then told us that he respected all of us, and wished us success throughout our careers. That made an impression on me because in those days, most senior officers enjoyed having us treat them like royalty. Mike was a man who realized we were all people first. He was the ultimate people person who treated everyone, regardless of job, title or rank with respect and dignity.

I also knew he was not just a talker, he was a doer. He had created the Police Employees Assistance Program (PEAP), to ensure that all employees were afforded respect during difficult times. Prior to the creation of PEAP, officers involved in traumatic events (officer-involved shootings, and the like) did not receive any form of counseling or assistance from the department. Mike was known around the LVMPD as a gentle giant who always had a big smile on his face. I knew that working for him would be an adventure, and the entire area command was going to benefit.

When I walked into his office, Mike immediately jumped up and gave me a bear hug. He told me that he had handpicked me to come to northeast because he knew I would make things better. We talked for about two hours, mainly about the problems in northeast and the lack of support from executive staff. Another reality was that the majority of people residing in northeast area command were living in extreme poverty, and northeast was considered to be the red neck's West Side. Mike said that most of the officers were excellent and wanted to make a positive difference for the citizens they served. He told me he trusted me as a leader and would not micro-manage. If I needed any help, I could always count on him.

As our meeting was coming to an end, the janitor popped his head in and asked if he could turn on the vacuum cleaner, or if we were still talking. Mike responded "Sure, go ahead. How's Michelle doing?" The janitor flashed a big smile and spoke for about five minutes about his daughter and the goal she scored last night in soccer. As the sound of the vacuum started, I said good-bye and went home. While I had heard only positive things about Mike in the past, his actions with the janitor confirmed them.

I drove home, and surprised Allison and the kids by stopping for pizza and ice cream. After I put the pizza on our table, I put my shiny new lieutenant bars on top. We had a great evening and I knew that Allison was especially happy that I was going back to patrol. We could now calm down when I was off-duty and not be constantly interrupted by my pager. Also patrol permits for a more stable family life, and I did not have to worry about bumping into people when I was off-duty. I was excited for three reasons: the chance to get back to patrol, being in charge of multiple squads and mostly, to work with Mike Jones.

My first command was northeast area command, swing shift (3:00 p.m.-1:00 a.m.) and encompassed the northeast quadrant of our valley. I had four squads reporting to me, three of which were highly productive. The other squad (NE31) was made up of a group of malcontents. My three superior squads consisted of proactive officers who truly cared about the citizens who lived in our area. The problem squad only cared about doing as little as possible. Unfortunately, because of my days off, I worked with NE31 only one day each week.

Additionally, two other challenges were complicating matters: the large geographical area and the requirement to be watch commander for half of the week. The size of my area made responding

Integrity Based Policing

to some calls a difficult task. When traffic was bad, it often took almost an hour to arrive on a situation. Serving as watch commander was also counterproductive to my role. In this role, I had to respond all over the valley to ensure certain types of situations were being properly handled. As watch commander, I also needed to complete a detailed log for the deputy chief to brief executive staff.

This watch commander's log had just started after I'd been a lieutenant for a couple of weeks, and I remember it being highly controversial. Bobby Bennet (my buddy and also a new lieutenant) called me and asked my opinion of these new logs that we were required to complete. I told him that I hated them, and they took away from my more important responsibilities. Bobby went on to say how he thought it was a great thing, and he liked being able to document all of the specific calls to which he had responded. I told Bobby that this was the difference in our personalities. We are both baseball fanatics, but our memories were different. I remember the first time I walked into Shea Stadium, I smelled the grass and saw my idols emerge from the dugout. His first baseball memories were of his sharp #2 pencil and keeping a meticulous scorecard. It is all a matter of individual taste!

Serving as watch commander was like being an overpaid secretary. All of the critical incidents were already logged by dispatch, and I believed a lieutenant duplicating this effort was counterproductive. I did not need to spend time with officers from other area commands, when it was my officers I needed to develop and mentor. While other lieutenants thought that completing a log was helpful because it gave them a written record to justify their activities, I believed that other important measurements existed, such as officer productivity, community policing projects, morale, crime rate and the level of citizen satisfaction.

I made it a point to spend the majority of my time out in the field with my officers because policing was always my passion. In the beginning, officers, and sergeants were suspicious of me always backing them on calls. I remember a family fight call where I was the first unit to arrive. As I arrived, both the male and the female were fighting on the front lawn. I jumped out of my car, and the fight was on. After a few minutes, I managed to get both parties in cuffs. I told dispatch that I was "code 4" and only needed a transport. When the officer arrived, he said to me, "How'd you get them hooked up?"

I looked at him and said, "What do you mean?"

He said, "I didn't think any lieutenants had handcuffs and you carry two sets." We both laughed and from that point on, my relationship with my officers soared.

The advantage of being respected as a "cops cop" is that your people trust you and will tell you what is really going on as opposed to what they think you want to hear. In evaluating how successful a leader is, it is equally important to evaluate performance when the person is not present, as well as when they are present. Subordinates will perform in a positive manner because they trust and respect their leader, and want to protect him or her. This will often include making sure their leader is notified of a problem before it becomes a crisis. This is a valuable tool for a leader with 24/7 responsibilities. As a leader, if you have the trust of your people, you will know what is going on even when you're not physically present.

One evening, I was having lunch with two of my sergeants at Denny's and sensed they wanted to tell me something. After we ordered our food, a sergeant finally said, "We're having serious problems on swing shift because of the crap that's going on with NE31." I asked him to explain, and he explained that, in the past, they had never been confronted because the squad was so senior, but their conduct was beginning to influence the newer officers. They told me that two officers from NE31 had gotten into a fist fight that past Saturday, and their sergeant was the one who physically broke it up. When they talked to the sergeant about it, he told them to "mind their own business."

As we talked in more detail, they also recalled having several NE31 officers reeking of alcohol, and their sergeant told them to "get some coffee and work the desk." Making matters worse was

Integrity Based Policing

that NE31 had often bragged that they were the "untouchables" because of their seniority and their close ties to members of executive staff. Their conduct was spreading, like a cancer, over my other three younger squads.

While it is certainly more fun to be out in the streets stopping cars and chasing bad guys, a leader must ensure that handling personnel issues take priority. Internal strife that is not effectively dealt with, often leads to a complete breakdown of the team. After learning this information about NE31, I decided that I would cancel my days off that week and investigate the alleged misconduct of NE31. Because NE31 was off the day I learned of this information, I was able to drive back to my office and get my "ducks in a row."

After I got back to my desk, I reviewed all the personnel files of the officers on NE31, along with their sergeant. I discovered that three of the officers had worked with each other for the past four years and landed on NE31 because they had been run out of another area command. In their files, none of these officers had had any prior discipline, only glowing evaluations. The sergeant was newly promoted and had actually worked as an officer on the same squad from which these three officers had escaped. The fact that three officers had nothing negative in their files did not surprise me. Failing to document misconduct has always been a major problem. This practice allows problem officers to transfer to different area commands and never receive corrective action. 'If it was not documented, it never happened.'

I called Captain Mike to advise him of what I had learned during lunch and my plan of action to ensure it was handled. Mike was happy to see that problems with NE31 were finally going to be addressed. He also advised me to consider the impact of their conduct on all the officers at NEAC. He finished by saying that he was 100% supportive and to let him know if he could help. My last phone call that night was to the sergeant of NE31. I told him that I had heard about the fight last Saturday, and needed to talk with him about it. His response was denial and he attempted to minimize it as innocent horseplay. I told him to be in my office at noon, and that we were going to discuss the conduct of his entire squad in detail.

Kids in Action

The next day, I began an investigation that would lead to the sergeant and several of his officers receiving suspensions. We were also able to make several transfers that led to making positive change. The advantage of allowing the chain of command at NEAC handle this situation, instead of having civilians getting into the mix, was tremendous. This entire investigation and the subsequent personnel moves took two weeks. Within two weeks, we resolved a serious problem and greatly improved things. With today's practice of utilizing civilian experts, this situation would have taken at least six months (if ever) to resolve. While internal investigations are not pleasant, they need to be done in an efficient and expedient manner. It goes back to the old phase: "If you have to make a cut, do it fast and with a sharp knife."

With the NE31 matter resolved, Captain Mike Jones advised me of a plan to improve utilization of lieutenants. The plan consisted of breaking down all patrol lieutenants into two branches: watch commanders and area commanders. Watch commanders worked out of specific area commands, but were only responsible for the operations of the entire valley. They would respond on all critical incidents and maintain the log. The area commanders would be in charge of a certain geographical area. This included the 24/7 responsibility for everything that went on in the area. One advantage of this was that all sergeants and officers, regardless of their shifts, reported to the same lieutenant (unity of command). The other big advantage was that the lieutenant could focus on mentoring and developing his/her people, as opposed to running all over the valley.

Captain Jones told me he wanted me to be the area commander of the Baker/David Sectors. These sectors were the poorest areas of town with the highest crime and gang problems. The biggest change was that now I was in charge of all three shifts, as opposed to just the swing shift.

This plan made sense because it was consistent with the tenets of "community policing." All the business owners and apartment managers knew I was the lieutenant assigned to their area. As a result of this new style of policing, crime was lowered and the quality of life in the neighborhoods greatly improved. Teamwork and communication escalated because separate shifts were not competing for resources. We now had all three shifts focusing on what was best for the people who lived in the area.

In my new role as an area commander, I decided to conduct bi-weekly meetings with all of my squads collectively. During one of these meetings, two of my senior officers (John Lybert and Nick Lucas), said, "The biggest problem for us is when school is out for the summer. The kids have nothing to do but rove the streets." The other sergeants jumped in and said that was why gangs were recruiting so many of the little kids. Gangs were using these kids to commit burglaries and other crimes because they knew nothing would happen to them. We discussed possible solutions, but really could not figure out how to resolve this. The bottom line was that when the schools were closed, the kids had nowhere to go. I told everyone to talk with their people and see if they could come up with any solutions.

Within two hours after we met, I was contacted by Officer John Lybert to meet him over at an elementary school (Sunrise Acres). John had spoken to the principal of the school (Dr. Montoya), and he had some ideas that could help us resolve this challenge. Dr. Montoya said he would allow the gymnasium and the outside playground to stay open all summer if we could provide adult supervision. He told me that UNLV could assist by providing students to oversee the site. Dr. Montoya said that the city of Las Vegas would also need to approve of the operation. Dr. Montoya asked me to let him make a few phone calls to see what he could do to help.

By the day's end, Dr. Montoya identified two other low income elementary schools (all in NEAC command) that wanted to participate. He had also coordinated with UNLV Department of Education and had a list of students who would staff all three locations. The city of Las Vegas approval was the last thing that we needed to make this a reality. The city was complaining about a slight increase in insurance that they would need to pay (approximately $2,000), but I did not think that was a major hurdle. The only challenge was that the school year was over in two weeks.

I spoke to the city councilman, and he was attempting to stall by saying, "There's no way to approve this so fast." I told him that Sheriff Alexander would be calling him to impress on him the importance of our new program. That scared the councilman and he told me, "Please don't call the sheriff. We'll ensure everything is a go from our end." When Sheriff Alexander was in office, all the local politicians feared his wrath and did not want him to be mad at them. Sheriff Alexander commanded respect as the county's top lawman, not just another political crony.

The magic of community oriented policing is that great things happen because people take action with little concern for who will receive credit. A seasoned officer sought the advice of an elementary school principal, with whom he had developed a relationship in order to make things better for the community. This created the magic that gave birth to Kids in Action. The other principals, who also wanted to include their schools, certainly were not doing this to pad their own resumes. They did it because they wanted to help the kids. In reality, the only person who was complacent was the city councilman who needed to be persuaded by my threat of a phone call from Sheriff Alexander.

The following week, a press conference was conducted to introduce "Kids in Action." It was a major success and continued for several years. While we only had one light duty officer assigned to this program, it benefited hundreds of local under-privileged kids. The best thing about it was that it all started with an idea from a stick and whistle officer, not somebody in their ivory tower. The measurements used to evaluate police effectiveness need to include more than just "bean counting" measures; they need to include public service. Without a doubt, "Kids in Action" was a major success on both fronts. The project lowered crime rates and improved the quality of life for people in the community.

During the late '80s and early '90s, the major philosophy that governed the majority of American law enforcement was

Integrity Based Policing

Community Oriented Policing (COP). COP was grounded in the principle reality that we (police) needed to work with citizens to combat problems in the community. Such problems included crime, social issues, quality of life problems and anything else that people in the neighborhood viewed as important. We (police) would work in concert with citizen groups, non-profits, other governmental agencies, churches, etc., to resolve the underlying problem. This resulted in identifying and fixing the true causation factors.

"Kids in Action" was an excellent example of why COP is essential for policing to be truly effective. The current driving philosophy in law enforcement is Intelligence Led Policing (ILP), which measures success and failure by looking solely at crime statistics. This is not accurate or inclusive of the other important responsibilities of the police. In COP the involvement of the citizens as part of the decision-making process is paramount, as compared with ILP where this involvement is not considered an important element. The biggest difference between the two can be summed up by saying that ILP seeks to please the bosses, while COP strives to ensure the community improves and the citizens are happy.

After I had handled the internal problems of NE31 and "Kids in Action" was up and running, life at work was almost on autopilot. I had more time to be out in the field with my officers and attend meetings with the citizens in my area. Most importantly, things at home were going great. All of my kids were attending Saint Francis De Sales Elementary School, and I spent most of my free time coaching soccer and t-ball.

A major downside of technology in the early '90s was the size of cellular phones and pagers. I remember coaching my son Patrick's t-ball team, the Padres, and worrying about leaving my phone in the car and having my pager during the game. On one night as I was coaching third base, I received a page to call dispatch with the prefix of 911. I immediately ran to my car and retrieved the cell phone, and called in to find out what was the emergency. I was told by dispatch that I needed to report and take command of swing shift; we were beginning to face civil unrest over the Rodney King verdict.

Fortunately, one of the other coaches gave Patrick a ride home. I remember driving to the station and I could not believe that people in our community were imitating the troublemakers in Los Angeles.

I drove to the station, threw on my uniform and was logged on within an hour. After I logged on, I was briefed by Deputy Chief Myers that several fires had been set and numerous incidents of looting had occurred on the West Side, and the intelligence was that protesters were going to march down Bonanza to Main and start rioting on Fremont Street. The intelligence indicated that the protesters were planning to start their march at 8:00 p.m. which gave us about two hours to prepare. My orders were to command the entire northeast quadrant of the valley. Under no circumstances were the protesters to be allowed to reach Main Street. We had other squads at D Street and Bonanza to stop them and end the march. I would need to have a second line of containment set up at Main and Bonanza, in case they broke through the initial line of defense.

I decided to have one squad assigned to handle calls for service, and the other three squads would be located at Main and Bonanza. Our command center was at Cashman Field and the entire valley was at call screening "0." This meant that top priority calls would be broadcasted. I briefed the three squads, and told them that we were the last line of defense. Under no circumstances would we allow the protesters to get past our line. Since we had no helmets or shields, I warned everyone to identify bottle throwers and we would send an arrest team into the crowd to make the arrest. We played the waiting game until 7:30 p.m.

At 7:30 p.m. we were notified that the teams at D Street and Bonanza were able to disperse the marchers and prevent them from continuing east. For the next hour, we remained at this location, until the command center advised us to break down the second containment. We were able to deal with all the incidents breaking out throughout the valley. The people protesting were not, in fact, protesting. They were just criminals who saw this as a great chance to burn and steal things. The sheriff was able to

Integrity Based Policing

impose martial law, which forced all citizens to be off the streets. That night, the entire West Side and most of the valley was in a state of chaos as numerous fires burned and we were getting shot at. This continued for the next three days and nights, until finally we could return to normal patrol.

Fortunately, despite all the rounds fired at the police and bottles thrown, only one officer was shot. Thank God, his injuries were not life threatening, and he was back to work within a few weeks. The biggest victims were the overwhelming majority of African Americans who lived in the neighborhoods that were burned. These rioters were just imitating the idiots in Los Angeles, who started rioting a few days prior. While Los Angeles experienced more than fifty deaths and thousands of serious injuries, we were fortunate that most of our damage was only to property. The true heroes were the many African American leaders who stood up and supported our department in our actions. I also firmly believe that our department's philosophy of community oriented policing was a major factor in the prevention of more serious injuries.

The next week, I, and one of my officers, Vinnie, were back coaching our t-ball team. I was hitting fly balls to the outfielders and Vinnie was playing catch near the dugout. I saw a young African American man running up and immediately perceived him as a threat. Both Vinnie and I put our hands on our weapons, which were concealed, and began to get all the boys behind cover as Vinnie and I tactically approached him. I ran toward the man and yelled, "What do you want?"

The young man asked me, "Hey coach, can I still sign my boy up to join your team or is it too late in the season?"

I told him, "Sure, we're always looking for more talent." Both Vinnie and I realized immediately that we were also victims of the Rodney King riots. The young man who ran up to us became one of our coaches, and his boy was our new first baseman.

Back at NEAC, things were going well. With the internal problem of NE31 resolved, Kids in Action running smoothly and the riots over, there was time to be out in the field mentoring my people. The biggest challenge was constantly going to internal affairs with my officers. In the majority of cases, officers were getting disciplined for allegations that never should have been sustained. One situation I will always remember was one where many people, including Captain Jones, thought my actions would land me in trouble.

Two of my younger officers received a sustained complaint from IAB for "use of force." My job was to decide upon the appropriate corrective action for the officers. This included going down to internal affairs and reading the investigative report. I also needed to interview the concerned officers to understand the best course of discipline. I went down to IAB and reviewed the investigative report and I could not believe the lack of quality and the opinions being portrayed as facts. I even spoke with the lead investigator to gain some clarification. I remember his shrugging his shoulders and telling me that it was not my job to question the quality of his investigation.

After reviewing the investigative report, I spoke with Captain Mike and told him that the investigation was a pack of lies and was in no way accurate. I told Mike that I wanted to have IAB answer some of my questions before I could recommend discipline. Captain Mike said he would check with Undersheriff Styles to see if this would be possible. Captain Mike then told me that if worse came to worst, I could give the officers an oral reprimand, and he would ensure this was overturned during the appeal process, resulting in nothing negative in the officer's personnel files. I told Captain Mike that if we approved this shoddy work from IAB, we are only enabling their substandard investigations. We needed to fight to defend our people, not roll over and play dead.

The next week, Captain Mike told me that the undersheriff had refused to review the complaint and I needed to complete my disciplinary recommendation within 72 hours. I advised Mike to tell the undersheriff that I would not give a recommendation on a bogus complaint. I added that if he wanted to open an investigation on me, I was willing to be held accountable for my decision. I felt as I had years ago when the DA demanded that I testify on the suspects from the bookstores. I wasn't going to budge. When the truth is in your corner, you have nothing to fear.

The next day, Captain Mike told me that thanks to my stubbornness we had to meet with the undersheriff the next morning. Mike also told me that this was the first time that the undersheriff was being asked to review a case before it was an official appeal.

The following morning Captain Mike and I drove down to the undersheriff's office in city hall. Most of the conversation during the 10-minute drive to city hall was Mike telling me that he believed the undersheriff was livid and wanted to get this matter over with. As we walked toward the elevator, Mike kept telling me to let him do all the talking. As we turned the corner and walked toward his office, I sensed, despite Captain Mike's anxiety this was not going to be a nerve-racking meeting.

After a few pleasantries, the undersheriff asked me why I thought the investigation was garbage and what I wanted him to do about it. Thank God, I listened to the advice of my father and always made sure to rehearse my position before the meeting. I went on for about the next twenty minutes on all of the items in the investigative report that were problematic. I explained how the physical evidence supported what my officers said during their interviews and how IAB decided to not consider this. I then told the undersheriff that he should overturn the IAB finding and exonerate both officers. During my conclusion, I ended by saying, "I know that you believe that integrity matters."

Both the undersheriff and Captain Jones appeared to be in support of my position from the head nodding. The undersheriff asked me why I thought IAB would misstate facts to sustain this complaint. I said that I did not know if these mistakes were intentional or if it were incompetence, but I thought that by giving a recommendation for corrective action I would be giving tacit approval to their investigation. The undersheriff took several deep breaths and said overturning an IAB finding, outside the appeal process, was something he was not comfortable doing. He stood up and thanked us for coming in.

Kids in Action

As I and Captain Jones were walking out, the undersheriff announced, "I decided to overturn this entire cluster-fuck. Thanks for bringing it to my attention!"

Both Mike and I felt like a ton of bricks had been dropped from our shoulders. On the drive, back to NEAC, we spoke about the changes that had to be made in the method in which IAB did their investigations. While we both knew it was too early to tell if our stance would result in any true positive change for the department, we knew we had done the right thing in fighting for justice.

After this episode, Mike would joke about how we both needed to be careful because we had pissed off IAB. While I knew Mike was joking, I made it a point to be extremely careful to ensure everything was documented and people did not complain. I had been a lieutenant for one year, and it was time to go up to the sheriff's office for my certificate and picture.

It turned out that my probationary year as a lieutenant was a tremendous learning experience. This was an exciting time because community oriented policing was the dominating philosophy and I was surrounded by great people. The ten lessons below would always prove to be beneficial to me throughout my career:

1. Treat others, regardless of position, with honor and respect. The manner in which Mike spoke with our janitor demonstrated to me that Mike had people skills all leaders must have.
2. Artificial barriers that hinder a leader from mentoring and developing his or her people need to be removed. After Mike decided to allow me to be an area commander, I was able to focus on my people. This resulted in positive change.
3. A leader must lead from the front. By constantly responding on calls, making arrests, and working alongside my officers, I developed a partnership with them that made everything flow smoothly.
4. Having a high level of trust is essential to be successful. Ensuring that the work environment was conducive to high

Integrity Based Policing

trust allowed me to know what was really taking place, as opposed to what they wanted me to hear. The situation concerning the officers on NE31 would not have come to light if trust had not been established.

5. While dealing with misconduct is not an enjoyable task, no true leader will shirk this essential responsibility. Ensuring a fair, thorough, and objective investigation serves to increase morale. When discipline needs to be exercised, it is to improve performance and should be meted out in a timely manner.
6. Whenever a leader is dealing with misconduct, he or she is being critiqued by everyone. While it may appear that others are not aware of the incident, believe me, in most cases they know all about it. Your reputation as a leader will be determined by your ability to effectively deal with these situations.
7. A leader must know that the best solutions often come from the street level. The concept of Kids in Action came from a veteran officer. It certainly wasn't the product of an executive meeting. A leader must LISTEN to his or her people.
8. A leader must know when to take action, even if 100% consensus has not been attained. With Kids in Action, I was not going to let one city councilman put a halt to this project. I knew the benefit to the kids was much more important than his ego.
9. A leader needs to protect his or her people and ensure they are not being treated unfairly. After seeing the shoddy investigation that IAB had completed on my two officers, I was committed to ensuring their rights were not violated. Believe me, your people will appreciate the effort.
10. A leader must have the courage to walk into his or her boss's office and confront them with the truth. Many people want to tell the bosses only what they want to hear. By meeting with the undersheriff to explain my position on the faulty

IAB investigation, I was in no way being disloyal. The opposite is true. By telling him to his face, I was being honest and showing him respect. The trick is to make sure you have facts to support your position.

Having my picture taken with Sheriff Alexander was a very important day for me. Sheriff Alexander was the type of leader everyone on the department respected, and getting the opportunity to talk with him was an honor. On that Thursday morning, as I walked into his office, he was sitting behind his desk and invited me to have a seat. He started out by congratulating me for making it off probation and said Kids in Action was his favorite program because it helped kids in low income areas.

After a few casual exchanges, he then told me that the one area of our department that needed an overhaul was internal affairs. He said the problem was that the people in internal affairs would not make a pimple on a good cop's ass. I laughed and said that I agreed. He then asked me, "Would you be interested in taking it over?" I told him, I was honored by the offer, but I really enjoyed patrol and wanted to stay there for a few more months. He said, "It's already decided, you're going to be the internal affairs bureau commander effective this Saturday."

I said, "It'll be an honor," and we shook hands. He told me to check in with Undersheriff Styles before I left the building.

9

ANNA BANANA

Undersheriff Styles was leaning against the doorframe of his office waiting for me to step into the hallway. When he saw me, he smiled and said, "You're in for the ride of a lifetime!"

After we were seated at the small conference table in his office he became serious. He advised me to always remain objective and seek the truth. We spoke for over an hour about the dismal reputation of internal affairs, and he offered some suggestions for improvements. He told me that I had been selected for this assignment because several people had recommended me. These recommendations stemmed from the manner in which I handled a few investigations, my people skills and the fact I was a "cops cop."

The undersheriff said that earlier in the day, he had advised the Police Protective Association (PPA) that he was transferring me to take over IAB, and they gave their approval. The PPA president said it was going to be nice to have a 'real cop' running IAB, instead of the stuffed suits who normally filled this position. My predecessor frequently refused to discuss cases with the PPA and had difficulty relating to police officers. The undersheriff warned me that he knew he was taking a big risk by selecting me; however, he was convinced he needed to do something drastic to improve IAB. The undersheriff candidly warned me that he would be keeping a close eye on me to make sure I was not overly siding with officers versus ensuring a thorough and objective investigation.

The undersheriff explained that he believed the reason IAB had such a dismal reputation was threefold: inexperience, lack of compassion and inflated egos. Because nobody assigned to IAB had lengthy experience in tactical or investigative units, their expertise was limited. This resulted in investigators who had no compassion for the officers under investigation. When investigators cannot relate to the officers being investigated, it is impossible for them to be empathic. Lastly, given that IAB was not amenable to honest feedback, they were not improving. Their perception and reality were polar opposites because they had such a distorted opinion of their own performance. Without open and candid feedback, IAB was in a downward spiral. Honest feedback is fundamental for reform; with little receptivity to constructive feedback, improvement is impossible.

Before ending our meeting, the undersheriff added he was disturbed about the number of officers being disciplined by internal affairs for minor infractions that would best be handled through their chain of command. The previous few months had seen the majority of sustained cases get overturned during the appeal process. This was a waste of time and money, and more importantly lowered morale throughout the agency. Putrid investigations resulted in a lack of trust, which lowered morale. Low morale equates to poor performance.

I felt like a relief pitcher in baseball being put into a tied game in the bottom of the ninth with bases loaded and no outs. After the manager hands over the baseball, smacks the pitcher on the butt and trots off the mound, reality sets in. The manager will be sitting comfortably in the dugout watching the events unfold as the pitcher stands alone facing the heart of the lineup.

I knew I was stepping outside my comfort zone by taking over IAB for several reasons. First, my favorite part of policing had always been working the streets, and in my new position I was stuck inside an office. Second, I loved working with other hard-charging police officers. In my new role, I was working with only three administrative sergeants. Lastly, I loved supporting police officers in defense

Integrity Based Policing

of their actions. In my new role, I would be in the opposite corner. As I drove back to NEAC to clean out my locker and tell Captain Jones, I was wondering, "What am I getting myself into?"

My mind raced back to 1980 when I was being interrogated by those internal affair investigators who wanted me to resign. I remembered how I knew they were nothing but bullies who sought to trick me into quitting. In fact, the very same office where I had sat while they screamed at me twelve years prior was going to be my new office. After I left the undersheriff's office, I said a few silent prayers and made a promise to God that I would never allow others to be victimized the way I was that day.

The internal affairs commander was normally the most hated person in our department. I had worked my entire career to gain a reputation for being a "cop's cop," and I was concerned about keeping my good name. When Captain Mike saw me, he ran up and said "going to IAB will be the best thing that ever happened to you and our department." He told me to "always do the right thing and don't worry about pissing people off. Your friends will understand you are doing your job, and the other people aren't worth worrying about."

I called my father to get his advice before I drove home to tell Allison. Even though my father had never been a police officer, he gave me the best counsel I had ever received, "Remember to serve the citizens you're sworn to protect, and don't worry about getting others mad at you. If you serve God first, nothing else matters."

Since IAB's reckless investigations had been detrimental for members of our department, I saw this transfer as a blessing. I believed it was God's way of telling me, "Okay Dan, you know I've been with you so far. I'm not going to abandon you now." I was energized about the new challenges that lay ahead and the positive changes I could champion. Since my role of IAB commander required wearing a suit jacket and ties, I decided to stop by the mall and get some outfits.

With my extremely limited sense of fashion, I probably should have waited for Allison to come with me, but I thought I would save some time and, besides, I figured it wasn't rocket science. I parked in the Meadows Mall parking lot and was thrilled about the adventure of shopping without Allison. The mall was almost empty. I could forget about all the problems needing attention at IAB, and just relax and do a little shopping. After thirty minutes, I had picked out a few jackets, pants, shoes, shirts, and several ties, all of which the saleslady said looked great on me. I was a happy camper as I walked out of the store, thinking, "I don't care what Allison says. I do have good taste in fashion."

When I got home and showed Allison my selections, she said the six words all men, like me, hate to hear: "I hope you kept the receipt!" I was so proud of myself for picking out what I thought was professional attire in record time, and Allison had burst my bubble. I argued with her, saying, "These look great and they send a professional message!"

Allison replied, "You're right. They do send a message -- the message that you have rotten taste in fashion!" We drove back to Dillards to return my selections in exchange for apparel that Allison approved of. Oh well. At least I kept the receipt!

I had prided myself on earning a reputation as always defending my officers against IAB's pathetic investigations, and now I was the man who would be responsible for overseeing those investigations. While I initially thought this might create a conflict in my new role, the opposite proved to be true. By ensuring that all investigations were fair, objective, and thorough, I was benefiting both the department and all the officers.

A leader has to be willing to do battle to defend his people, and I viewed IAB as hassling good hardworking police officers. Several IAB cases that I voiced concern over left IAB personnel with egg on their faces, so I knew these same people were not happy to see me as their new boss. In fact, I think the many battles I had with IAB proved to be the primary reason the sheriff and the undersheriff selected me. I believe they both were saying, "Let's see if you can do any better, since you were our major pain in the ass."

When I assumed command of internal affairs, it consisted of me (a lieutenant), three sergeants, and two clerical positions. I knew going in that one of the three sergeants was not happy to have me as his new boss. This sergeant had been the lead investigator on the recent case that I fought to have overturned by the undersheriff. This sergeant often complained that I went to great lengths to defend my people. Although I personally took this as a compliment, he believed it was a negative trait. This type of thinking was the main reason I questioned whether he could remain part of IAB or needed to leave. I had the answer to this question very early in my tenure over IAB.

Just as I predicted, the sergeant I anticipated having problems with came in and did his best to avoid me. He had been in IAB for five years and was used to being left alone. Another sergeant, Larry Spinosa, came in and said how happy he was that things were going to improve. Larry told me something that puzzled me at the time. However, after a short period, I realized it was sound advice: "To survive in IAB, you have to do a good job. However, make sure it isn't too good of a job."

My new secretary, Marie, had been in IAB for her entire career (fifteen years) and while she was very loyal to my predecessor, she would do whatever I needed her to do. Marie could give me a look that let me know exactly how she felt. Her knowledge and experience would prove to be vital in making positive improvements. After about two cups of coffee, I decided that I needed to call everyone together.

I told everyone to come into my office at 10:00 a.m. for a quick meeting, and began fumbling through the in basket. At 10:00, everyone was sitting in my office except the sergeant who had issues with me. I walked down the hall and told him it was time to begin the meeting. He jumped to his feet and followed me into my office. After everyone was present, I started the meeting by saying, "Today is a brand-new start for all of us and we need to work together." As I was saying this, I could see from his facial expressions this one sergeant thought I was wasting his time.

I asked him, "What do you think we can do to improve things?"

He sarcastically replied, "Lieutenant, I have two investigations I need to send up to the undersheriff today and I don't have time for this."

I told him, "From this point on, no investigations will be sent out of this office unless I approve them."

He replied, "This is the way we've always done things here. Don't be changing things on your first day." I told him that my order was effective immediately, and if he did not like it, I had a list of qualified sergeants to take his position. The rest of the meeting went much smoother. Before concluding, I told them that our priority was to conduct objective, fair, and timely investigations and that, from then on, all cases needed to be approved by me.

After lunch, my problem sergeant handed over the two case files that he had just completed. Upon reviewing them, it was obvious that, while this sergeant had put in extensive effort, the investigations were far from being fair and objective. It was obvious from reading both of these investigative reports that this sergeant had made up his mind that the officer was guilty before he even began the investigation. This was apparent from the leading questions and the assumptions made based on his opinion, not the proven facts.

To ensure a fair and objective investigation, an investigator needs to go into a case with an open mind. Acquiring a slant in either direction, guilt or innocence, only leads to shoddy investigations which are damaging for the employee, the department, and the community.

I walked into the sergeant's office and told him that we needed sit down and discuss the cases before I could approve them. He went into a hissy fit, saying, "These cases are solid, and I am not going to do any more on them!"

I told him I was ordering him to, and that if he did not want to make corrections, he would be out of IAB. He told me, "That's it. I'm going to transfer out." I told him that was fine with me.

The sergeant who took his place was a 25-year veteran who was a cop's cop. Replacing my problem sergeant with him was like replacing a moped with a Porsche. I knew going into this job that, to make improvements, I needed to get the right people on my team. This new sergeant was certainly the right person to improve the quality of my team and send a clear message to the rest of Metro: IAB was serious about making positive reforms. Word spread like wildfire that IAB was no longer a group of hatchet men in wingtips. IAB had transformed into a team of respected veteran street officers who did objective and thorough investigations.

We were able to implement the necessary personnel changes within several weeks, which quickly and greatly improved IAB. With the support of the undersheriff, I could make the needed changes in a timely manner. In today's world of micromanagement, with the inflated roles of human resources, labor relations, and the associations--these needed changes would have taken years to make.

After we had our team assembled, we decided to take a critical look at how we were managing our time. The reality was that IAB was wasting too much time handling investigations that they had no legitimate reason to be conducting. Minor complaints (discourtesy, minor excessive force, uniform appearance, etc.) are best adjudicated at the area command level because they can handle these efficiently. IAB needs to be paying attention to serious violations and criminal acts, and training supervisors to police their own people. With the talented and respected group of sergeants I now had, we could train supervisors throughout the department on how to conduct top quality investigations. As a result, IAB had more time to thoroughly monitor and investigate areas of the department engaged in serious misconduct and criminal behavior.

With the support of the sheriff and undersheriff, we rewrote the IAB manual to mandate that other sections do their jobs and handle minor complaints. The reality is that making positive change is very easy once you have the right people on your team. The credit for the positive change belongs to Sheriff Alexander and Undersheriff Styles. They listened to their people and recognized that internal affairs needed reform. They also were receptive when subordinates told them that I was the person they needed to transfer in. This was out-of-the-box thinking because I was just off probation and had a reputation as a police officer with lieutenant bars. They took a big chance and were nothing but supportive of our innovations.

After a couple of weeks, the daily briefings were modified to weekly meetings. At 7:00 a.m. each Friday, I would meet with the sheriff and the undersheriff to brief them on the status of the investigations we were working. Since neither of them wanted to hear about minor details, most of this time was spent discussing global issues and the importance of family. I would still immediately brief them when a major case popped up or when any person of rank was suspected of serious misconduct. The bottom line was that they trusted me to do my job, so they did not need to know all the minor details.

After we had quality investigators in place, we began to hear about things that had been going on around the department for many years, but were never investigated. Plain clothes units had always received little attention from IAB because they hardly ever generated citizen complaints. The overwhelming majority of our complaints involved uniformed officers (patrol and traffic). The reason for this is simply that uniformed officers are always visible and constantly dealing with the public. It is also a fact that most of these complaints were best handled by their own chain of command. Given that patrol was now investigating their own minor complaints, IAB now had time to examine other bureaus. This made many people (outside patrol) very uncomfortable.

One night just before I headed home, I received a call from a lady who claimed she worked as a manager at a local strip club. She advised me that at least ten different officers (all ranks) were going into the back room and getting blowjobs from her dancers. She told me that in return for the sex, the police were supplying the club with information on vice enforcement. While the overwhelming majority of these complaints are bogus, this one made me concerned because the female gave a large amount of detailed information. I told her that we needed to meet in person and we arranged a time and location.

I called Ted, one of my sergeants, and told him to come with

Integrity Based Policing

me to meet this lady. At 8:00 p.m. that same night, at a TCBY Yogurt Shop, we first met the female making these allegations. She would not give us any identification, but only stated that her first name was "Anna." She was in her early 40s and still had an outstanding body. You could tell immediately that she was a high maintenance whore who would not be seen on Fremont Street. She was from Costa Rica and resembled the lady in that old Tropicana Orange Juice commercial, so we decided then to refer to her as "Anna Banana."

As Ted and I were sitting there talking with her, I realized that we must have looked like two perverts trying to work out a price for a date. Both Ted and I had coached our children's T-ball teams and were still wearing our dirty coach's uniforms (t-shirt, jeans, and sneakers). Anna Banana was wearing a sexy outfit, six inch heels and had the makeup and hair appropriate for a night out at your favorite strip joint. Her two biggest assets were hanging out, so both of us needed to focus and stare at her forehead.

After a few minutes of chitchat, I learned that she had been a high roller prostitute in town for over ten years. Throughout this time, her only arrest was for a DUI and she had managed to remain drug free. The club owner, who had known her for many years, believed she would be a big help to his club by playing Mother Hen for the young dancers. Even people in the flesh industry are cognizant of the importance of maintaining a clean and sober workplace.

She handed me a list of about twenty names of "who's who" in Nevada, including some high-ranking members within our department along with some elected officials. She said that these were some of her prior customers, and that she always maintained meticulous records.

I asked her, "What specifically can we help you with?"

She said that so many officers were coming in for blow jobs that it was hurting her business. She could not provide any names, only generic descriptions of some of the officers, except one. She gave me a very detailed description of this officer, even that he had shaved himself in an effort to look more erotic. She admitted she knew this because he had been her lover for the past six months.

After about an hour, we ended our conversation. I knew her allegations needed to be fully investigated, and yet I sensed that her motivation was that she was a scorned woman.

The next morning, I went up and briefed the undersheriff on the information we learned the night before. I showed him the list she had handed us with her alleged customers. The undersheriff said this was the type of case that could easily blow up on us if we did not conduct a thorough and objective investigation. He told me to work on an investigative plan and to make sure we got to the bottom of this as quickly as possible.

The first thing we needed to do was verify the allegations that Anna Banana was making. I decided to have surveillance conducted at the strip club during the hours that these alleged acts were taking place. We also conducted a complete background on Anna Banana. We arranged for a black and white to conduct a traffic stop on her and forward us a copy of the citation. The most important interview would be with the officer she had identified. However, this could not be completed until after we learned whether or not the acts were legitimate. If we had called the officer in before we determined if other acts were taking place, he could have burned our investigation by telling others involved. The same is true of the names on the list. If we approached them, they could easily subvert our efforts to discover the truth. The most important task at this point was to maintain confidentiality while corroborating her allegations.

Her background came back clean with the exception of a DUI and some traffic citations. She also had a sheriff card that allowed her to work at this strip club. We decided to conduct surveillance from 10:00 p.m. through 4:00 a.m., which were the hours she alleged the officers were coming in. After two full weeks of surveillance and no suspicious activity, I decided to contact the identified officer. I was all set to send out the notification for an interview when I received a 911 page from Anna Banana.

She told me that word had gotten out to the officers, and she was receiving threats to shut up or she would end up with a bullet

Integrity Based Policing

in her head. I told her we needed to meet and clear up some things. The good news was that she had no idea that we had been conducting surveillance at the strip club. I was confident that she would lie and confess her entire story was bogus. Unlike our first meeting, this interview would yield the truth. Or, so I hoped!

When conducting any investigation, maintaining confidentiality is a major challenge. I could monitor internally, however, I couldn't prevent Anna Banana from opening her big mouth. She had already told numerous people, including cops, that she had been working with IAB and many officers were going to get fired. I even received calls from several reporters that Anna Banana was telling them everything.

The interview was going to take place at 2:00 p.m. the next day. My sergeant and I had already written out all our questions. We were going to ask her about things that happened this past week, so we could catch her in a lie. Once we caught her in a lie, getting the truth would be easy. We also had other questions devised to get some details on the other officers involved. This entire interview was going to be recorded, so we had the exact words prepared, as opposed to some hastily written notes.

When she came into my office, roles had been reversed from our last interview. Both the sergeant and I were dressed professionally in our suits, and she was wearing jeans and a t-shirt. We started out by asking about activity during the past two weeks. She told us that no police officers had been in because their favorite girls were not working. She went on that she believed some of the officers were aware she had contacted internal affairs because cops were always following her. She also admitted that she had never received any threats, but was frightened by all the police cars she was seeing. No doubt she was a whacko, yet she was honest about the prior week. Before we finished, she also handed us some photos of her partying with the identified officer along with numerous off-duty officers. These Polaroid pictures also gave her story a degree of credibility.

Because we didn't catch her lying, we decided to run the covert surveillance for another couple of weeks before we called in the identified officer. That next week, we did see numerous on-duty officers come into the strip joint; however, none of them went into the back rooms or engaged in any questionable activity. Most of them came in and talked with some employees for a few seconds and left within a few minutes. Another piece of information that came to light was that the club was very police friendly and even sponsored a few police softball teams. By doing this, these types of places made a good investment. Having numerous officers as friends is a valuable thing to anybody engaged in nefarious activity.

I remembered as a kid, my Dad telling me after seeing a group of New York's finest, sitting in front of a mob-owned pizza parlor on Flatbush Avenue, "those cops are worse than the bums that own the place." I also flashed back to when Bobby Bennet and I got banished off the Strip because we did not give preferential treatment to certain people. The reality is that things have not changed and sleaze-balls will always be looking for a chance to buy law enforcement officers. Police, district attorneys, and politicians, are valuable commodities in the world of crime, and some can be bought for a very cheap price.

The next week, we decided to call the identified officer in for his interview. The officer was a young patrolman stationed out of the northwest substation. He had been with our department for three years, and had been assigned to northwest since graduating from field training. Prior to joining our department, he had served in the United States Air Force and had a Bachelor's Degree in Criminal Justice from UNLV. He was also single and the only bachelor on his squad. When I called his association representative to let them know we were sending out the notice of interview, he laughed and said Anna Banana had already called him several times.

The time and day of the interview was set for Wednesday at 7:30 a.m. The reason for this is that interviews designed to gain additional information are best set for early in the morning. At this time of day, the mind is normally the most acute and clear. As my sergeant and I crafted our strategy for the interview, we vacillated

Integrity Based Policing

between confrontational and compassionate. The confrontational approach was by far the easiest, i.e. "you are an asshole and we are going to fire you." The compassionate approach required letting him know "you are a victim of circumstances, and we are going to help you save your career, as long as you're honest with us." We decided to start out with the compassionate approach, with the idea that we could always turn the heat up.

As he walked into the room, he looked like a calf being led to slaughter. His eyes were halfway shut, and you could see he needed a good night's sleep. After I read him his Garrity warning, police officer bill of rights, and told him it was being recorded, he started to give a very detailed response regarding his relationship with Anna Banana. He said that he met her at a softball party at the strip club about six months ago. He went into great detail as to how he was immediately smitten with her because of her enormous tits, Latino accent, and seductiveness. He was confronted by Anna Banana and told that she was going to teach him things about pleasing a lady he had never learned in the police academy. He admitted that he was very drunk at the time, and the next thing he knew he was peeling Anna Banana and engaged in the best sex he had ever had.

They began a romantic relationship and for the first few months it was great. Because Anna Banana lived alone in a beautiful house, he decided to move in and enjoy the good life. This lasted for several months until he realized that this cougar (Anna Banana) was not the lady he wanted to settle down with. During the several months that he was living with her, numerous police softball parties were held at the house. This certainly explained the Polaroid pictures of all the officers partying down with Anna Banana. He also said that many of the officers stopped by the strip joint because of the friendships they had developed.

I asked him why he was dating an ex-prostitute. He told me he did not know about that for months. That was a main reason why he decided to end their relationship. He admitted having suspicions from the beginning, but she was such a great liar that he discarded those thoughts and decided to enjoy the experience. He also said that he ran a background check on her and the only prior was a DUI. He ended his contrition by saying he was more than willing to take a polygraph test regarding this relationship. At the end of the interview, I was confident that he had answered all of our questions truthfully and knew that this was a scorned woman who was looking to use IAB to get payback on her ex-boy toy. After several more interviews that verified everything the officer told us, the officer was cleared of any wrongdoing.

This case demonstrated the dangers of police officers fraternizing with strip clubs. In response to this case, we went out to all area commands and spoke about the dangers of being associated with people in the flesh business. We could not create a more stringent policy on consorting because department attorneys were fearful of First Amendment challenges. We were also unsuccessful in crafting a policy to forbid officers from accepting comps. How can we tell officers to stop accepting free coffee, when the top brass was enjoying trips, golf outings, contributions, and other such perks?

During my first few months as the commander of internal affairs I was fortunate to witness several examples of powerful leadership. I am confident that while these examples of sound leadership involved law enforcement, they could also apply to other professions:

- Good leaders must be willing to take chances and think outside the box. When the undersheriff selected me, he took a gamble by not seeking somebody with more seniority. Instead of picking an older, administrative-minded lieutenant, he selected a young lieutenant who was a proactive officer.
- The undersheriff knew that serious problems existed in IAB, not just the surface issues. Good leaders need to dissect challenges if they seek long-term solutions.
- Leaders must be willing to give people a chance to succeed, but not let them subvert positive change. When I first started, I knew that this sergeant would be resistant to reform. However, I decided to let his actions determine his destiny.

My plan was to start fresh, and unfortunately for him, he was not willing to change.
- Leaders should use their own experiences to empathize with others. I know that my experience with IAB back when I was in field training made me more sympathetic to officers sitting across from me.
- Becoming a better leader requires a person to venture outside his or her comfort zone. While at first the challenge of transferring to IAB seemed daunting, it served to broaden my view and made me a better leader.
- While most change is best if it is incremental, at times a leader must be decisive to maintain control. The decision to transfer out the problem sergeant so quickly was one that his conduct dictated.
- A leader must always strive to make sure the right people are working with his/her team. After the right people are on your team, life gets much simpler.
- The power of trust makes things go smoothly. After the undersheriff trusted me in my new position, we could meet on a weekly basis. The fact that he did not have to micromanage made everyone happy.
- All leaders must make sure that they are setting the example of ethical soundness for their employees to follow. As I learned, "How can an officer be ordered not to except gratuities from night clubs, if his/her bosses are accepting free gifts from these same people?"

10

CROSSING OVER THE RUBICON

Despite working in a tiny office and juggling heavy caseloads, IAB was a fun place to work. We were veteran investigators who all were working for positive reform, and we were making things better. Our mission was clear, and we took pride in focusing on serious misconduct and corruption, as opposed to harassing hardworking cops. Besides investigations, we also made changes in the way we treated our fellow employees.

One afternoon, Patti, one of my office assistants, said she wanted to discuss something. She told me about an officer who had resigned from Metro prior to my transfer to IAB. He had been under investigation for several months concerning a complaint alleging excessive use of force. The complainant was a wealthy casino executive who had "juice" (favor) with the sheriff. It was obvious the officer did nothing wrong, but IAB refused to exonerate him. This lasted several months. As a result, the officer was on administrative leave. During this timeframe, nobody from Metro had contacted him. The officer eventually resigned and joined another department back East.

"We lost this officer because nobody cared enough to call him and check on his welfare," Patti said. I agreed. I thought about the time Undersheriff Dennison called me when I was in field training. Prior to this call, I was contemplating enlisting in the military and leaving Metro. Before Patti left my office, we had already drafted a new policy. This policy mandated at least weekly contact between the investigating officer and the targeted employee. This policy was created for the employee's well-being. This contact and conversation would not influence the outcome of the investigation, but was conducted solely for the welfare of the officer under investigation.

After the Anna Banana investigation was completed, I began receiving calls from strippers and prostitutes complaining about our officers' conduct. It did not take long before I realized that IAB needed a person with expertise in the 'world of prostitution' to join our team. The justification was clear: the flesh trade is sleazy, and it takes years of experience. An experienced investigator is able to focus in on the truth and not waste time chasing down falsehoods. Prostitutes are experts in deception and use their street smarts to their advantage. Nobody assigned to IAB had this type of experience and I knew that, without it, we would be operating at a major disadvantage. Fortunately, a veteran vice detective called to ask me if he could join our team.

The undersheriff and I said yes.

With the addition of this seasoned detective, IAB could now be proactive in dealing with police corruption. Having an experienced detective allowed us access to undercover investigations and confidential informant files, without first notifying the covert section. Notifying the targeted section allows reports to be changed or destroyed, thus increasing the possibility of cover-ups. While this transfer was viewed as a positive thing by reformers, many others saw this as dangerous and jeopardizing the status quo.

Another benefit of adding a seasoned vice detective was that it gave IAB a level of credibility with the prostitutes. We never had that before. Historically, we received filtered information, which limited our operational effectiveness. After this in-the-know detective joined internal affairs, some officers in plainclothes details became fearful. They were no longer operating in anonymity. In fact, IAB could be watching them. Despite warnings from the sheriff and the undersheriff about actions that could provoke scorn from other sections, I knew that in order for internal affairs to best serve our community, we needed to have complete access to all covert operations.

Undersheriff Styles and Sheriff Alexander led the way by allowing internal affairs to amplify its reach. In the past, IAB focused solely on responding to citizen complaints and media concerns, without regard for organizational soundness. Having a totally reactionary IAB may please the public in the short-term because trivial complaints by uniformed officers are their sole focus. Allowing IAB to be proactive meant that all the areas of the department were now being watched, which benefited our community by fostering organizational soundness.

Morale increased on the department. The organization seemed fairer. Patrol officers understood that all officers would be held to the same high standards, including detectives in covert assignments. The credit goes to leadership at the top because often issues will be uncovered that will rock the boat. Leadership has to support those occasional rough waters. Just because everything appears to be going along smoothly, does not mean that there is no corruption. Corruption is like a cancer in that the earlier it is identified and treated, the greater likelihood for a return to organizational health.

A month after completing the Anna Banana investigation, I received a phone call from the attorney general's office about one of my academy mates. This officer had testified in Federal Court that, as part of his normal duties, he routinely shared criminal history information on individuals he accessed through NCIC with a local attorney. His actions violated federal law, and the FBI was threatening to discontinue our department access to NCIC. The officer was a foot patrol officer in downtown and was a close friend of this attorney.

Sharing information this way was not his job; in fact, it was a violation. When I interviewed the attorney, he acted as if he were above the law. He was upset that I had the audacity to even conduct an investigation because he claimed "we've always done this." This attorney made a career of befriending officers and using them. The only difference between this lawyer and the strip club owners was his "Attorney at Law" sign in front of his office, instead of one with naked ladies. Because my academy mate was honest and admitted his error, he received minor discipline and became more selective in picking his friends. The FBI was satisfied with our corrective actions, and we maintained our NCIC privileges.

Then there was the time when the former vice detective, who was assigned to IAB, told me that he had been getting paged by a prostitute. She alleged that a vice detective whom she had been in a relationship with was taking money from her. Making matters worse, the suspected detective was his ex-partner, and they were still friends. I told him that we needed to investigate. Taking money from a prostitute was a felony crime.

The expression on his face reflected that he was still harboring something he wanted to get off his chest. He told me, "I know for a fact that her accusations are true." He told me about a breakfast conversation where the suspected detective showed him some cash she had given him. He said he told this detective to immediately impound it and do an officer's report, but he didn't follow up or notify his chain of command. Clearly, no curative action had been taken.

I told my detective that he should have made sure that procedures had been followed.

His rationale? He did not trust the leadership in vice and was confident the young detective would do the right thing. He said he thought it would look better for the detective to handle this matter himself, instead of ratting him out. I advised him that, while I believed he should have done more, I was confident he did what he thought was right. I told him that I needed to run this by the undersheriff before we proceeded with the investigation.

It was late Friday afternoon when I met with the undersheriff. He was not very happy to see me.

"Can't this wait until next week?" he greeted me jokingly.

I explained the situation and its urgency. When I told him about the detective's breakfast conversation, he asked, "What do you think?" My detective was clean. I explained that he did not trust the leadership in the vice section. The undersheriff agreed.

"See if we can corroborate this and make sure we get this on video," he directed. I left his office knowing that we had a busy night ahead.

I returned to my office, called in two of my sergeants and the detective, and told them we needed to set up a meeting between this detective and the prostitute to see if he would take more money. My detective paged her. She replied quickly. She said that she was supposed to meet her detective friend at a bar inside the Sands at 2:30 a.m. She added that he had been calling her because he needed cash for a business venture that he and his brother were undertaking.

The timing was perfect for us to complete a quick recon and set up a surveillance plan before heading home to grab a bite to eat. Our intelligence section helped us get the video and camera set up by 5:00 p.m. This type of case is sensitive, so only a limited number of individuals outside IAB could help. After this was done, I told everyone to go home and meet back in the rear parking lot of the Sands at 1:00 am.

I could not help but feel bad for this detective whose career was about to go down the drain. He was twenty-eight, a former Marine, and married with two babies. I wondered how a kid like him got involved with a stupid whore. He was in vice because he was good buddies with the sergeant and lieutenant. A kid his age with only four years' experience had no business being in a covert assignment. He looked young, so he had no problem getting soliciting cases on the girls, and unfortunately, he was transferred into the vice section with no regard for his lack of maturity or experience. I thought back to my days as a young kid working undercover in the bookstore caper. Thank God I was never tempted to go back. I also felt bad for my detective, who had been his senior partner. I could not imagine the guilt of thinking, "I wish I had done more to save him."

That night, the plan went down exactly as expected. At 2:30 a.m., the young detective strolled in and sat down next to the whore. The whole thing took just five minutes. She said to him

Integrity Based Policing

"Here's the money you wanted," and handed him $1,000 cash. He took the money and finished his drink. As he was leaving, he turned to the woman and said, "I feel like shit taking money from you." As he walked out the casino door and headed to his car, one of my sergeants walked up to him and told him to come with him. His eyes welled up with tears.

"I'm glad you caught me," he said.

This entire episode was a painful experience for everyone involved, except that sleazy broad. I remember seeing her face with an expression of satisfaction after she knew we caught the detective red-handed. In her sick mind, she was happy that he fell for the trap she set for him because he did not want to continue a relationship with her.

When we got back to the office, the detective took complete responsibility for his actions and offered to resign immediately. I told him to wait until after he met with his attorney or at least somebody from his chain of command. He became even more adamant about giving a complete confession and resigning. I was equally as insistent. He should talk it over with someone first. So, I called the lieutenant in charge of vice, my former sergeant, Billy Elders, and asked him to serve as a representative. As I expected, Elders did not care about how this detective was doing. He was mad at me because I did not warn him beforehand.

The detective confessed and resigned. During his interview, he went into detail about how he first met this whore and that she was his informant on several pandering cases. He always met her with his partner until one night when she paged him at 4:00 a.m. She was crying and insisted that they meet alone. She told him that one of the pimps she had informed on had put a contract out on her, and she was afraid to leave her apartment. She insisted that this detective come by himself because she did not trust his partner. He complied against his better judgment. When he got there, it was clear to him that she wanted to have sex, but he refused, he said, and they talked for several hours. He felt obligated to help her, since he had built several major cases from her information. He told me that they never had sex. He confessed they did become close – way too close. From that point on, they always met alone.

During one meeting, she slipped him $200 to buy his wife an anniversary present. He argued with her about the money, but she insisted. Their relationship had taken a disastrous shift from officer and confidential informant to an unwholesome friendship. As time progressed, the money became larger in denominations and increased in frequency. He said that breakfast when he told my detective about taking the cash from the whore was the last time, prior to this night, he had taken her money.

I listened to his emotional confession and watched the tears drip down his cheeks. I realized this outcome was determined the minute he decided to meet with her by himself. His decision to meet her "one on one" was like when Julius Caesar led his army across the Rubicon in 49 BC. He had passed the point of no return. His career was over.

This whore had strategized every move, and he was like a dumb puppy naively navigating through her maze. What whores lack in morals and decency they compensate with their street smarts. Once he met her alone, she knew his badge was hers, and she could take it at any time. When he decided to end their relationship, she simply pulled the switch.

After the interview, Lieutenant Elders and I returned to my office. Elders was red as a beat and I could sense he was upset with me for not giving him a head's up. I told him that I could not tip him off or I would be part of the cover up. I knew Billy Elders couldn't understand my reasoning. He was already in the damage control mode and cared only about his reputation.

I checked in with the detective the next morning to see how he was doing. He wanted to make sure that his wife knew that he had never had sex with this whore. So, I spoke with his wife in person at their home. We talked for about an hour. While I certainly could not excuse his conduct, I respected his willingness to accept full responsibility. This case was about a young man who went down the slippery slope by feeling so comfortable with this whore that he would

Integrity Based Policing

meet with her alone. The department's error was allowing a young kid to transfer into the vice section without adequate supervision.

The next week was already going to be busy, and this latest case just added to my workload. I knew that both Lieutenant Elders and his captain were upset that I had not warned them, and I had already heard reports that they both were spreading rumors about what a sloppy job we did. On the other hand, I received many phone calls from others in Metro saying they were happy that IAB was finally being proactive.

The sad fact was that Billy Elders and his captain were blaming internal affairs for this incident instead of holding themselves accountable. Because there was a complete lack of leadership in the vice section, this was no surprise to people inside the LVMPD. I hoped that Billy and his captain would put safeguards in place to prevent similar incidents in the future.

I was about to discover that improving the organizational soundness within the vice section was not a priority.

At the end of the day, my cell phone rang. It was the undersheriff. He asked me how I was holding up dealing with those crybabies in vice. He told me that they had been bugging him and the sheriff all day. He said that he mentioned to the captain how my detective was apologetic that he had not done more when he first learned about the detective's actions. The undersheriff said that the captain then went nuts and told him he wanted my detective to be fired for not notifying the chain of command. The undersheriff then told me to contact the captain and get this thing worked out.

My very next call was from the captain, and he was screaming.

"You better fire that fucking detective you have up in IAB. He knew about it and didn't tell anyone."

I tried to explain as calmly as possible that the reason it was not reported up the chain was because he did not trust his higher ups. I also said both the undersheriff and sheriff agreed with my reasoning for not charging him. Despite my attempt to reason with him, he was not listening. He continued his rant until I ended the phone call.

Crossing Over the Rubicon

I hung up the phone and finally went home for the day.

But the phone calls were not over.

That night I got a call from the undersheriff. This captain was driving him crazy and had even called him at home. I explained that there was no reasoning with him. The undersheriff agreed but he ordered me to go the vice narcotics bureau the next morning to smooth things out. I think what put both the captain and Billy Elders over the edge was that this was the second major cluster for them in the recent past. A suspected pimp who died during a vice encounter was still fresh in people's minds, and this was yet another sign of their failed leadership.

When I arrived at the vice/narcotics bureau the next morning, I had to wait in his assistant's office for a good twenty minutes. The captain was supposedly having a meeting with Billy Elders. I could not believe that this was the same place I worked just two years before. Then I was a part of the family; now I was being treated like an enemy. I knew having me wait in the outer office was the captain's way of disrespecting me.

I got up and stormed into the captain's office. The captain and Billy Elders looked stunned.

"Please go outside," the captain blurted out. "We aren't ready for you yet."

I told him, "No. Quit wasting my time. You can stop by my office later in the day."

He started out by reminding me that I was only a lieutenant, and he was a captain – I was being insubordinate to him. The reality was I did not report to him. The captain then started screaming again.

"I don't know who in the fuck you think you are, not telling us about the investigation until it's over!"

I told him that I would never advise people of a covert internal investigation in advance. The captain said he could have straightened things out, and this detective would still have a job. I was dumbfounded at this – thinking, "Why would you want a person who committed a felony to remain in the department?"

After that part of the discussion was over, he began screaming at me to file a complaint against my detective. He told me that I should not have any detective assigned to IAB because we were just trying to mess with undercover operations. I told him that we had already decided not to file a complaint against my detective. His anger escalated. He blamed the entire episode on my detective and me. I argued back that the absence of leadership in the vice section was responsible.

That sent him over the edge.

I told them the decision was final. The captain said, "This discussion is over." Fortunately, I had a sergeant with me. He grabbed me and escorted me out of the office.

While the captain was unhappy, the undersheriff was pleased. He told me that the reason he wanted me to handle this was for my own professional development.

"Danny, you're a nice guy and it's essential for you to learn how to deal with conflict, both inside and outside the department," he told me.

He was right. I also thought back to the counsel my father had given me, "Serve the public and don't worry about pissing people off." I felt good about that decision and I slept well that night.

While the overwhelming majority of people on Metro were supportive of the reform efforts, some like Billy Elders and his captain longed for the bad old days. Filing charges against my detective would have deflected the blame from them. In these good new days, they could not deflect blame as easily as they had previously.

I was truly enjoying my role as IAB commander for all the good that we were accomplishing. The down side? I was cynical and distrusted people, except for my family and closest friends. Officers tend to isolate themselves by only befriending other cops. When you are assigned to IAB, you do not even want to socialize with other cops and believe me, the feeling is mutual. As a result, Allison and I stayed busy with kids' activities and our house became our fortress. Our big nights out were taking the kids out for pizza and mixing some pina coladas after the kids went to bed.

Because the majority of IAB cases were confidential, I would often get calls at home from people whom I had not talked to in years. Most of these conversations would go something like, "Hey Dan, how are you doing? By the way, I heard that my sergeant might be in a jackpot. Is that true?"

I would always tell them, "If you have a question about him, call him not me." Eventually, the calls became fewer and fewer. Finally, I would turn off my cell and let the calls go to voice mail.

Conducting fair and objective investigations was the easy part of my job. The hard part was dealing with the people who believed they should be treated differently. The officers being investigated appreciated our focus on uncovering the truth. It was the higher ups who were resistant to this goal. The investigation with the vice detective is an excellent example. The detective was actually thankful and accepted complete responsibility. His bosses – Elders and his captain – viewed this as an attack against them personally and thought IAB should not have investigated the incident without first warning them. While this case did serve as an 'eye opener' that not everyone values integrity, I was confident that the majority of people were supportive of our efforts. I learned some important realities during this period of my career, both organizationally and individually.

The reality is that internal affairs must have access to all files in an effort to maintain organizational soundness. Police agencies need to ensure that all areas (including covert sections) are subject to random drug testing, audits of bank accounts, confidential informants' files and other measurements to ensure they are sound. While some will argue that covert assignments cannot be as transparent as other areas, I would say they must be even more transparent. This will not only help the agency, it will benefit all of the members of the covert section. I have seen throughout my career that the only people who resist transparency are those with something to hide.

Integrity needs to be the cornerstone upon which police agencies are built. Because the vice hierarchy sought to deflect blame as opposed to providing leadership, a talented officer lost his job. When the facts indicate command level officers are tolerating and justifying corrupt acts, they must be held accountable. The attitude that was prevalent in the vice section should not have been tolerated by the executive staff. While demanding organizational soundness might make some uncomfortable, the benefits are worth the effort.

To be proactive, agencies must ensure safeguards are in place to minimize the opportunity of corruption. It is critical that officers who are not mature or experienced enough to join a covert assignment are ineligible to test for these positions. The time to create proactive policies is before a major incident occurs, not as a response to a scandal.

Not only did I feel bad for the young vice detective, but also with the detective who was informed months earlier and did not follow up. While the advice to impound the money, and do an officer's report was good, without follow-up, it did nothing to remedy the situation. The detective should have personally made sure that the situation was resolved by impounding the money and going with the detective to inform his chain of command. When misconduct or a criminal act becomes known, you have both a moral and legal obligation to ensure it is properly reported.

While I personally liked this detective and was saddened by this situation, my oath required that I objectively investigate it and take action. This situation was painful for me; however, I knew I had no other choice. Leaders have an obligation to let the truth surface and allow the chips to fall.

This young detective did not stand a chance against this lady of the evening. This detective was toast after he decided to meet her by himself. All officers must remember that confidential informants are not your friends, especially when they are the opposite sex. Good officers know to keep them at an arm's distance and never trust them. I can still remember the ugly grin on her face when she saw him get busted.

In Chapter One, I said that dealing with bullies is the most important part of an officer's job. This is even true within the department. In dealing with the captain of vice, I needed to be loyal to the citizens of Clark County, not people in positions of power. While I certainly did not enjoy having to argue with the captain, it was therapeutic. I realized that while it is part of life to disagree, it is most damaging if you refuse to confront the conflict. While nobody with a sane mind looks forward to a heated argument, it can serve as medicine for the soul.

With the improved reputation of IAB, many incidents that happened years ago were re-surfacing. People trusted us now. They were not afraid to call. Such was the case one Friday evening as I was getting ready to take Allison out to a French restaurant. The caller was a lady who said she was from Georgia.

She told me that her sister was a civilian employee of Metro and was on the verge of a mental breakdown. Her sister had reported that a detective – who of all things investigated sexual assaults – had been molesting a young boy. She had reported this crime to my predecessor; however, nothing was done to remedy this disgusting conduct. Her sister believed that the department had covered it up. I collected the information about her sister. Before I hung up she said that her sister was excited that I was in charge of IAB because I was a Christian.

I called Allison and told her that I might have to work late again, and we may need to take a rain check on that date. She started laughing.

"Why am I not surprised?" she replied. I asked her if she needed me to cancel the reservation.

"I didn't make one," she said, "because I figured you would get tied up at work again."

11

DOING TOO GOOD OF A JOB

I called the number and was happy that it went to an answering machine. "Hi, this is Dan Barry the lieutenant from IAB, and your sister said I should give you a call. Please call back. You are not in any type of trouble. God bless, thanks."

I was hoping that she would wait until Monday to return my call. Unfortunately, I had a pretty strong suspicion that my dinner with Allison was not going to happen. I heard my cell phone ring while driving home and knew who was calling.

The female caller asked if I honestly wanted to hear the truth. She was worried this was just another cover-up and was suspicious of my intentions. I knew from the outset that I needed to earn her trust. I told her I cared about uncovering the truth and was concerned about this young boy. As the conversation progressed I sensed her relief as she began to trust me. I was trying to do the right thing, not just patronize her. During our initial phone conversation, we forged a mutual trust for each other. So she told me her story.

A couple of years ago, she met Steve, a sexual assault detective, and developed a close friendship. As time progressed she started to wonder why their relationship had never become romantic. They were not kids – both were in their 40s – but despite their dates, Steve never made any romantic gestures toward her. She began to think that Steve was most likely gay, so she decided to end their relationship.

When she told Steve it was over, he said that he was not gay, just cautious. So she decided to give him more time. Finally, after one date, Steve asked her to come to his house. She thought that this would be "the night." He was so nervous on the drive to his house that she thought he was just acting like an awkward teenager.

At the front door of his ranch-style home, she was curious as to why Steve did not use his keys. He rang the doorbell.

"Who's in the house?" she asked him.

"A kid I'm watching named Randy."

After a few seconds, the door was opened and a little boy was standing there naked. She described the boy as about ten years old.

Steve was nonchalant when she asked him about Randy. Steve answered that Randy's mother was a crack head and an unfit guardian who allowed him to be sexually assaulted by a male friend of hers. Steve was the detective assigned to the case, and he had become close to Randy and his mother. The mother asked Steve if he could help her watch Randy, because she could not properly care for him. So, Randy began staying at Steve's house.

As for the nudity? Well, Steve said he was a naturalist and insisted she get naked if she wanted to come inside his house. After she refused to disrobe, their romantic relationship ended and Steve drove her home. Even so, she and Steve remained in contact because she was concerned for Randy's welfare.

Randy confided in her that he slept naked with Steve and they massaged each other in bed.

That is when she called IAB to report this activity. But instead of an investigation being launched, she was patronized and in essence told her fears were unfounded. She was told that Steve was a great man, a super detective and was a mentor for Randy. She was notified that the department would not take any action to intervene, and she needed to mind her own business.

Despite her relationship with Steve being over, she felt guilty because this young boy was still being molested and the department had failed to intervene. When she heard that IAB was under new leadership, she hoped justice would be done. I gathered all the important information – who Randy was, who his mother was – and decided that we needed to start an immediate investigation. I contacted Bob, one of my sergeants, and called Allison to confirm that I would not be home for dinner.

Bob and I developed an investigative strategy. As we were discussing this case, we both recalled rumors about Steve that had been circling around Metro for many years. We heard that he may be gay. He was in his late 40s, had never married, nor had he been in a serious relationship with a woman. That had people wondering about his lifestyle. He was a 25-year veteran of Metro and had worked SWAT prior to becoming a sexual assault detective. He was currently assigned to the airport and had been there for just under a year. He had been transferred to the airport immediately after the initial complaint was made.

To say that he was highly regarded within Metro was an understatement. Since he was single and loved the outdoors, he had all the gear that most married guys with kids could only dream about having. I confirmed that he had taken members of Metro leadership on hunting trips at his ranch in Idaho. Most of the rumors began on these hunting trips when he would parade around naked in front of the other hunters. His excuse was always that, because he was a naturalist, being naked was normal. It seems that some people would turn a blind eye, so long as they could ride his ATVs and use his expensive hunting gear.

I decided we would meet with Randy and his mother to introduce ourselves and possibly conduct some interviews. Their apartment was in 'Naked City,' which was the most dangerous part of town. We decided to talk with his mom first, and if we had time, we would talk with Randy. As we walked to the apartment door, I heard some noise and saw a large mutt charging at us. I hit him with a rock and he scampered off. The door to the apartment was wide open. Kathy, Randy's mother, screamed for us to come on inside.

The apartment was a pigsty, and the smell of dog piss permeated the air, making me glad that I had not eaten before the interview. The mother looked as I suspected she would. She was a "Rock-stitute," which meant an admitted prostitute who was hooked on rock cocaine. She was wearing extremely short cutoff jeans, and had a wife beater t-shirt without a bra. She told us that she had to leave in a few minutes to meet some friends. Because of the condition of the apartment and the lack of adult supervision, I told her we would be taking Randy to Child Haven. To my surprise, she was ecstatic. Having Randy at home was like a noose around her neck, she said.

Kathy began by telling us that she was very upset with Steve because he had stopped giving her money. She said that several years ago, her ex-boyfriend had raped Randy. She did not know about it until Randy was taken to child protective services after he told his teacher about the sexual assault. The boyfriend was prosecuted and Randy went with her to the detective bureau. Detective Steve conducted the interview. According to her, Randy immediately bonded with Steve and looked up to him as a male role-model.

After the interview, Steve told her that he wanted to have Randy stay with him for a couple of weekends. He said that Randy needed to be a strong witness, and he wanted to form a close bond with Randy.

She said she told Steve that he could have Randy any time he wanted. It would make her life much easier.

For the next few weeks, Steve had Randy stay over at his house and the two of them became extremely close. Steve would take Randy on hunting trips and bought him an ATV. Every time Steve would drop Randy back home, he would have gifts that his new best friend had purchased for him. Randy was an outstanding witness at the trial and the suspect received a lengthy sentence. After the trial, the relationship continued to grow and Randy and Steve were sleeping naked in the same bed. Steve was also paying the mother to help her out with the bills. The only requirement was that Randy be allowed to spend time with Steve. She said she suspected that something weird was going on, but Randy was getting to live a life that she could not provide for him.

This went on for almost two years.

Then Steve stopped calling and having contact with Randy. But Kathy was accustomed to the extra cash and freedom from Randy. She was upset, so she contacted our department. According to her, this got Steve transferred to the airport. Steve again began having Randy stay with him, but now there were several other kids staying with them. She also told me that she had received a call from Steve this week, and she had yet to return the call. The reality that he attempted to reconnect with her was evidence to me that Steve was afraid she would contact IAB. We ended the interview and I told her we would be back in contact with her.

Then we asked Randy if he wanted to talk with us in the apartment or did he want to go with us to Denny's? He did not hesitate. He requested Denny's and he asked if he could have a strawberry milkshake. We also told him to throw some of his clothes into a bag because we would be taking him to Child Haven. This made him even happier because he would be leaving his Mom's smelly apartment.

Randy was twelve and yet appeared to be a little con man.

Randy spoke about Steve as if he were a 25-year-old woman discussing her soul mate. He sipped his milkshake and told us that he and Steve were in love and that other people were attempting to block their path to happiness. He used terms like, snuggle partners, honey bunny, and other phrases you would not expect to hear from a 12-year-old boy.

Only when he was with Steve was he truly happy, he said. Sleeping naked in bed with Steve was just one part of their relationship. To Randy, it was emotional and physical. Randy's aspiration was to move in with Steve. After taking a few pages of notes, my sergeant and I drove him to Clark County Juvenile Home and booked him into protective custody. I also ensured that the only people who could have contact with Randy were me and Bob.

I drove home that night with a sick feeling in my stomach.

The next week, I enlisted the help of two veteran child sexual assault detectives, Roy Chandler and FBI Agent Roger Young, to help us interview Randy. Both told me that this seemed to be a classic case in that Steve used his position of power to entice a young child for his perverted pleasure. We got Randy to admit masturbating together with Steve while they were naked in bed. Both Roy and Roger told me that in all likelihood there were many other victims, but they doubted if any would ever come forward.

I learned about the demented lifestyle of pedophiles from these experts (Roy and Roger). Pedophiles are attracted to children within a specific age group. In the case of Steve and Randy, the fact was that Randy had matured since the beginning of their relationship which resulted in Randy no longer being sexually attractive to Steve. This reality caused Steve to develop wandering eyes. It is common in many cases for the child who has physically matured to become a recruiter to bring younger kids into this disgusting circle.

As we tried to interview some of the detectives and supervisors in sexual assault, I could not believe their lack of candor and honesty. Most of the supervisors and detectives blamed the child and his mother for allowing Steve access to this young boy. They all said that they knew Steve was a strange bird, and letting him have unlimited contact with Randy was too much for him. I was also stonewalled at the district attorney's office and could only find one individual, District Attorney Scott Mitchell, who had enough integrity to take this to the Grand Jury.

Based on the advice of Roy Chandler, Roger Young, and Scott Mitchell, we decided to do a search warrant on Steve's house first. I was skeptical that we would get any evidence from inside the house because I knew we had many internal and external leaks. I was advised by both Chandler and Young that, because Steve was a true pedophile, important pictures and other such trophies would still be in the house. The fact that I could not trust the sexual assault bureau meant keeping them in the dark. I even used sexual assault to spread misinformation because I knew it was all getting back to Steve. A few days before we were to execute the warrant, I told the sexual assault section that our investigation was over because of Kathy's lack of candor and her drug use.

Integrity Based Policing

The next step was to obtain a warrant. We knew we had probable cause. When the district court judge signed the warrant, she was crying. Nobody enjoyed this case. It just had to be done. To ensure the entry would be tactically sound, I had Steve's own lieutenant call him and tell him he needed to be at the airport in thirty minutes. We were conducting surveillance on his front door from the desert area with our binoculars. Within a couple of minutes, we saw his front door swing open as Steve jumped into his Ford pickup. We had a black and white pull him over a few blocks away from his residence as he was heading to the airport.

Then we confronted him.

I walked up to Steve and told him that we had a search warrant for his residence. Steve did not look at all surprised.

"It's about time," he said.

I took Steve with me, we drove back to his house, and he gave us the key. We recovered many photos of him with young boys in various stages of nudity, and we also recovered numerous love diaries of his sick relationships with many young boys. After we finished serving the warrant, we decided to not arrest Steve, but encouraged him to contact a defense attorney.

The next day, Steve resigned. After his resignation, we submitted the criminal case to the Clark County Grand Jury. He was convicted of a lesser charge and served just thirty days in the Clark County Detention Center.

But we weren't done. Next, we started the internal investigation of the cover-up.

We had to interview several members of the executive staff. We knew that the sheriff and undersheriff were not happy, although they did not stop the interviews. The reality is that people say they are in favor of complete accountability and transparency until it hits too close to home. I started to notice obstacles. I thought back to my first day in IAB, when Sergeant Larry Spinosa told me the secret to success in IAB is, "Do a good job, but make sure it's not too good of a job."

During the child molestation investigation, it was obvious that

Doing Too Good of a Job

Steve's entire chain of command either had strong suspicions, or knew for a fact that Steve was a pedophile and made the decision to conceal it. Steve had been involved in his criminal and perverted conduct for many years, but nobody wanted to confront it. Steve was good at his job and personally well-liked, and all of his young male victims had inadequate parents. It made them vulnerable. Finally, Steve had juice (favor) with many members of the executive staff and with the district attorney's office, making it difficult to shed light on his actions. While I still believe that Steve should have been sentenced to a much lengthier prison term, I was at least satisfied that he was convicted and that he resigned from Metro and moved out of Nevada.

Sadly, the members of sexual assault involved in the cover-up were not disciplined. This was no surprise to me after the vice incident. In fact, people both inside and outside his chain of command that covered up his crime received no discipline. The only person who sought to conduct an honest investigation, a sergeant, was kicked out of the detail as soon as his superiors became aware of his intentions. This wasn't just a case of turning a blind eye. Some people were actually playing an active part in keeping it quiet.

After this disgusting case, I realized that some members of the executive staff were afraid that they could not control our investigations. While some of Metro's top staff applauded us for holding vice, narcotics, and the detective bureau accountable, they were also afraid that the next door we might be knocking on would be theirs. After Steve was charged criminally, several people I had always liked were upset with me for going after Steve, and said they thought the kid and his Mom were the real culprits! I couldn't understand their rationale, and realized our organizational soundness was in dire need of an overhaul.

This investigation took its toll on me, too. My effort at work was bleeding into my home life. I was so busy that I had stopped coaching and Allison was the one driving the kids all over town. Even when I was home, my mind was often still at work. I found myself drinking more. The stress of being the IAB Commander was well known within our department and typically it was only a two-year assignment. I had just finished my second year. But I knew I would stay until Sheriff Alexander retired, which was still eighteen months away. Still, I was starting to think this was the time for me to transfer out of IAB to save my family and career.

The pressure I was feeling was not from the cases we were investigating. It was from the unhealthy work environment that rewarded supervisors who looked the other way. I knew that, at best, IAB was seen by the executive staff as a necessary evil. If they had been committed to reform, they would not have allowed supervisors who covered up misconduct to go unpunished.

Fortunately, I had a great team and our mission was going after the truth.

I was meeting with the sheriff and undersheriff in one of our weekly meetings, when something changed my thinking.

"I'm worried about you. Are you okay?" Sheriff Alexander asked.

"Yeah," I said, "it's just starting to piss me off to see all the shit that goes on."

Alexander laughed.

"You're going to go home and take the next week off."

They both told me I needed to remember that my family was the most important thing in life. The sheriff told me that he wanted me to stay until his term was complete, and he appreciated the job I was doing. I left that meeting with a renewed sense of duty and knowing I needed to improve balance in my personal life.

During that week of vacation, I made time to do things with Allison and the kids. We found that holding weekly family meetings was a great way to share information. Every Sunday after Church, we would get donuts and hold our meeting. Everybody had to participate by saying what we were doing well and what needed improvement. For the first couple of meetings, all the kids said that I was always angry. I remember how that hurt to hear, but "out of the mouths of babes come words of wisdom." I found that by prioritizing my family first, my performance at work also improved. I made it a point to be out of the office on time, not just sitting around and doing busy work. I also made it a point to work out every day and cut back on the drinking.

It did not take long for me to begin feeling better and actually having more time to relax. Every day from 11:30 a.m. until about 1:00 p.m., the gym in the basement of city hall was packed with cops working off stress and pumping iron. While lifting weights was great, I always preferred running several miles and getting outside the building. My running buddy was Greg, our homicide lieutenant, and we were also each other's sounding boards. We were both Christians, we shared common values, and this made both of us better.

12

YABBA DABBA DOO!

Working out has always been my way of reducing stress. Besides the physical exercise, during this time it provided an opportunity to talk with other officers of all ranks which seemed to make stress disappear. Inside the gym, everyone spoke from the heart without concern regarding political correctness. It was a form of therapy that made the rest of the day more bearable. One advantage to life back in the 1990s versus today was that we were not slaves to technology as we are now. When a person was out of the office, it meant they would respond after they physically returned to the office. The only device that I carried on me was a pager that would display the number of the party calling me. My secretary knew when I needed to immediately handle something, and when those issues arose, she would call me on the only hard line inside the gym. Everyone in the gym referred to this phone as 'the bat phone.'

My inbox was a very important item. Most of the interoffice communication consisted of small yellow notes that my secretary would fill out and place in my brown metal inbox, strategically positioned on my desk. On most days, my objective was to have my inbox empty before noon and get my daily workout in. Normally, after returning from my workout, I would have several new items in my inbox to deal with. I can still remember the delight I felt when I looked at my inbox and saw it was completely empty. That's when knew I was done for the day. It was similar to the introduction to the "Flintstones" when Fred would slide down the tail of the dinosaur after hearing the pre-historic bird screech.

Back in the 'good old days,' before our world of hyper-dependence on iPhones, Blackberries, and instant messaging, if you called somebody and were told they were out of the office, you would expect a reply only after he or she returned. We all know that in our modern world of technological advancements, saying that someone is not in the office only means you will be put through to his or her cell phone. In the '90s, stepping out of the office meant you could take a breather. This temporary break from stress allowed a person to maintain sanity and improve performance. If you left the office, you could actually relax and get away. In today's world, to unwind you cannot just leave the building -- you need to get out of cell range. I am convinced that the benefits of instantaneous communication have been minimal. I'm equally confident that our immediate-response society has resulted in many early deaths, health problems, early retirements, and other societal maladies.

My workouts are still the best part of the day. Working out is medicine for both the body and the mind.

When I was running or lifting, I was not worried about dealing with idiots or attempting to justify my actions. Besides, during physical exercise it was enjoyable to be able to talk with others in an informal setting. One of my friends, Greg, who was the homicide lieutenant, also worked out during his lunch breaks. Because we were in stressful lieutenant jobs, working out benefited us both psychologically and physically. Another advantage was the fact we were both Christians and these workouts also helped spiritually.

One afternoon, after running five miles, both Greg and I were paged to come up to the undersheriff's office. We were wondering why the undersheriff wanted to see us both at the same time. Greg said, "Maybe he is going tell us we're both fired," and I replied, "I don't think we could be that lucky."

As we walked into his office, I saw Deputy District Attorney Dave Roger, Deputy Chief Dick Marshall and the undersheriff sitting around

Integrity Based Policing

a small wooden conference table. I was thinking, "Maybe one of the homicide detectives got arrested for DUI or beat up his wife." Unfortunately, this problem would be more complicated and would involve the two subjects that I maintained a solid D- average in throughout my high school days: Biology and Chemistry.

Back in the early '90s, DNA was a brand-new technology for law enforcement. Metro only had a handful of people who possessed any level of expertise and they were assigned to our forensic laboratory. Deputy District Attorney Dave Roger was set to begin trial the next week on a murder case in which DNA evidence would be critical for a successful prosecution. In this case, the suspect was accused of killing a prostitute. He then used a large butcher knife to chop her body into small pieces and stuffed her body parts into an old suitcase. The suitcase was found next to a dumpster on East Fremont, behind an old fleabag motel.

The homicide detective wanted DNA extrapolated from the blood and hair inside the suitcase to be compared with the DNA taken from the suspect. The lab director sent only two items (the piece of blood stained clothing and hair found inside the suitcase along with the blood collected from the suspect) to a laboratory in Virginia for DNA analysis. Dave Roger had just learned that the result of the analysis showed that the suspect's blood did not match the DNA on the blood stained clothing and hair inside the suitcase. He was afraid that the jury would believe that someone else may have been involved in this murder.

When he initially read the laboratory report, Dave was baffled and wanted a scientific explanation as to what, exactly, these results meant. Dave contacted our lab and spoke with the director who told him the reason for the confusion was that the victim's blood also needed to be analyzed because it had been mixed with the suspect's blood. She told the deputy district attorney that he needed to subpoena the chemist who actually performed the test, and she could explain the results in front of the jury.

Dave was outraged because he was confident this director had intentionally created the confusion in an effort to make this detective look incompetent. Dave believed that our director knew that by sending only the suspect's blood for comparison, the results would be misleading. Because her relationship with this detective was so putrid, she saw this as an opportunity to make him look stupid. Her personal disdain for the detective resulted in creating major problems for successful prosecution and violated her professional responsibilities. In the early 1990s, these DNA tests often took months to complete, and the trial was set to begin in only a few days. This confusion would postpone the case.

The policy for detectives to obtain DNA was relatively simple. All they had to do was inform the lab director of potential DNA evidence at the crime scene, and because she was the person with the most knowledge, she would make the determination as to which items needed to be tested and send them off. Because DNA was such a new and expensive technology, only the scientists in our lab knew what items were best candidates for testing. Worse yet, the director and the detective hated each other. When the detective asked for testing to be completed in this case, the director knew for a fact that the victim's blood needed to be sent back to obtain an accurate scientific report. Everyone who knew both of them understood that she was just doing exactly what he requested, even though she knew it would lead to an erroneous report, just to make him look stupid.

The undersheriff asked me if I thought we should open an investigation for "neglect of duty" against the lab director. I told him definitely. If police officers cannot trust forensic experts to give us accurate advice, we are in big trouble. I was also confident that this director, who had a PhD, had such a large ego it would be easy to obtain a confession.

I returned to my office and had all the notifications sent. I personally called the director to inform her of the investigation. I had known her for the past several years. It was clear to me that, if she was half as smart as she thought she was, she would be twice as smart as she really was. She thought that all officers, regardless of rank, were complete idiots, or so said all of the employees who worked for her. Her biggest personality flaw was the horrible way in which she treated her own employees. Her lab people were not even allowed to talk with officers unless they told her first. I knew her arrogance would bring her down.

As I suspected, her reaction was extremely patronizing.

During our first conversation, I played up to her inflated ego. I explained that I was confused about her actions, along with many aspects of DNA technology. I wanted her to explain the protocol for DNA testing. She told me that she appreciated my confusion, and she would be happy to educate me. I told her I would schedule her interview in a few weeks, and advised her to obtain an attorney. I also admonished her not to discuss this investigation with anyone. She told me she understood and hung up.

The next week I began calling some of the laboratory chemists in for interviews. They all confirmed what we had suspected – that the director was trying to make this detective look stupid and purposely sabotaged the report. The fact that both the victim's and suspect's blood needed to be sent back for testing was common knowledge. I also learned that this director had been calling people into her office and asking them if I had contacted them and what they said during their interview. When I heard this, I decided to have her placed on administrative leave.

An acting director replaced her until the investigation was complete, and guess what? The work environment in the laboratory immediately improved. The dedicated professionals assigned there were no longer being bullied. I received many phone calls from people assigned to our laboratory thanking me for helping them.

My job was to prove that this director's actions were intentional beyond a "clear and convincing" standard of proof. To do this, I needed to have her admit that she knew that by not sending the victim's blood, the results would be erroneous. Knowing this would create reasonable doubt in the jurors' minds about the suspect's guilt or if he were acting alone. She also knew that to counter this, the state would need to test the victim's blood and have an expert flown in to testify and explain away the original findings. In short, her actions screwed up the whole trial. I needed to make that clear.

Yabba Dabba Doo!

The local media was running the story, and she had retained a prominent defense attorney. The media's slant was that a highly-educated woman with an outstanding reputation was being mistreated by a group of dumb cops. I decided to use the old Colombo strategy and just allow her ego to do the rest.

The Colombo strategy was named after the TV character that solved his crimes by allowing the persons being interviewed to think they were the ones in control. Colombo encouraged suspects to gloat about their brilliance. Suspects unwittingly confessed as they inflated their own ego. In this case, I was fortunate that the scientists were able to make me knowledgeable in the area of DNA, so I knew the protocol. I also reviewed the director's resume with a fine-toothed comb and knew all of her degrees and certifications. The night before the big interview, I felt as I had the night before my promotional test – nervous, but extremely confident.

The interview was set to begin at 10:00 a.m. but I was at my office at 6:00. I had arranged everything in my office to gain a strategic psychological advantage. I had stacks of forensic books and journals on my desk, folders of interviews with other employees, and other items pointing to her guilt spread across my desk. Many of the folders had labels with the names of forensic experts on the front. Some of these experts were not even interviewed, but these props give the interviewer (me) a big psychological edge. The closer it came to the interview, the more my stomach hurt and I was thinking, "I hope I don't get sick." I am a thick-headed Irishman and I did not want to tell anybody how I felt. So, I just sat there and hoped the feeling would go away. After ensuring my office had a major home field advantage, I walked into the reception area.

At about 9:45 a.m. my stomach was hurting so much that I thought I may have gotten food poisoning from breakfast. Everybody was trying to leave me alone that morning because they knew I needed to focus. But Bob noticed that something was wrong.

"Dan, are you okay?" he asked. "You look like shit!" Being totally honest was one of Bob's attributes that I admired the most. I told him my stomach was upset, but I was sure it would go away. I went to the water cooler. I thought a drink might help. My mouth was filled with water when Bob produced two Alka-Seltzer tablets and said "these will help." Without even thinking, I popped those two very large pills in my mouth.

My mouth began to foam immediately and I ran down the hall to the men's room to spit it out.

As I jumped into the hallway, the attorney and the lab director were just stepping in.

"Dan, we can reschedule!" the attorney said. Because I was in no condition to have a discussion with him at that moment, I ran down to the men's room and cleaned myself up. The foam had oozed its way all down my shirt, soaking it and my Tasmanian devil tie. I went back to my office anyway.

"Dan, we can come back tomorrow," the attorney offered again.

"No, let's get this thing over with," I insisted. "I always get like that before important interviews."

That eased my tension and I felt better in a couple of minutes. Enter "Columbo."

I started by apologizing for the confusion, but because this new DNA technology was complicated, I needed her to clarify a few things. I complimented her on her extensive background and asked her to describe the relationship she had with the lead detective in this case.

"I have limited knowledge of him," she said, "because he was only a detective, and I am a civilian director."

This contradicted my other interviews in which I learned that she openly criticized him in front of her staff. So, I asked her about this discrepancy.

"They never should have told you what we spoke about in confidence," she replied. She begrudgingly admitted she thought the detective was a complete asshole, and she believed he had been insubordinate to her on many occasions in the past.

I decided to turn up the heat. I asked her, "Who is the leading expert on DNA in our department?"

"I am the person who has the most knowledge and experience," she replied. So, I told her about my contact with other scientists and what they had said about cross-contamination of blood samples. Most of the scientists said even a novice bench chemist would know that both the victim and suspect's blood samples needed to be sent for comparative analysis with the blood and hair evidence inside the suitcase.

"Was this just a mistake based on your lack of knowledge concerning DNA evidence, or was it intentional?" I asked.

"That detective never requested I send the victim's blood for testing, only the suspect's!" she shouted.

"I guess you just dropped the ball because you don't have the basic knowledge, that without sending the victim's blood, the results could be misleading?" I waited for her answer.

She was getting really upset; angry tears began to flow down her face.

I continued.

"Maybe we just need to enroll you in a basic DNA class at the community college."

After thirty seconds of awkward silence she screamed back, "Of course I knew that the victim's blood needed to also be tested, but why should I help that stupid bastard?!" She went on about his lack of respect and admitted knowing that the test results would be misleading. The interview lasted two hours. When it was over, both the lab director and her attorney could have used some Alka-Seltzer.

She resigned after the investigation was complete.

About this same time, the political season was heating-up. Sheriff Alexander announced that he would not seek another term. Undersheriff Styles, who was thought to be the next in line for sheriff, surprised everyone when he said that he was retiring along with Sheriff Alexander. The election was less than a year away and no viable candidate had stepped forward to take Alexander's place. The only person who even showed interest in filling the position was Mike Jones. I supported Mike because I knew what a great leader he had been as captain at northeast area command. I was confident that Mike was going to be the man to get our department

Integrity Based Policing

on ethically solid ground. I called Mike and offered my complete support.

Mike appreciated my endorsement and congratulated me on our progress in IAB. Mike promised to continue the positive changes and said he would continue to support IAB reforms after winning the election. As a matter of fact, he was planning to have IAB report directly to him to reduce the filtering of information. He told me that the case involving the lab director was an example of the type of work IAB needed to pursue. Even though he was close with the former lab director, he understood that it was the right thing to do. He also told me that he was going to transfer me out of IAB after he was elected because he did not want to burn me out.

That was a great day at work. I had just learned the resignation of the crime laboratory director had been finalized and the acting director had been made permanent. The new director was Linda Kruger, a woman who had the integrity, intelligence, and qualifications needed to take our crime laboratory to a higher plateau. She would encourage her people to work hand-in-hand with all other bureaus and improve the quality of our department's crime laboratory.

I was winding down my last few months in IAB. It seemed my department was starting to move in the right direction. While ethical soundness was still not yet a reality, I thought we were at least heading in the right direction.

I was proud of some of our chief accomplishments during my time in IAB. A major problem when I was first transferred into IAB was that the investigations were taking several months to reach completion. Even after these lengthy investigations, most of the sustained cases were being overturned during the appeal process. We had made major improvements in both the quality and expediency of internal investigations. This was accomplished by improving the morale and getting the right people on my team.

We were completing all internal investigations within thirty days. This reduced stress on everyone involved. Effective discipline must be timely, and having investigations completed in a timely manner meant that the concerned employees could move on. This also meant that everyone in IAB carried a caseload of ten to fifteen cases. We were all working hard, but nobody complained because morale was sky high.

Contrary to the former IAB department, our hard work paid off because none of our cases were overturned during the appeal process. This raised morale throughout our department. Some police administrators will argue that morale is not an important factor. I think that is only because they cannot achieve it. Effective leaders value high morale. An administrator who does not see low morale as a cancer in the organization is like a gambler who thinks as long as he is not gambling away the rent money, he does not have a gambling problem. When people are treated fairly at work, they will produce great results. I am confident that maintaining high morale is not just important. High morale is essential for organizational success.

In August 1993, Allison called me at work to say that her father had just passed away. Allison's Dad, Joseph Gautie, was a World War II fighter pilot and Harvard graduate. He was a great man, and his death at age 73 was unexpected. The undersheriff told me to drop what I was doing and get home. Allison and I flew back to Schenectady, New York for the funeral and I took the week off. When I came back and turned in my vacation slip, the undersheriff tore it up, meaning that the time was not subtracted from my vacation leave.

"You work way too many hours as it is," he told me.

I was optimistic that things would go smoothly during the homestretch of my days in IAB. I anticipated that my remaining time in IAB would be uneventful and I could hand off the torch to another person who would continue to improve our department.

Unfortunately, a phone call in the middle of the night would undercut my plan.

13

NO GOOD DEED GOES UNPUNISHED

Las Vegas is hot. It's in the desert. Surviving our summer heat is probably the most difficult part of adjusting to life in Vegas, but it is well worth the effort.

Staying hydrated and using sun block is just a part of the daily grind for all of us who call Las Vegas "home." The thermometer often hits 110 degrees in the middle of summer, and it stays hot long after the sun goes down. The best strategy is to stay inside air conditioned comfort and only venture outside in the early morning or late evening hours.

One hot Friday evening, I was relaxing by our pool with my family when the ringing phone interrupted the evening's solitude. Allison ran inside to grab the phone. I could tell from the look on her face that it was not good news. Our friend, Mary, was calling to tell us she had just discovered her yellow lab, Lacy, lying on the bottom of her pool. Making matters worse, her husband was in Carson City and she was alone with her five kids. The kids and Mary were frantic and they were afraid to go into their backyard.

I drove to Mary's house, pulled the poor dog out of the pool, wrapped her up in a bed sheet and put her in the back of my SUV. It was about 9:30 p.m. and I asked Mary what she wanted me to do with the body. I was hoping that she was going to have me take the corpse to an animal hospital for cremation. No such luck. Mary asked me to bury the dog in a desert lot her family owned in the extreme southern edge of the valley. After retrieving a pick and a shovel from her garage, along with detailed directions, I was off to take Lacy to her final resting place.

The drive was at least forty-five minutes, most of which was over dirt roads without any signage. When I finally identified a row of mailboxes with Mary's last name, I knew I had located the parcel of land. The spot was in a mountainous area and the lights of the Strip were barely visible. I had to park my SUV in a position to use my high beam headlights as my source of light. After I identified a flat piece of dirt, I began to dig the hole. Making matters worse, I was wearing flip flops, and the ground was as hard as cement. The rocks caused most of my pick strikes to result in sparks flying. I was banging away for over an hour and I was covered in sweat and dirt. The sound of coyotes howling prompted me to keep my .40 Glock within arm's reach. I was almost done when I noticed the Metro helicopter in the desert sky. I assumed they were just on a routine patrol.

After finally digging deep enough, I picked up Lacy and placed her in her grave. I was covering her up and I thought the hard part was over. I was beginning to enjoy the peace and solace of the desert night as the temperature had dropped to the mid-80s. The stars were so plentiful that I wished I had taken my camera. I was totally at ease as I lifted the last few shovelfuls full of dirt to level the ground and cover the grave. Suddenly, I heard a distant siren.

The next thing I knew, two black and whites were shining their spotlights on me and screaming "Show us your hands."

I did. After they recognized me and I explained what I was doing, we all began to laugh. One of the young officers joked, "Gee, lieutenant, you must be having a ruff night."

They told me that the air unit had reported a suspicious situation, and they were sent to check it out. The officers even helped me select a large rock to mark the spot of Lacy's resting place before they went back on patrol.

I drove home, took a shower and could not wait to get into bed. As I dozed off, I was thinking about the events of the day. It was only midnight, but it seemed much later.

It must have been 2:00 a.m. when the phone rang. I was sore and tired that night, and I wrapped the pillow around my head and hoped Allison would not answer it. Then I heard her say, "Just a second. I'll get him."

The dispatcher on the other end of the line informed me that the sergeant in charge of our evidence vault had just committed suicide. Information indicated that he had shot himself in the head while sitting in the cab of his pickup truck. The dispatcher further advised me that several ripped open evidence bags were scattered on the truck's floorboard. It turns out that more than $100,000 in cash had been emptied.

This would only be the tip of the iceberg.

After I arrived at the scene it was obvious that this case would require an extensive investigation before we could determine its magnitude. The stolen money had been impounded for safekeeping. It had been taken from dope dealers. This meant that the cash would never be claimed by a concerned party and would be automatically turned over to the general fund. Dope dealers arrested for trafficking drugs do not file a claim for their money because they cannot legally account for its origin. Because our internal tracking system was almost nonexistent, learning the total amount would be difficult.

One of my sergeants responded with me to the scene, and we would not be home for the next forty-eight hours. Earlier in the day, the decedent had been notified by his lieutenant that he was under investigation for taking extended lunches. It was suspected that this sergeant had a gambling problem, but nobody knew he was stealing money from the vault. We were not only dealing with the tragic death of a veteran sergeant, but also beginning an investigation that could affect the entire criminal justice system in Southern Nevada.

The reality was that many of the employees at the evidence vault knew their sergeant was spending more than two hours at lunch, but said nothing. The day of his suicide, the sergeant was finally confronted by his lieutenant about his alleged misconduct.

No Good Deed Goes Unpunished

During the investigation, we learned that many people had suspicions for months about his conduct, but did not think it would do any good to report it. This lack of trust in their superiors again played a major role in the misconduct being unreported. I thought back about prior cases involving the vice section and sexual assault section, in which the same justification was offered for remaining silent. When somebody finally did speak up, the sergeant was beyond the point of rehabilitation.

The next morning, we searched his home and two storage sheds that he had rented. We also went to the evidence vault, which was in a state of complete disarray. Bags of evidence were torn open with the contents scattered everywhere. Inside the sergeant's office, ripped-open evidence bags covered the carpet. Right away we knew that the amount of money stolen was well over the original estimate. We did not even know where to begin our investigation because everything was in such disorder.

Many department employees volunteered to assist us in organizing the evidence vault. We needed to go through each individual item impounded and make sure it was accounted for. To accomplish this, we needed to create a spread sheet with all the event numbers of everything impounded. We needed to compile a second list of the event numbers on evidence that was possibly stolen or tampered with so we could determine the total amount stolen. This process was laborious, but it needed to be complete and accurate.

We found empty evidence bags in the most unlikely of places – at his home, in the restroom of the evidence vault, in storage sheds, in several department vehicles, and in dumpsters. Evidence was also being stored at an offsite location that our department had vacated several months prior. Instead, it resembled a swap meet. Several employees had keys to this building where items of value were being stacked. There were firearms, cash, narcotics, appliances, electronic equipment, and tools.

At this point we were confident that the deceased sergeant could not have been the only person involved. We highly suspected that other people were involved, too.

After several weeks of painstakingly going through all of the evidence and creating some type of order, we formulated our investigative strategy. My investigators had created a tentative timetable for the interviews, and although it was a time-consuming process, we were making progress. If I had learned anything from my experience, it was to never rush into an investigation without a well-thought-out plan. I was confident this investigation would be lengthy and complex. However I was also confident the truth would surface.

When I received a call from the undersheriff requesting that I brief him on our progress, I was not overly concerned. As I walked into his office, I could see from his facial expression that he was not happy. He told me that I looked as if I had not slept in days. I responded that we all had been working around the clock. I asked him if he wanted the good news or the bad news first. He said, "Tell me the bad news first."

I reported to him that this incident was not pretty. In fact, we were very confident that others were involved in the thefts and still others had to have known it was going on. At this point, we had not identified any specific parties involved; however, we had not begun our interviews.

He asked how I could be confident that others were involved before we talked with them. I told him that because torn evidence bags were laying out in open view throughout the vault I was convinced others knew something was wrong. Even the vehicles that were shared by other employees had empty evidence bags inside.

Also, other employees had spare keys to this supposedly empty off-site location which was being used as a storage facility. This made their involvement a very strong possibility. The undersheriff just buried his face in his hands and asked, "Is there anything more?"

I told him, "Because the vault was in such a complete state of disarray and their chain had been neglectful in their supervision, we need to do an internal investigation to hold them accountable."

The undersheriff asked me what he could do to assist us

with the investigation. I told him that all we needed was some additional clerical help to assist us. I said the good news is that we were making headway, and I was confident the truth would surface.

He told me he needed to make some decisions and would be getting back in touch with me. As I left his office, I sensed that the truth was the last thing he cared about. His only concern seemed to be putting this ugly mess behind him. His voice and demeanor were solemn as if he needed to break some bad news, but did not want to tell me yet.

I had never seen this side of the undersheriff before. I waited at the elevator door and tried to reassure myself that it was just my imagination. The undersheriff was going to ensure that an honest, thorough, and objective investigation would be done. But I could sense during my briefing that he did not like what I was telling him. I thought he might want to take this investigation away from internal affairs.

I was right.

As I was driving home from the office, my cell phone rang. It was the undersheriff. I noticed immediately that his voice was no longer depressed. In fact, he sounded 'chipper.' Because it was less than five minutes since I left his office, I thought he must have received some good news.

"Dan, I decided that you and your guys are just too busy to handle this investigation," he said. "I decided to have Captain Kirk take this case over."

No surprise here. He did not want another major embarrassment. I was sick to my stomach, but I knew that all my arguing would not change anything. I could understand this administration not wanting another 'black eye' so close to the end, but this decision left a sour taste in my mouth. I realized that they knew me well enough to know I was going to unveil the truth. After a few seconds of awkward silence, I responded.

"Whatever you want. You're the boss."

"Dan, don't let this get to you. You've done a great job and we have other fish to fry." He told me to turn all our investigative files over to Captain Kirk. The next day, I handed the case over to Kirk. I knew the truth would never surface and that was exactly what the tower wanted. To nobody's surprise, he completed the investigation within several weeks and exonerated everyone except the deceased sergeant.

I believe that covering up the truth is horrific for any organization because it erodes trust and destroys the organizational soundness. A person's integrity can be measured in what he or she does when nobody is watching. Maybe our department manual needed to be replaced by Plato's Republic. In Plato's Republic, a story is told about the Ring of Gyges. This magical ring makes the person wearing it become invisible. The dialogue challenges the reader to determine if such a magical ring truly existed, whether or not an otherwise honest person would behave in an unethical way if he knew that, because he is invisible, his acts and words would never be attributed to him. Unfortunately, the truth is often not considered important.

By now, I could not wait to leave IAB. The reality is that the truth was not as important as public perception and personal agendas. The best policy needs to be focused on uncovering the truth and let the chips fall where they may. Police departments may suffer from a scandal, but it is their response that determines organizational soundness.

The election was only a few months away and I could see the light at the end of the tunnel.

In the race for sheriff, it was starting to look like Mike Jones was a sure bet to be our next sheriff. I was confident that he would be a great sheriff and would be supportive of a strong and independent IAB. I hoped that after Mike took office, things would improve. Mike had developed a reputation for being a people person, and it was anticipated he would bring about positive change in our department.

A few weeks before the election, I received a phone call from a supervisor in personnel. She told me that copies of the written test for the lieutenant's examination had been compromised by one of the clerks. The written test was scheduled for the following Saturday morning, just two days away. I jumped in my car and drove over to personnel. The supervisor who contacted me said that we had a serious breach of confidentiality. After I learned the facts, I agreed with her assessment.

A female clerk had downloaded the test and made copies of it. We had no idea what she did with the copies or if she handed them out to friends scheduled to take the examination in two days. We had no way of determining how many of the candidates might have been given a copy of the examination. We also could not simply change the questions. Civil service rules required this test be given as written and approved by the civil service board. It was obvious that to ensure integrity of the process we needed to postpone the examination and rewrite the questions. The civilian director was adamant that this was too much work.

Because Mike was still the deputy chief over personnel, I called him to discuss the need to postpone the test. We met at a Winchell's near his campaign headquarters. He agreed to postpone, thanking me and saying, "This is a no brainer. We need to postpone the test."

I drove the five minutes back to my office and discovered that Mike had changed his mind. The test was going ahead as scheduled. I guess, after I left, Mike spoke with the civilian director who pleaded with him about not changing anything. That was my first indicator that the positive change we prayed for was not going to be a reality anytime soon.

As anticipated, Mike won the election by a landslide. When he announced his executive staff, people began scratching their heads. He announced his selection for undersheriff would be Dick Marshall. Another big surprise was that Captain Kirk was being promoted to deputy chief. I knew that any chance for positive reform was dead.

Rumors began to circulate throughout the department about the organizational changes that the Jones administration was going to implement. One of these rumors was that IAB was going to be assigned under a deputy chief. This was in complete contradiction to the reform that Mike and I had spoken about. I went to talk with Marshall about this, and he would not even consider changing his decision. After about an hour I realized that I was getting nowhere fast and left. It was clear that he was still upset with me because I wanted to do an honest and legitimate investigation of the evidence vault. Fortunately for him, he was not held accountable in this incident. Instead, he was promoted to undersheriff.

The next week, I bumped into Mike in the hallway. It was the first time I had seen Mike since he was elected. He shook my hand and asked for a few minutes to chat. He said that he was moving me out of IAB and wanted to thank me for the great changes I had made. He asked for my opinion about having IAB report to a deputy chief. I told him it was a bad idea. It would result in more cover-ups and lack of integrity. He smiled and said that is exactly how he felt. He said that IAB would report directly to him to keep it heading in the right direction. I left his office and was very happy. Maybe things would get better. This decision did not sit well with the incoming undersheriff, however.

Mike decided to follow my advice and have IAB report directly to his office. Because of this, I received many congratulatory calls. I also had calls from people who told me that I had damaged my career. It was too late to worry about winning a popularity contest. I thought about the advice my father gave me when I first took over internal affairs. He said, "As long as you can look in the mirror and know you've done the right thing, you have nothing to worry about."

Toward the end of my tenure at IAB, I could sense the tension between incoming members of the executive staff and me. I even called Marshall to let him know that Mike was the one who asked me about where IAB should report in the chain of command. I was trying to keep communication clear, but I knew pay back was coming.

My new job threw me to the dogs.

That is, my new position was lieutenant in charge of the resident and canine sections. This was a dream job compared with the last one. My new position didn't require me to micro-manage, because all of my officers and sergeants had seniority. The best part was that my deputy chief was Mike Hawkins.

On my last day at IAB, I spoke with the incoming lieutenant, Randy Whitney. We laughed and reminisced about how he guided me through the Bob Samuels fiasco. I was confident that by having IAB reporting directly to the sheriff, things would continue to improve. Randy had confidence in Mike Jones, but worried about some of the bozos he picked for his executive staff. I was relieved that I was leaving IAB in skilled hands; however, I was still worried about organizational soundness.

Transferring from IAB commander to the resident/canine section, was like going from piloting a fighter jet to paddling a canoe. The pace was so much slower that I thought I must be missing something. Most of my time was spent driving to meetings all over the county. My new captain, Billy Elders, and I would meet on a weekly basis. I was out of the loop of the daily operations of the major events taking place. But this transfer was a major break for my family.

I had sacrificed being actively involved in my kids' lives during my time in IAB, so this was a needed move. I had plenty of time to be with my kids. Being able to see the kids and reengage with them was tremendous. All four were attending Saint Francis De Sales School, and this allowed me to volunteer there. I was involved with Adopt a Cop, which was a program similar to DARE, where I actually taught several classes and walked around the campus regularly. Being in charge of canine was also great because I had annual canine demonstrations for the kids' classes. While my children sometimes complained about having their dad in their classrooms, they were excited whenever we did a canine show.

I always enjoyed teaching in Catholic schools because I could discuss the importance of being Christ-centered, as opposed to being politically correct. While people love to hear all the exciting "stick and whistle stuff," they also need to hear about how survival is only possible through a powerful spiritual connection with Jesus Christ.

Integrity Based Policing

It had only been a few months, and things at Metro were already sailing off in the wrong direction. Sheriff Mike Jones reversed his decision to have IAB report to him and instead had it report to a deputy chief. His official excuse was that he did not have the time, but he really just wanted plausible deniability. My mentor and replacement, Randy, had retired because he was not getting the support. Obviously, the flip flop on having IAB report to a deputy chief was a factor in his decision to leave.

Randy had attempted to run IAB just as I had. Sadly, he did not have any support from the new sheriff. All of the progress that had been made to improve IAB over the past three years was over. The new mantra seemed to be "plausible deniability always trumps organizational soundness." The deputy chief and others could fire up the spin cycle before the sheriff needed to get involved.

While this made the sheriff's life easier, it proved toxic to organizational soundness. It would be as if a brain surgeon asked nurses to close the incision and put a clean bandage on the patient before the doctor examined him. While the surgeon will keep his or her hands clean, this does nothing to remove the tumor that is growing beneath the bandage. Any hope that I had for this new administration to be successful was gone.

My new section was running smoothly. I had the best lieutenant job in the department. Most days were spent meeting with community members from rural communities in the morning and attending K9 demonstrations in the afternoon. I also had great officers and sergeants committed to community policing.

The resident section was divided into three separate areas. Each area was commanded by a sergeant and consisted of six to eight officers, depending on the size and population of the area. The Overton area included Overton, Logandale, and Moapa. The Mount Charleston area consisted of Mount Charleston and Indian Springs. The busiest area was the Jean area, which encompassed Blue Diamond, Jean, Sandy Valley, and Prim. Several brand new casinos had just been opened in Jean that created a major demand for our services.

No Good Deed Goes Unpunished

The joke around the department was that the resident section had not changed since the Wild West days. The reality was that most of my officers were more like Sheriff Andy of Mayberry, and the rest of our department was a different world. To be assigned to the resident section, officers needed to live in the community they served. They were known on a first name basis by the citizens in their communities, both good and bad. They also received 20% additional pay because of the job's challenges. This made being assigned as a resident officer a prestigious and rewarding career path.

What I loved most about the resident section was that it was truly community policing. My officers would know when Mr. and Mrs. Jones were having health problems and make sure that they stopped by and checked on them. They would also know when some new troublemaker moved into town. They would ensure that the troublemaker knew about the difference between living in a small town and living in a big city. In most cases, the troublemaker would move back to the big city after a few heart-to-heart talks. The crime rate in the resident area was so low that many people claimed we had too many officers. The reason crime was low was that we had seasoned officers who practiced true community-oriented policing.

My biggest challenge was posed by the economic boom. Casinos were spreading out all along I-15 south to the California border. Casinos and quiet communities did not mix. While residents of towns like Sandy Valley were used to having their resident officers patrolling their streets, officers now were often assigned to calls at one of the large casinos. This created pressure from many of the locals. We had numerous town hall meetings to ensure the citizens knew that we were still committed to protecting and serving them in these rural communities.

The county commissioners, who had never concerned themselves with the resident area before, were showing a keen interest now because of the influx of cash from new casinos. The economy was in full throttle, and everyone thought that the entire I-15 would

Integrity Based Policing

soon be an extension of the Las Vegas Strip. Commissioner Erin Kenny previously did not care about the citizens of Sandy Valley, but was now concerned about their welfare. She wanted to placate the new casinos -- certainly not the people who lived there. After all, these folks were low income and not politically active.

Fortunately, I had one of the best sergeants I have ever worked with assigned to this area: Sergeant Greg Weeks. Greg was an intelligent and a gifted communicator. He had been telling me how Erin Kenny had been blaming Metro for all the problems in the area. Greg thought it was funny because he knew the people in the area and they hated Commissioner Kenny. Because Greg and I knew what the community thought of Kenny, we were not concerned about her big mouth.

One afternoon, I received a call from Captain Billy Elders who spoke to me about working with Commissioner Kenny and her staff to improve our relationship. He suggested that I have Sergeant Weeks take Kenny's liaison for ride-alongs to mend any hard feelings. I laughed to myself and told Billy that I would think about it. I never even mentioned the suggestion to Greg, and I thought that would be the end of it. I knew that Greg and his team had such a positive relationship with the citizens that he did not need to be chauffeuring Kenny's liaison around.

Erin Kenny's liaison was an older lady who never wasted money on her appearance. She was over six feet tall and must have been pushing 300 pounds. It was a common joke that when she came into town, the locals hid all their cattle! Personally, she was friendly enough, but it was obvious that she was an Erin Kenny supporter and hated the police.

One Wednesday night, Billy called me in a panic and said that we needed to be at a citizens' forum the next week. He said that he had learned that Kenny's office had set up this meeting to show how Metro was not serving the community. We had to be at the meeting at the Nevada Landing on Friday.

"Sure, I'll be there," I told Billy, "but I don't think it's a good idea to have Greg Weeks attend." I told him that I had followed his advice and had Greg take the liaison on several ride-alongs. Unbeknownst to me, Greg, who was single, and this liaison had begun an erotic affair. Once Greg broke it off, they could not stand to be in the same room together. Billy started laughing.

"Quit fuckin' with me. Just make sure you and Weeks are at that meeting."

I never told Greg about the joke I pulled on Billy concerning him and this fictitious fling.

That Friday the meeting place was packed with citizens from Sandy Valley and Good Springs. The meeting began with the Clark County people claiming how much they cared for the people of the area, but that Metro wasn't doing enough. Both Billy and I spoke for several minutes about the department's commitment to the area and the need to keep working together. Then, I called Greg to the microphone and for the next forty-five minutes, he dismantled everything that the county had been telling residents. He was like a rock star and the entire room was on their feet applauding him and our department. Erin Kenny and her liaison hid their faces and slipped out of the meeting room.

As Greg was winding down, Billy and I were smiling in the back of the room. Greg finished his oratory and walked back to join us amidst a standing ovation. As Greg reached Billy and me, Billy shook his hand and said "Great job!" As the last of the citizens were talking, Billy looked at Greg and me.

"Kenny's liaison is a real knockout!"

Greg did not miss a beat.

"She's not much to look at, but she sucks a mean dick!"

Billy turned purple, began spitting out his mouthful of coffee and began screaming, "You've got to be fuckin' me! You didn't, did you?"

Both Greg and I were busting up laughing and I never even mentioned to Greg what I told Billy about the week before.

It is that kind of humor that has been a stress reliever for me. It is equally important that you must be able to take a prank as well as give one. When this is not true, the supervisor will lose credibility with his or her people. After it was over, Billy kept telling Greg and me that we had gotten a good one over on him.

I was enjoying being in this new position that allowed me time to slow down and work with my people and the citizens in the outlying communities. My deputy chief was Mike Hawkins. Mike was a war hero in Vietnam, and he continued his warrior ethos throughout his career as a policeman. Mike had experience in all facets of police work – patrol, undercover and investigative. He was one of those men nobody expected to be wearing deputy chief stars. He was a man of complete honesty and was the quintessential "cop's cop." I enjoyed talking with him and knew that he would give me good solid advice.

My new assignment was also great for my family. I was home every night for dinner and played an active part in my kids' lives. Allison and I were taking Elizabeth trick-or-treating one Halloween when Elizabeth was seven. That night she was dressed up as a princess. Elizabeth asked Allison to feel a small lump she had on the side of her neck. I could tell immediately that Allison did not like what she felt. Allison asked her how long she had the lump.

Since kindergarten, Elizabeth told her.

At first, we assumed it was swollen glands. After a week with it not changing, we decide to have it checked by a doctor. I was concerned, but not overly, thinking it was probably nothing. However, the family did go into our heavy prayer mode.

I was doing my best to keep it light with my sense of humor at the doctor's office. We sat there quietly in the waiting room. I was a wreck on the inside. In the examination room, Elizabeth took a seat in a large chair that looked like one you would see in the dentist's office. The doctor asked us a few questions and felt her neck.

He did not like what he felt either.

He told us it was a mixed cell tumor and that it was very unusual for a child her age. He said that there was about an 80% chance it was benign, but she would need more tests. He said he would schedule a needle biopsy and then would schedule surgery to remove it during Christmas break. Elizabeth, Allison, and I were all basket cases after this appointment and couldn't wait to put this thing behind us.

I called Billy Elders and explained the situation. He was extremely supportive and told me not to worry. He promised he would cover anything I needed and to just focus on my family. Words cannot express how much that means to you when you are going through an ordeal like that. The needle biopsy was completely benign, but they did see some shadows on the film. It was decided that the tumor would be removed on December 20th, because this would give Elizabeth time to recuperate before she went back to school.

The surgery went perfectly, and the tumor was completely benign. The danger was that its position was surrounded with facial nerves. Seeing Elizabeth smile and talk after the four-hour surgery was the best Christmas present Allison and I ever received. That Christmas was the best we ever had, and I will never forget the support I received from all my brothers and sisters at Metro. Every year since, December 21st is officially "Binky Day" for our family. It is Elizabeth's special day for the family to give thanks to God for having Elizabeth. Being the baby in the family is something Elizabeth has always used to her advantage, and as her Dad, I would not have it any other way. The fact is, even though she's an adult, happily married and thirty, she still has me wrapped around her little finger.

14

PAYBACK

It was nice having my office several miles from headquarters. This meant that, at least physically, I was removed from all our "top brass." In the resident/K9 section, we were in our own little world. Our section was small and specialized, so the majority of problems within Metro had little impact on us. My sergeants and officers had a wealth of experience and were committed to making a positive difference. Because all resident officers received twenty percent additional pay, they knew they could be transferred out if they were not productive.

I was aware that elsewhere on our department, things were going downhill fast. Two off-duty officers had gunned down a Hispanic gang member and were awaiting trial. Another example of the downward spiral was a sergeant and two young officers who were sitting in the county jail over an incident at the Horseshoe Hotel. Predictably, because internal affairs was reporting to a deputy chief, the spin cycle was operating at full speed. All the positive changes that had been made were now history. Once again, IAB was circling the wagon for the sheriff, as opposed to ensuring organizational soundness.

I decided that the only way to improve things within our department was to get promoted to captain. I knew that I had been transferred into my current assignment for one reason: to keep me far away from executive staff. Ethical lapses rarely come to light when people are afraid to speak the truth. Our organizational culture was shifting in a dangerous direction. Civilians had garnered increased clout over the decision-making process. This shift in power from commissioned officers to civilians decreased morale and polluted our organizational culture. Because the next captain examination was still two years away, I set two goals for myself: graduate from the Federal Bureau of Investigation National Academy and begin working toward my master's degree.

My first challenge was selecting a major for my master's. Many people advised me that criminal justice would be the easiest choice and would help with my career. I disagreed from the beginning. I already had my bachelor's in criminal justice, so perhaps another major would be more advantageous. Others suggested an MBA. While I agreed that it would be a good selection, I believed our agency was overly focused on the business side. We really needed to ensure ethical soundness as a required ingredient in the decision-making process.

I still had a few weeks before the application deadline for graduate school when I bumped into Sergeant Chuck Jones. Chuck had worked with me in narcotics, and we both appreciated the need for ethical reform within our department. He told me about a graduate program at UNLV that he was considering. UNLV was offering a new major, "Ethics and Policy Studies." This was a novel program that concentrated on the importance of maintaining ethical standards when creating policy and making decisions. Chuck and I realized that this would be more beneficial to our department than any other field. Before we officially committed to this major, we met with Dr. Craig Walton, chairperson of the Ethics and Policy Studies Program.

Getting into Doctor Walton's office was not easy. His small office was so cluttered with stacks of academic papers, magazines and books that Chuck and I had to walk sideways and step over mounds of academic journals to even get to our chairs. His secretary lightheartedly said, "Have a seat and Dr. Walton will be here when he gets here. That could mean anywhere from fifteen minutes to an hour. Dr. Walton functions in his own time zone."

Like many scholars, Dr. Walton was not a punctual man. His

mind was filled with big ideas, and playing slave to a wristwatch was not a priority for him. It was half an hour before he strolled in.

He looked like a hybrid between a cowboy and an old NFL linebacker. He had a full head of wavy grey hair and a beard that looked as if it had not frequented a barber shop since President Nixon was in the White House. His brilliance was obvious when he started to speak. He possessed a genuine desire for society to rediscover its ethical soundness, and this became more obvious with every spoken word. After our meeting, my decision was cemented. I would enroll in the ethics and policy studies.

To be accepted into the EPS Program, I had to take the Miller's Analogy Test (MAT). The MAT differed from other entrance examinations and focused on logic and association skills. Dr. Walton said that Chuck and I should do well on this test because of our investigative experience. The next week, Chuck and I completed the Miller's Test and were accepted into the EPS Program. Because the program was created for working adults, classes were on weekday evenings, 7:00 to 10:30 p.m. I needed thirty-three credit hours to graduate. I figured that if I took one class each semester and two during the summer I could finish it in three years. The last nine credits were to complete my thesis and have it approved by the EPS Board of Directors.

The first classes included logic and philosophy. These classes taught students how to construct a valid argument and the vital role philosophy played in creating our democracy. The Founding Fathers used the words of the great philosophers as a roadmap to create the Declaration of Independence and Constitution. The rest of our classes were targeted at the works of great philosophers and how these needed to serve as steppingstones for ethical soundness as we forged ahead in the 21st Century. We spent many classes discussing a contemporary subject and evaluating it from a philosophical frame to measure ethical soundness.

We read Aristotle with the understanding that virtue is a matter of hitting the mean. Extreme actions cease to be good or virtuous. Looking at courage, for example, we can understand that the excess of courage is recklessness and the lack of courage is cowardice. A person who runs into a burning building to rescue a bag of marijuana is considered a reckless fool. On the other hand, if he runs into the same burning building to save a child, he is a hero. This is an example of the "pleasure pain test." It is important to identify the motivation of an act to evaluate its ethical soundness.

Our Constitution and Declaration of Independence called upon the works of Hobbs, Locke, and Mill as the foundation for our democracy. With our fast food mentality driven by desire for immediate gratification and instant pleasure, it is convenient to forget about ethical soundness. Today, media sound bites and political expediency are often the primary driving forces, and we forget to consider ethical soundness.

I was fortunate that my department paid for tuition and books for my master's, but I needed to attend classes and do all the work on my own time. Most of the time, this was not a challenge. I went to class one night each week and did my homework assignments on Saturdays. Some weeks, the projects took more than a day to complete, and this meant cutting back on sleep. Since Chuck and I were taking the same classes, we would always meet beforehand to discuss the upcoming projects. Most classes had six to ten students. If you missed an assignment, everybody knew it.

One week, I was assigned to lead an hour-long discussion on John Stuart Mill's utilitarianism. Unfortunately, three major events unfolded in the rural area that week and I never had time to crack a book. The project was also 20% of our final grade. I told Chuck before our class, I was going to tell Dr. Walton that I was not prepared and let the chips fall where they may.

"Don't say anything," Chuck said. "I'll handle it."

I felt like a school kid hoping that his teacher forgot about last night's homework assignment. My stomach was growling and my palms were sweaty as I pondered how I was going to tell Dr. Walton that I was not prepared. Then I heard Chuck's voice, "Dr. Walton, do you think that our local government officials follow the path of Nicomachean ethics or are they mainly concerned with serving their own self interests?"

At that moment, I knew I had dodged the bullet.

Dr. Walton was a genius and I could see his blue eyes gaze upward as he went into a lengthy dissertation about the lack of ethics in our local government. For the next two hours, he lectured us about the need for improvement in the arena of public policy. As I listened intently, I noticed that our class was almost over. Almost in mid-sentence, Dr. Walton looked at me and apologetically whispered.

"Dan, I am so sorry but we ran out of time," he said. "Will you please give your presentation next week?"

"That'll be fine," I said. After class, I told Chuck that I owed him lunch for pulling that off.

Dr. Walton never held a political office, yet he was an exceptionally powerful man. He was the voice of the people when it came to ethics. He used his razor-sharp intellect to examine public policy issues at all levels. He used his writing skills to explain in layman's terms the ethical soundness, or lack thereof, in relation to local government. I was honored to have had the good fortune of such a graduate school mentor. Nevadans lost a great man and moral warrior the day Dr. Walton passed away. An article from Dr. Walton would make any politician accountable to the public. Since his death, accountability has been agonizingly deficient in the public arena.

After class one night, Dr. Walton pulled me aside and asked if I had given serious thought to the subject of my thesis. I told him that I wanted to examine how police handle misconduct throughout America. He approved and said he could not wait to read it. Dr. Walton cautioned me that he believed this subject would put me at odds with other police executives. I told him that because of my experience in internal affairs, I could not avoid the subject. Within two weeks, I selected a committee of faculty members to participate in reviewing all chapters of my thesis to be titled, "Handling Police Misconduct in an Ethical Way."

About this same time, Deputy Chief Paul Conner, who was my sergeant back during my academy days, asked me if I would be

Payback

interested in attending the Federal Bureau of Investigation National Academy (FBINA). He told me that, in addition to its being great for my career, I could also knock off six credit hours needed for my master's degree.

I told him that I would be honored to attend; however, I needed to check with Allison and the kids first.

Before I officially accepted the invitation to attend the FBINA, I wanted to make sure my family approved. Because our children ranged in age from nine through fifteen and would be out of school the entire eleven weeks of the academy, I knew this would mean more work for Allison. In 1996, we did not have the instant connectivity as we do today with cell phones, texting, Facebook, or email, so being 3,000 miles away was a major challenge for us. As I drove home that night, I was thinking of the best way to advise my family.

Telling Allison and the kids was much easier than I had anticipated. After I explained to them that this experience would help my career and give me a chance to see my parents on weekends, they all agreed that this was something I needed to do. We decided that, as a family, this would be a challenge, but one that would make us stronger.

The captain's examination would be four months after I returned from the FBINA, so I would still have time to prepare.

The hardest part would be spending eleven weeks away from my family. Even though the kids were not babies, the long separation would be hard. Allison and the kids understood that this was a great opportunity for me and fully supported my decision to attend. The only consolation was that my mother and father lived in Myrtle Beach, S.C., and I would be able to see them on weekends. The next morning, I called Deputy Chief Conner and officially accepted the invitation. I still had several months to prepare before I left for the academy.

I received another surprise when I was asked to drive an unmarked car to Quantico and leave it back there for other LVMPD students. The reason for this was that it allowed FBINA attendees to travel and see sights outside the Quantico Marine Corp Base. I was given four days to drive the 3,000 miles and enjoyed the solitude and beautiful sights. Lacking a formal itinerary was great because if I wanted to stop and play tourist, I could. I remember one afternoon when I pulled over to a batting cage in Oklahoma and realized I could no longer hit 80 mph pitches and had to use the 60-mph cage.

The best part of my drive was its restorative value. At this point in my career, I was becoming increasingly distrustful of others and questioned many in my own department. I thought about the reason I became a police officer in the first place and if I had made the right decision. In the class I had attended the day before, Sergeant Hoye proclaimed that "we became police officers because we hated bullies." This seemed even more undeniable as I cruised eastbound on US-40. Without the distractions of everyday life, I recommitted myself to always fighting bullies and said prayers of thanks to God for allowing me to be a part of American Policing. As I pulled off US-95 and entered the Quantico Marine Base, I recommitted myself to the noblest of all professions: policing.

Entering the academy was like entering a high security prison. The academy is on a Marine Corp base, only a short distance from our nation's capital, so even police officers were subject to tight security. This was strange in the pre-9/11 world. However, in a short time, I got used to it and had a great time.

My roommate was from a small town in rural Kentucky, and he drove home every weekend to be with his wife. It never was boring because most of my 250 classmates of the 186th Session formed a close bond. It was a good thing because without email, text messaging or Facebook, my contact with the family was extremely limited. We had one phone on our dormitory floor. It was next to the stairwell so it was always very noisy. I would call home several times each week, but the first few weeks were tough. Most weeks, I would leave the academy on Friday morning after my last class, and drive the eight hours to Myrtle Beach to spend the weekends with Mom and Dad. I would drive back to the academy on Sunday afternoon after church. Those treasured weekends were a gift from God.

The workload was manageable. Normally, I spent a couple of hours after class working on papers and completing assignments. I still had time to work out and toss back a few beers in the board room (the tavern) before going to bed. I took six graduate credits from the University of Virginia, which resulted in an increased workload; however, these classes allowed me to complete my master's degree on schedule.

I made the right decision to attend. I spent quality time with my parents while receiving outstanding training. I also made contacts with police leaders from all over the globe. These relationships remain an important part of my life today. I also realized that despite coming from different backgrounds and parts of the world, we all shared a common brotherhood and disgust for bullies.

Once the academy was over, I could not wait to get back home. I was extremely happy to be with my family and friends again. Right away I learned that things were not going well within Metro. The sheriff had been hiring other civilian experts to further water down the role of commissioned leadership. Sheriff Jones hired a labor relations expert who oversaw the disciplinary process. The organization chart of Metro looked like a Fortune 500 company instead of a police department. IAB went back to being a secret society at the beck and call of executive staff. In coping with the changing organizational culture, I focused on my role in the resident/K9 section and prepped for the upcoming captain's examination. Believe me, it wasn't easy.

My life had many ups and downs.

My master's program increased my knowledge and awareness. Dealing with the lack of ethics in the department brought me down. I realized these poor decisions and policies were signs of ethical decay, not innocent mistakes. I decided that I would never sidestep ethics for popularity with top brass.

An important part of being a leader is holding your people accountable. Part of this means imposing corrective action when it is needed. Since the department had a labor relations director, important disciplinary decisions were being handed off by administrators.

This minimized the important role that commissioned officers played in the disciplinary process. The role of labor relations on paper was only advisory; however, it did not take a rocket scientist to realize that they had become the alpha dog with all disciplinary decisions. Worse yet, labor relations reacted exclusively from a legal framework as opposed to an ethical one.

Another example of the contamination of our organizational culture could be seen in the new role of the Public Information Office (PIO). Historically, the chain of command handled most press releases. They were closer to the events and could give the most accurate and candid responses to the media outlets. At this time, the civilian-run public information office served as another layer between the citizens and their police. This absence of transparency diminishes trust and hampers the partnership between the community and its police.

This paradigm shift began in the late 1990s. The organizational shift in decreasing the power of commissioned officers while increasing the influence of civilians was very gradual. I am reminded of the comic strip with the little boy staring into a goldfish bowl. The little boy asks the goldfish, "Is the water cold? "The fish answers, "What water?" The reality is that when people become accustomed to their surroundings, they accept it as normal.

While many believed these internal changes would not significantly change the level of police service within the community, they were wrong. In fact, this shift dramatically changed the role of police. Because this change in leadership philosophy was subtle, it gradually impacted the organizational culture and the level of service provided by Metro. This change resulted in minimization of the role of all commissioned officers, including the sheriff. As opposed to the powerful sheriffs of the past, we currently have top cops who seek consensus from certain key individuals instead of making decisions based on the public good.

The strong sheriff model is where the sheriff acts as the person who is ultimately responsible and accountable to the citizens. An example of this was the command presence and decisiveness

Payback

Sheriff Lamb showed when he refused to allow members of the Hell's Angels and organized crime families to set foot in Clark County. Other examples can be seen when Sheriff Alexander decided to take back the Strip from the pimps and prostitutes. His decision to put undercover officers in our high schools is another example of this model in action. Tough decisions need to be made in the interest of public safety. A strong sheriff focuses on doing what is right, not winning a popularity contest.

Conversely, with the corporate model, the sheriff seeks consensus for all important decisions. This consensus includes not only executive staff and elected officials, but also the money people. This model lessens public safety and jeopardizes homeland security. Las Vegas is a potential target for terrorism, but the hotel owners on the Strip do not want the public to be afraid to visit. When there is a threat to our valley, representatives from all the power houses collaborate on how best to respond.

This unhealthy influence was especially evident when FEMA scheduled a training exercise in Las Vegas in 2010. It got canceled. Multiple agencies had planned the event for months. Because the Las Vegas Convention and Visitors Authority and Hotel Association protested having the exercise, public safety took a back seat. The public might think the city was a safety risk, they argued. So, they put pressure on Senator Harry Reid and the entire exercise was cancelled. No matter that it would have benefited first responders. The fact that the sheriff is elected and doesn't report to Senator Reid is not a factor.

So much for the safety of Clark County citizens. If the power brokers on Las Vegas Boulevard do not give their blessing, it is not going to happen.

This was the department I was returning to, but I was fortunate to have the best sergeants in our department working with me. They made getting back into the flow of things after the FBI Academy much easier. After a couple of weeks, it was as if I had never left.

I was focused on my master's and beginning to pull references together for my thesis. My committee was in place. They just needed to approve my chapters and they acted to support me, not serve as a barrier. I wanted to truly gain knowledge about ethically handling police misconduct – not just get it done. Besides the academic challenges, I also had to prepare for my captain's examination which was just four-months away.

I was motivated to pass the captain's examination because I wanted to help my department get back to being ethically sound. I believed that I could make a positive difference as a captain. I saw how our administration did not have a clue about organizational soundness. In fact, we were heading in the opposite direction.

I was not traveling this road alone. Many others shared this concern, including my closest mentor, Ted Farrell.

Ted was in his mid-fifties and was a 'real deal' Red Sox fan. He was the smartest person in our department and definitely honest. He was the civilian who oversaw our budget and risk management. He had his master's degree in accounting, and I know that he had wanted to be a commissioned officer. I teased Ted that he was really a police officer trapped inside a civilian's body. He was an Irish Catholic and shared my passion for ethics. We would always discuss the lack of organizational soundness and the critical need for reform.

I respected Ted and I constantly sought his advice. We enjoyed philosophical discussions over lunch or a beer. Ted told me that I needed to be careful because I was known as "a bull in a china shop." He told me, decisions made in IAB, like the evidence vault, vice, intelligence, and the child molester, made members of top brass nervous. Ted and I possessed similar views on the importance of integrity. I believe this is the reason why, despite having superior intelligence and talent, Ted was never a member of the true inner circle.

Ted taught me much about the civilian side of our department. The more he taught me, the more confident I became about finishing near the top of the list on the captain's test. I already had a solid background in the area of tactical operations. In addition to helping me prepare for the test, Ted was also helping me with my thesis preparation. He would challenge me on arguments that others had not even thought about, making my thesis solid.

I finished first on the written examination. That was nice, but it did not matter much. The written was only 15% of our final grade. The remaining 85% would come from the assessment center. The high written score helped because only the top ten scores would be eligible to compete in the assessment center. The assessment center was an examination that put candidates through a series of exercises. Candidates would be graded on the way they handled each exercise and the total from all the exercises would comprise the final grade. Because, all the graders were from different agencies and would discuss their grades with executive staff before submitting them, the process was a sham. While many protested the process because they knew it was imbalanced, we all had to live with it.

Everyone knew staff had private conversations with the raters, but I hoped if I did well enough, I would be in the top four. I had already participated in two previous assessment centers and I knew what I was doing. It had been four years since my IAB days and I just hoped that the harsh feelings with members of the executive staff had dissolved. All I wanted was a fair shot. I remembered advice from when I was a kid boxing in an opponents' hometown: "If you don't knock him out, don't shed tears about losing the decision."

The day of the assessment center went by like a flash. I felt as if everything in the exercises had been part of my preparation materials. I knew I had done well on all six exercises and I believed that I was going to be near the top. During the final interview, I learned that the three raters were all former IAB commanders. I was confident as I left Cashman Field, and felt that I had scored a knockout. Still, I would wait two days before I was notified of my standing.

I was sitting at my desk when I received the call from personnel telling me that I had finished number four. The top three were being promoted immediately after the list was confirmed, and this was a two-year list. That meant I was definitely going to get promoted. I got phone call after phone call congratulating me and telling me I was going to make a great captain. I could relax and just focus on my current assignment while I waited to make captain. I was sure that my days in the penalty box were over and I would be a captain before this list expired.

The next week I went out to lunch with Ted, and he was ecstatic over where I finished. His advice was to lay low for the next year and not stir the pot. This was a great time to work hard on my thesis and also push to get things accomplished in my section. I was not even stressing over the decisions being made by our administration. Work was fun again, and I looked for ways to help our community.

One afternoon, two young officers, Eric Fricker and Kelly Korb, brought me a proposal for a new Mounted Patrol Unit (MPU). Other large departments across the country already had mounted units and our department certainly could benefit from having one, too. A mounted officer can safely maneuver a crowd more easily than twenty officers and makes rescuing an officer in trouble much easier. Selling the Mounted Unit idea to the executive staff was a piece of cake. The MPU became a reality within a month. Deputy Chief Mike Hawkins taught me the importance of collaborating with members of Executive Staff in making this happen so swiftly.

The new MPU would fall under my section. We did not have a budget, so everything we did was through a partnership with the community. Citizens donated horses, equipment, and feed. The county even donated space at Horseman's Park for our new unit. Our first big event would be the National Finals Rodeo (NFR), and we were confident we were going to make a positive impression.

That was the good news. The bad news is that horses a have terrible habit of leaving their droppings in the most obvious places. On our first night of the NFR, we realized we needed somebody with a pooper scooper to follow us. Unfortunately for me, I was the only one without a horse. So, I told the guys that I would handle it. That night was enjoyable and I know all the officers enjoyed seeing me with the pooper scooper.

Payback

I think that all good leaders are constantly in possession of an invisible pooper scooper. We are always cleaning up the messes and putting them neatly into a container, outside the public's view.

Being number one on the captain's list with eighteen months until the list expired was great! I was confident that I was getting promoted and because the rank of captain is the highest commissioned rank, I did not have to worry about taking any more promotional examinations. One captain had already announced he would be retiring within the next year. Time was winding down on my days as a lieutenant. I was excited about finishing my thesis and getting that promotional phone call.

I continued to wait with anticipation. One night, a phone call took the wind out of my sails.

I got a phone call from a friend who told me about a rumor he had heard. Word on the street was that the sheriff would not be promoting me. Instead they were replacing the retiring captain with a civilian. This civilian would become the special project director reporting to Undersheriff Marshall. The undersheriff had a long memory and was going to do whatever he could to ensure he kept me in my place.

I told Allison.

"I knew they were going to pull this," she said. As a couple, I was always the optimist, and she was the realist. She knew that the administration was looking to promote people like themselves – "yes men." She told me that I could not survive in an atmosphere like that so perhaps being a lieutenant was the highest rank I would achieve.

We said some prayers for all the great things God had given us.

On Monday morning, I was at Captain Billy Elders' office at 8:00 a.m. sharp. I asked him if there was any truth to the rumor that I had heard.

"Yeah, Dan," he said sheepishly. "They are fuckin' me, too. They are moving me to vice/narcotics!"

We must have talked for an hour. Most of that time, he was crying about his impending transfer. I knew this was payback for not

Integrity Based Policing

supporting the cover up of the evidence vault investigation, and I told him so. After both of us were through venting, I drove back to my office to figure out a game plan.

It must have been 5:00 p.m. when I got a call from Deputy Chief Hawkins. He was pissed. Billy had called him and told him I was bad mouthing Sheriff Jones. I told him that we needed to meet and discuss this entire conversation in person. We set a meeting for 7:00 a.m. the next morning and agreed Billy would not be there. Before I left the office, I called Billy's cell phone to tell him that I was meeting Chief Hawkins the next morning. I could tell from his shaky voice he was nervous and asked me if I would call him after my meeting with the chief.

The next morning, I waited outside the chief's office for him to arrive. Mike Hawkins was the one person in executive staff I still trusted as both a police officer and a man. I was going to be totally honest with him.

He started off by telling me that Billy told him that I had said that Sheriff Jones was an asshole and I no longer supported him. He also heard that I said the decision to pass me over on the captain's list was payback for my IAB days – that I thought this new civilian position was needed as much as "tits on a bull."

Then, he told me that he always thought I was a team player and was upset because I was crying "sour grapes'" instead of just blindly trusting our sheriff.

I stayed calm.

"Chief, I am going to be honest with you because I respect you." I had never told anyone about the entire evidence vault caper or my other conflicts with the undersheriff because I hoped that these issues were behind us and we could move forward. It was obvious they had not and were still harassing me. I also told him that I didn't know if the sheriff was a part of the decision, or if he was just naïve to the underlying reasons behind this decision.

I was relieved to see that Mike understood when he heard my side of the story. I asked him if he would come with me to talk to the sheriff and confront him with my concerns. Before leaving, he asked me, "What did Billy have to say?"

Payback

I declined to repeat our confidential conversation. We shook hands, and he agreed to come with me to talk with the sheriff. I was glad that Deputy Chief Hawkins was no longer upset with me and I was even happier that I still respected him.

My next move was to call the sheriff's office to arrange a meeting. I purposely never called Billy because I wanted to keep him in suspense. Besides, I knew he would be calling me later in the day. He finally did call me at 5:00 p.m.

"Did you get everything square with Mike?"

I told him that we had cleared up some confusion and he and I were both meeting with the sheriff on Friday morning. He said that he hoped the meeting with Sheriff Jones went well, and he was glad I had spoken with Mike. I knew Billy well enough to know that he was now stressing over what I would tell Sheriff Jones.

On Friday morning, I met the deputy chief at his office and together we took the elevator up to the eighth floor. Mike asked for a minute as he finished something on his computer. After a short time, the sheriff asked why I wanted to speak with him -- as if he did not already know.

When I stated my case, and made an argument for my promotion, Sheriff Jones denied any agenda to pass me over and said he needed to support the desire of his undersheriff. He gave me his word that because the list still had three months before it expired, he would promote me upon the next opening. The reality was that no additional captain openings were anticipated for the next year. In five minutes, the sheriff jumped up, looked at his wristwatch, and said he had an important meeting to attend. Deputy Chief Hawkins and I left the office.

"I really hope you get promoted," Mike said. We shook hands and smacked each other on the back. I went back to my office. I was glad to have met with Sheriff Jones and at least he was put on notice. I was still unsure if he was an active participant in the payback or just naïve.

New Year's Eve was only a few short weeks away and I needed to put this behind me and focus on my next major event – showing off the mounted patrol. I had to prove that this new endeavor was effective. I spent the next few weeks with the MPU and enjoyed getting away from my office to ride horses. I had to ensure that all of the mounts were trained and that none of the riders would be injured. One false move and the new unit would be dead.

On New Year's Eve, the entire event went through without a hitch. The MPU performed brilliantly and even rescued several officers pinned down in the record-setting crowd. The local media loved the MPU and I knew that we had both the public and department support we needed to survive. The Clark County Commissioners requested a report on our new unit's strategic plan. They wanted to know how they could support us financially. I drove home that night knowing that the MPU had definitely hit a grand slam and would become a permanent section. I was happy to have the next day off, but I could not wait to start on the memo to our commissioners. This document would serve as the official document creating our new unit.

The MPU had scored a major victory during its debut, and was now a reality as opposed to an experiment. I was proud of the great job that the mounted unit did during the event and I was excited about moving it forward. My two oldest daughters, Rosie and Caitlyn, were both attending Bishop Gorman High School and driving. My son, Patrick, and youngest daughter, Elizabeth, were still attending Saint Francis De Sales and growing like weeds. It had been only a year since Elizabeth gave us the scare of our lives with that benign tumor, and we thanked God every day for the great result. I realized that Allison and I had much to be thankful for, and in the scheme of things, making captain was not even an issue.

I remembered what my dad told me many times, "Enjoy what you have today, because it'll be over in a flash." I felt guilty about stressing so much about not making captain, and just wanted to enjoy all that God had already given me. As a Catholic, I needed to realize that God is in control, so why sweat the small stuff?

On January 2, 1999, I got to my office early to prepare the memo for the Clark County Commissioners. My secretary, Sharron,

Payback

was at home caring for her sick sons. It was just 10:00 a.m. and I was nearly halfway finished with the report when the phone rang. Usually another staffer would grab the phone when Sharron was out, but this time, I needed a break from working on the report so I answered the call myself. It was the sheriff's secretary.

"Hi Dan," she began, "the sheriff wants to talk with you. Can you hang on for him?"

I held the phone for a couple of minutes, thinking that the sheriff probably wanted to congratulate me for New Year's Eve, or he wanted to see the after-action report I was writing before I sent it to the county commissioners.

"Hi Dan, this is Mike Jones," he said. "I was just informed that Paul Conner has retired to become police chief in Round Rock, Texas. So I'm promoting you to captain and Billy Elders is becoming a deputy chief."

I was in a state of shock and did not even respond.

The sheriff went on to say that because Chief Conner had already left, my promotion date was immediate and I was taking over the downtown area command. I needed to report to my new command and prepare for "first Tuesday" (a local monthly public event) that night at 7:00 p.m. I was in such a state of disbelief that I only told Sheriff Jones thanks, and did not even say good-bye.

It turned out that Deputy Chief Conner, my old sergeant from the academy, had been the leading candidate for this position in Texas for several months. He had kept it a complete secret from everyone at Metro until his appointment was officially announced. All the worrying and stress I had gone through the past few months was for nothing.

God taught me an important lesson about putting my faith in Him, not in people. Matthew 6:34 teaches us, "Therefore do not be anxious for tomorrow, for tomorrow will care for itself. Each day has enough trouble of its own."

I drove to supply and got my captain bars and new badge, and turned in my lieutenant badge. My cell phone was ringing so often that I had to turn it off. Word spread throughout the department so fast that I was afraid Allison would hear about my promotion from somebody else. Allison was teaching that morning at a school less than a quarter mile from my house, so I knew I could talk to her during her lunch break.

Both Pat and Liz were in school so I knew I could not tell them until they got out. Rosie and Caitlyn were both off school that week for Christmas break. Rosie was at her friends' house, and Caitlyn was working her part-time job at a fast food restaurant. I decided I would stop by the restaurant and tell Caitlyn before I went home to tell Allison. I walked into the restaurant and waited for Caitlyn to see my new captain bars. When she saw me, she did not even notice the bars but could tell from the look on my face that I had some good news

"Dad, what's up?" she asked. I pointed to my new bars, and she did not have a clue. I then pointed to my new badge that said "Captain," and she immediately started crying and ran around the counter to give me a hug.

I went home and waited for Allison to arrive. I had left a message on her cell that I needed her to come home because I needed her to sign an important document. As her car pulled into the driveway, I walked out to meet her. She immediately noticed my new bars and screamed, "How did this happen!"

I explained what had transpired, and we both hugged and felt as if a ton of bricks had fallen from our shoulders. I told her that I had a million things to do and would not be home until late because of my "first Tuesday."

The rest of that day was a total blur. Everyone was shaking my hand and smacking me on my back. I called Billy, who was also busy getting ready for his new job. He congratulated me and I congratulated him, and we were both caught totally off guard with these promotions. I was also called by the captain who was taking Billy's old job, wanting to know who I would recommend to take the position I was vacating. I told him that Tom Smitley was the person who could come in and do a great job. The captain agreed and selected Tom to take my place.

The rest of the day was spent getting boxes packed and swapping out offices. I had not even had time to meet with Frank Barker, the captain I was replacing at DTAC, to be briefed on the status of my new command. I knew that I was extremely fortunate to be taking over the busiest area command in our valley. DTAC was a beautiful building that had been the Old 5th Street School. While many said, it was an old building, to me it was an historic building that would house the best area command in the history of Metro.

I was introduced to Annamarie, my new administrative assistant. She had been Paul Conner's secretary for the past several years and was one of the most talented administrative assistants in our department. The two of us worked together moving in boxes and getting our new work areas set up. As I finally sat down behind my desk, I noticed that it was already 6:00 p.m. and first Tuesday was only an hour away. Since, I had been working hard all afternoon, I was lucky my new station had showers and I could clean up before facing the crowd of citizens.

First Tuesday is a monthly event at all of LVMPD's Area Commands. First Tuesdays serve as an opportunity for the public to come inside stations and talk directly with officers of all ranks about the crime and quality of life issues facing their neighborhoods. It was something that Mike Jones began the first week of his new administration, and it was still going strong. At downtown area command, most of the people who regularly attended came mostly for the free food. I could hardly believe what had transpired that day, and could not wait for the meeting to start.

After I had taken a shower and changed into a new uniform, I made a few notes of items to mention as I kicked off the meeting. I had met many of the 120 people assigned to my new command, but I had few names memorized. As I was getting ready to start the meeting, one of my senior lieutenants handed me a note that said, "The speaker from sexual assault will not be attending." I looked out at the audience of about forty people and took a deep breath as the events of that day finally sank in.

That morning, I awoke thinking that being a captain was never going to happen. Little did I know, by the end of the day I would be standing at this podium as the new captain of DTAC. Again, I realized that all the worrying did not accomplish anything. It had been in God's hands all along.

15

THE MAGIC OF TRUST

DTAC was new. It only had been in existence for two years before I took command. Police services before then had been based out of the northeast area command. When DTAC was opened, officers, sergeants, and lieutenants were taken from other area commands. Since other captains selected who was going to staff the new command (DTAC), they selected those they perceived as their weakest links. As such, DTAC was nicknamed "the land of the broken toys." As a newly promoted captain, I could not have been happier to be taking over this gifted group of people.

As I looked out over the packed room, I noticed that most of the people in the audience looked confused. They appeared to be wondering who is this new guy standing at the podium and where is Captain Barker?

"I'm not a Captain Barker impersonator," I began. "My name is Dan Barry and I'm the new guy."

Some of the people in the room started to laugh. That broke the tension and helped me to relax and have fun. I introduced myself and told everyone the presentation that had been scheduled was canceled, so we were going to spend time getting to know one another.

We divided the room into four small groups and made a list of the top five challenges facing the downtown area command. In the final thirty minutes, we compared and contrasted the lists from all four groups, and we ranked the top five challenges. All the groups came up with the same top five challenges facing us – gangs, violent crime, prostitution, narcotics, and the homeless. Even though this list was compiled more than 18 years earlier, I had no doubt that the same problems would lead the list today. After my first "first Tuesday" was over, I stayed around, and talked for a couple of hours. I got home that night after 11:00 p.m. and despite my 16-hour day I was so excited that I could not get to sleep.

My first couple of weeks at DTAC went by in a flash. I was working long hours while rarely taking any breaks, and it was a blast! In truth, DTAC was notorious for always ranking highest in violent crime while possessing the scarcest resources. Even our office furniture was secondhand. The majority of our desks and chairs were donated by other area commands because they had purchased new furniture. Nobody at DTAC cared because morale was high and having a pristine building was not a high priority. At DTAC we cared about people and making our community a safer place to live, even if we were working out of an old building in serious need of a makeover.

During the work day, it was the epicenter of our valley, but after 5:00 p.m. most people went home to other area commands and DTAC was empty. This lack of ownership meant that the DTAC was the area command that nobody cared about. We always had the fewest officers and lacked resources when compared with the other area commands. We needed to increase the sense of pride in the downtown both internally and externally.

On most days, I attended all three briefings (graveyard, day, and swing) and spent a great deal of time going to community events. During my first few weeks while visiting briefings, I would constantly hear how terrible things were at DTAC and how all of our equipment was secondhand. I figured out quickly that this attitude was the driving force behind our low morale. Before we could move forward, we needed to change the belief that DTAC was the "land of the broken toys."

We made positive change by concentrating on our biggest asset

The Magic of Trust

— our people. Having officers and civilians determined to make DTAC the safest command in our valley made my job easy (and a lot of fun!). To accomplish this, I needed to increase trust at DTAC and encourage innovation. Whereas it was commonplace to hear about all the mistakes, little was ever said about all the great things we were doing on a daily basis. I was confident we could turn things around.

We improved the culture of DTAC by shifting our self-perception from "victims" to "victors." The phrase "DTAC Pride" was all over our command. We celebrated our victories. We focused on the positive things we accomplished. It made people take notice.

I remember one series of robberies that occurred when I first started at DTAC. A group of thugs was hitting all over the valley and was growing increasingly violent. During their later crimes, they tied up the victims and pistol whipped them for no apparent reason. I believe they had pulled at least fifteen robberies in all area commands. One night, after a robbery in the southwest part of town, one of my graveyard guys spotted the suspect vehicle driving on US-95 at Charleston several hours after the robbery. After a short pursuit, he took all four of the suspects into custody. One suspect was handcuffed and sitting in the back seat of a patrol car when he was overheard telling his partners, "Damn, I knew we never should have come downtown. Cops in downtown are hardcore!"

This spread like wildfire throughout all of patrol, and fostered healthy competition. Officers from other area commands would brag to my guys about their beautiful spacious stations and their fleet of shiny new vehicles. DTAC men and women began to take pride in working out of a building that should have been condemned and our cars that all had more than 100,000 miles on them. Despite these factors, we were still putting away more criminals than all of the other areas. The other commands were known to DTAC as country clubs, while we were known as the ghetto cops.

All of our significant arrests were proudly displayed in front of the briefing room. Credit was always given to the team and this made all our people closer. The term "DTAC Pride" was not just a

Integrity Based Policing

slogan. It became the reality. Officers were truly proud to be on the DTAC team. Better still, executive staff left us alone. The sheriff and staff were so busy trying to keep all the Strip properties happy, they did not have the time or the inclination to worry about DTAC. Probably our biggest asset, besides our great people, was having Oscar Goodman as mayor.

Mayor Goodman was a former mob attorney prior to getting elected as mayor. Many, including myself, were suspicious about having a man with his background in such a powerful position. History would prove these concerns unfounded, and he became the greatest mayor in the history of Las Vegas. He was already financially independent. He was never concerned about placating special interest groups or prostituting himself to the money machine. Whenever I needed his help, I would call his office and got it immediately. Even though Mayor Goodman was a liberal Democrat and I was a conservative Republican, it did not matter. All we cared about was helping our citizens.

After I had been at DTAC for a couple of weeks, Undersheriff Marshall called me and invited me to lunch. We had a great lunch at Chicago Joe's and discussed topics such as our families and the future of our department. When lunch as over, we had the real talk.

"I guess you know now that I wasn't trying to block your promotion by passing you over," the undersheriff said.

"I was promoted because Paul Conner left our department to become a chief in Round Rock, Texas. It certainly was not because you wanted to make me a captain," I said, "but that's all history now. It's over -- let's move on." We shook hands and went back to work. It's not easy being honest, but I was not going to start playing games at this point in my life.

To make long-term change, we needed to increase Community Oriented Policing (COP) in Downtown. DTAC did have a successful COP team, but we needed to incorporate COP into all squads. Having a close relationship with the mayor and the city council allowed us to accomplish a great many things in a short period. Instead of just arresting our way out of problems, we used the holistic approach by getting citizens involved.

One of our early successes was on East Fremont where prostitution and drug sales had taken over. Certain low rent hotels were actually renting rooms out on an hourly basis to hookers and other nefarious characters. These criminals capered on East Fremont and left the area after they had finished. Because many of these low-life characters did not have cars, they often took the bus. We set up video cameras all over East Fremont and conducted sting operations. Along with many successful arrests and prosecutions, we identified the businesses that were involved in criminal enterprises. With the help of the mayor and the city council, we went after them. In many cases, we were able to criminally prosecute the employees and successfully put them out of business. The best part was watching the fleabag hotels being bulldozed after the city took ownership. Within six months, East Fremont had improved and good citizens were taking back their neighborhood.

Predictably, the criminals moved their operations to different locations in other area commands. Executive staff started to blame DTAC for the increase in crime. Instead of ensuring other area commands were using COP effectively, it was easier to blame DTAC for displacing the criminals. That was fine with me so long as the citizens who worked and lived in DTAC were safe and happy. Unfortunately for our department, Deputy Chief Walt Myer, COP's best champion, had retired to become chief of police in Salem, Oregon. With Chief Myer's retirement, all of executive staff's knowledge of COP went to the great Northwest.

The relationship between Sheriff Jones and the city of Las Vegas was tenuous, at best. Besides Mayor Goodman, another major source of irritation to our sheriff was that Mike McDonald, a former patrol officer, was elected to the city council. Mike had been a hardworking patrolman. He was not intimidated by Jones and would often make public statements about problems within Metro. The sheriff's main focus was on placating the power players on the Strip, which is in Clark County, and this created a major problem. Because DTAC was within the jurisdiction of the city of Las Vegas, Sheriff Jones saw us as a burden.

Integrity Based Policing

Everyone recognized this uneasiness, including my people at DTAC. We took pride in having the lowest crime rate in our valley, despite operating on a shoe-string budget. This tense relationship kept executive staff away from "first Tuesdays." Nobody from executive staff wanted to be seen talking with the mayor or Mike McDonald, or having to explain to the sheriff why they were consorting with the enemy. The local media was acutely aware of this ongoing feud between Jones and McDonald.

Mike McDonald loved seeing his name in the headlines of the Review Journal, and never backed down from a good fight. He would fuel the fire by making comments that sent Jones and his minions into "high speed wobbles." One of these comments came after a reporter inquired about the possibility of him running for sheriff. Mike responded "Why would I want to move down two floors?" This was because his office was on the tenth floor of city hall and the sheriff's office was on the eighth. It also implied that he had more power than the sheriff.

Jones' antagonism made this period of time even more stressful for everybody at DTAC. The mayor and city council were calling me directly to handle issues instead of the sheriff's office. My job now was to act as go-between and ensure that things went smoothly. Mayor Goodman showed his political astuteness by purposely avoiding this dispute.

One afternoon, two of my swing shift officers came into my office with a bombshell of a question.

"Are we going to be joining the new city police or are we remaining on Metro?"

I thought they were joking, but I could tell from the looks on their faces that they were serious. They told me that they had seen Mike McDonald on the afternoon news holding a press conference about deconsolidating the LVMPD. I told them not to worry. I was sure this was just a political ploy that could never happen. After they left my office, I called some people to learn whether or not this was a joke.

It was not.

The Magic of Trust

Councilman McDonald had conducted a study which demonstrated that, while 40% of the LVMPD budget was paid by the city, they were really receiving a much smaller portion of the budget. He had planned to go to the Nevada Legislature and have the LVMPD deconsolidated. This sent shockwaves through the department and the community. Rumors were circulating around the agency that the decision to break up LVMPD was a done deal and that all DTAC would join the new city of Las Vegas Police Department.

I was confident that this was politically motivated, but I was concerned that the putrid relationship between our department and the city could turn this into a reality. My official and personal position was that the LVMPD needed to remain one organization to best serve all citizens. Mayor Goodman was wise enough not to take a public position and was working behind the scenes as a mediator. Politically, this was a genius move. Here was the newly elected mayor acting as the only adult standing in the room and breaking up the fight between Mike Jones and Mike McDonald.

I was busy ensuring that my people at DTAC were not worried about this issue and continued to work hard. I also spoke to citizen groups to explain why deconsolidating our department would be devastating. The community support for Metro was solid, making the break up highly unlikely. I also attended every one of the monthly "meet the mayor" meetings, which showed the public that we were working together.

Many inside Metro thought I was siding with the enemy; however, I knew it was the best thing for our department and the citizens. After several months, the idea was scrapped thanks to public outcry, the effort of Mayor Goodman, and the hardworking officers in DTAC. This resulted in fostering a high trust level between the mayor and me, which served us both well.

After that, many thought that we did not need to worry about the city. In reality, this proved that by working with the mayor and other council members, Metro could improve the service provided to all citizens. The heroes were Mayor Goodman and the hardworking men and women of DTAC who ensured that the people of Las

Vegas benefitted regardless of the political posturing occurring behind the scenes.

The neighborhood located northwest of Sahara and Las Vegas Boulevard was known as "Naked City." It was so dubbed in the '60s when many of the showgirls who worked on the Strip lived there and would often sunbathe in the nude by the pools of the many apartment complexes. Eventually, this once beautiful neighborhood turned into a cesspool of hookers, drug dealers, illegal immigrants, and gang members. It was so dangerous that few people would walk the streets there, even during daylight hours. It was the most dangerous area in our valley, and efforts to improve it were futile. Because this was the most dilapidated section of town, it was also where many of our low-income citizens – including seniors – resided. My plan was to keep a lid on the violence by assigning several two man units, but I will admit, I never expected to have a major impact on this area. It was too far gone.

At a first Tuesday, a sweet little older German lady named Gertie wanted to talk with me. She had lived in Naked City and emigrated to the U.S. from Munich many years ago with her late husband. It was such a beautiful place to live when her husband was alive, she said, but over the last ten years, it had changed into a living hell. She couldn't move because she was living on her husbands' social security check, and it was all she could afford. She babysat, but had to keep the kids inside her tiny one-bedroom apartment because of all the violence on the streets – even in the courtyard of her complex. She pleaded with me to do something; she did not want to end her life living in the prison cell she called her apartment.

I told her that I would visit her the next day and see if we could do something. The next morning, after coffee, I told Lieutenant Curt we needed to check on Gertie to see if we could do anything to help.

Her apartment was in the 100 block of Chicago Avenue. It was nearly 10:30 a.m. as I drove my unmarked Chevy to Gertie's apartment. The drug dealers were already scattering like cockroaches when the lights are turned on. All the block walls were covered with

The Magic of Trust

gang graffiti and junky old cars were parked everywhere. I could smell the garbage and I could see people's eyes peering through their windows at us like dogs locked inside kennels. I noticed that all of the doors and windows were fortified with bars. Her building more closely resembled Indian Springs Prison as opposed to a senior citizen apartment complex. I rang the doorbell several times before we saw Gertie opening the door. As Curt and I waited to be let in, I was wondering what in the world we could do to improve things.

She was excited to see us and gave us each a big hug. Inside the apartment, it was immaculate with pictures of her late husband and family members decorating the walls. The three-beautiful little Hispanic girls Gertie was babysitting were sitting quietly on the couch watching television. She told us about all the shootings and gang fights that had taken place on her street. A young boy she used to watch was killed several weeks ago by a stray bullet fired by a 28th Street gangster at a BNC member. Since then, all the kids in the neighborhood were afraid to venture outside. Gertie did not care about her own safety. She was worried about whose child would be next to die from a stray bullet.

We talked for about an hour. On the way out, I noticed one of the black and white photographs. It was a picture of a beautiful young lady and a handsome soldier.

"Is this you and your husband? "I asked. She told me it was taken before they were married, after her late husband was injured during World War II. I knew we owed it to both Gertie and her late husband to make her life better.

Lieutenant Curt and I had planned to go to lunch at the Golden Nugget. We got into the car, took a deep breath and were quiet for a few minutes. I broke the silence.

"Let's skip lunch." I said. "We have work to do."

"That's exactly what I was thinking," Curt said. "Wow, here's a man who was injured during World War II, and his poor bride can't even go for a walk in her own neighborhood."

I responded that all the good things we had accomplished at

DTAC meant nothing if we could not protect people like Gertie. We went right back to the office and sat down to start on what we initially named the "Gertie Project."

I called several COP cops to come into my office. I was fortunate that one of my COP officers was a retired Army officer named Dan who had worked under General Colin Powell at the Pentagon before joining our department. He was an expert in planning and logistics, and would be the ideal person to develop the detailed plan we would need. I was also lucky to have Officers Eric Fricker and Angelique Dominguez, who both knew all of the key players in Naked City.

The support from other levels of government was tremendous! Mayor Goodman, Councilman McDonald, and Councilman Gary Reece couldn't do enough to help us in this effort. Councilman Reece even allowed us to have a liaison, Suzie Martinez, assigned full-time to ensure it was a collaborative effort. Dr. Pricilla Lopez of the Clark County School District let us have Spanish classes and interpreters at our disposal. These women gave us credibility with the large Hispanic population. This was certainly a team effort--all because Gertie wanted to make things better.

First, we spent hours walking around the neighborhood to learn as much as we could about the people. On the corner of Fairfield and Cleveland, I introduced myself to a man in a wheelchair, Don Damitz. I quickly realized that he was a very powerful man.

Don was a double amputee who had lived in this dangerous neighborhood for over a decade. Despite his physical challenges, he got up early every day and took the bus to volunteer at University Medical Center (UMC). After spending a full day at UMC, Don would sit outside his complex to keep the gang bangers and the drug dealers away. Don and I immediately became friends and spent many hours together discussing ways to make things better.

One afternoon while talking with Don outside his apartment, I saw a small pickup truck park on the curb in front of Don's apartment. An attractive young middle-class white lady popped out with a bag of groceries. I thought, "What is she doing over here? She

The Magic of Trust

must be lost." I was surprised to learn that she was State Legislator Chris Giunchigliani. She routinely stopped by to check on Don's welfare. I introduced myself and warned her to be careful coming to this neighborhood until we had a chance to clean it up. Chris knew the danger, but she cared enough for Don that she was willing to take the risk.

Gertie's project had us going door-to-door to talk with the people who lived in the community. We discovered that the overwhelming majority of the people who lived there had great ideas and only wanted the police to work with them on improving their neighborhood. We warned them that before we would see positive results, we had to get all the gang members and criminals out of the area. They let us use their apartments to do surveillance on suspected criminals. We arrested hundreds of criminals and had them evicted from the neighborhood. We also learned that the people in the neighborhood preferred it to be called "Meadows Village." The term "Naked City" had a negative connotation. The official name of the project was changed from the Gertie Project to the Meadow's Village Initiative.

The Meadow's Village Initiative resulted in numerous apartment complexes being seized under the chronic nuisance laws and being torn down. These buildings were converted to ownership that cared about the tenants' safety and well-being. We partnered with the Crime Free Multi-Housing Program, and as a result, the quality of life improved and the crime level fell. It did not even cost much. Officers at DTAC accomplished this without overtime. Squads voluntarily adjusted their shifts to keep the criminals off guard. The three phases of the plan were: information gathering, saturation enforcement, and maintenance.

The Meadow's Village project was successful because of ownership and trust. Everybody assigned to DTAC took ownership in the neighborhood and did all they could to make it succeed because everyone cared. We cared because we got to know many of the residents as people. They were not just numbers. When the residents became confident we cared for them, they were willing to help us.

Once the relationships were established, a mutual trust developed that was magical. Residents knew we had their backs.

It made our jobs easier.

After a short three months, we were confident we could scale back our presence, allowing them to take back their streets. However, we knew we needed to maintain a strong presence or the neighborhood might regress. We were able to get one of the apartment owners to give us an apartment in the complex. We decided to put a satellite LVMPD office at the donated apartment to complement our normal patrol efforts and to provide a constant presence inside Meadow's Village. This owner was so happy to work with us that he even had it furnished for us.

Near the end of the initiative, I stopped by Gertie's apartment. She was ecstatic about the improvements and even had the bars removed from her windows. She was allowing the children she was babysitting to play outside in the courtyard. She also had started a small garden outside, just as she had when her husband was alive. That was all the payback I needed to justify our efforts. With all our success in Meadow's Village, I still heard complaints about displacing criminals. If I learned anything during my career, it is that success comes only one neighborhood at a time. This project proved that trust is magical and can turn even the most dangerous neighborhood into a safe community.

16

"READY, FIRE, AIM"

Next on my list: completing my thesis.

Things were progressing smoothly at DTAC. I was able to devote more time to finishing my thesis. The toughest part of completing my thesis was not the research or presenting my arguments, it was making sure the final product was in the required format. After my committee had approved it, I had to get it past the "ruler lady." She actually used a ruler to guarantee the borders, margins, columns and spacing met every requirement.

With my abysmal computer skills and ADHD tendencies, this proved to be a monumental task. I was fortunate to have Annamarie as my secretary. She was not only a talented wordsmith, but also an expert in Word Perfect. I decided to pay her to review the 148-page document to make sure it was good enough to get past the "ruler lady." Thanks to Annamarie's hard work, I was able to get it approved on November 15, 1999.

So, my master's was complete and work was going well. Finally, I was able to relax and enjoy being a captain. In the late '90s, being captain was like being a chief of my assigned area. Trust was high all through the department, regardless of rank. In those days seeking advice from a superior was a sign of teamwork, not a sign of being indecisive. I would call my deputy chief on a regular basis to discuss issues. This type of communication resulted in better decisions and fostered innovation. Not every idea resulted in a homerun like

Integrity Based Policing

Meadow Village and East Fremont, but we built upon our mistakes. Under the tenets of COP, I needed to think outside the box and encourage all my people to do likewise.

At one of our weekly meetings, my deputy chief told me that he and several other chiefs had to go to New York City to meet with Chief William Bratton to observe a new process called "COMSTAT." This was a process in which captains needed to report on all crime in their areas to top brass on a weekly basis. Because New York City Police Department had major corruption, as noted in the Mollen Commission Report, COMSTAT was needed for their agency. Fortunately, the LVMPD did not have these problems and we did not need the same prescription. The LVMPD had little in common with the NYPD and to duplicate COMSTAT was a big mistake for our department.

Historically, measuring police effectiveness has always been a serious challenge. How can variables such as fear of crime, crime prevention programs, community satisfaction, youth diversion programs and other vital roles of police be accurately measured? The only quick and easy measurement is examining reported crime.

The Uniform Crime Reports (UCR) serves as the repository for crime statistics. The FBI oversees UCR and departments across the country supply them with the crime statistics within their jurisdictions. Even UCR has its shortcomings. The main problem is that statistics are misleading. Unreported crime and the reclassification of crime make its accuracy highly suspect.

As we saw during the Meadows Village initiative, crime statistics require analysis to be interpreted. Before we began the initiative, reported crime in Meadows Village was high, but stable. Many crimes were reported by a third party who witnessed the crime, but did not live in the area. Most property and violent crime went unreported. Citizens did not report these crimes because they did not trust the police and feared retaliation. A person who became victimized feared the suspects might return to injure them if the crime was reported. Also, most victims did not want to be labeled snitches. If a person was looking to score drugs or get a prostitute

"Ready, Fire, Aim"

and the person was beaten or robbed in the process, calling the police is normally not on his/her short list. There are many other reasons why people do not report crime, and this calls into question the accuracy of crime statistics.

In Meadows Village, crime actually went up when we first gained the community's trust. It was only after we developed trust that citizens began to report crime, which was both predictable and positive. Within the next few months, the numbers decreased drastically and leveled off. This resulted in an honest reduction.

Soon after this, Sheriff Mike Jones decided that we would begin conducting weekly COMSTAT meetings. Some of his original justifications, such as increasing face time between executive staff and area commands, and focusing on crime reduction, seemed reasonable. However, this shift in our organizational philosophy seriously injured our neighborhoods by reducing police and citizen interaction. Before this paradigm shift, focus was on improving the quality of life. After this shift, it became pleasing the sheriff by focusing solely on numbers.

It seemed that the majority of departments across the country sought to replicate what the NYPD was doing with COMSTAT. Unfortunately for the men and women of the LVMPD, this included the LVMPD. Although we would call these Crime Management Meetings (CMS), they were replicas of COMSTAT. In reality, these were nothing more than "dog and pony shows" designed to placate executive staff.

Every week, we highlighted a designated area command and the captain had to give an hour and a half long presentation on all the crime in his or her area. In DTAC, Sunrise and 28th Street, was a haven for violent crime and gang activity. This area was loaded with illegal immigrants and gang members, but reported crime was relatively low. A major reason for the lack of reported crime was fear of retaliation from street gangs. Another major factor was the fear of deportation, since the majority of the population were not living here legally. I spent many hours trying to enlighten executive staff as to why I needed to deploy additional resources to this area.

Obvious in this situation was another example of the dangers of relying solely on crime statistics, resulting in a false sense of confidence. I noticed that during a two-month period, we had only two room burglaries on Fremont Street. I thought this was tremendous. Those security guards must be doing an outstanding job. During a meeting with all security chiefs, I congratulated the chiefs for doing an outstanding job, and they laughed. They told me they were not filing police reports on these crimes because they did not want to wait for our response. I told them that they needed to file these reports because we needed an accurate picture of the crime on Fremont Street. We worked out a plan to ensure that all the crimes were documented. The following reporting period, we had more than 100 room burglaries. Executive staff could not understand why I wanted the 'real' numbers instead of the lower (fictitious) ones.

These meetings took time away from being able to interact with my officers and the citizens. Preparation normally took up to twenty hours, and that is not counting the additional workload on my lieutenants, sergeants, and officers. Preparing for these meetings took face time away from the neighborhoods. Using statistics as the sole measurement was a set-back and it is still hurting our neighborhoods today.

Street cops noticed the change right away. Things got worse. Top brass thought things were getting better. I remember during one of my presentations, fourteen robberies showed up at the intersection of Main and Carson during a 28-day-period. I knew these were from homeless people getting into fisticuffs and taking bottles of booze inside a homeless encampment. We took these reports because we were measuring the homeless problem in DTAC. I briefly mentioned this and moved on to a more serious problem we were having concerning gang violence in the area of 28th and Sunrise.

The sheriff was upset and demanded I immediately assign officers to combat this imaginary crime spree. I reiterated these events were not a crime series, and we needed to focus on the 28th and Sunrise Area. I was then ordered to schedule additional officers to combat these robberies. Following this order, we did several

"Ready, Fire, Aim"

directed patrols without any results. The area of 28th and Sunrise had numerous shootings, including a homicide. During the next few CMS meetings, executive staff kept their "peanut gallery comments" to themselves.

After several months, the success in Meadows Village was remaining constant. I had one officer assigned to the satellite office in addition to our normal patrol, and I envisioned keeping this level for another six months. Several staff members began to ask me about shutting down our satellite office and transferring the officer to a regular patrol squad. I was adamant about keeping the satellite open and told them it was necessary to ensure the area did not relapse.

The only positive that resulted from CMS meetings was the comic relief it provided for all the non-Kool-Aid members in attendance. The funniest part of the weekly CMS meetings was studying the deputy chiefs as they sought to strategically position themselves close to the sheriff. The sheriff would make it a point to sit at different locations and normally would take his seat at the very last-minute. Several deputy chiefs would follow him and seek to take the seat next to his. Watching these non-sanctioned "musical chair" competitions unfold was at least a form of entertainment. Some people would actually bet on the 'brownie of the week.' The scene reminded me of watching nervous high school boys scoping out the prettiest girl in the class, hoping she would sit next to him in the cafeteria.

I had been at DTAC for only eighteen months, but I wanted to escape from all the craziness going on in patrol. Chief Hawkins was over the special operations division, and it was very rare for a new captain to transfer into his division. The coveted bureau was Organized Crime Bureau (OCB). When I learned that the captain of the OCB was retiring at the end of the month, I did not think I had a chance of taking his position.

Of all the six other patrol captains, I was the most junior by several years. I had worked for Mike Hawkins for several years as a lieutenant, but I still did not think I was on the short list to transfer to OCB. After a CMS, Mike asked me if he could talk with me in my office.

He asked if I would be interested in taking over the OCB. I told him absolutely. I loved DTAC but I was sure that our successes would go up in smoke because of this new CMS philosophy.

Then it hit me. I would have to tell my people that I was leaving DTAC. We had accomplished so much during my 18-month tenure. I was confident that being over OCB would allow me to do even more to help DTAC. Besides, the transfer date was still three weeks away and I had time to meet with all squads. They were all sad to see me leave, yet they knew with me over gangs, intelligence and special investigations, DTAC would get the attention they deserved.

At the last city council meeting I attended before leaving DTAC, Mayor Oscar Goodman surprised me with a proclamation from the entire city council and himself. September 6, 2000, was proclaimed as "Captain Dan Barry Day" in the city of Las Vegas. The proclamation noted the low crime rate, the Meadows Village Project, successes dealing with the homeless population and the reduction in gang violence.

My days at DTAC would always be the best days in my career.

My new office was in a brand new lavish building near McCarran Airport. I was impressed. The office was about three times the size of the one I had at DTAC. It was also in an executive complex and surrounded by beautiful landscaping. In my new position, I commanded the Gang Crime Section (GCS), Criminal Intelligence Section (CIS) and Special Investigations Section (SIS). I was extremely comfortable with gangs, but criminal intelligence and special investigations were new to me.

Mickey was the lieutenant over CIS who had been there for several years. He was a solid cop. But he was best friends with Mike Jones and did not conceal this fact. I also had two lieutenants in gangs, both of whom had great reputations and I knew I could rely upon them. My focus would be to ensure all enforcement squads were in targeted gang-infested neighborhoods. Most nights, GCS was using a shotgun approach, simply waiting to be dispatched to

"Ready, Fire, Aim"

shooting calls. We also needed to improve our method of tracking gang members.

Special investigations was the section that I knew the least about going into OCB. The majority of their work was business licensing and reporting their findings to the county commission and city council. My lieutenant was solid, but several of his key people would be retiring soon. This lieutenant was also getting ready to transfer to another assignment. I had two main objectives: succession planning for the key people leaving and improving communication between SIS and CIS. Many major CIS cases are first identified in the paperwork of SIS, specifically those dealing with organized crime profiting through the sex industry.

My major challenge was to ensure that everyone in my bureau, despite dissimilar missions, worked for the common good. In patrol, it does not matter if you are working day shift or graveyard, you still have the same goal: 'put assholes in jail.' But in OCB this was not the case. A detective in CIS working a Ponzi scheme does not care about a gangster slinging dope. I needed to get the message out that we were all in the same bureau and we needed to communicate. I decided to give ethics training to my entire bureau, and mix up different sections.

I created a four-hour lesson plan on ethics, and it was well received. It also gave many of my people the chance to get to know each other. While I was happy in my new position and learning many new things, I was sad to hear that DTAC was going downhill. Even Meadows Village had returned to its prior condition because my successor had immediately shut down the satellite office and moved several COP officers to patrol squads. This was done to conform to the CMS model. I knew that without maintenance, Meadow's Village would return to Naked City in a short period of time.

The best part of being out of patrol? I no longer needed to give CMS presentations, although I still needed to attend them every Wednesday morning. It frustrated me to listen to the new DTAC captain gloat about how great things were going, but I knew otherwise. I thought about Gertie again being locked inside her apartment.

Integrity Based Policing

One of the men I respected most, Ted Farrell, had just retired from Metro. He was the man who helped me survive my time in internal affairs and was still the man I went to when I needed an honest opinion. He was a Christian and also loved philosophy. I went to him for help with my thesis. One afternoon I called Ted to invite him to lunch. We decided to meet at Nikki Lee's on Friday at noon. I could not wait to hear his opinion on some of the issues facing me in my new position.

Ted was already in a booth at Nikki Lee's when I arrived. We talked for about an hour. He was going to the doctor later in the day because he had been experiencing severe headaches and dizzy spells for several weeks. I figured that he was just getting used to his recent retirement. We finished lunch and went on with our day. The devastating news came the next week: Ted had an inoperable brain tumor. He had less than six months to live. I had the privilege of seeing Ted several more times before he went to be home with the Lord. The day he died, I lost a great friend and mentor.

Within a week of Ted's funeral, another one of my mentors passed away. Father Tom Holland was always my spiritual compass and I considered him a part of my family. My only comfort with the passing of these great men was that I had no doubt they were at peace with God. Suffering the two deaths within such a short timeframe taught me that life is precious. I should enjoy every minute.

I had settled into my new routine. On a Thursday afternoon, one of my female CIS detectives walked into my office and told me she wanted to transfer back to patrol. I informed her that the procedure was to submit a transfer request. I would make it happen within the next month as soon as we found her replacement. She gave me a look.

"I want to be back to my old squad by this Saturday,"

I told her, "That isn't going to happen. It will take at least a month to replace your position." She stormed out of my office and waddled down the hallway.

No wonder she was in the middle of her fourth divorce, I thought.

Less than a half hour later, this same detective was back. This

"Ready, Fire, Aim"

time she was holding a large binder, which she plopped down on my desk. She asked me to read it. Then she walked off again. I read the binder, and it was obvious she had been taking copious notes on her squad members' conduct. She had planned to file a diversity complaint, which would allege that her sergeant had made repeated inappropriate comments toward African Americans, Hispanics and gays. The last memo said that if she were not transferred immediately she would hand this complaint to the EEOC Office.

I saved her the trouble of filing the complaint with the EEOC by immediately contacting them and filing it for her.

The investigation took less than a month and the sergeant admitted to making some derogatory comments. The female detective had been involved in a romantic relationship with this sergeant, and made the complaint after he broke up with her. The EEOC director did not like the sergeant, so he was demoted to officer. I could not understand why this newly created office had the power to make this egregious decision. We had a 25-year veteran sergeant who had always been a great cop and leader getting demoted without any prior warning.

Sheriff Jones agreed with the findings, and I was ordered to tell the sergeant that he was being demoted. I decided to advise him of his right to appeal, too. Late in the day, Chief Mike Hawkins called. Mike and I vehemently disagreed with the decision to demote. How could they demote him when he had a stellar record and had never even been warned before? We both said that we would support this sergeant throughout the appeal process and would meet at my office to advise him after our weekly CMS.

This incident signaled a dangerous turning point within our department. On one hand, Deputy Chief Billy Elders and Mike Jones went along with the decision to demote. On the other hand, Mike Hawkins and I along with other senior people disagreed. Mike believed that by blindly obeying the EEOC Board's decision, he was protecting himself. In the end, Sheriff Jones made the choice. It is easier simply to go along than to do the right (ethical) thing.

I experienced a pain in the pit of my stomach. It would be my

Integrity Based Policing

job the next morning to tell the sergeant he was being demoted. Despite his outstanding career and proven leadership, he was no longer going to be a sergeant. I never felt more like a Nazi. At least Mike Hawkins would be there with me. As I pulled into my driveway, I tried to forget about the entire subject and just enjoy the family. At dinner, Allison asked me, "How are things at work?"

"Nothing new, but I can't wait until the weekend."

That night I had a difficult time getting to sleep. It was about midnight when I was finally able to nod off. Unfortunately, around 3:00 a.m. the phone rang. Allison grabbed the phone and I was thinking that this was one of those typical calls – dispatch telling me of a situation I needed to know about: an officer involved shooting, major complaint, or an accident are only three of the possibilities. Allison said, "Excuse me, who is this?" She handed me the phone.

The voice on the other end was an older female who said she was my parents' next door neighbor in Myrtle Beach. The lady advised me that my dad was in the hospital with an ulcer attack. She told me not to worry, and she was sure it was not an emergency. I called the hospital, but could get no information because of privacy laws.

I called my brother Pat. We had both received the same information. My sister, Debby, called from Texas and said that she had learned from the lady who called that my dad had severe stomach pains and my mom had driven him to the nearest hospital to have it checked. We decided to go on as usual, say a few prayers, and we would adjust after we learned more details.

I could not get back to sleep. I decided to head into my office early and prepare for a presentation I was giving at CMS. I said about three Rosaries for my dad. I was confident he would be fine.

At work, I called Pat and Debby several more times, but nobody had heard anything new. I planned to keep calling back to Mom and Dad's throughout the day. I turned my attention back to the unpleasant task of demoting my sergeant after the CMS meeting.

At around 10:15 a.m., my entire body started to shake and I knew Dad was gone.

"Ready, Fire, Aim"

I got up from the crowded CMS meeting and ran out to my car. I then looked down at my pager, and it went off with a 911 on the window. I immediately called Debbie and her daughter, Andrea, answered the phone in hysterics. She could not say any words, but I knew my dad had gone to be with the Lord. Prior to this, I never believed in all those stories about the emotions you experience after a loved one dies. Now I know.

On my drive home, I called my secretary, Annamarie, and told her the news. She was great and told me not to worry about anything but my family. Mike Hawkins called me to express his condolences. Mike had just lost his father several months before, so he knew what I was going through. I called Allison to have her get plane tickets to fly back that night. She told me not to drive, that she would pick me up, but I insisted I was fine. I never broke down until after I was inside my house.

It was Christmas week and the kids were out of school. Rosie and Caitlyn were now junior and senior respectively at Bishop Gorman High School. Pat and Elizabeth were still attending Saint Francis De Sales. They were all upset at home, but knowing my dad was a man of God made us all strong. I began telling the kids that my dad would have wanted to go out fast, just like he did. I realized I had not broken down yet, but I knew that would come. When I spoke to my mom on the phone, the floodgates opened. She was the composed one, telling me that, "Daddy is now with the Lord" and "don't be upset." Allison got tickets for me to fly out on the redeye.

After my brother, Pat, and I arrived in Myrtle Beach, we drove to my mom's house. Once we reunited with Debby and my mom, we learned the details of my dad's final hours on earth. He had gone bowling that night and rolled three of his typical 200 games. When he got home, he told my Mom he thought he was coming down with the flu, so he had a cup of tea and went to bed early. Around 2:30 a.m. he told my Mom he needed to go to the hospital. This was very unusual for my dad, because he never went to the doctor's office. On the 30-minute drive to Georgetown Hospital, my Dad did not talk and was very pale. As my Mom pulled their car to the front of the hospital, my dad immediately walked right into the emergency room. Before going inside, he told my mom, "Call Monsignor Duffy, and tell him I will need somebody to take my place at Mass this Sunday."

My dad walked into the emergency room and never spoke to my mom again.

Mom was busy signing paperwork when the doctor came out and told her that he had suffered a major aneurism, and there was nothing that could be done. When my mom reached his bedside, my dad, Patrick Joseph Barry, had died.

I know that my dad's last words to my mom were a going away present for us all. As Monsignor Duffy said at his funeral, "Any man whose last thoughts are about his church obligations, knows exactly where he's going." Dad's funeral was on Christmas Eve, and my brother and I flew back to Vegas on Christmas Day. In a short six-month period, I had lost my three mentors – Ted Farrell, Father Holland, and my Dad.

Who would I talk to when I needed advice?

Fortunately for me, the next week at work was New Year's Eve, so I was extremely busy. I was responsible for all the intelligence and ensuring the fireworks went off without any issues. In a pre-9/11 world, it was easier than it is today; however it still required 12-hour days during the week before the event. The entire event was uneventful, except for the normal drunk idiots getting into fights.

I heard a rumor that my Deputy Chief Mike Hawkins was going to retire in the next few months. Nobody could even come close to filling his shoes. Deputy Chief Kirk was also retiring to take a lucrative position at a large Strip property.

I remember grasping that our department had lost its sense of direction. The art of policing, which encouraged officers to use sound discretion was being replaced by a set of overly restrictive rules. I also feared that the goalpost was moving. Historically, public service meant serving all citizens regardless of their annual income. It seemed that our new target was aimed at serving the elite and not average people. While many laughed and predicted that we

"Ready, Fire, Aim"

would get back on target after a few months, I was not as confident. It was like going to the range and not thinking about site alignment or trigger control, and then wondering why you did not pass the qualification – Ready, Fire, Aim!

17

OLD YELLA

The main ingredient needed for any successful team is a high level of trust. While a high level of trust was the norm inside both gangs and special investigation sections, in Criminal Intelligence Section (CIS), the opposite was true. The lieutenant over CIS (Micky), was a pleasant guy and a solid cop, but he used his close relationship with the sheriff as a tool to promote himself. The culture in CIS was to keep Sheriff Jones happy instead of serving our citizens. This created a form of mission creep that made the role of CIS mucky. Was their mission to investigate organized crime, or appease the sheriff by targeting his enemies?

The sheriff's biggest nemesis was Councilman Mike McDonald (the former patrol officer) and this made him 'public enemy #1' for CIS. Their major goal was to develop probable cause to open a criminal case against McDonald. Despite all the resources expended to make this happen, a criminal case was never opened. I decided that I would focus my attention on the important work my gangs crimes and special investigations sections were doing to make our streets safer.

During this time, special investigations was investigating corruption involving several of our Clark County Commissioners and the Galardi family. The Galardi family had been identified as being connected with organized crime and were receiving preferential treatment from our county commissioners. Former police officer and ex-County Commissioner Lance Malone was suspected of being the bagman facilitating these illicit activities, and county bureaucrats were obstructing our investigators.

The gang crimes section was busy attempting to put a dent in gang violence, and had partnered with the FBI on a joint investigation directed at a violent street gang known as the Rollin 60s. The Rollin 60s had been terrorizing the northeast portion of Las Vegas for the past several years. Lieutenant Lew Roberts coordinated with our federal partners and determined that by utilizing Racketeer Influenced and Corrupt Organization Act (RICO), we could dismantle this group of thugs. While RICO cases took several years to complete, it was (and still is) the most effective method to obliterate any gang. With attention deficit disorder apparently influencing members of our executive staff, they never supported this endeavor.

Regrettably, the rumors that had been floating for a few months were confirmed when Mike Hawkins called me into his office and confirmed that he was retiring. His replacement would be Billy Elders, and I feared that, with Billy's weak leadership, things would only get worse. Because I tend to be an optimist, I was hoping that Billy might have changed. However, I soon realized that would not be the case. Even before he was officially transferred to the organized crime bureau, Billy was already strategizing how to gain allies.

Prior to Billy's transfer in, we agreed that the CIS lieutenant (Mickey) needed to be transferred, but we realized that we could never transfer him out because of his intimacy with Sheriff Jones. Mickey was there to stay. Billy showed his shrewdness by becoming extremely friendly with Mickey, and therefore getting even closer to Sheriff Jones. Fortunately for me, I never worried about kissing ass. Police work was always too much fun.

One Friday afternoon, Billy, Mickey, and I, were called to the sheriff's office. In his office, we were briefed that the FBI had an informant in San Diego who was providing information about corrupt activity involving several political figures. This informant also said several Clark County Commissioners were receiving payoffs.

Mike ordered us to assist the FBI on this case, but I could see he was nervous. It was obvious from the outset that Mike was not excited about having his department working with the FBI on a caper that could send members of the Clark County Commission to federal prison. The only thing that seemed to pique his interest in "Operation G Sting," was the possibility that Mike McDonald could become one of our targets.

Before leaving the sheriff's office, we decided to assign two of our most experienced detectives to participate in this investigation. Because this investigation was so confidential, we knew we needed detectives with experience and a solid reputation. One of our detectives would be Larry Hanna. Larry was a solid veteran whom I had known for over twenty years. The second detective would be Paul Evans, a man who could also be trusted.

The two FBI Agents (Chris Byers and Joe Dickey) were also solid in my mind and I never doubted they would both keep this confidential and do an excellent job. As months rolled by, it became obvious that Mike McDonald was not going to be a target of this investigation. The reality was that Lance Malone, an employee of Mike Gilardi, was our main target. The two sitting commissioners that we believed to be corrupt were Erin Kenny and Dario Herrio. It seemed that as the potential of criminal culpability of Mike McDonald diminished, so did any interest in this case from Sheriff Mike, Billy Elders, or Mickey.

As months passed by, little activity had taken place on the wire concerning our commissioners. We began to suspect that, because those involved were so suspicious, somebody must have leaked information. Our targets were so paranoid they were changing cell phones on a regular basis. Whatever the reason, it looked as if the San Diego case was solid, but our Las Vegas investigation was barely crawling along. The only targets where probable cause existed that would support indictments were Galardi and Lance Malone. All of our sitting Clark County Commissioners had limited conversations and were extremely guarded with the words they used.

With Rosie and Caitlyn both attending the University of Reno

Old Yella

and Patrick and Liz at Bishop Gorman High School, the reality that time was flying by sank in. Allison and I were making the drive up to Reno on a regular basis, and we were still heavily involved with the activities of Patrick and Liz. The kids were growing up too quickly, and nothing could slow that reality down. Every night, I would attempt to forget about work and just enjoy the family, but that was impossible. It troubled me that our department had shifted away from an environment of trust to a climate where I was suspicious of others. I found myself questioning the motives and integrity of my fellow officers, especially my superiors. Trust had become the exception and certainly not the norm within our agency.

The summer of 2001 was a busy one in the area of gang violence. It seemed that we had gang shootings every night. The good news was that most of our victims were gang members. Probably the funniest incident from that summer was a door kick when my guys hit the wrong door. I received a phone call from a reporter friend, who told me that Channel 13 was going to run a story on the evening news concerning gang officers kicking in the wrong door. Unfortunately, the incident happened on the 4th of July and after the door was kicked, an old mutt hobbled outside the apartment. The elderly lady who resided at the apartment was not at home, and when she returned, she found that her apartment had been boarded up with a note from the LVMPD. She also noted that her 14-year-old dog was missing. After making about five frantic phone calls, I learned that my guys had hit the wrong door and the dog must have slipped out without anyone noticing. The Channel 13 story was set to tape in two hours, so we needed to find the dog and return it to the old lady in a very short time frame.

I grabbed Jimmy, one of my lieutenants in gang crimes, and we drove over to the animal shelter. On the drive, I called the dog's owner and told her we were looking for her dog and asked her for a description. Unfortunately, her recollection was not even close to what the dog actually looked like. She told me the dog looked like a collie and had a red collar with no tags. The only useful clue was that the dog was deaf and blind, and it had great difficulty walking.

Integrity Based Policing

When Jimmy and I got to the shelter, it was packed with dogs and cats--all victims of the commotion of the 4th of July.

I noticed one old dog with a pinkish collar lying in the back of a large kennel. The dog did not look anything like a collie, but the collar could be described as reddish. As I went into the kennel, I called out to it and snapped my fingers, and it became obvious that the dog was deaf and blind. Because we were running out of time, I figured we better hope this is the one. We had to pay about $50 to bail the dog out of doggie jail, and I still did not know if this was our escapee canine. As Jimmy and I drove to her apartment, Jimmy kept singing, "Who Let the Dogs Out." As I pulled in front of her apartment, I saw the Channel 13 news crew already set up. I went up to the door and asked the lady to look at the dog to see if we had the right one. She walked to my car and immediately started crying, "That's my Misty!"

The film crew was already set up, so they asked if I would do a live on-camera interview with the lady and the dog, saying how everything turned out just fine. I gladly accepted and opened my car door for the mutt to jump out. It was obvious that Misty could not lift herself up so I picked her up and carried her inside the apartment. As I was transporting her, she pissed all over my shirt. This happened literally seconds before we went on live television for the interview. Luckily for me, my shirt was bright yellow and nobody saw the piss stain all over my shirt. After the interview, we drove back to our office, and Jimmy and I were laughing so hard that we were both actually crying. Jimmy gave me a new nickname: "Old Yella."

The lack of activity on our wire was making everyone suspicious. While I and others blamed the inactivity on Lance Malone and the other targets being paranoid and switching out phones on a regular basis, I was not sure if some information may have leaked out. To ensure that we minimized the opportunity for information to get out, I normally dealt directly with the detectives and the FBI agents working the case. I was also careful of the types of things I briefed up the chain. The distrust within the organized crime bureau resulted in the most confidential meetings taking place at offsite locations. At least this was good news for Starbucks.

Old Yella

On the morning of September 11, 2001, I had gotten up early to cover for Billy at executive staff briefing, which started at 8:00 a.m. Billy was going on a hunting trip to Alaska for a couple of weeks, and had appointed me as acting chief. I was getting dressed when my son, Patrick, ran into my bedroom and told me, "A plane just flew into one of the Twin Towers!"

At first, I thought it was an MTV prank--until I ran out and looked at the TV. I saw the second plane hit, and any hope I had of this being a sick media prank was over. I ran out and headed to main station for executive briefing. Thinking back, that entire day went by like a big blur. On a personal level, I was afraid because my sister, Debby, had an office in Manhattan and I was worried about her safety.

As I pulled into my parking space at lower-level, Sheriff Jones was still sitting in his truck. I walked with him to the elevator and both of us were anxious. On the ride up to the eighth floor, he took a deep breath and said, "It's time to be a leader."

The manner in which the sheriff acted that grave morning will always be embedded in my mind. The sheriff's conference room was packed with everybody in a state of complete panic. Mike used his deep voice to take control and took complete command. This was the same man I had worked for a decade ago--his actions made everyone focus and ensure that our valley would be safe.

It was decided that I would lead the intelligence operations out of my building. The sheriff even ensured that the FBI and all other agencies were working in unison. He coordinated a joint press conference for all agencies to ensure the public knew they were safe. That entire day was spent on the phone with multiple agencies to establish our unified command. I received a call in the late afternoon that my sister, Debbie, was fine, although she had lost many coworkers in Tower 1. As the horrific events unfolded, I thanked God that Mike Jones was our sheriff that day.

Pulling into my driveway that night after the day of hell, I knew that we were at war and life was never going to be the same. I sat through dinner with Allison, Patrick, and Elizabeth, and tried to make them all feel at ease. Rosie and Caitlyn were safe up at UNR, so I told them, "We have to be thankful everyone in our family is fine." After dinner, we watched as the events were played over and over again. The only solace that day came from the surge in patriotism that seemed to explode. It did not matter what political party, religious group or music you liked. We were all AMERICANS!

The next few weeks at work were spent restructuring our department to ensure the homeland was secure. We decided to divide CIS into two sections: criminal and homeland. Sheriff Jones hosted a meeting for all police chiefs and sheriffs in early October to ensure we had a national unified plan. This meeting included leaders in law enforcement from across America. At this meeting, Mike again showed his ability to command as he told everyone, "Our greatest chance to be successful in homeland security will be a renewed dedication to community oriented policing. That's our greatest defense." I had a renewed respect for Mike and thought, "We may again be heading down the right path--a return to public service."

After several months, our department had adjusted to our new world reality. We formed an entire team of officers with a sergeant assigned to the Joint Terrorism Task Force (JTTF). All officers and civilians were trained on responses to acts of terrorism and the different threat levels. Although things would never return to normal, we could at least get back to policing our community.

The decision was made to move Lieutenant Mickey to take over the homeland section. This decision seemed to make sense because he and the sheriff were inseparable. "Operation G Sting" had taken a back seat for several months, and finally we were able to revive it. A plan was devised to have Lance come to my office for a meeting. Since 9/11, we had a new security policy in our building where all cell phones and pagers needed to be checked in at the front counter. The game plan was to meet with him about loosening some of the county codes concerning strip clubs in response to the economic downturn after 9/11. When Lance would come to our building to meet with me, he would have to check his cell phone in with the receptionist. While Lance was in my office, a new electronic device would be implanted in his phone that would work even when the phone was turned off.

I called Lance, and he was only too happy to come out to talk with me. After he arrived, he gave his phone to our receptionist and walked into my office. We talked for over an hour and the device was implanted. He seemed in high spirits when he left. He retrieved his cell phone and did not seem suspicious. As I saw him drive out of our parking lot, I assumed our plan had worked masterfully. Unfortunately, I was wrong. He drove directly to the Nextel Office and swapped out his phone. The funny part was that the device, which cost thousands of dollars, was gone, and we were back to square one.

Any hope that I had for us moving in the right direction was gone when the sheriff decided to hire an outside consultant. It was obvious that this consultant was only a conduit between all the power players on the Strip so they could have direct access to the sheriff. The first time I saw Rick (the consultant), it was clear that he was a snake oil salesman, and our sheriff was buying it by the barrel. The biggest advantage of having Rick on board was that the sheriff no longer needed to meet with the hotel bosses directly because Rick was his crony.

Mike tried to sell Rick and his team to the department as if they were going to take our department to a new level of excellence. The reality is that they did take us to a new level, but in the wrong direction. As opposed to us reengaging with the community and each other, we were more concerned about spending money on buildings and things.

I remember the first training session we had at DTAC with Rick. He had all of us broken into small work groups making paper airplanes. The saddest part was that, while we sat inside DTAC playing these childish games, less than two blocks away, the owner of a jewelry store and her mother were murdered. If some of the sixty supervisors had been working the streets instead of building paper airplanes, maybe we could have done something. Looking back on

Integrity Based Policing

it, this change in organizational culture began years before. Things like the weekly CMS meetings, hiring a labor relations director, legal counsel, and a civilian public information director, were all designed to create a certain perception and control the message. When you control the message, you control the masses. Unfortunately, organizational integrity and trust are not important to everyone.

Joe Dickey and Larry Hanna came into my office frustrated because our case had flat-lined while the San Diego case was proceeding smoothly. We talked about all the evidence we had confirmed, ensuring that we had several dirty commissioners. For some reason, they were not having many conversations on the wire about their corrupt activity. Larry said, "I wish we could just dump all this shit in their lap and see what happens." At that point, a light bulb went off and we all said, "Why not?" It was decided that I would address the entire Clark County Commission and lay out many of the facts we had showing the widespread corruption.

After Larry, Joe, Paul, and Chris prepared my presentation, we decided that the best way to accomplish this, and still conform to the regulations of the county, was to submit an application with the recorder's office. Because all citizens have the right to present their case to the commissioners during an open zoning meeting, we decided this would be ideal. I went down to the recorder's office in plain clothes, without my badge showing, got in line and completed the necessary paperwork to address the commissioners. I never indicated on the application that I was a captain with the LVMPD.

On the morning of my appearance I was in full LVMPD uniform and as I walked up to the podium, I could see the commissioners squirm in their seats. During my presentation, I told them how LVMPD had already identified Mike and Jack Garlardi as members of organized crime. I said that the commissioners were hampering our efforts to investigate criminal conduct by not approving the travel requests. I also told them about some changes in ownership involving LLCs, which they approved, that were illegal. I also told them that we were suspicious of their relationship with the Garlardi family members and wanted to learn more about these relationships.

Old Yella

As I was speaking, one of the known corrupt commissioners (Herrio) walked out of the room in a huff. Erin Kenny kept trying to interrupt me, and I had to speak over her on several occasions. Kenny being ignorant was not a surprise to me because I knew she was one of our main targets. The only surprise was Commissioner Mary Kincaid-Chauncey, because we had not thought of her as one of our targets. She chastised me, stating that this was not the proper forum. At that moment, it became obvious to me that she was also engaged in criminal activity. Erin Kenny asked me at the end of my presentation, "Are you here as a captain with Metro, or as a private citizen?" I answered her, "Both. As a citizen, I can't tolerate corrupt politicians, and as a captain, I'm paid to investigate them and put them in prison."

As I walked out of the chambers after my presentation, a friend of Erin Kenny's followed me. He told me, "You better be careful. Erin is going to call Sheriff Jones and say that you were disrespectful." I told him, "Go fuck yourself, and tell Erin she's going to federal prison." When I arrived back at my office, everyone was slapping me on the back and thanking me for getting this thing going again. I said, "Believe me, this was fun!"

I had to tell Billy and Mike about my appearance in front of the Clark County Commissioners. I knew I was in a "win-win" situation because neither of them could reprimand me for doing what I did. I also knew they would not be happy. I told Billy that I stirred the pot and the commissioners acted like a group of scared teenagers. He smiled and said, "Be careful of those feds. After they leave, we need to clean up their mess." I never even talked with Sheriff Jones. I'm sure his phone was ringing off the hook. I knew we already had enough wires up to make him guarded in all his conversations.

Following my presentation, the wire fired up and quality cases were made on all of the crooks (Garlardi, Malone, Kenny, Herrio, and Kincaid-Chauncey). I knew that this investigation would make positive changes in local government. Because our corruption case was running smoothly, I was now able to spend more time with my gang section. My gang officers had been firing on all cylinders and were getting guns, drugs, and thugs off our streets on a nightly basis. It was great. Finally, I had time to go out and participate in some operations. The fun part of policing is definitely found out in the field, not sitting behind a desk.

The largest problem we faced in gangs was not having a computer system that would aid us in identifying gang members and their turf. One of my lieutenants contacted LAPD and identified a system known as LAGANG that they had been using for years and which would meet all of our needs. Unfortunately, the startup cost was prohibitive, so this took several years to bring to fruition. The gang section was still relying on the old pin maps common during Prohibition.

As the end of Sheriff Jones' second term came to an end, it was assumed throughout our department, that Mike would seek a third term. As the sheriff's press conference began, he announced he would not be seeking a third term and the silence was deafening. He also said that he was giving his complete support to Billy Elders. People inside Metro were scratching their heads wondering – "What will be our next surprise?" The concern within Metro was the lack of transparency and trust that was hurting morale within the entire department. I still hoped that things were going to improve as we headed into the future. I guess Allison is right – I am an optimist.

18

WEDDING BELLS

By now, it was common knowledge that Mike had positioned himself to land a high paying job in the private sector. Billy Elders was the anointed person to take Jones' place, and had no difficulty getting all the cash he needed for a successful campaign. The strip/political machine was now firing on all cylinders. The major competition for Billy Elders was Randy Oaks, a respected veteran captain. Randy was a strong candidate, but without the Strip machine behind him, he was not a serious contender. Working for Billy during this time was a challenge because I always needed to anticipate his ulterior motives. He did not care about anything unless it might impact his campaign coffers.

One night, my gang section was working together with members of our SWAT team, attempting to track down a murder suspect. This suspect was extremely dangerous and had vowed not to be taken alive. Their manhunt led them to a complex in Meadows Village, which had about ten different studio apartments. After checking several apartments without any success, my officers decided to move on to investigate other locations in Henderson. As my gang officers were getting into their cars, a young Hispanic lady walked up to them. In broken English she told them to make sure they checked inside a certain apartment. With a trembling index finger, she pointed to an as-yet-unchecked apartment. Because the SWAT Team had already driven off, my four remaining gang officers decided to check the address before heading to Henderson.

The decision was made to conduct a 'knock and talk' as they wanted to make sure all possible hiding places were checked before leaving the neighborhood. The gang officers tactically stacked up at the door, knocked, and announced themselves. It was about 2:00 a.m. and the apartment was completely black. They were all surprised to hear the sound of the tumblers disengaging the apartment lock. Two visibly nervous Hispanic women stood inside the doorframe. When one of my officers showed them a picture of our suspect and asked if they knew his whereabouts, they both said "no." But one of the women hand motioned and pointed to a closed door inside the dark apartment.

Working in tactical unison, my team quietly entered the apartment and posted themselves on both sides of the doorframe. The darkness was an asset. Once they entered, they could control visibility with their flashlights. After the signal was given, the breech man turned the knob and pushed the door open into this 12"x10" room.

As the light illuminated this small room, all four officers tactically made entry and sought cover. The only thing inside the room was a mattress against the back wall. Two people were lying on this mattress – a man and a woman – and the man had the woman in a headlock, a knife against her throat. He was the murder suspect. All officers began shouting commands for him to drop the knife.

The female victim leaned back as the suspect's attention was diverted to my gang officers. This created a small window for my officers to take a shot. They got him. My officers did an outstanding job saving the victim and killing the suspect.

The next week, news spread that a lieutenant who was not even at the scene had been spreading vicious lies claiming that one of my officers fired thirty seconds after the suspect had already been killed. To compound the gravity of the situation, this lieutenant blatantly lied during his internal interview. I decided to terminate him, and only needed Billy's concurrence to proceed. At first, Billy was 100% in support of my decision, but he had not yet obtained the key endorsement of the Police Management and Supervisors Association (PMSA). At this time, Billy's only concern was getting elected and because the decision to fire this lieutenant was not politically expedient, Billy began to have second thoughts about supporting his termination.

Billy asked me to check with our director of labor relations before proceeding with the termination. Because we were only supposed to seek the director's opinion on contractual issues, I knew that Billy was just shielding himself from making this disciplinary decision. I went to the director's office, and he said he was against termination. His reasoning was that, even though he lied, we should give the lieutenant a break because of his seniority. I could see the director was in an awkward position. I spent about thirty minutes trying to persuade him, but I could tell he was afraid. Billy was using the director as his "fall guy." Based on Billy's decision, this lieutenant was allowed to keep his job. Billy eventually got the PMSA endorsement. Four years later, in the first weeks of the Murphy administration, this same lieutenant would resign in lieu of termination for submitting fraudulent overtime slips.

Well before election day, it was painfully obvious that Billy Elders would be our next sheriff. He had the money machine and the kingmakers behind him. In Las Vegas, three people have always been behind successful candidates. These three have the inside pathway for all the hotels, local media, and unions, and without their backing it's impossible to win any county-wide election. The problem is, after the election, these three are still pulling the strings. So after Billy Elders won, little changed and the machine kept churning. Former Sheriff Jones was rewarded with a very high paying position working for a major casino.

After the election, Billy Elders decided to divide the organized crime bureau into two different bureaus: homeland/criminal intelligence and the gang/special investigations. I suspected that he did this because he wanted control over the ongoing corruption case. He knew that my loyalty was to the people of Clark County, not to Billy Elders or the machine. I was not in the least surprised when he told me that Lieutenant Mikey was being promoted to captain over homeland/criminal intelligence bureau. On the bright side, I loved putting gangsters in prison and respected the job that our gang officers were doing.

During my vacations, I normally would rotate the role of acting captain between my lieutenants. The acting captain had to take my seat during CMS meetings, which was always a major pain for the person selected to fill this position. Our RICO case had just ended, resulting in sending more than forty of the most violent criminals in the valley in for lengthy prison terms. The Rollin 60s, the most vicious gang in Las Vegas, were completely dismantled because of the partnership between Metro and the FBI. The week of the bust-out, I had Lew Roberts fill in for me, and he gave a brief overview of its success during CMS. New Sheriff Billy Elders went nuts.

"Why in the fuck are we working with the FBI?" he shouted.

"It was approved two years ago and it was the right thing to do," Lew explained.

When I returned, Billy would not even discuss the issue. I knew that he did not want the FBI to share the credit. Executive staff avoided the press conference, too, for the same reason. I was honored to have been there and I am happy that those thugs went to prison, regardless of who took credit.

Most people inside Metro who knew Billy and the new direction for our department certainly were not surprised that he won the election by a landslide. The question that most people were asking was, "What will be the first thing he does to embarrass himself and the department?" The reality was that Billy had surrounded himself with a very thick layer of insulation to protect him. He had several sections just to shelter his public image. Legal counsel, the PIO director, the labor relations director, the intergovernmental affairs executive director, internal affairs, and Undersheriff Dan Murphy, were like the offensive line on a football team. Their job was to keep Billy from getting sacked. The tragedy was that the enemy was the public and truth became their biggest nemesis.

The "new normal" within Metro was that trust was low and spin

Wedding Bells

was high. Since I was no longer in charge of criminal intelligence, I did not know the status of the county commissioners' investigation. I was delighted to finally learn they had wrapped up their case and Dario Herrio, Erin Kenny, Mary Kincaid-Channesy, Lance Malone and Mike Galardi, had all been federally indicted and were all looking at prison time. Knowing Billy Elders and the other members of executive staff, G-Sting was not something they wanted to be associated with.

The gang crime section was under the leadership of Lieutenants Lew and Cyndy. We were making solid arrests and impounding firearms on a nightly basis. Dismantling the Rollin 60s had also made the streets of our valley much safer. However, a group of rich white kids that lived in the upper middle class community of Sumerlin would create media frenzy as I had never seen. The press could not get enough of these punks known as the "311 boyz."

This gang was composed of rich white kids who attended Centennial High School in this upperclass neighborhood. They had videotaped each other in several acts of violence, including beating the hell out of other high school kids. The gravest of their crimes was a rock throwing incident that destroyed the face of a handsome young boy. Given that these criminal acts involved rich white kids, the "311 boyz" were labeled as public enemy number one. Thanks to the solid work of some of my detectives like Pete Calos and Tom Bateson, the "311 boyz" were all arrested within several weeks. Although I was happy that the public outcry was great to dismantle these rich white kids, I could not understand where the rage was in our minority communities. Every week, young Hispanic and African American kids were being slaughtered and I never saw this type of anger.

Because our kids were attending college, Allison decided it was time to keep the promise she had made to her father twenty-five years earlier. She enrolled in college at UNLV and finished her bachelor's degree in Elementary Education. In December 2004, Allison graduated from UNLV at the same time as our niece, Dawn.

One morning, a friend from the county licensing called. He

asked if I knew who was representing Mike Galardi during his upcoming business licensing case. I did not, but suspected it would be one of the thousands of ambulance chasers who practiced in our valley. He told me that Gilardi's attorney was Jimmy, a very close personal friend of both Billy Elders and Undersheriff Dan Murphy. Jimmy had a reputation of associating with members of organized crime and other nefarious figures, and he was close friends with Billy and Dan. Jimmy was deeply imbedded in our department and was a part of several Metro oversight boards. He was also the same attorney who befriended one of our officers to do background checks for him when I was in internal affairs. Realizing this potential embarrassment for Dan and Bill if this fact were made public, I knew I had to tell them.

My Deputy Chief agreed with me that this could get ugly, and I decided to call the undersheriff. As a courtesy, I called my assistant sheriff and could not reach him. I then called Dan Murphy to let him know that the press may be calling him. Dan was very grateful and told me, "It's not really Jimmy. It's his partner who is representing Galardi." He thanked me for covering his back, and I thought that this was the end of it.

Later in the afternoon, my assistant sheriff staggered in and started screaming at me for "implying Jimmy was in bed with Mike Galardi."

"I was not implying anything," I said. "But I was protecting the sheriff and the undersheriff."

It was then I realized that even when I tried to protect Dan and Bill, their minions would go ballistic. Since Jimmy's close relationship with members of the executive staff was certainly nothing new, why make a big deal about it now?

The next day, my Deputy Chief and I spoke about our assistant sheriff's tantrum and my response. He said he supported me and my actions despite the tantrum. Even in the polluted organizational culture of this administration, it was still good to work with a man of honor like Deputy Chief Bill Conger.

In this rancid organizational culture, it was important to shield my people so they could remain focused on their jobs. This was easy because I had two great lieutenants working with me. Our enforcement teams wore green battle dress uniforms (BDUs), which made them stand out from normal patrol officers. These greens looked sharp and had the gang section emblem prominently displayed on the front. Gang members ran like scared rats when they saw the "greens" roll into their neighborhood because they knew we would get them. Since most patrol officers were busy handling calls and lacked the training, gangsters were not as afraid of them.

Wearing the "greens" made my people proud of being a part of a special unit. With the enforcement teams keeping our neighborhoods safe, I fought to ensure "greens" remained their normal uniform. The only other section that was authorized to wear "greens" was our SWAT team. Rumor had it that SWAT was upset because gang officers were also wearing "greens." I was not concerned about this and told my people so. I decided that the ego of some individuals was not as important as maintaining high morale within the gang section and keeping our neighborhoods safe. In reality, I have always seen our goal as keeping people safe, rather than being focused on "what not to wear."

My assistant sheriff strongly disagreed and wanted to have them switched back to the standard uniform. I maintained that as long as the greens were feared by gangsters, I wanted my people to keep wearing them. The enforcement team reciprocated by keeping the heat on the gangsters and I was happy to tolerate my assistant sheriff's little hissy fits.

The problem of not possessing a computer system to track gang members was hampering our enforcement efforts. Lieutenant Cyndy made this a priority, and located funding through a Byrne Grant, which paid for this new system and the training on how to use it. Cyndy's tenacity and her commitment to detail enabled us to complete the transition to our new system within six months.

This silly disagreement with the assistant sheriff over greens meant that my days were numbered. When Billy Elders called me and told me he was transferring me to the Special Operations

Bureau (SOB), I was not surprised. When I told Billy I did not want to transfer there, he seemed taken aback. SOB was the easiest captain position on the department. All four of the sections (SWAT, Air Support, Resident, and Laughlin) were self-sufficient. Besides having coffee with my lieutenants, there really was not much to do. I knew that putting another captain over gangs would allow them to micromanage.

When word got out that I was leaving gangs, the talk was about who would take my place. Executive staff wanted a puppet that would be blindly obedient to their whims and never stand up for the men and women. Forcing my guys to stop wearing BDUs made no sense to me and I was not going to do it just to please my bosses. When I learned who was taking my position, I certainly was not surprised. He was a new captain who was my former trainee. He certainly was not going to make any waves with executive staff.

Before the transfer, I spoke with him and advised him not to change uniforms.

On his first day, he told all the sergeants and lieutenants in gangs, that he would not be putting our enforcement team in uniform. They could keep wearing the greens. The very next day, after meeting with the assistant sheriff, he told all the enforcement teams to turn in their greens and start wearing the standard uniform. His credibility was shot, and the quality of the gang section went down. The next day, Lieutenant Cyndy transferred out because she could not work for a weak supervisor. In the next few months, many experienced and talented people bailed out of the gang section. I guess executive staff really put those gang guys in their place! As a result gang violence sky rocketed, and it continues to be the biggest crime problem facing the citizens of Clark County.

My transfer to support services put me in a place where I would have minimal contact with Sheriff Elders and his executive staff. In SWAT, I had a lieutenant I liked, but who lacked patrol experience. His biggest asset was his "juice" in the LDS community and his influence with Senator Harry Reid. The SWAT command mobile post, which cost more than $550,000, was paid for from an earmark fund courtesy of Harry Reid. The political contacts that this lieutenant had made him the sheriff's "go to man" whenever he needed a favor from the LDS community.

The K9/resident section was commanded by an outstanding lieutenant. He was an old-school cop who was very engaged with his people. Whenever I needed a question answered, or had a suggestion, he was always on top of it. Under his leadership, the K9/resident section was elevated to a new level and all of his people benefited.

The Laughlin section also had a great lieutenant. Because Laughlin was 90 miles south of Las Vegas, this lieutenant was really a small town police chief. He was also a solid leader and I never needed to worry about getting blindsided. Probably the greatest thing about Laughlin was that it was good old fashioned COP. Everyone in Laughlin knew their cops, and crime was low and the quality of life was excellent. I would often drive to Laughlin just to escape from the craziness happening in our department.

The air support/search & rescue section was led by one of the hardest working lieutenants on our department, Lieutenant Tim. Tim would often work 60-hour weeks, and never put in an overtime sheet. He told me on many occasions that he had dreamed of being in this position and his goal was to make the most of it. Tim's only problem was that he was not a kiss-ass, and whatever he accomplished was through his own hard work. I saw similarities between myself and Tim, and realized he was in for many unexpected hurdles.

After my first few weeks, I realized, with all the "juice" in SWAT, K9/resident and Laughlin, it would be easy to obtain resources for those three sections. SWAT had an open checkbook on anything they wanted. K9/resident had just gotten a new building built for them and never had a problem going over budget. Laughlin had so many toys that they were the envy of all other bureaus. However, air support/search & rescue was in dire need of a larger hanger and manpower. Since their lieutenant wasn't well-liked by upper brass, I knew getting what was needed would take a miracle.

Despite all the justifications that Tim and I would send in with our requests, the answer was always "No." The fact that we were keeping two of our 2.5 million dollar helicopters parked on the tarmac wasn't even enough of a reason to get a larger hanger. Both Tim and I came to the realization we were not going to get another hanger or additional people. Our goal was to ensure safety and be productive with the resources we had. It was so obvious that Tim was not getting any support that, at meetings, the other lieutenants would jokingly pass a collection basket around the room for Tim's new hanger.

I would talk candidly with Tim about the reality of his situation. The strained relationship between Tim and upper brass made his job impossible. We were both aware that they were looking to blame him for a mishap so they could justify booting him out. I advised Tim that it would be better for his career if he left and went back to patrol. Tim's passion for his section and his attention to detail allowed him to remain there for two full years. Inside, both Tim and I knew, it would be only a matter of time before they would find a reason to boot him out.

When one of Tim's senior sergeants, a seasoned pilot, retired unexpectedly, Sheriff Elders wanted to replace him with another sergeant who had left the section several years ago. Elders and the assistant sheriff got into an argument over this, and somehow Tim was blamed for putting the idea in the sheriff's head. Tim was transferred back to patrol. Tim's replacement was a close friend of the sheriff, Joe. He had been the sheriff's executive lieutenant and I was confident that new hanger, new helicopters, and additional pilots might become a reality in the very near future.

Lieutenant Joe had been in the section for only a month when Sheriff Elders miraculously approved $14 million to build a new hanger. We also purchased two new helicopters and added four new pilots as the new lieutenant was still unpacking the boxes in his office. Tim returned to patrol and continued to be an outstanding leader. Credit for the improvements in the section went to Lieutenant Joe, but they rightfully belong to Tim.

On the home front, my oldest two daughters, Rosie and Caitlyn,

Wedding Bells

had graduated from University of Nevada at Reno and were both planning to marry. Rosie's fiancé was Brent Suerdieck, a U.S. Air Force officer. They had dated for several years and I could not have picked a better son-in-law. Rosie and Brent were married on January 6, 2006 at Our Lady of Las Vegas Roman Catholic Church. The wedding was beautiful and the reception went great. The only sad part was that they would be living in Minot, North Dakota and not in Las Vegas.

Caitlyn was marrying her high school sweetheart, Andrew (Andy) Kano. Andy had attended Saint Francis De Sales Elementary School and Bishop Gorman High School in Rosie's class. He had just graduated from the U.S. Naval Academy at Annapolis when he called me and Allison to ask for Caitlyn's hand. Caitlyn and Andy were married by Father Corey Brost at Annapolis on April 23, 2006. Andy was attending TBS in Quantico when they were married.

During this period, the organizational culture within the LVMPD was deteriorating. People appeared fixated on protecting their jobs instead of serving the citizens of Clark County. This resulted in a breakdown in communication, and staff telling the bosses what they want to hear. The major achievement during those four years was the "more cops initiative." This created an additional state sales tax to hire more officers. The city and the county had always paid for police officers before. Because the Strip properties supported it and R&R Advertising pushed it through, the voters approved the initiative. Because our department had moved to micromanagement, as opposed to COP, many new positions were required to fund "cops on dots."

As Elders neared the end of his first four-year term, few doubted that he was going to run again. During the last week of filing for office, Billy Elders held a press conference at which he announced that he would not seek a second term. He threw his support to Dan Murphy. This was the same trick that Erin Kenny had pulled four years prior to ensure that Mark James would fill her shoes as Clark County Commissioner. The only difference was that Kenny was convicted for corruption, and Bill Elders was still the Sheriff of

Clark County. Before Bill ended his term, he coordinated with the Las Vegas Convention and Visitors Authority to build the new convention center area command. The LVCVA would pay for the bricks and mortar, but the officers needed to staff it would be pulled from other area commands.

Members of Metro were not surprised when they heard of Bill's last minute decision not to run. They figured he had a job lined up in the private sector. Many, including me, thought that he had subverted the will of the people by announcing he wasn't running for a second term with only a few days left to file. This tactic served to reduce the chance of any serious opposition for his protégé, Dan. In truth, candidates for sheriff need to raise money for at least one year before filing. An incumbent who pulls out on such short notice may not be committing a crime, but he is not acting ethically.

Dan Murphy became our next sheriff. The machine had again anointed Sin City's next top cop.

After Dan took office, I asked to leave the special operations bureau and return to patrol. In January 2006, I was transferred to the southeast area command.

19

NEIGHBORHOOD PRIDE

It was great being back in patrol.

I loved working with the young hard-charging officers who were assigned to southeast area command. Whereas many of my generation of Baby Boomers allege that this younger generation of Millennials lacks the enthusiasm that we had when we were new officers, I need to call bullshit! I know that the majority of these young officers are every bit as motivated about putting bad guys in jail and serving the good citizens in our community as we were thirty-five years ago. The difference is that my generation has let them down by providing weak leadership and ignoring their creativity. In reality, because we (Baby Boomers) are in charge, the blame needs to rest with us.

I was reenergized by working with this team of dedicated officers and I knew that we could make a positive difference in our community. My first priority after arriving at southeast area was reconnecting with citizens in our neighborhoods. At that time, the SEAC Community Oriented Policing (COP) team was a group of officers lacking any direction. It was not their fault that our department no longer understood or practiced the philosophy of COP. Without leaders who could teach COP to these officers how could they be successful? Within my first two weeks, I identified a young graveyard sergeant who had a solid background in COP. I asked Sergeant Tony Longo if he would take over the COP team, and he accepted. The officers on my COP team were ecstatic to have a leader who understood COP and could train them to be successful.

In just a few weeks, we were accomplishing things others thought were impossible. Crime had begun decreasing at a rapid pace among the hotels along Boulder Highway and in the apartment complexes. It was obvious that our successes were making members of executive staff edgy. It did not take long before officers from other area commands started complaining, "Why can't we practice COP like the officers at SEAC?" When the benefits of practicing COP were identified, people wanted to shift away from the corporate/military philosophy which executive staff insisted upon. Fortunately for staff, the climate within our department had already become so sullied that nobody would dare challenge the status quo. Unfortunately, the atmosphere within Metro more closely resembled the "Stepford Wives" with their robotic behavior than the great department we had been in the past.

One of our most successful projects was the Crime-Free Multi-Housing Program (CFMHP). CFMHP was a program used to ensure that apartment complexes and other multi-housing units were practicing crime prevention and communicating with the police. Within the first six months of this initiative, we had reduced crime more than 40% in our complexes. Part of this program included an advertisement which ran in two magazines that recognized the participating complexes. We had agreed from the start of this initiative that the minimal cost of the advertisement would be rotated between the two Clark County Commissioners, the apartment association and LVMPD. The cost was only $1,000 for three months. It was a great investment. Unfortunately, when the time came for LVMPD to pay the $1,000, our civilian financial officer said she would not allow it. Because the LVMPD would not participate, the entire program ended.

Since the COP efforts at SEAC were driving crime down, we became victims of our own success. To staff the newly created convention center area command, officers were being taken from SEAC. The argument was that because crime was down at SEAC, we did not need all those officers. It was a way to sabotage COP efforts at SEAC and minimize our positive results.

My balance came at home. Allison and I had just become grandparents! Rosie and Brent had a beautiful little girl named Gracie. Caitlyn and Andy had a cute little boy named Bryan. I still loved being a police officer, but I was aware that other things in life are much more important. I was upset that our staff was taking people from SEAC, but I didn't blame them personally. They were just trying to pacify the sheriff.

The reality is that for COP to flourish, trust needs to be high throughout the agency. The lack of trust throughout our department was so serious that I knew we needed to focus efforts within our command boundaries. I was hoping SEAC could serve as an example of the benefits of the COP philosophy and that the other area commands would soon follow. Unfortunately, I soon realized that despite our successes, the toxic organizational culture conflicted with the philosophy of COP. As opposed to a healthy collaboration, our environment fostered conflict and competition which is contrary to the tenets of COP.

The weakness of our internal affairs bureau had become obvious within our department. Internal affairs had no regard for the truth, and the quality of their investigations was pathetic. For example, there was an incident involving one of my senior officers. His son was being bullied by a student at Las Vegas High School. The bully had stolen his cell phone and iPod, and the campus police officer refused to investigate. The juvenile suspect was a star track athlete and the campus officer was the track coach, so no investigation was conducted. IAB disregarded the facts and refused to insist that school police do their job. Despite efforts to communicate with IAB, I was ordered to leave it alone. Morale at LVMPD was extremely low. The word "on the street" was that officers could not be proactive without IAB going after them.

I had four outstanding lieutenants, and each of them were committed to COP. These lieutenants made it a point to ensure that COP was practiced by all their squads and their officers responded. We knew that, at the rate people were being transferred out of SEAC, crime was going to be a challenge for us. Despite our challenges, morale was high, and we continued to be the best area command. That was another source of irritation for the executive staff, and it was obvious during every CMS meeting.

For example, we discussed a series of burglaries that had been committed at several apartment complexes on East Sahara during a CMS meeting. Kerri Farley, one of my COP officers, noticed a spike in burglaries when the series' first started. Investigation revealed that several inmates, all gang members, had been released from prison and had moved into one of the targeted complexes. They had recruited several juveniles in the complex to commit these burglaries for them, and they were fencing the stolen property. Besides recruiting for this gang, they were spending money on drugs and other juveniles were eager to join this motley crew. Through the COP relationships we had developed, we designed a plan of action and identified and arrested all of the suspects. Since the reporting period for CMS ended two weeks prior to the meeting, the fact that the burglaries had stopped was not included. We had made multiple arrests, gotten confessions and recovered all the evidence. I knew this crime series was over.

When I reported on the burglaries during my CMS presentation, I said that this series was over, and the burglaries were not an ongoing problem. A member of executive staff challenged me.

"You can't say for sure that the series is over since we didn't have physical evidence (such as DNA or fingerprints) to match with the suspects." I knew we had confessions and had recovered the stolen property. As I sat there getting ready to respond to that without being too sarcastic, I heard the voice of one of my lieutenants.

This lieutenant was normally a quiet man who never spoke during CMS meetings. He was sitting in the far back of the room in the peanut gallery and when people heard his deep voice, everyone in the room turned around, and he immediately became the focal point. I was thinking to myself, "Don't do it!" This lieutenant shouted his response.

Neighborhood Pride

"That's probably the dumbest thing I've ever heard!" He continued, "How can we match physical evidence when nothing was left at the scenes since the suspects always wore gloves?"

He explained about the confessions and all the property being recovered. I never had to respond and the sheriff quickly shifted to another subject. The entire room went quiet, and I know that of the 100 or so people in the room, everyone had been thinking exactly what this lieutenant said. While I always thought of this lieutenant as a true friend and warrior, he became a "rock star" in my book for covering my back and being honest!

When that CMS was over, we headed back to SEAC, and this lieutenant was the man of the hour. All my other lieutenants were imitating the expressions on the faces of Dan and his minions as my lieutenant was making his comments. I was biting down so hard to keep from laughing that I actually had a sore mouth. Lieutenant Chris Carroll, who is probably the funniest man I ever met, kept singing that old Joe Cocker song, "You Are So Beautiful To Me." That had become our theme song for CMS meetings, to describe the way everyone tried to suck up to the sheriff. As Chris was singing, all of us were laughing and we were just glad we were together as a team.

I enjoyed that day, but I knew that SEAC had just become the next target for executive staff to implode. Despite having a great station with no problems, we were in their crosshairs because we were 'not drinking the Kool-Aid' and were seen as competition to the status quo. Crime was down. Morale was high. COP was in full swing and others were starting to say, "Why can't we do that?"

The next week, CMS was canceled. In its place, we would have a captains' retreat to develop plans to make these meetings productive. After three weeks of retreats, it was decided that only two changes would occur. The term "CMS" (Crime Management System) was going to be replaced. The new name for these meetings was "ACTION" (Acting on Crime Trends in our Neighborhoods). The second change was that we would now be having another meeting to prepare for ACTION the day before the ACTION meeting. It would generate another report for the meeting.

Integrity Based Policing

I told my lieutenants about the change from CMS to ACTION. I thought it would be at least a few days before a joke was created to mock the new acronym. The lieutenants had said that CMS stood for Captains Massaging Shit. Certainly they would not think of anything that quickly for ACTION--not for at least a couple of days. I knew I was in trouble when I saw Chris pull out a yellow legal pad and pen, and begin to write at a feverish pace. Within two minutes, he proudly announced what ACTION really stood for: "Asses Clinched Tightly In spite Of Numbers!" Everyone knew that, despite the change in name, nothing had changed.

You can put lipstick on a sow and it's still a pig.

Another benefit of practicing community oriented policing is that elected officials will do whatever they can to support you. Improving quality of life and reducing crime takes a community effort, not just a police response. We were working closely with Commissioner Chris Guinchillino and the entire Clark County Commission. This relationship was another source of tension because Sheriff Murphy did not trust or communicate with Commissioner Guinchillino.

The sheriff had created the "office of intergovernmental affairs" to serve as his method of dealing with other entities of local government. Once, while meeting with Commissioner Guinchillino, I got a call from the intergovernmental office asking that I have a representative from their office at these meetings with me. The representative from intergovernmental affairs showed up at the next meeting. When the commissioner would not let her attend the meeting, I knew that the sheriff would go into high speed wobbles. I was right.

I could read the 'handwriting on the wall' and knew my days at SEAC were drawing to an end. I still believed that, before I was transferred, I would get a phone call from the sheriff. Considering that I was a 29-year veteran captain, I thought they would at least extend that minor courtesy.

Retired Chief Kirk, who worked at the MGM, decided that he wanted to retire. One of the assistant sheriffs was announced as his replacement. This was the same assistant sheriff who had been

Neighborhood Pride

busy staffing the new convention center area command from the other area commands. This meant that another shakeup would take place to fill the vacancy. When Sheriff Murphy made the announcement, he laughed about the MGM announcing that same day that "200 employees were being laid off." Sheriff Murphy sarcastically said, "They need to fire all those people to be able to afford Tom's salary." The room erupted in phony laughter at Sheriff Murphy's feeble attempt to make a joke, but I was disgusted that Sheriff Murphy would joke about people losing their jobs. I guess virtues such as compassion and kindness are not important to certain people.

After a meeting with my team, we decided to grab lunch. Just as I got into my car, my cell phone rang. It was an assistant sheriff who told me I was being transferred to the crime lab. I told him that I did not want to transfer, but he insisted. He told me the sheriff wanted me to use my leadership skills to improve morale at the crime lab. At that point, I knew he was blowing smoke because morale was never important to Sheriff Dan Murphy.

As I joined my lieutenants for lunch, they knew something was wrong. I told them about my transfer, and we tried to focus on other more positive things. The transfer date was not for another two weeks, so I would have time to get with all my people before the move.

When I arrived back at my office, the chief called. I figured he was calling to say he was upset over my transfer.

"I already know about the transfer." I told him that I would be going to the crime lab to start the move.

"You're not going to the crime lab," he said. "The sheriff decided he wants you in patrol services." He said that he would confirm that the sheriff did not change his mind again, and call me back.

Patrol services was a gofer job for executive staff. It was an umbrella bureau for many of the small sections that service all of patrol. These sections included field training, major events, saturation teams, youth education section and the administrative section. With me there, every one of the area commands now had captains who drank the sheriff's Kool-Aid. I knew that COP had just suffered another blow and wondered if it would ever recover.

Late that same day, Lieutenant Chris Hoye called and said he was transferring to patrol services to head the saturation teams. I was happy about this. I knew that continuing to work with Chris would make my new assignment more bearable.

This move was almost fitting at this point in my career. My new office was on the second floor of city hall, next to the ACTION room. The worst part was not the small office space. It was the closeness to the executive staff. I'd be the first person that they would see after leaving their staff meetings, and they would dump their projects in my in-basket. Here's how it would work: the sheriff would ask some question about a project or an article that he wanted to learn more about. The chiefs would then quickly raise their hands and tell the sheriff they would research it and have an answer for him later. As soon as they left the meeting, they would pass my desk and toss it into my inbox.

Because my office was only a third of the size of the one at SEAC, only a few of my things would make it into the new space. Most of my things went right into a box and into my garage. Other than a few pictures of my family and the yellow brick from the FBINA, my walls were bare. I quickly realized that the less time I spent in the office, the fewer projects were dumped in my inbox. PSB was newly created, so we needed to be resourceful, which was a challenge. Because the saturation teams were created to be proactive, they were making solid arrests and getting guns and drugs off our streets. The major obstacle for our saturation teams was that our organizational climate encouraged other sections to find fault with them.

Since our entire department revolved around the ACTION meetings, most effort went into preparing for these worthless meetings. During many ACTION meetings, captains would blame their increase in robberies on the saturation teams not being assigned to their area. To defend my people, I made it a point to keep stats on the activity of my saturation teams and would "call bullshit." Soon,

Neighborhood Pride

the captains would blame their crime increases on other factors, like the weather and the horoscope.

This reminded me of when I was a young sergeant over the newly created gang unit. Other officers would say that the gang officers were a group of do-nothings who were not accomplishing anything. We made it a point to attend as many patrol briefings as possible and share information with all the other officers. That was exactly what we did to turn things around for the saturation teams. Unfortunately, despite improving our reputation among the officers and sergeants, many in executive staff would take pot shots at the long-term effectiveness of the saturation teams. It seemed that they couldn't grasp that the purpose of any saturation team is "shock and awe," not long term maintenance. I attempted numerous times to have other captains ensure their COP teams would coordinate efforts with us. It fell on deaf ears.

Any veteran officer knows that, regardless of jurisdiction, certain geographical areas will be high in violence and crime. These areas are known as "hot spots." For long-term success, COP needs to be an important weapon in the jurisdiction's arsenal. Without COP to provide maintenance, neighborhoods will decay.

The most notorious "hot spot" in Las Vegas was once a beautiful neighborhood. During the '70s and '80s, as the Las Vegas Valley spread, the area surrounded by Desert Inn and Flamingo on the north and south, and Swenson and Paradise on the east and west, experienced a mass exodus. This area had many apartment complexes and the majority of people moved out in droves to neighborhoods farther away from the Strip. The mass vacancies forced the landlords to lower rent. The new residents lacked any connection with neighborhood. The influx of illegal immigrants, gangs, and the lack of community pride turned this neighborhood into a haven for criminal activity. Worse still was that this area straddled three separate area commands.

One afternoon, I asked my assistant sheriff to let me try something different. Up to this time, all of our deployments were inside one geographical area. I requested permission to embark upon this neighborhood for 90 days. I would work with the other bureau commanders and the crime analysis, to reduce crime and improve quality of life in this historic neighborhood. The assistant sheriff was 100% supportive and operation "Neighborhood Pride" was launched.

My secret weapon was a young patrol officer named Brooke Lavin. Brooke had been a part of my COP Team at SEAC and had been moved back to a regular patrol squad. I asked Brooke if she would work with me again to partner with my saturation teams and improve this neighborhood. I knew this would be the last COP project that I would command.

Brooke's tireless work made "Operation Neighborhood Pride" a huge success. Elders families could walk the streets at night in this formerly dangerous neighborhood. We reduced crime in this area more than half and made quality of life improvements. The apartment dwellers were thrilled. This neighborhood was once again a place for good people and criminals were vacating this neighborhood. I thought Sheriff Murphy would take notice. Unfortunately, I was wrong. When the deployment period ended, the sheriff ended the operation and the neighborhood returned to its original state of decay.

Meanwhile, my son, Patrick, was a 2nd lieutenant in the U.S. Army. He got the news that he was being deployed for one year to Iraq. Even though he was already away from home in Germany, knowing that he was being deployed made me realize that time was moving fast. Even our youngest, Elizabeth, who was a teacher in Los Angeles, had left the nest. She and her fiancé Matt were going to be married next summer. As for Rosie and Caitlyn, they each had two babies and Rosie had number three on the way. I was driving back to Vegas from Yuma, after my grandson, Owen's, baptism, when an epiphany hit me like a bolt of lightning.

It was on a Sunday at about noon, and I was driving home alone. I was experiencing the same sick feeling I often felt on Sundays, dreading the thought of going back to work the next morning. It had shifted away from the vocation I loved to a burden that I now had to endure. I was getting ready to take a break at a small store in Quartzite, Arizona, when it hit.

I could retire.

My 30th year with LVMPD was approaching. For the next hour drive until I hit Needles, I thought about giving up the career I had always loved.

At a McDonald's in Needles, I called Allison.

"Dan, you cannot stop being a cop!" She knew how much I loved Metro and being a cop, and thought that I had at least five years left to go. I also think she was afraid that I would start trying to be a handyman around the house. Unfortunately, when God was handing out carpentry skills, I must have been on a different cloud. Most guys who retire have a long "honey do" list. In my case, it was a "Honey DON'T" touch that" list!

The next morning, I told everyone about my decision to retire. Everyone was happy for me and said that they could not wait until they had enough time in to leave our department. My last few months went by like a flash, and I honestly felt sad for the brothers and sisters I was leaving behind. Working those last few months, I experienced a whirlpool of emotions and I knew our department had lost its direction. As opposed to treating people (inside and outside) with respect and compassion, they were now seen as expendable objects.

20

A MATTER OF TRUST

My retirement party was on Valentine's Day, 2010, and love was just one of the many emotions I experienced that day.

The best part of my retirement party was that my daughter, Rosie, had just given birth to our newest grandson, William, only two days before. During the party I was thinking about traveling to Los Angeles the next morning to see him for the first time. There was no denying that I would miss policing, but I was excited to begin this new chapter in my life.

Seeing many of my friends who I had not seen in years was fun, but no consolation for giving up life as a police officer. I did my best to appear in high spirits while listening to several presentations, but I felt as if I were witnessing my own funeral instead of just leaving a job. The worst part was the realization that the vocation I loved had morphed into a bureaucracy that cared little about people.

I kept asking myself, "Did I do enough to fight the good fight, or did I just sit idly by as our organizational culture became toxic?" My memories raced over the numerous times when I fought with members of executive staff, only to be told, "No." Their typical response was that because they were on top of the organizational chart, only their decisions mattered. Of the many skirmishes I had with executive staff (i.e., the organizational shift away from COP, defending an officer who was being railroaded by a shoddy investigation or

A Matter of Trust

other ethically questionable activities), their refusal to explain their position was most frustrating. Candid disagreements are healthy for organizations when both sides honestly communicate, but that had not been a part of our organizational culture for many years.

At that moment, I realized the answer to my question was a definitive, "I'm not sure." I knew I had battled many times to defend people from injustices; however, success was infrequent. Although, I know people appreciated my effort, a loss is a loss. I looked around the room and saw many young officers. The majority of them were the same ages as my own kids. An inner sadness engulfed me as I contemplated how these young officers may never experience the fun and job satisfaction that I had enjoyed.

After all the speakers finished, the master of ceremony called me to the podium to say a few words. This was a unique occasion to give my own eulogy and still be breathing. I did my best to talk for about five minutes. Most of my chatter was spent thanking others and regurgitating a couple of amusing stories that left the attendees laughing. I was happy to discover that others in the room did not know that I was fighting back tears the entire time. I could not wait for this thing to end.

I made a final check of my office to ensure that my things were cleaned out. All I had to do was leave my proxy card and keys on the desk. After turning off the lights, I tried to divert my thoughts to the fun things that Allison and I would have time to do. A few days later, it hit me that I was no longer a slave to my Blackberry or the alarm clock.

I often joked with Allison about most retired officers looking alike because they all grew goatees. Most of my colleagues and I had joined the department in our early 20s. Because of appearance standards, we could not have any facial hair, except for a small moustache. The new liberty to grow some facial hair seemed to be part of the retirement process. In addition to no longer needing to answer my pager, not shaving was another perk of retirement.

Despite Allison's protests, after several weeks as a retiree I was sporting a goatee. I thought that it looked cool. In Allison's effort to

Integrity Based Policing

have me go back to the clean shaven man she married over thirty years ago, she mocked me, saying that I looked like a Schnauzer. After several months of working to maintain a neatly trimmed goatee, Allison's teasing paid off and I agreed to shave it. I must admit that after returning to being clean-shaven, I realized how much work it was to maintain that goatee.

One of my favorite movies has always been the "Jackie Robinson Story." Besides this movie showing the adversity Mr. Robinson encountered as the first African American to play major league baseball, it also depicted a memorable conversation. In one scene, Robinson is talking with the owner of the Brooklyn Dodgers, Branch Rickey. In regard to baseball he said, "In order to be great, you have to play it like a man and love it like a boy." While he was referring to our great American pastime, I am confident this statement can also be said about policing.

I have had the privilege to work side-by-side with true public servants who saw their job as a way to help others. One consistent difference separating great officers from the others was their passion for the job. Their faces would light up like a Christmas tree whenever they recounted how they tracked down a suspect or handled a domestic fight. For great officers, it is not just about staying out of trouble and getting a paycheck. It is about making a positive difference.

To a great police officer, there is nothing more exhilarating than making a major arrest or recovering a large amount of evidence during a search warrant. I remember many times during my career when the officers on the scene looked more like a little league team that had just won a big game than a group of highly trained professionals. If a person is not emotional about victory or defeat, maybe he or she should look for another line of work. Enthusiasm is an attribute which needs to be encouraged, not stifled.

In the early '90s, Deputy Chief Myers always seemed to enjoy his work. Myers truly loved policing and the people we served. He would often ask me questions about the challenges I was facing. It did not matter if it were 3:00 a.m. or p.m. Myers would take the

A Matter of Trust

time to make sure he answered my questions. I normally feared calling a deputy chief at home during the graveyard shift, unless it was Myers. His love for policing and his outstanding people skills always served as the model I sought to emulate.

In 2007, when I was captain at southeast area command, Sergeant Tony Longo and his team lowered the crime rate and improved the quality of life for all of the residents living in apartment complexes. His love for policing was obvious to others and he helped countless people. While Tony often worked more than sixty hours each week, he seldom submitted for overtime or complained. His passion was contagious and made everyone on his team shine. The joke around the southeast command was that whenever somebody had a big smile on their face, they caught the Tony bug.

Two other important attributes of a great police officer are resiliency and perseverance. Mistakes need to be viewed as learning opportunities, not reasons to throw in the towel. Dealing with adversity in a calm and ethically sound manner is a requirement for any true leader. A person who has never had to deal with adversity, does not have the experience to be leading others, especially police officers.

I am a fan of the great former heavyweight boxing champion, Floyd Patterson. Patterson was not only a great fighter inside the ring but also a true gentleman outside the ring. He once was interviewed by an announcer who sarcastically asked, "What's it like to be the champion who has been knocked down more than anybody else?" Without hesitating, this great champion countered, "You say I was the fighter who got knocked down the most, but that also means I got up the most."

The importance of resiliency cannot be overstated. During my career there have been many times when I had to go through adversity. The challenges that I faced after I arrested the suspect in the bookstore knocked me to the canvas. In Chapter Five – Three's a Crowd – we learned that Randy Whitney and Dave Groover's leadership and support during this tough time is something I will never forget. While this period was not fun, it did not last forever. I learned to shake off the cobwebs and move forward with my career.

Unfortunately, I have seen situations in which an officer gets him- or herself into trouble and never recuperates. It is imperative for all of us to look out for each other and assist people going through difficult times. In a healthy work environment, officers of all ranks look out for each other. The importance of a phone call or a pat on the back to a person going through hard times can be immeasurable. Despite being retired, I will never stop caring about the men and women who wear the badge. I also understand the critical service that police provide for all Americans and thank God for allowing me to be a part of our noble profession.

During my 30-year career, I have seen major improvements in technology that contribute to making our communities safer. In the 80s, officers rarely had access to portable radios and many officers did not wear bulletproof vests. In today's world, all officers have portable radios and are issued bulletproof vests. Having immediate access to SWAT, canine, and air support are other examples of technological advances that make policing safer and more effective in today's world.

Unfortunately, I have also seen major setbacks in the way we serve the community and treat people, including fellow officers. The shift to the business (or corporate/militaristic) model has resulted in cookie cutter administrations that fail to weigh mitigating factors during the decision-making process. Virtues such as care, compassion, and kindness have been replaced by objectiveness, political correctness, and detachment. The challenge for today's police leadership is to make the most of our technological advances and treat people as gifts from God, not faceless widgets.

The path of reform must be considered from an ethical, and not a solely legalistic frame. While it is tempting to look for answers in crime statistics, the absence of trust is the real reason for our downward spiral. As we forge ahead in the 21st century we need to rediscover our ethical balance. True leaders always lead from the front and strive to serve others.

In our final chapter, I want to introduce the acronym TRUST to lay out a roadmap to help restore our ethical balance. These recommendations will prove to be advantageous because they embrace three main elements: (1) They are consistent with the original mission of American policing: "Keep the peace by peaceful means" (2) they are not expensive to implement and (3) all five virtues are beneficial both internally and externally. Probably the greatest benefit is that by focusing reform on these five recommendations, departments will amplify trust.

TRUTH	Departments need to ensure the truth is certain.
Respect	People deserve to be treated with respect.
Understanding	Always strive to understand the other position.
Stability	Make sure that decisions are not just knee-jerk reactions.
Transparency	Trust can never exist if people are operating under the cloak of darkness.

These values are essential to improve policing. To implement these reforms and move forward, police departments must recalculate. Of course, "recalculate" has a new meaning in our world of electronic devices. Positive reform requires leaders with courage, skill, and understanding to improve American policing and best serve our communities. These leaders will encourage innovation and restore TRUST in our sacred vocation.

Even before I retired, I knew that I was technically challenged.

Allison and the kids still tease me about an incident in May 2008, which demonstrates my lack of technological skills. My son-in-law, Brent, had been assigned to San Pedro, California, for a few months when my granddaughter Dani was baptized. My son, Patrick, who at the time was a senior at University of Nevada at Reno (UNR), was on spring break and would be joining us at Dani's baptism. Allison and Patrick headed off to San Pedro in the middle of the week, but unfortunately I needed to wait until the weekend to drive down. I was excited during the five-hour drive and could not wait to see my new granddaughter and enjoy her baptism. I also knew that I had to

Integrity Based Policing

be back in Vegas at 11:00 a.m. on Monday for an important meeting with all of the apartment complex owners in my area command.

At Rosie and Brent's house I was ecstatic to see my family, especially our new granddaughter. After the baptism, I told everyone about my scheduled meeting. Allison and Patrick said that they wanted to stay a few extra days, and we decided that I could use Patrick's GPS to guide me in driving home, so I wouldn't be late for this meeting. Plans were made to leave San Pedro at 5:00 a.m., and I would be back in plenty of time. Before I went to bed on Sunday, Patrick reassured me,

"Dad, don't worry, the GPS will tell you exactly where to go."

The next morning I awoke an extra hour early before turning on the car's ignition. I turned on the GPS and, with great confidence in my new best friend, began the drive. At first it seemed that all of the LA traffic was heading in the opposite direction. I did not need to travel less than 65 mph and I was thinking that I would have time to go for a run, stop for breakfast, and still easily make the meeting.

After about two hours of this stress-free driving, I began to wonder why things did not look familiar. I thought the GPS was taking me to I-15 by an alternate route as nothing looked recognizable. I saw a sign that made me panic, "Reno 340 miles." I got off the next exit and called Patrick. After I told him of my dilemma, he asked me what I had done before I started on my trip. I told him that I simply programmed the GPS to go "home" and followed the directions since then.

"Dad, I live in Reno," Patrick said calmly.

After he talked me through how to reprogram the device and entered *my* correct address, I was on the road again. Unfortunately, my ETA was an additional three hours, and there was no way I was going to make it home for this important meeting.

I sat back and blamed the GPS for causing me to miss this important meeting. After several minutes of screaming at the "Garmin from hell," I realized I had nobody to blame but myself. I made my second dumbest mistake of the day by calling Lieutenant Jeff Whitehead and telling him exactly what had happened. Of course, I

A Matter of Trust

became the laughingstock of everyone at southeast area command. The lesson I learned from this was the importance of combining common sense with technology. We cannot have blind dependence on technology and disregard the importance of the human factor.

After the incident with Patrick's GPS, I have certainly learned how to operate my own GPS. In fact, I always make sure that I have my GPS with me when I travel. Being retired, Allison and I are able to travel all over and not worry about getting lost. The best part of my GPS is that even when I do make a wrong turn, it will correct me and get me back on course. That annoying little voice, "recalculating" is not a sound that I enjoy hearing, but I know I had better listen to my GPS. Unfortunately, in dealing with other things in life, we do not have that annoying mechanical voice telling us we have gotten off course, and how to get back on track to achieve ethical and legal soundness.

In my life, I have always heard another internal voice that lets me know when I need to make adjustments. Being a Christian, I always pray and look to Scripture to serve as my internal GPS. Organizationally, we need to ensure that our agencies are sound from both a legal and ethical framework. While many attorneys are employed to make sure actions and decisions squeeze within the legal framework, I can tell you that, from my experience, not enough (if any) consideration is given to ethical soundness, especially the manner in which we treat other people. The need for police to increase ethical soundness and improve the way we treat others, both internally and externally, has never been greater in America. In an effort to recalculate, American policing needs to make use of the acronym TRUST (Truth, Respect, Understanding, Stability, and Transparency) as a guide to get us moving in the right direction.

CPSIA information can be obtained
at www.ICGtesting.com
Printed in the USA
FSHW021430010720
71701FS